ORCAS
INTERMISSION

Books by Laura Gayle

The Chameleon Chronicles:
Orcas Intrigue
Orcas Intruder
Orcas Investigation
Orcas Illusion
Orcas Intermission

Tales from the Berry Farm:
Orcas Afterlife (forthcoming)

ORCAS INTERMISSION

Book 5 of
The Chameleon Chronicles

Laura Gayle

BOOK VIEW CAFE

Book View Café Publishing Cooperative

Orcas Intermission, by Laura Gayle

Cover art and design by Mark J. Ferrari
Interior design by Shannon Page

Second Edition

ISBN: 978-1-63632-097-7

BOOK VIEW CAFE
www.bookviewcafe.com
Book View Café Publishing Cooperative

To JoJo Brixton

Even though you hate yourself,
you're still everyone's favorite

CHAPTER 1

"I told you I had reasons," he said soberly. "Very compelling ones."

JoJo Brixton's grave expression melted into an impish grin as he gazed up at me from his seat at a conference room table deep in the bowels of Friday Harbor's courthouse.

I sank into the chair across from his before my legs failed me, the implications cascading through my mind. "How long?" I finally managed.

He cocked his head. "You mean, how long have I been *helping* the nice Feds?"

"Yeah...that."

"Hmm." He pretended to think. As if. "Remember that day at our house?"

Our house? I'd never lived with JoJo—and then I understood. "Your parents' house? When they searched it, last December; and you made me lunch, pretending not to know why pâté is expensive?"

JoJo shrugged. "I still maintain that every animal has a liver. But yes. Veierra and McMichaels had just had words with me, right before you arrived. Perhaps I seemed uneasy?"

"Oh yeah." He'd been so testy that we'd almost had a fight. Lisa Cannon's acting troupe had just trashed the house before haring off to party elsewhere, and I'd been worried about losing my job as the Brixtons' caretaker. "You did seem…not quite your usual careless self. But why'd they search it if they were there recruiting you?"

"Misdirection, my dear." He leaned back in his chair. "They didn't want *you* guessing the reason for their visit. I really can't overstate how relieved I am that I can be honest with you at last."

Did he sound almost serious? I didn't know which of his stories to believe anymore. I rubbed my eyes, having been whisked out of my house and carted over here to San Juan Island before I'd even had coffee. "Okay, but…why are you working with them?" JoJo Brixton just didn't seem like the 'FBI mole' type.

Wariness flickered across his face, as if he were weighing his next words.

"You did just say you're going to be honest with me now," I added.

"I did, didn't I?" He grimaced. "Well then…can we just settle for an admission that the Feds might have discovered a thing or two about me which I'd rather not see them pursue?"

"They have something on *you*?" I leaned forward. "What is it?" When I'd first walked through the Brixton house as caretaker last November, JoJo's room had smelled faintly of pot. But that was legal in the state of Washington now. Alcohol was the only substance I'd ever seen JoJo use to excess, but…had he been involved with some worse drug?

"Cam, my dear," he said, shaking his head, "it can't come as a surprise to you that I'm not exactly a stickler for the rules."

"Well, no. But which rules are we talking about, exactly?"

"*Any* rules." He gave me a bright smile. "So, what shall we talk about now?" He cast a quick glance toward the security camera above the door, then looked back at me.

Oh. Of course. Gosh, I really needed that coffee. "Okay," I

said. "So, then...you've been spying on...who, exactly? Wait! Was it *me*?" I suppose this should have occurred to me sooner, but, see above re: coffee. Remembering everything that had happened the last few days got me creeped out all over again. "Oh, JoJo, do they know about Marie's boxes from my trunk?" I shot a glance back up at the security camera, horrified. If they hadn't, they did now. My arms even started tingling. Who knew what I might blurt out next if I didn't get some caffeine soon?

"Relax, Camikins." He put a hand on my arm briefly. As if he somehow knew about my chameleoning. (*Did* he?) "Of course they know about the boxes. I brought them straight over here for analysis—do you have any idea what an important piece of evidence they are?"

I nodded, dumbfounded. "Yes, I do, which was why you were going to destroy them!"

He shook his head again, still smiling. "Which I might actually have done if those boxes were evidence of some wrongdoing on your part; but they aren't, and everyone knows that. You're not in *any* trouble, dearest. Didn't Veierra and McMichaels tell you that? Everyone—even Sheriff Clarke—knows you're not the bad guy here."

"Well, yeah," I allowed. "I just...I guess I'm having a hard time believing it. Believing any of this whole situation, to be perfectly honest."

"I understand," he said gently. "You'll have a lot of things to rethink now."

Who knew JoJo could be so sympathetic? I'd always liked him, of course (even when I hated him). But I'd met a different side of him just a few days ago, when he'd whisked me off to Seattle in a freakin' *helicopter* and spent the day being the fairy godmother to my Cinderella; and now...here was yet another new side of him. My brain was struggling to keep up. "Okay, so you've been spying on me, but everybody knows I'm not the bad guy, so—who else? Lisa?"

His expression softened even more. "You know how much I love Lisa. I have only ever wanted to protect her." His glance darted to the camera once more, then back to me. "Lisa Cannon is as innocent as—well, no, no one's as innocent as you are, little lamb. But she's close, and my only concern here is to help catch the *real* bad guys and clear Lisa's name." He blinked his ridiculous, lovely lashes at me.

Somehow, the more absurd his claims became, the more I believed him, and yet… "Clear her name, and save your own skin, of course," I reminded him.

His smile widened as he gave an insouciant shrug. "Well, naturally there's something in it for me too, my dear. That's a given in anything I do, isn't it?"

Oddly, I found this admission just as hard to swallow as any of his others. Whatever the FBI had on him must be pretty dire if it had made him willing to answer to them. The JoJo Brixton I knew didn't answer to anyone, slippery charming eel that he was. "So who's the real bad guy?" I asked. "Lisa's ex-husband?"

"Oh honey, there are so many of them." He shook his head; his perfect hair reflected even the fluorescent lights gorgeously. "This whole mess is so much bigger—and darker—than you can imagine. Derek is just one small worm in a much, *much* bigger can of them." He leaned forward and held my gaze, looking very nearly earnest. "That is why I tried so *very nobly* to get you off this island and out of harm's way." He frowned, theatrically, before smiling once more. "Though, selfishly, I'm glad my efforts failed—especially now that we can share my secrets. You're such sincere and entertaining company."

"Well thanks." I wasn't about to say the same thing to him… not just yet, anyway.

He sobered again—emotions flitted across his face like an unsettled weather system. "Even Lisa has no real idea how much danger she's actually in." He patted my arm once more. "Another reason I'm happy to have you working with me now. Two can watch her back more effectively than one."

Dang him, he was softening me, no matter what my rational mind might warn me to remember. I gave him an uncertain smile. "Do I have *any idea* who you really are?"

He paused, studying me. "You're thinking of all those things I told you about myself over lunch in Seattle, aren't you."

"Well, yes; that, and all the other stuff you've told me—like pretending to be drunk so you could apologize to me, because I'm your only real friend. I mean, JoJo, really?"

"Yes, really. I meant everything I said that day, and I mean what I'm saying now: you know me better than nearly anyone, actually." He laughed sadly. "I mean, you've *met* my family."

"I have indeed." I shook my head. His sister was as callous and cutting as JoJo, but without the charm; his father was inattentive and ineffectual; his mother—my old boss Diana—was...I shivered. The less I thought about brittle, demanding, exacting Diana Brixton, the better. "But why do you pretend to be such a—I don't know—such a jerk?" I burst out.

He spread his hands. "Because I'm a jerk!"

"JoJo..."

He sighed. "Okay, protective camouflage then."

"To hide you from what? From people caring about you? Actually getting to *know* you?"

His eyes crinkled with his smile. "And see, this is exactly why everyone loves you, Camikins. I know you're holding as many secrets as the rest of us, if not more—but nothing ever even dims your sweetness! It's, it's, I don't even have words for what that means to me—to everyone who meets you."

Not everyone, I thought darkly, recalling Kevin, and Colin... and Kip too now, probably.

"From the moment I learned to talk," he went on, "I could see that sincerity just made me vulnerable, even deep within the bosom of my ever-loving family. Exposing any feelings, any desires, any honesty, was simply setting myself up for betrayal, damage, hurt—and not even for any reason with a name, but just because that's how my family is. I learned very early to hide behind a JoJo face that charmed everyone and let no one in. And," he added, leaning forward and dropping his voice, "I believe that you, dear Cam, are the first person I have *ever* said that out loud to." Before I could find any response, he brightened up dramatically. "And now that you are *on the team*," he gushed, practically sparkling, "I don't have to keep deceiving you—about anything!" He put on a sad-clown face. "You can't imagine how hard it's been to keep this all to myself."

I was getting whiplash. Was this performance yet another mask? For all I knew, he'd been performing for so long that even *he* didn't know.

I really, *really* needed some coffee.

"Well, I'm happy to help," I said, "especially if it means helping Lisa. I told them," I waved vaguely toward the door, the camera, at all the important official authorities out there, "that I'm absolutely not going to spy on her, and they all assured me that I'm not expected to. So I'm glad to help clear her name and flush out whoever is really behind all the intrigue."

JoJo nodded soberly. "Lisa has never deserved any of the trouble swirling around her."

"So—I guess the sheriff is going to give me an orientation, but—what's it been like for you, being a double agent?"

JoJo chuckled. "Dearie, it's just 'agent'. We're not 'double' unless we're spying on two different masters for each other."

I nodded, suppressing a grin.

"But, for me, it's been a whole lot of pretending not to be interested in the dramas and mysteries around me, while managing as best I can to be in the middle of all of them with eyes and ears wide open."

"Right." I was already there, whether I'd intended to be or not.

"The only place I dropped the ball," he said, "was with you. And that was precisely because I slipped and let myself care about you—far too much. I very nearly tipped my hand trying to get you out of danger, which made Agent Veierra quite unhappy with me. It was touch and go there for a few months. She made me leave the island altogether for a while, just to play down my indiscretion before you or someone else took notice."

Ohh. "So that's why," I murmured. "Honestly, getting your mom to fire me hurt twice as much because of how you just vanished afterward. Like we were never friends at all. The way you just kept posting about going to parties and on trips and buying new ridiculous clothes, without ever writing me or anything…"

He nodded, his gaze soft, even a little—abashed? "I hated to do it, Cam," he said quietly. "Well, except for the clothes part. I do love clothes. But I couldn't step too far out of character without arousing suspicion from…the wrong sort of people. Even writing to you would just have ticked Veierra off even more, and risked drawing unwelcome attention to you from…all sorts of bad directions. I wasn't going to put you in danger that way, or endanger my own position in—" he waved a hand "—this giant web of intrigue."

"I see that now, I guess." So many moving parts to keep track of.

"It wasn't that I didn't care." He held my gaze. "You see that too, don't you? It was that I care more than I was ever supposed to."

And…what was *that* supposed to mean? Was this scene for the benefit of our observers? Or were we heading for another uncomfortable "Colin moment"—this time captured on tape? I could not imagine JoJo having any romantic designs on me. At least, I sure hoped he didn't. I certainly felt no spark of attraction for him; and he was way too smart not to know that. Wasn't he?

No. He couldn't. I would know.

This *was* a scene.

Well, despite JoJo's belief in my sincerity, I'd been playacting my whole life. I nodded, watching his eyes. "I care about you too," I said, letting my voice go soft with emotion, just like he had. "That's why it hurt so much when I thought you didn't."

"I know." And then, because JoJo Brixton could not be serious for more than thirty seconds without rupturing something, he suddenly beamed at me and said, "Okay then! Is it time to place you back into our esteemed sheriff's indelicate grasp?"

"Not yet—I have a few more questions first." I would have even more later when we weren't sitting in a bugged room, but this one seemed safe here.

JoJo leaned back in his chair and faux-grumbled, "Just when I thought I might finally get that Bloody Mary."

"Bloody Mary?"

"You know. Red drink, a little spicy, filled with vodka. And that yummy celery stick."

"I *know* what a Bloody Mary is. You think they serve them here?" I stifled a giggle, imagining a courthouse Bloody Mary. If I'd thought the substation's *coffee* was disgusting...

JoJo snorted. "Of course not, Camikins. I meant down the street at Piquant. They serve a perfectly luscious one!"

"Right." I shook my head. "So, since they're not expecting me to spy on Lisa—or on you, obviously—and they made it real clear they're not looking into Jen either, do you have any idea who they do want me to spy on? I mean, who else do I even know?" Paige Berry? Perish the thought.

He shrugged his fine shoulders. "You'll have to ask them that. But if I had to hazard a guess, I'd look in the direction of your play."

"My play?" My mind immediately went to my cast of characters: Felicia, Martin, Kristoff and the gang. But they were all fictional, so...

"The play you wrote," he said patiently, "which is being produced *this summer*, am I right? And heading into rehearsals very soon now?"

"Oh. Oh! The troupe!" Several of whom had just recently been hauled off by the cops—for suspicious behavior in the hospital room of poor Marie… "Of course." I leaned back and rubbed my forehead, feeling stupid. "They'll want me watching the actors."

"That would make sense," JoJo agreed. "You'll have the perfect excuse to spend all sorts of time with them. A new play being produced for the first time? How many community theaters are lucky enough to have the playwright *right there* to consult?" His grin widened. "I imagine Lisa will want you around for every minute of it."

"Yeah," I agreed. "Especially since—" I caught myself just in time to change course. "—since I'm her assistant now. There are probably all sorts of…notes she'll want me to take, or something." Lisa and JoJo were close; he probably knew more than I did about her business and the threats against her from Derek and whoever else. But she'd been very clear with me about not blabbing her secrets to *anyone*. Including, I supposed, the fact that she didn't know who else among her actors might have been working for her ex-husband. I gave JoJo what I hoped was a guileless smile.

He gave me a thoughtful look, then leaned forward with a bemused grin. "Camikins! Are you being *discreet* about something? With me?"

My dang poker face! Would I ever get ahead of it?

"Charming," he mused, as if I were a precocious toddler who'd just done something clever. "But that's actually not a bad topic to tie this meeting up with. I'm sure the sheriff will explain all this during your orientation, but even though you and I will be working together now, the team will want our reports *untainted* by each other's observations. So we should probably avoid discussing whatever we may discover, to avoid accidentally warping each other's perceptions." He gave me a subtly odd look. "Do you see what I mean?"

"Well…sure." We might even end up being witnesses in a trial someday. "I get it."

"I knew you would." His smile broadened as he looked back up at the room's security camera. "And, for the benefit of our handlers who are no doubt following this conversation with rapt professional attention, let me just state for the record how very, *very* seriously I take *all* the rules and strictures they've established here—despite my little joke to the contrary a few minutes ago. Whatever my demeanor may suggest, I understand the rules just as clearly as I believe Cam does now; and I meant it to the bottom of my eager little heart when I told Agent Veierra that I'd learned my lesson." He looked back down at me with strange intensity. "So our glorious overlords can rest assured of our *complete* discretion—even with each other—at *all* times and in *all* places; right Cam?" Then he gave me a perfectly transparent look conveying the message *Not here, not now.*

I just stared back at him, wondering how he could possibly imagine they weren't seeing his hyperbolic insincerity just as easily as I was. I finally blinked at him and said, "Of course. I'll follow the rules as well or better than you do. You know that very well. And so do they, I think."

He offered me a prim little grin. "Of course we do. I just wanted to be sure that was absolutely clear. For the record."

I couldn't figure him, and I didn't want to make myself crazy trying, so I just nodded. "I guess I should call the sheriff in," I said, picking up the pager that Veierra had given me, "and let you get on with your very important Bloody Mary business."

"Oh, I shall." But instead of getting up, he leaned in once more, his expression suddenly all sincerity again. "Seriously, though, Cam: it really is nice not to be alone anymore."

"And it's nice to know you're not a jerk after all," I fired back at him.

"Oh, I'm still a jerk." We both burst into laughter. JoJo shook his head. "Are you sure you don't want to skip the orientation and come get Bloodies with me?"

"Dude, I'm still waiting for my first *coffee* of the day."

He smirked. "I'm sure they could bring you a cup. I'd be happy to ask for one, if you…"

I was already making desperate *No* motions with my hands. "Ugh, please, seriously! I had no idea you even got up this early, much less that you'd be ready for happy hour already."

"In general, I make it a point *not* to be up this early," he assured me. "Which is why I'm in such *desperate* need of a drink."

I was turning the pager over to see how it worked when there was a gentle knock on the door, followed by the unmistakable voice of Sheriff Clarke. "Don't mean to interrupt if you're not finished yet."

"And that's my cue," JoJo murmured, getting to his feet. "Come on in," he called. "We're done."

The door opened and the sheriff walked in.

"I'll be down the street if desperately needed," JoJo said breezily, heading for the door. He turned back and gave me a saucy wink as he passed Clarke and sauntered out.

I handed the unused pager to the sheriff, who watched JoJo leave, *Lord help me* written all over his craggy face.

"He's a character, all right," I said.

Sheriff Clarke turned back to me. "That he is."

❧

The sheriff let me take a short break before the orientation. I needed to process a bit, walk around outside.

And I really, really, *really* needed that coffee now.

Friday Harbor was just waking up; it was still early, despite everything that had already happened. Out in the harbor, I could see a ferry pulling in; a line of cars waited in the holding area, ready to drive on board.

I found a cute café across the street from the ferry landing, and ordered a coffee and a cardamom bun to go. Then I walked along the water's edge. I spotted the restaurant where JoJo had said he was going to get Bloodied, but I didn't see him inside.

By the time I got back to the courthouse, refreshed, fed, and invigorated, I was ready to learn about becoming an agent.

♋

After several intense hours, Sheriff Clarke summoned a deputy to motor me back to Orcas Island. "Let's get you back to your normal life before Ms. Cannon gets home from her errands on the mainland," he explained as we waited for the deputy to arrive.

Gosh, they sure did seem to know a lot about Lisa's whereabouts and activities. I wondered whether I should feel worried or relieved that the authorities seemed much more on the ball than anyone was giving them credit for. Anyone *I* knew, at least.

"But remember, not so much as a hint about your involvement here," he added, "even to the officer who's escorting you back. He's been told no more about why you're here than anyone else should know. Understood?"

I nodded, trying to fortify my poker face as my escort knocked at the door.

He was quiet on our trip back through the islands, leaving me alone with my thoughts.

The orientation had been pretty straightforward, even anticlimactic. So many pieces of paper to sign; so many lists of rules and regulations to carefully read, and then have explained to me anyway. So many steps that had to be gone through before I would officially start my confidential informing duties. Background check, identity check, drug test, photograph—we'd only gotten the process started today. It would be weeks before I was cleared to begin.

Oh, and I wouldn't be *paid* anything. Confidential informants performed this work out of the goodness of their hearts. Fortunately, Lisa paid me more than enough; JoJo wasn't hurting for funds either.

There were a million other details. "I know it's a lot," the sheriff had said at one point when he could clearly see my mind was reeling, "but we've found it's better to give too much information than too little. So there's no questions later."

And so you don't get sued, I'd thought.

Before I left, he had reiterated yet again that I was in no way expected to spy on my boss Lisa, and that furthermore, she was to never suspect anything. "You must never give her the impression that you are assisting our investigation in any way, is that clear, Ms. Tate?"

"Yes, that's clear," I'd assured him. "Crystal."

He refused to tell me who I would be paying the closest attention to. "Not until you're official." It had to be the troupe, though.

The sheriff had told me that, once we got underway, I would be brought in periodically for "questioning," and to report my findings. This would not only be a convenient cover story, he said, but it might even lead the actual bad guys to think that law enforcement was focusing on me instead of chasing down the true villains. "Who knows?" Clarke had mused. "Might even make some of them careless, if they think we're barking up the wrong tree." He'd grinned. "Incompetent rural force that we are."

"Right," I'd said. "So I'll be sure and act scared whenever you guys haul me 'downtown.'"

"Or just frustrated and confused. Pretty much anything but overjoyed to see us when we come for you. Don't overdo it. Less is more when it comes to believability."

"I think I can handle that."

I'd probably sounded confident when I said that. But could I? I was no actress.

As the young deputy motored slowly into Massacre Bay and approached the Brixton dock, I couldn't tell from down here on the water if anyone was home in either of the great houses. Was JoJo still on San Juan? Still drinking? Or had even that been just another mask?

He definitely drank; I'd accompanied him enough times to be

sure of that. But there'd been that faux-drunk act just the other day...

Was there any point in even trying to guess which of JoJo's faces were the real ones?

The deputy handed me onto the dock, lifted his hat politely, and motored back out into the open water. I stood on the dock, watching him go as the sound of the boat's engine receded and the ripples on the water smoothed and stilled.

It was a pretty day. The sun was higher overhead than it had been all winter; we were a month into spring by now, and the days were growing noticeably longer, though still not a whole lot warmer. But the sun felt nice on what little skin I had exposed. I turned my face up to the light and closed my eyes, bathing in the vitamin D.

I'm a secret agent, I thought. *I'm a spy!*

Then I hiked up the hill to go feed my pets breakfast—well, lunch—as even spies must do from time to time.

⟡

James and Master Bun were, of course, delighted to see me, and even more delighted when I saved them from near-certain starvation. And from freezing to death, too; I gave in and lit a fire in my woodstove, despite the lovely sun outside.

Once my leggy orange cat was grooming his fur by the fire, and fluffy brown Master Bun was dozing under the dining table, I began to pace around my small house, still trying to figure out just how the heck I was supposed to deal with what had just happened to me.

"I'm a *confidential informant*, James," I told my cat. "Did you know that?"

He licked all the way down his tail, then started at its top again.

"The sheriff himself. You should have seen him and all his paperwork. He was so official, and so serious; I wonder if he feels empowered by having the Feds here on his turf, helping him with such an important case; or pushed out of his own investigation, like Lisa seems to think. Or have we all just watched too many cop shows?"

When Master Bun wandered out from under the table, nose twitching, I scooped him up and carried him outside to his hutch. This was about the time after a meal when he'd be looking for a place to deposit his little poop-pellets. When I came back in, James had finished with his tail and started on his paws.

"I wish there were somebody I could talk to about this—any of it," I told my cat. "But, you know, *confidential*." I sighed. "I mean, you and Bun are wonderful conversationalists; don't get me wrong. I'd be perfectly happy just to stay at home and talk to you all day, forget other people completely." I sighed again. "But while I'm sure no one could give me better advice than you could…I'm not as fluent in your language as you are in mine."

James tugged on a claw with his teeth; something must be stuck there. Cats, honestly. It looked uncomfortable. My own nails began to itch in sympathy. I turned away and gazed out the front windows.

"I guess I could talk more with JoJo—assuming I could find him—but…I've kinda had enough JoJo for the moment. If only I could just call Jen and…" That's when I remembered what I'd learned this morning that she *did* need to know. I grabbed my phone and touched her name.

"What's happening?" she breathed, without even saying hello. I could hear the panic in her voice. "Are they coming for us?"

"No, Jen—I mean, not today, at least," I started.

"What do you *mean*?" she whisper-screamed. "Not *today*?"

I took a breath. "Hang on, just listen to me a minute, okay?"

"Okay…"

"So, I got called in for questioning again this morning and—"

"Oh no!" she cried. "I knew it! We're all going to jail!"

"No we're not!" I cried. "Jen, relax. They know all about your cloak-and-dagger work at the inn, and—"

She wailed incoherently.

"Jen!" I was now totally yelling. James stared up at me, alarmed; had I ever screamed in his presence before? *"Will you just listen?"*

Jen caught her breath, gasping. "Okay. I'm trying. Jeez, Cam."

"They're not going to do anything—to either of us," I blurted out in a blind rush, desperate to short-circuit her flailing panic, "as long as you cut it out right now, okay?"

Silence. "They…they know, and they don't care?" she finally asked, her voice heavy with doubt. "They *told* you that?"

"No, you're still not listening. They know, and they *do* care, in fact kind of a lot. Which is why they want you—*us,*" I quickly corrected myself, "—to cut it out. If we do, they are willing to overlook our little…error in judgment."

"Forever?" she asked. I could hear the hope in her voice.

"Forever, yes, if we *cut it out,*" I repeated. "So no more Trixie Belden and Honey Wheeler. Are you getting me?" I pressed. "Jen?"

She exhaled heavily. "Oh, thank goodness. Oh, wow." She sighed again. "How on earth did you convince them to let us off?"

I tried not to chuckle. *Oh, Jen, how I wish I could tell you…* "I didn't convince them of anything. They brought *me* in to convince me that we really need to stop poking into these things. They know we're not the bad guys here, but our 'investigation' has been a serious interference in the *real* investigation, and they want it stopped. You're hearing this, right?"

"Right," she said quickly. "Oh yes. Wow. I have *so* learned my lesson, Cam, I cannot even tell you."

"Good." If I believed her, which, knowing Jen…

"I'm so sorry you're the one who got hauled in to talk about it," she went on. "Was it Larissa again? Was she pissed?"

"I, ah, it was the sheriff, actually," I stammered.

"The sheriff on Orcas twice in one week!" she said, astonished.

"My goodness. We must really rate."

"Yeah, well."

"I so owe you, Cam," she said, sounding more like herself. I told myself this was good news—that she believed I got brought in just to have this warning delivered.

But whew, keeping this giant secret from my best friend was going to be a challenge.

"No more spying, anywhere, I promise," Jen was saying.

"Good," I said, forcefully. "So—" and then I got the beep of an incoming call. I glanced at my screen. "Oh hey Jen, I have to take this, it's Lisa."

"Right! You go! We'll talk soon!"

"Bye."

I clicked over to Lisa's call. "Hi!" I said, brightly.

"Cam, hello," came her warm voice. "I just wanted to let you know I'll be home this evening. I'm on the six-thirty boat, and assuming it's on time—"

We both chuckled.

"Right," she said, after a moment. "In any event, shall we meet tomorrow after breakfast to get started? Say nine o'clock?"

"That sounds good. Have a nice sailing!"

"I will. See you tomorrow then."

"Yep."

I tucked the phone into my pocket, still smiling. Lisa and I were overdue for having a formal discussion about the rest of my duties in my new capacity as her personal assistant—now that I'd finished writing my play for her. I was excited, and a little nervous. We'd been dancing around the remaining details of my job description for months now. It was hard to believe this was finally going to happen.

Assuming nothing *else* showed up to delay us, yet again. Nothing bigger than a late ferry, anyway.

I spent the rest of the day trying to enjoy my last few hours of leisure, as Lisa had encouraged me to do more than once. I scrolled through social media on my phone till my finger got sore; I tried to read a book, but couldn't get into the story; I went for a walk down on the beach, until the sun set and it got too cold.

Back home, I rekindled the fire, and took my time cooking a dinner of wild-caught salmon filet with fresh rosemary, a cinnamon-baked yam according to my mom's recipe (I made two, so I could have one for breakfast), and a green salad. It felt comforting to fiddle around with all the details, to concentrate on the prep and make a pretty plate. It was so soothing that I wanted to laugh at myself as I sat down to eat. "I just don't know how to relax," I told James. "I'm going to be sorry I wasn't better at this when I get all busy. I'll think back on these days and be very disappointed in myself."

He stared up at me, obviously wondering which part of what I was saying meant *I'm going to give you some of this salmon*. When it became clear that the answer was *None*, he gave up and wandered over to the stove. The A-frame was cozy and toasty, the fire crackling merrily. It wouldn't be long before I wouldn't need fires…at least, I hoped so. I didn't have a lot of firewood left.

And I couldn't ask Colin where to get some more now.

I brought my dinner to the table and dug in, almost too distracted to taste it. Colin had been happy to carry my firewood when he'd also been carrying a torch for me, but after my having finally made it clear to him that there wasn't anything between us, I couldn't keep calling him for help around the place now, as I would a friend. He pretty clearly hadn't seen me as a friend the night he'd stormed out of here.

I sighed. Why did things always have to get so complicated?

I'm a spy, I thought again. *I'm a secret agent*. It was a quiet mantra running behind all my thoughts. *Okay, "confidential informant," whatever*.

I just hated being left alone with this situation. Tonight was one of Jen's bartending nights. Should I drive into town and have a drink at the Barnacle? Just…to take pleasure in her company?

No. That was a terrible idea. She would read all over my face that I had something else on my mind, something I wasn't telling her. I should never try to be sneaky—I knew this, everyone I ever met knew this. *You should never play poker*, more than one person had told me that.

So why in the world do the Feds think it's a good idea to make me a spy?

In spite of all of the morning's conversations, I still had no answer to that.

CHAPTER 2

Lisa ushered me into her bright dining room the next morning. A stack of binders and loose papers sat at one end of the long table; she showed me to a seat at the other end, then sat across from me.

"Coffee?" she asked, with a warm smile.

"Please," I told her. "Do you want me to get it?"

She was already on her feet, patting my shoulder gently as she passed into the kitchen. "No, no. Cream, sugar?"

"Just cream."

A minute later, I was sipping something amazing. Rich, bold, yet smooth and somehow…nourishing? Could coffee be nourishing?

"You're going to give me a list of where all the amazing food and wine and coffee and everything comes from, right?" I asked her. "As part of my training?"

Lisa gave her tinkling laugh. "I think I made it clear that grocery shopping is *not* one of your duties. You'll be busy doing more important things—so let's just jump right in, shall we?"

I nodded, and took another sip as she waved at the pile of materials beside us.

"Most of that is from when I and my assistant were based in

the city," she said. "Some of it might be useful, but here on Orcas, my focus is on Island Rep."

Orcas Island Repertory Theater Company. *Her* company. The one producing *my* play.

"So you know," she continued, "we aren't a community theater. We're a *regional* theater."

"There's a difference?" I hated to reveal my ignorance, but I had to fess up.

"Yes. My actors are paid, for one thing. We produce four plays a year, so we almost always have something in progress. And, while I am the producer and director of this production, I will need *you* to be responsible for much of the day-to-day tasks. Your official role here is production manager."

"Wait, so I'm the playwright *and* the production manager?"

"Absolutely." She smiled brilliantly. "Think of it as an opportunity to completely control your first official production."

Or completely *destroy* my first production, but I didn't say that out loud.

"I think you'll enjoy this work. But—forgive me if I'm mistaken—I'm assuming you have no experience in theatrical production?"

I squirmed. "Um, no. I thought I was writing a screenplay, when I started…"

"Of course," she agreed. "And starting fresh is a good thing, actually. Island Rep is…a little different than most regional repertory theaters, so I like that you aren't coming in with a lot of ideas about how things are *normally* done." She gave me a kind smile. "I'll give you the thirty-thousand-foot overview now; later we can dive down into the details. Do you need more coffee?"

I glanced down into my empty cup. "No, I'm good." I was already jittery.

She set her own cup aside and tented her fingers in front of her face; her grey eyes unfocused for a moment as she thought. "All right: a successful production is a time-consuming and complex endeavor. The performances are just the tip of an iceberg of work, decisions, and design. *Normally*, everything begins with securing the rights to the production." Here she smiled again. "But this time I'm lucky to have an 'in' with the playwright. Since this is an introduction of a previously unpublished work, however, we'll need copies printed up. Then, the real work begins."

"The real work," I said apprehensively.

"Yes. There's set design and construction. Then sound and lighting, and props. We usually recruit our volunteer stage crew from the high school. And then there are the costumes, of course. We have volunteers for those too. Then there's hair and makeup; I do hire that out, and I'll introduce you to Lana later. She's spectacular. Petra can serve as both stage manager and prop master; you'll meet her when we start rehearsals in earnest. I'm still making up my mind about dressers, though Petra may be able to fill that role too."

"Dressers? Like…with drawers?"

"No, no." She chuckled, clearly under the impression I'd been joking. "The need for help dressing the cast varies from production to production. But we do have two multi-role tracks this time—which might mean lots of fast changes off stage. I'll need to think on that a bit more."

I leaned back in my chair. "Wow."

Lisa's smile was distracted but kind. "Wow is right, Cam. Do you see why I need you? Fortunately, I've been doing this for a few years; you won't have to invent the wheel. The venue provides a crew to run the tech, lights, sound, and so on. And Orcas is full of creative people who are ready to work for nothing."

"Nothing?"

"Nothing." She smiled patiently. "I pay a few, but just a few, and not handsomely. The theater is a registered nonprofit, but it's a point of pride that it generally runs in the black. I economize where I can. I rent storage space at the venue for flats, doors, window frames, anything reusable in the way of lumber and molding and whatnot. I try not to store too much, or the rent would cancel out the value of whatever's in there. Sometimes it's more economical to buy what I need, then donate it somewhere after the show. But you'd be surprised what the set designer can do with basically nothing."

"I bet you don't have salon chairs and sinks and a big mirror," I said ruefully.

"My set designer has ins with theater companies all over the Puget Sound area. He can rent, borrow, or steal. He's a genius."

"Who's the set designer?"

She gave me a level look. "Roland Markus. Have you met him?"

I'd met so many people on the island, but that name didn't ring a bell. "I don't…think so?"

Why was she watching me like that; what was I missing? "He's tremendously talented." After the briefest pause, she went on. "There are a few people on the island who can fill the other roles I've told you about—I'll give you the list of names—and find out who's available and interested for this production. Let's see, what am I forgetting?" She pursed her lips and stared into space for another moment.

I hadn't been to one of Island Rep's plays yet. "You said the venue. Is that Orcas Center, or the Grange?"

"Oh!" She laughed. "The venue: of course. Orcas Center and the Grange are wonderful spots, but they have their own boards and committees and all the inevitable complications that come along with competing agendas and consensus decision making. I've assembled my own board, who give me the freedom to do things my way, and work with whomever I choose. I think the results speak for themselves." Her smile was proud now. "So, we have an arrangement with Madrona Farm down in Crow Valley. Do you know them?"

"No, I don't think so."

"It's an old, non-working farm; the family has converted the barn to lovely event space. They hold weddings there, and corporate retreats, and my plays, of course. They have a large stage with first-rate lighting and sound systems. No curtains, though—which our production designs must always take into account."

"No curtains? How do you do curtain calls?"

"With big smiles and deep bows." She shook her head. "You have no idea what it costs to install curtains, and then the fire marshal is involved, and there's testing and...trust me, it's such an arduous process." Theatrical curtains must be pretty dang expensive if even Lisa Cannon was balking at the cost. She went on. "It helps with costs to bring in community volunteers for every role I can."

My head was swimming. "What other roles *are* there?"

"So many. I have a wonderful volunteer who designs the posters and programs. I have an eager cadre of volunteers to get the posters printed and put up all over town. They also usher, take the tickets, run the concessions during intermission—in fact you know one of my volunteers, Paige Berry."

"Oh! Yes. Wait, she does concessions?" I thought about what kinds of "concessions" Paige would provide. Broccoli-bean cookies? Goat milk wine? Kale cupcakes? I stifled a shiver—and some inappropriate laughter.

Lisa didn't miss my expression though; her eyes sparkled with amusement. "As a matter of fact, she is my concessions coordinator. Paige and her crew enjoy helping out, and of course volunteers get to see the shows for free, which they love. Using volunteers not only saves money; it also keeps the community invested."

I nodded. "I get it."

"Good. Because volunteer outreach will be one of your duties. There's also the sale of tickets on the company's website and through key businesses around town. I'll want you to handle that yourself, as funds are involved. So, are you ready to resign yet?" Lisa actually sounded a little worried.

But though I was anxious, I was also intrigued. "Putting a play together sounds like an enormous puzzle, and I'm ready to get started."

"Excellent!" Lisa's smile was dazzling. "You will be working very closely with Madrona Farm in the next few weeks as we get this all worked out in time for rehearsals to begin. I'll help wherever I can since this is your first production, but I warn you right now, I'll have less bandwidth than usual while dealing with...my current interruptions. I'll be relying on my production manager."

"Right. I'll do the best I can," I assured her.

"I know you will—and that you'll know to call me when you can't." Her grin grew wry. "I probably don't need to tell you that the world of theater is filled with...outsized personalities. Some are problematic. Quirky. I'll try to give you a heads-up whenever possible, but you'll run across some interesting folk." Her wry smile ripened. "Above and beyond the usual helping of island eccentricity. But you'll be fine. You have a way with people."

I felt myself blushing. "Uh, thanks."

"Just the simple truth, Cam. Your ability to get along with so many different kinds of people is one of your greatest strengths. I noticed it the day we met, and my confidence in you has just grown ever since."

Ugh, I was terrible at taking compliments. I wanted to sink through my chair, all the way to the center of the earth. I forced myself to keep smiling and focus on the stunningly overwhelming volume of information Lisa had just breezily rattled off. "Um, so, is this all written down somewhere? I'm not sure what to do first..."

She laughed gently. "I know. Yes, it's a lot; and no, I'm sorry, there isn't a handbook." She tapped her temple. "It's all in here, but I'll feed you your assignments in manageable bites. I just wanted to give you an overview so you'd have a sense of the scope. You weren't required to remember it all."

"Whew."

"By the time you've done a half a dozen plays, it'll all seem natural as breathing to you." She gave me a reassuring smile, and I did my best to look reassured. "So, your first assignment is to drive out to Madrona Farm and check on the venue. Introduce yourself to Erin and José Salazar, the owners; they're lovely people. You'll be working most closely with José; he's the hands-on fellow in the barn itself, and all the outbuildings. And an absolute wizard at tech. He runs the boards and lights."

I nodded, guessing that the "boards" had something to do with lights, not with the stage floor.

"The production dates have been planned out more than a year in advance," she said. "But you'll want to double-check that they're on target, since we'll be starting rehearsals on the twenty-ninth and running through most of next month."

By this time, I had taken out my phone and opened the notes app, and was writing all these names, dates, and details down. Lisa noticed and nodded.

"Good idea. Again, though, you're just confirming that there aren't any issues, and familiarizing yourself with the venue—and meeting the Salazars, of course. I'll shoot Erin a quick text to let her know to expect you."

"Thanks," I said while typing away.

"After that, and this doesn't have to be today but it should be this week, I'll give you the contact information for Roland Markus. You'll want to set up a meeting with him as soon as possible."

Her lips pursed as she said his name, and the lines around her eyes became just the tiniest bit more pronounced. I remembered her odd look from a few minutes ago. "Will he be expecting my call?"

"He *should* be expecting your call." She exhaled through her nose. "I hate to throw you into the deep end right away like this, but it can't be helped." A quick, bright smile. "At least everything will seem easier after him! Roland is absolutely brilliant at design, and he combines that with the rare ability to construct a set within budget. He contracts with Orcas Center and the Grange, though they also have in-house staff and some materials of their own. So he's very…in demand, even though he can be somewhat opinionated." She gave a soft sigh. "He's simply the best, and he knows it. He worked for years on Broadway. I can't imagine using anyone else."

"Oh, I get it," I assured her. Brilliant. In demand. *Opinionated.*

She nodded. "I believe you'll handle him beautifully."

"I hope I can. I mean, I don't really know anything about set design…"

"Oh Cam," Lisa said. "You know what a salon *feels* like, and how your play should strike the audience when they enter the theater. So take a little time before you meet with him to think about the kind of mood your play and its characters should evoke. Get the feel of it in your heart and your mind, just as you did when you wrote the play. You envisioned it, yes?"

"I did," I admitted. "I saw it all clearly in my mind."

She nodded. "Exactly. So think this through, and you'll be ready for any pushback from Roland."

Pushback. My favorite. "Do you want to send me his number?" I asked, stifling a sigh. Ugh, I was not looking forward to him.

"I will. And the last part of your first tasks involves the script: we'll need a dozen copies, spiral-bound. Which reminds me." She reached down the table and dragged a slender laptop over from where it had sat next to the pile of materials, and opened it up. "I'm emailing you the latest version of the script. I've added in some very basic set descriptions and notes about blocking. You know what blocking is, right?"

"Uh, I think so—figuring out where everyone stands on the stage?"

"Where they stand, where they move, and when. It'll change in rehearsal, but early blocking notes are crucial for the actors. They tie physical movement to learning their lines. You'll see. What

I've added here will be enough to rehearse from." She turned her attention to the screen, typed and clicked and clicked again, then shut the laptop. "There."

My phone gave an answering chime. "Here," I said, glancing at it.

"Take that file to the Office Cupboard," Lisa said; "the company has an account there. When you have the printed copies, write up a letter to everyone in the cast letting them know who has each part, when read-throughs and rehearsals are to begin, and asking them to confirm their acceptance of the roles and the production schedule—in writing." She smiled again. "A formality, of course, but the businesswoman in me insists on paperwork."

"Okay. But…" I was puzzled. We were missing a step, a very important one. "What about auditions? Don't we need to find replacements for Bella and Petey?"

Lisa smiled indulgently. "Repertory is different. I almost always know who plays what."

"But…are there members of the troupe I haven't met then?" I had totally written the part of Felicia—the "me" character—with Bella in mind. Even though she was at least ten years older than me, she had the presence, the energy; I could just tell she was the best actress of the bunch, and she was super pretty. Not that "super pretty" should be a requirement for the role, I supposed, but…when one imagines a character based on oneself, one imagines someone gorgeous, right?

Sadly, though, Bella had been arrested in Seattle, and would not be appearing in any play for the foreseeable future, except maybe *Jailhouse Rock*. And if there was anyone else in Lisa's troupe who could fill her spot now, I sure hadn't met them.

Lisa's smile grew mysterious. "No auditions. I recruit the actors I want. And frankly," she held my gaze, the smile now gone entirely, "I don't want to risk giving Derek and his moles another shot at me."

My heart sped up, with fear and surprise. "You think he

would…I mean, could he do that again so quickly?" She'd told me that Derek had planted Bella and Petey as moles in her acting troupe. They'd been working for him the whole time! It was still hard to wrap my brain around. They'd seemed so much like… well, like actors. But I supposed that's what moles had to do, wasn't it? Put on an act.

Then again, *I* was secretly working for the Feds now… And I forced that thought right away, along with all its unwanted implications. "Moles" had nothing to do with me. Not here. We were just producing my play, written by no one but me with my own ten fingers.

"I'm sure Derek knew about their arrests before I did," Lisa said. "In fact, if I know him at all, he's expecting me to hold auditions to replace my two *best actors* as quickly as possible. They both joined the troupe last year at the same time, and they were so *good*. Oh, Derek made sure the bait would be taken." She nodded, speaking more to herself than me at this point. "He'll have sent new bait up here. But I won't bite this time." She smiled softly.

I suddenly remembered JoJo's remark yesterday morning, about the investigation being about so much bigger and darker stuff than I knew. Had he ever actually answered my question about who the real bad guys were? I didn't think so. Derek, obviously; but he'd made it clear there was more to it than just an ugly divorce and an angry ex-husband. Did even Lisa know who or what she was really up against, or was that something only a mole for the Feds would be privy to?

"Well!" Lisa said brightly. "None of that matters anyway, because I've already found perfect replacements for Petey and Bella. People I know and trust implicitly."

"You have?" Oh, of course she had; Lisa Cannon would have a huge network of talent to draw from.

Still smiling, she got up and walked to a pile at the far end of her dining table, came back with another sheet of paper, and handed it to me. "Here's all the scheduling and location information you'll need, along with the cast list and their email addresses. Make sure they have each other's contact information. They should already have it, but you know actors." Oh, she could not stop grinning. What in the world…

I looked down, skimming past the contact information for Roland Markus (ugh) and a few of the other people she'd mentioned, to find the cast list. The first role on it was Martin, the male lead—and my mouth fell open. *JoJo Brixton?*

I looked up at her, stunned. "He's agreed to this?"

She nodded happily.

Well, of course he would, I thought. He was a born actor—and this way he could spy on everyone in the troupe. What a tricky fellow JoJo was turning out to be.

"I'm sure you know that JoJo is a pitch-perfect performer, even in his sleep," Lisa said, echoing my thoughts while making me wonder, yet again, how familiar Lisa was with JoJo's sleeping habits. Would I ever find out?

Oh, you have no idea what a performer he is, I thought, glancing further down the list to see who she'd found to play Felicia.

At first, the name I saw just confused me.

Then I gasped.

And then I just froze, caught between laughter and horror. "You're…joking?" I finally managed to squeak out.

Lisa's delighted laugh tinkled through the room, and though it was the middle of the morning, I desperately wanted a glass of her fine wine. "Not at all!" she said merrily. "Who am I going to find—here or anywhere—who knows this character better than the woman who *wrote* the part, after *living* her life?"

"Oh my…no, no! Lisa, I can't *act!* In front of a *room full of people!*" My arms were already starting to tingle. "I couldn't stand up on a stage and read a birthday card aloud. There's no way on earth that I can—"

"Oh yes you can!" she sang, still bursting with great good

cheer. "I know you don't think you have it in you, but I can spot potential, and you—"

"No!" I actually interrupted her back, shocking myself, but apparently not her.

"Yes!" she parried, cheerfully. "You don't know it yet, but you have all the resources a good actor needs! The rest is just confidence."

"Of which I have zero!" I cried, unable to stop myself. The tingles up and down my arms worsened—I could *not* vanish in front of Lisa! Not here, not now, not anywhere ever! Oh, why weren't we having this terrible, dreadful, impossible meeting at cocktail hour? "Less than none! Way, way less, Lisa!" I was begging now, nearing total panic.

"Which is why this is exactly what you need to do, Cam," she said, a little more seriously, though still absolutely delighted with herself. "As you already know, I'm committed to mentoring young women with outstanding potential—like you. And I want you to try this. In fact, I'm making this play, and your *acting* in it, a central feature of your work for me."

"That's not fair," I murmured, barely able to find my voice. Oh, I had so wanted this job, had been so proud of myself for stepping out of my old life and into this shiny new one, of becoming a well-respected (and well-*paid*) personal assistant to the great Lisa Cannon. And now...

She was looking at me kindly. "You're right," she said, almost apologetically. I felt a *thunk* of relief. I'd gotten through to her. "It isn't fair, you're not wrong there; and I understand how frightening this will seem to you at first. I *respect* that fear, Cam. In fact, I respect it much too deeply to enable it."

My gaze shot from the folded hands in my lap, back up to her. For a moment it had sounded like she'd heard me, but no. No.

She continued to look at me kindly, gently. "You'll never become who you truly are unless you discover what it's like to break *through* that fear."

I opened my mouth to say something—to plead, to disagree, I didn't even know what—but she continued before I could get anything out.

"*But*, because I do respect your fear—and *you*—I'll make you a bargain. So you don't think I'm a villain." A warm smile. "I'll be your understudy. As director, I'll be at every rehearsal, and know every one of your lines, every detail and nuance of your whole play, as well or better than anyone else in the cast. And, if you still feel as frightened one week before we open as you do now, I'll step in and play the part myself."

"You…you will?" I stammered.

She nodded. "I will—if it comes to that. I'm too old for the part, and I won't be anywhere near as good at it as you're going to be. But I'll do a decent job, and I won't think one bit less of you when all is said and done—as long as you really, honestly tried. Your job with me will be as secure as ever, and there will be nothing for you to explain to anyone—ever. Is that fair?"

"That's more than fair," I managed, feeling both relieved and ashamed at the same time, and also somehow—goaded? But in a good way. Propped up. *She's good*, a small part of my brain whispered. I saw now how she pushed her "promising young women" into achieving things they hadn't ever dreamed they could.

Too bad it hadn't worked on Marie. But then, she had been up against more than just a lack of self-confidence, hadn't she?

Would I be her next failure?

"I want you to try this, Cam," Lisa said, more softly. "Truly try it. I promise, there is so much more to you than you know." Then she winked at me, literally winked.

I still couldn't find my voice.

"And now," she said, as if I had agreed, and the matter was all settled and behind us, "I need to ask you for some of that discretion we talked about, in regard to what I'm paying you."

"Oh. Oh!" I said, caught off guard by the change of subject. "Yes, of course."

She smiled. "No one else in the cast is getting paid as much for doing this play as my new production manager/lead actor will be." And then her smile grew. "Of course, no one else will be working nearly as hard as you, so you're earning every cent of it."

"Right. So, um, about that..."

"Of course." Lisa chuckled, and pushed back from the table as she drew her slender smartphone out of a pocket of her jeans. "I'll send a quick text to the Madrona folks."

"Right," I said again. My head was still spinning as I got up too, and numbly took the materials Lisa handed me. Including this absurd, impossible cast list.

Oh my freaking gosh, I thought. *I'm a secret agent* and *an actress. All in one day! I hope my head doesn't explode all over Lisa's lovely dining room.*

At least my arms had stopped tingling.

CHAPTER 3

I walked almost blindly back down the path to my little cottage, but once there, I didn't go inside. I needed a moment to regroup. I continued on the path through the woods, skirting the creepy little house where Sheila had lived.

The same creepy house where I'd been held captive. Where I'd first found the earliest vestiges of my strength, of control over my own life…over my own supernatural disability.

Where I'd escaped from Sheila.

I shivered. It was still unsettling, and trying to talk myself into feeling better about it wasn't really helping. I walked on, just breathing the fresh outdoor air, trying to blank my mind.

That lasted all of thirty seconds. I couldn't act in a play! How could Lisa think I would be any good at it? She was crazy, she was projecting, she didn't know me…she was just doing this so she could take the role herself, that's why she'd offered to do it if I was too scared…

But that was silly, wasn't it? She could just have taken the role if she wanted it. There'd been no need to put me through this torture and then swoop in to save the day. I could imagine the kind of person who might do something like that, and it wasn't Lisa.

I just had to take her word for it, didn't I? I just had to believe in her confidence in me.

Ugh.

I circled back through the woods and walked to my car, got in, and drove up to Crow Valley Road.

The farm was easy enough to find, now that I knew where to look. It was completely picturesque, even this early in the spring, when leaves were starting to bud out on the deciduous trees and the fields were still muddy.

I drove down the long, well-graveled and graded driveway and found a large flat parking lot with spaces delineated in white chalk. Very fancy! I parked next to one of the bright red barn's three sets of big double doors, and was out of my car before I noticed the smaller door off on the far right-hand side. The one sized for people, not for tractors and horses.

Oh well.

I walked over to that door prepared to knock, but it opened and a middle-aged redheaded woman stepped out. "You must be Camille," she said with a bright smile.

I held out my hand and she shook it. "Call me Cam," I said. "And you're Erin?"

"One and the same. Come on in—José is up on a ladder, of course, so we can talk till he comes back down to earth."

I liked her immediately.

She waved me through the door into a well-lit hallway paneled in clean but rustic wood, and led me to a second door on the left. She beckoned me into a much larger and darker space, which I realized was right behind the three sets of large double doors I'd seen from outside. As my eyes adjusted to the dimmer light, I liked what I saw, including rustic metal chandeliers and restroom doors at the far end.

"This is our lobby space," she said, turning to smile at me. "The large outer doors are opened for events, filling this room with light and fresh air. The smaller doors over there," she gestured toward three more sets of more finished-looking double doors on the opposite wall, "lead into the larger event space you'll be using for the play. Shall we go take a look at that?"

"Yes, please."

She pulled open one of the center doors and led me through. Now I could see very clearly that we were in a barn. But even this cavernous room was nothing like what I'd been imagining—starting with the absence of any smell of hay or animals or machinery. It had definitely been repurposed for people. People in dressy clothes and impractical shoes. The floor was concrete, but polished to a high sheen and stained a soft green, and looked clean enough to eat off of. The walls were age-bleached wood, with knotholes artfully scattered about; the roof was high, almost too high to see clearly in the dim light, but I would have bet there weren't swallows or bats nesting up there.

Incongruously, there was a stack of hay bales in the far corner, but I wondered if they were even real. They looked clean enough to decorate Lisa Cannon's living room. (Or to perch on in a white lace wedding dress, perhaps.)

"This way," Erin said, after giving me a moment to gaze around. "There are rooms with a more human scale here too."

She led me across the giant room, and through a large arched gap on the opposite wall into a hallway running along the back side of the building past lots of doorways. "These will be your dressing rooms and cast restrooms," she said.

Eventually, we turned right at the building's corner and entered a small office, where Erin offered me a chair, and took the one beside it. "So you're Lisa Cannon's new assistant," she said warmly. "We just love hosting Island Rep's plays. It makes such a fun change from executive board retreats…don't ever let anyone know I said that, though."

I smiled back at her. "Don't worry—your secret is safe with me."

"Great." She leaned back. "So how long have you lived on Orcas?"

"Since last fall."

We chatted for a few minutes. I usually found small talk challenging, and I'd have thought I would have found it even more difficult now that I had so much stuff to remember, and so much more I had to very carefully avoid even hinting at, but Erin made it easy. I could see why she'd gone into the events-hosting business. She was just telling me about the year's schedule when a middle-aged man stepped into the small office. He was sturdily built, with a ready smile and kind eyes. "Ah!" Erin said, her face suffusing with joy. "And here's my better half."

I stood up and shook hands with José, noting the familiar rough calluses of an island man. It made me think of Colin for a moment, and of how JoJo's hands were flower-petal soft. "Nice to meet you," I said.

"You ladies need another minute to finish up?" he asked.

"Oh no," Erin said, "we were just gabbing. I only brought her in here so she wouldn't have to watch if you fell off that joist."

They both laughed; clearly an old-married-couple joke, even if it made me shiver. "Not today, my dear," he said lightly. "Better luck next time." Then he turned to grin at me. "Ready to have a look around?"

I followed him back out into the vast openness of the barn; Erin moved behind her desk, already tapping on her computer keyboard as we exited.

"There's your stage," José said, leading me toward a large, broad platform at the far end of the space, beside the weirdly pristine hay bales. "As you can see, it's wider and shallower than a lot of stages, which works well with speakers, but it means your design needs to be wider and shallower, too."

"I'm sure Roland Markus knows what we need?"

"Whoo! Him." He shook his head. "Let's hope he remembers."

Well, that was encouraging. "It's going to be a beauty salon, so I think…"

José's eyes lit up. "Oh, are you doing *Steel Magnolias*? Erin and

I saw that a few years ago at the Grange and we loved it!"

"It's…"

"Yeah! It's a great play! I heard it sold out, too. Not a dry eye in the place during that second act. It was a real winner, not like that *Amber Waves* Lisa did a few years ago. That play was a bummer. So depressing. No, you're much better off with something like *Steel Magnolias*, even though that one girl, you know, dies." He gave me such an open, happy smile that I hated to burst his bubble.

"It's not *Steel Magnolias*. It's a different play called *Salon Confidential*."

"Hm. Never heard of that one."

"No one has. It's new."

"A premiere, huh?"

"Yeah."

In the awkward silence that followed, we stared out into the space that would eventually hold an audience, an audience that would be looking at me. I decided it would be better to panic about that a little later, when I was alone.

But I felt a little dizzy, so when he hopped down from the stage, I followed him. "We set up the chairs starting about here, making two aisles, going back to about…here. And your tech booth will be on scaffolding, up there." He pointed up at a spot about halfway up the back wall, between two sets of lobby doors. I wasn't sure what a "tech booth" even was, but there'd be time for that later, I was sure. I didn't want to advertise what an amateur I was.

He walked back to a point about midway through the barn, and I obediently followed, looking here, there, anywhere but at the stage and the idea of me up there.

"We set up the chairs depending on ticket sales, of course; so we start with not as many. She likes it to look full, but there's plenty of room to add more if it's a popular show. Like the Christmas shows, she always sells out those." He pondered a moment.

"When she does a Christmas show, that is. Not sure what the thinking was this year."

"She was traveling for business," I said, as if Lisa Cannon needed defending.

"Your concessions will be set up in the lobby, of course. As I guess you saw, we have lots of room there for folks to stand around while they have their snacks and gab. Ticket sales only bring in so much money, you know. Wine and snacks go a long way to help support a local theater."

"Yes, Lisa mentioned the concessions."

"Every play's gotta have an intermission," José went on amiably, as if continuing some argument with someone who wasn't here. "Two intermissions is even better, if you can swing it. Then folks who were trying to save money or calories during the first one will have sat there through the second act smelling chocolate-chip cookies and fresh-brewed coffee and hardly able to stand it. You need a nice long intermission, too; the crowd is a little older. That's why we have plenty of restrooms, too. The last thing you want is folks waiting in a restroom line for the whole intermission and not buying any snacks."

"Uh-huh." Boy, this fellow had some passionate opinions about intermissions. "My play—our next play, that is—definitely has an intermission." Could I rejigger the scenes and have two? I wondered.

"Worst kind of play of all is a one-act," he went on. "You go to one of those experimental theaters down in Seattle, you know the ones, you walk in and look at the program and if it doesn't mention an intermission, whoo-hoo, you want to just turn right back around and leave. A play without an intermission is a play that doesn't have the confidence in itself that it can hold an audience. They know most people are too polite to get up in the middle of the acting and walk out, even if it's terrible, but they'll slip away at intermission without a look back. Nope. Most folks' time is too important to waste on bad theater. If they'd be happier at home in their PJs in front of their televisions, that's where they'll be."

"Okay," I said. I could certainly see why these people were so delighted to fill the barn with people, though; if I wasn't careful, José would have me here all day. "I, um, do have to get up to town pretty soon," I told him. "So if there's anything I should really see before we go over the schedule of dates—"

"No problem," he said. "There *is* one little thing over here I'm working on that you're probably gonna want to mention to Miz Cannon, bit of a deal with the breaker capacity…"

☙

I drove away an hour later, my head filled with…well, everything.

I was still in shock, processing the *I'm going to be an actress* part of all the past two days' surprises. Strangely, it helped a little to have a tangible place now to envision that actually happening. At one point, when José had been called away by Erin to take a phone call, I'd stood in front of the stage and looked back across the huge, empty room. It was dusky enough that I could squint and envision rows of portable chairs, first empty, then filled with people. People all looking back at me, pleasant anticipation and expectation on their faces.

My heart had sped up at this, in the familiar fear and alarm, but also, just maybe, a little bit of…excitement? To be sure, nothing like the excitement Lisa had shown when she'd dropped this terrible horrible no-good very bad idea on my head this morning, but maybe…just a sliver?

(Was I entirely sure that Lisa didn't have some strange supernatural power herself? I had my chameleoning, Paige Berry had her…whatever she had. Was Lisa's ability to make her young mentees believe in themselves some kind of magic?)

I drove up Crow Valley Road toward Eastsound. I planned to grab lunch before stopping at the Office Cupboard, which also gave me a little frisson of excitement. After the tangible effects produced by standing in the venue and imagining it all, what would it feel like to hold *actual printed copies of my play* in my hands?

I was so distracted by this vision that I forgot to pick up lunch and drove straight to the little stationery/office supplies/print services shop next to the post office.

And there the reality of it hit me all over again. I could not, could *not* do this…

Since Lisa was not safe to whine to, I pulled out my phone and called Jen. "Oh thank goodness you're there," I said when she picked up. "I am in *such* trouble."

"No!" she cried. "Are the Feds coming for us after all? Oh, I knew it was too good to be true! They were probably luring us into a false sense of—"

"It's not the Feds. This is way bigger trouble than that!"

Thankfully, she fell silent. I'd stunned the great Jen Darling into silence—if only for a moment. "Oh honey," she nearly whispered, sounding horrified. "Are you all right? What on earth could be bigger than the Feds…is it Kevin?"

"Ha! Who cares about Kevin?" I scoffed. "No, listen: Lisa is making me *act!* In *my own play!* She says I have to play the *lead*— that it's part of my *job as her personal assistant! Like she might even fire me if I don't do it!"* I was nearly yelling by now, closed up in my car, but people were still noticing as they walked by on their way into the post office. I tried to get a hold of myself.

"Girlfriend!" Jen cried, now sounding delighted. "That's amazing! You are *exploding!* Like a firecracker! This is fantastic!"

"What? No, it's not! It's terrible!"

"No, no, now you wait and listen to me, honey. Seriously!" She laughed. "I have never seen anyone bust out like this before! I'm in awe!"

"You're crazy!" I shifted the phone to my other ear and tried to keep my voice lower than a shriek. "I called you for support and you're just as wacko as Lisa!"

"Hon, Cam, no, please," she said more softly, though she was clearly still just beside herself with glee. "I hear you, I know, this is scary. But I see where she's coming from. Take a deep breath, okay?"

Because I love Jen, I did so, and then another for good measure. "So," I said sullenly. "Tell me why you're taking that madwoman's side against your very best friend in the whole wide world."

She chuckled. "Cam, sweetie. I am your best friend, and I've known you since almost when you first got here. Which, I admit, hasn't been all that long, in the grand scheme of things—but what I've seen in, what, six months maybe? is simply unbeliev-able."

"Yeah, a lot has happened, hasn't it?"

"Yes, but that's not what I'm talking about. I mean *in you*. Just your life since you moved here in November—the things you've faced, the things you've accomplished. You've investigated mysteries, and even solved a few. You've written a play! You've told off your ex-boyfriend! You've straightened things out with both Colin and Kip, and I know that took some rare courage. You've told off Diana Brixton, and then landed a much better job with Lisa Cannon. You've even gotten JoJo Brixton to humbly apologize to you and spend all day and a great deal of money trying to win your friendship back. Cam, hon, what in the world makes you think you *can't* just waltz onto a stage and absolutely kill it?"

"Because I'm not an actress, Jen," I said.

"I think they're all just called actors, Cam, and you're young enough to know that."

"I know zero about theater. I was hired to be a caretaker, and I somehow turned into a personal assistant and a playwright, and now I'm a production manager and an actress. I mean, actor."

"You weren't any of those other things either, and now you are. All you had to do was try, and boom, you nailed it! Acting will be no different."

"But it will!"

"Okay," she said, "it will be different: it will be better. Easier—because you wrote the play, so those are your own words. And bigger—because this play will be a sensation. And even more fabulous because it's *you!*"

I rolled my eyes. "You don't think you're laying it on a little thick there?"

She laughed. "Oh hon. I'm just trying to talk you down from this ledge you've climbed out on. You've totally got this. Seriously: this play is golden, and you're *on fire.*"

And she didn't even know the half of what was freaking me out. Seriously indeed: nothing was turning out the way I'd imagined it would when I'd finished writing the play a few weeks ago, then started—as she put it—telling people off, taking a stand in my own life. Oh, how I wished I could tell her the rest…but she'd probably just tell me I was going to make the best, most kick-butt confidential informant that ever walked the face of the earth, that ballads were going to be sung of my exploits around campfires for a thousand years to come…

"And I'm sorry," she went on, "but I've got to drop off these dogs and get on to the Goose—I'm almost late. Let's touch base later tonight, okay?"

"Dogs?" I asked.

She chuckled. "That's right, I guess I forgot to tell you—I got another job."

"*Another* one? What's that now, four?"

"Something like that. I'm a dog walker a couple times a week. The pay is great and the dogs are sweethearts—Rufus, down!—well, mostly sweethearts. I'll call you later, okay?"

"Uh, sure."

"Rufus!" The phone went dead. I stared at the screen for a moment, then stuck it back in my pocket. I took another deep breath, pondering her words.

Yeah, I supposed it probably looked like I was "busting out" all over, from where *she* stood. But Jen did know me better than most. So she should also know that, whatever was going on, it wasn't *me* to be so...I don't know, big in the world.

It wasn't an accident that my supernatural disability was a penchant for disappearing. It also wasn't an accident that I'd decided to try my hand at writing—the world's most solitary art form, right? I liked being behind the scenes, watching from a safe distance.

I didn't want to be on stage.

With a heavy sigh, I opened my car door and got out.

The automatic door slid aside, allowing me into the hallway in front of the Office Cupboard and the antique store next door. But just then, the stationery store's door opened too, and who should walk out but Deputy Kip Rankin, with a big shopping bag in his arms. I could see some of those little notebooks all the deputies used in such great quantity, sticking out of the bag. "Um, Miz Tate!" he said, his blue eyes widening. "Er, Camille, rather. Hello."

"Uh. Hi, Kip." My face was flaming, my arms tingling. We both stood frozen, staring at each other. I mean, of course we were going to run into each other around town. The island was small, and Eastsound was tiny. But why did it have to be so *soon*—and *today* of all days? There was a legal blood alcohol limit; shouldn't there be a daily trauma limit too?

"I, uh, see you've been doing some shopping," I said, stupidly, wanting to smack my own forehead.

"Right, yep," he said. "Uh, nice day for it, huh? I guess."

I should just step around him and go into the store. Do my business, leave him to his. So why couldn't either of us move??

"Yeah, it is," I said. "Well."

"Well. I, uh, really should get to the substation with these." He jiggled the bag a little, as if to verify his point somehow. I could hear those little notebooks rustling around in there.

"Yeah, wouldn't want those office supplies getting stale or anything." Now I nearly needed to physically restrain my own hand from reaching up to slap myself in the head. *Shut up, Cam! Just shut up and let him go!*

He gave me a wavery smile and nodded. Those eyes, those curls, that mellifluous voice…

No.

"Right," he said, and moved to step around me. Of course, that was right when I unfroze and started to step around him. We did the world's most awkward little dance until I finally escaped around him and nearly ran smack into the Office Cupboard's door before realizing that it had an actual doorknob that required my hand to open.

Once safely inside, I ducked into the art-supply side of the store just to pull myself back together. *Good gracious*, I thought. *Could that have gone any worse?*

No, no it could not have. And yet. It was over, and I had not died.

In spite of my still-waning panic, I could not help thinking that Kip had looked…really good.

And that ship had *so* sailed. Now I needed to focus on the very real and compelling business that had brought me in here.

But it still took me a few more minutes before I could manage to go to the clerk and arrange to have the play copies printed up.

୧✌୨

I stopped by Lisa's place on my way home to report on my progress, and she seemed pleased. "Give Markus two, maybe three days before you try him again," she said. "Escalate from there if he ignores your second message."

"Escalate. Will do." How did one escalate, I wondered. "So what should I do next?"

She glanced at her watch. "It's nearly four; I do have one last errand for you, if that's not too inconvenient?"

"Oh, sure," I said. "What?"

"Remember that binder I left in your keeping?"

"Oh. Yes, of course. Do you need it?"

She nodded. "I do. If you wouldn't mind getting it for me before the bank closes at five? As discreetly as possible, of course," she said, giving me a wink.

"No problem. I'll do it now and be back in half an hour."

"Oh, no need to rush back. I'm actually heading out any minute now for an early dinner with a Seattle business associate who's on the island for a yoga retreat. Let's just touch base in the morning about your next round of tasks, and you can give me the binder then, okay?"

"You bet," I said.

"Thanks, Cam."

When I got home from the bank, I tucked Lisa's binder onto a shelf in the little closet where I kept the litter box, still a bit nervous about leaving it where anyone might happen to see it. Then I plopped into my chair beside the wood stove. After the day I'd had, it was an amazing relief to be back inside my adorable little cabin, with only a cat and a bunny rabbit for company. They were the *best* company. They wanted very simple, very predictable things from me. Things I could provide. I wasn't letting them down.

Okay, I wasn't letting Lisa down either.

But, while my pets were world class listeners, I really did need some clear advice, from someone who could talk back to me. I thought about Jen, but she was probably busy, or she'd have called me back by now. Who else could I share my overstuffed mind with—who would take me seriously—and respond with something like intelligence?

JoJo seemed constitutionally unequipped to take anything or anyone seriously.

We could talk about the play—he was slated to play the other lead, after all. But if I called him and poured out my fears and anxieties now, I'd probably just end up berating him for knowing all about this the other day—because, looking back now, he so clearly had known all about it, the wretched sneak—and not giving me a single word of warning!

Oh he was a jerkface, that JoJo. What a lot of fun he must have had, going on about how Lisa would want me there for every minute of it all.

And if I was stupid enough to open up about the panic I was feeling now, he'd just tease me for it. Then I'd feel even more embarrassed and helpless. Funny how Mr. Sad-eyed Clown was so happy doing to other people exactly what his dreadful family had done to him, I thought, with all his sober confessions about the dangers of vulnerability, and his need for protective camouflage. *To hide you from people like yourself.*

"Well, James," I said, rubbing him about the ears as I sat in my comfy chair, "I guess I'm just lucky to have you, kiddo."

He purred in great appreciation of this.

"I wish you were bigger, then you could play Martin instead of JoJo Jerkface." I thought about it. "Well, bigger and also able to talk." I scratched his chin. "And you'd probably have to be able to stand up on your hind legs too, and hmm, you'd need opposable thumbs for all that hair-cutting that goes on, and stuff like that."

He continued purring. No problem is insurmountable when you're a fuzzy orange cat.

And then, I realized who I could talk to, and nearly slapped myself across the head again.

My mom! Duh.

The confidential informant stuff was off limits, of course—but I could tell her a lot more than I had already. In fact, I already should have by now, really. I touched base with Mom often, but usually by text, and almost never about anything big—mostly because I didn't want to keep alarming her and Dad after last Thanksgiving. That was when Sheila's cousin's dead body had washed up on the beach, forcing me to admit that it wasn't the *first* dead body that had turned up around here...and then that

I'd been kidnapped briefly, and was still healing from a gunshot wound in the arm.

That hadn't gone so well. And I'd been careful to tell my folks only the nice, quiet things that were happening in my life... which had also been the only things, thankfully, until the last few weeks. I hadn't told her yet about Marie's sudden illness, or the Feds on the island. I hadn't even told my folks about the azalea caper last winter.

I should have. Not just because Mom would be understanding and sympathetic, but because not telling her—or Dad—when I was in peril had been what bothered them most about last winter's episode. Protecting my mom from unpleasant truths wasn't going to help either of us.

This, after all, was the woman who had rescued me from my childhood. She knew more than almost anyone else in the world what I'd been through—what I'd survived, how I'd struggled. She'd never pushed. She was just always there, loving me, supporting whatever bargain I managed to make with the world around me.

I knew she had been baffled when I'd thrown over my Seattle life with Kevin and bolted for Orcas Island, but all she'd done was cheerfully bundle up herself and Dad and an absurd amount of groceries and come all the way out here to celebrate Thanksgiving. (Well, and ignore my instructions about taking the ferry, so that they ended up missing *two* boats in a row.)

I pulled out my phone and punched her number.

"Well, hello dear," she said, sounding happily surprised.

"Hey," I said. "Are you in the middle of things?"

She chuckled. "Always, but nothing that's more important than talking to my daughter. What's up?"

After months of basically texting cheerful emojis, I didn't think I could just dive into the bigger stuff. "Oh, nothing much—just hadn't heard your voice in a while. How are you?"

"Well, I'm fine. But how are *you*? Settling into that adorable little cabin all right? It isn't too small for you and all those pets?"

I rolled my eyes; good thing we were on a voice call and not FaceTime. "The cabin is perfect, one hundred percent perfect, Mom. I own basically nothing, and you know how I've always liked cozy places."

"That's all true," she allowed.

"You do need to come see it," I said. "These front windows— when the sun comes through the trees outside, it's like nothing I've ever seen before." *Nothing like Wenatchee*, I thought, feeling a little sorry for my parents. Sure, rural eastern Washington had its own beauty, but I'd take this place over anywhere else I'd ever been.

"Should I start looking at the calendar?"

"Sure, why not? I miss you guys."

"And we miss you." She paused, then said, "Cam dear, though it truly is marvelous to hear from you, my mother's intuition wonders if something's wrong."

Ugh, I couldn't even do "poker face" over the phone. "Well, no," I sighed, "I mean, yes, but not really wrong, I mean not to me…" I stumbled to a halt. "Hang on. Let me start over."

Mom laughed softly. "Honey, whatever it is, you can tell me."

Nope, I can't, I thought. *Not all of it.* "So um, the first thing you should know is that Marie—remember Marie?"

"Yes, I do. That poor little mouse, is she still texting you every ten minutes?"

"She's—oh Mom, I'm sorry I didn't tell you about this sooner, but Marie was airlifted off the island a few weeks ago…she was really sick, and now she's in a coma at a hospital in Seattle."

"Oh my goodness! Sick with what?"

"Well, see, that's the other thing. It might not just be…sickness. They think she might have been poisoned, or something like that. That it wasn't just a normal illness. And I might as well tell you that I saw a prowler around her house right before she fell into the coma."

Mom paused for only the briefest moment. "The prowler didn't see you, I hope?"

"I'm safe, don't worry. I called 911, and they searched the woods and didn't find anyone." I squirmed in my chair. "I don't know why I didn't want to tell you, but, I just…didn't."

"I know why." Her voice was kind. "And I understand. I'm glad you're safe. And, honey?"

"Yeah?"

"It's all right. You don't have to tell me everything. You don't have to tell me *anything*, in fact; but I'm always glad when you do."

"Um. Thank you."

"Of course." Gosh, she sounded so calm, so sympathetic. "I haven't forgotten what happened when your dad and I overreacted last Thanksgiving. I knew it even then, but once the momentum got going…well, you know how it is. And you know how your father gets."

"I do," I said slowly. He loved me so much. He always wanted to protect me.

"We were frightened for you, of course, but it was a mistake to try to get you to leave. I knew that, but old habits die hard." She gave a quiet laugh. "I've been protecting you since you came to us, and the first time you tried to step out and do something new and different, I was ready to pull you right back under my wing. The truth is, nowhere in this world is completely safe—Orcas isn't any different from anywhere else."

I was utterly astonished. *Mom* was apologizing to *me* for trying to take care of me?

And that's when I realized we'd been stuck in this feedback loop—hiding from each other in order to take care of each other. I'd tried to protect her (and Dad) from worrying about me, even as she'd tried to protect me from—well, from the whole world. When I was a helpless child, I'd needed that protection. But I'd outgrown that.

And Mom knew that.

"You've been growing into yourself all winter," she went on. "Writing your play; getting this new job with Lisa Cannon. Telling Kevin to take a hike. I'm so proud of you, honey. You're really stepping up and starting to star in your own life."

"Um. About that…" I began. Because if that wasn't an opening, I didn't know what was.

"Yes?"

I took a deep breath and told her what this "wonderful new job" was really going to entail…*acting*. On a *stage*.

"Cam! That's so exciting!" she said when I'd blurted it all out. "How wonderful!"

"*No*," I almost moaned. "Not you too! Don't you see? I'm *not* an actor, I don't *want* to be on stage!"

"Well, it's not anything you've done before, and I'm sure that's a little nerve-racking—"

"It's terrifying!"

"—but, as I was just saying, it's perfectly in line with everything I've been watching you do all winter. Honey, this is amazing news. Lisa is kind of a genius, giving you this. And now I know what dates we'll want to visit. Oh, I wonder if your brother can get over here from Thailand. You'll let us come see you in the play, won't you?"

"Well—of course," I stammered. "But Mom—I'm glad you think I'm strong and capable and all that, and I don't want to sound ungrateful that you want to come see it—but I'm just… it feels like I'm stuck in some kind of anxiety dream. You know?"

"I might," she said calmly. "But explain to me what you mean, exactly, so I can be sure."

I took a breath. James had fallen asleep in my lap, which was comforting. I wished again that I could tell her the rest of what I was coping with—but this part would have to do. "So, to me anyway, it feels like this. Lisa's amazing, and I love her to pieces, and she's been so, so good to me, really from the day I met her.

Okay? And all those months ago, when I told her I was writing a screenplay, she took me seriously. She asked me a few questions and asked had I ever considered writing a *stage* play? Well, I hadn't, and I didn't even really know the difference other than the obvious, but she explained it to me and encouraged me and told me that she'd be delighted to take a look at it when it was done."

"Mm-hmm," Mom said.

"And before I was even done writing the play, she hired me to caretake for her when it all fell apart with Diana Brixton, and gave me a stupid big salary. She paid me to do hardly anything all winter but sit around and finish the play. Then when I finished it, she did read it and she loved it! Except she suggested some changes—which were actually *perfect*, they made the play so much better. And now she's going to produce it! And direct it!"

"Yes, you've told me all this," Mom said patiently. "I'm waiting for the anxiety dream part."

"Don't you see? It's all Lisa. *I'm* not doing any of this—I mean, I am, sure; but she's the driver behind everything. It's all her idea, her encouragement, her mentoring. Her house and her grounds and her actors and her whole world! And now it's her idea that I should go up on that stage and act out the part myself!"

"Hmm," she said. "I see what you mean, but…there's another way to look at it, honey."

"Okay, like…?" I waited.

"First of all, the play itself—or screenplay—was *your* idea, *your* creation. Based on your own life experiences, written full of details that only you know. And you've done *all* the work of writing and rewriting it."

"That's true," I admitted.

"And," Mom went on, "I remember all the actual caretaking work you did last winter. Above and beyond the whole leak-flood-water-damage-complicated-repair situation that led to your taking over the job, you told me about your walking the grounds, checking water pipes during a freeze, getting mail over icy roads, taking deliveries, all the things that happen with a house in the middle of the woods in wintertime. Not to mention keeping her expensive house warm and occupied and safe. That's not nothing, dear. How was it *her*, not *you*, doing all that?"

"Hmm," I said.

"Maybe your salary is generous, but Lisa has plenty of money, and she trusts you. If I had her money, I'd pay more than the going rate for a personally vetted individual to live in my extra house while I was sunning myself in Bermuda."

I smiled at the image.

"So I don't actually see this as the Lisa Cannon Show, starring Lisa Cannon and all her money and influence, with her loyal assistant, Camille Tate, in a small supporting role. No, I see this as the Camille Tate Show, featuring Camille Tate as the star of her own darn life, supported by a generous grant from the Lisa Cannon Foundation. Do you see the difference?"

Mom and her PBS. But she had a point. "I do. Everything you say makes sense, Mom, always. But I still don't want to get up on stage and act. I can't imagine doing it, and I'll hate it."

She replied without hesitation. "Think of everything you've done since you moved to Orcas. How much of that did you ever imagine doing, much less enjoying?"

"Well...okay, but—"

"Cam. You know that you've always been kind of...timid... about yourself, and about life in general. For good reasons, of course," she added quickly. "You don't need me to tell you what those were."

No, I don't, I thought, remembering my meltdown just the other night. When I had finally let myself revisit what had happened on the night I'd watched *that man* kill my birth mother. The skin on my arms lifted and crawled in the familiar prickle, and I knew I would be unable to speak until I could get myself back from this. But I didn't have to speak, because Mom went on.

"You survived a nightmare. But honey, don't you see? The important part of your past isn't the nightmare. It's the survival. I'm finally seeing you step out of the shadow of your past, and step into—whatever else is out there for you. And it's really, really exciting."

"I don't feel excited, Mom," I said, somehow both frustrated and relieved. I felt like she was hearing me, and yet... "I think I've been carrying a whole lot more of that...old stuff...than I ever even realized, all my life. Maybe we should have talked about it all more—I don't know."

"Do you want to talk about it now?" she asked, very softly.

"Not right now, but...maybe soon? I'm feeling a little raw at the moment. Good, though," I hastened to add. "Just...kind of inarticulate. I think I need to think about...a lot of things...a bit more."

"Take all the time you need," she said. "I'll be here, whenever you want to talk."

"Thank you, Mom."

"Well, of course. That's what I'm here for."

"Okay, but I don't take it for granted," I said. "It means a lot— so many people don't listen. Even good people, who mean well. My best friends sometimes. People just get—all caught up in their own minds and their own business, and it makes it hard to listen. No one *hears* me."

"It's true," she said. "Listening is a skill. But so is speaking up, and it's one you're learning. And you're right: it's the easiest thing in the world to decide that you know someone and stop listening, or seeing them evolve. We all get set in our ways, and sometimes it takes a crisis to break out of old channels."

"A crisis like being shoved on a stage," I grumbled.

Mom laughed aloud. "Oh, Cam. You really are going to be wonderful at it. You know why?"

"Why?"

"Because your heart will be in it. Yes, any good actor can step into a role and inhabit it, but you wrote it, you know the material. And, in your quiet way, you've always brought everything you had to everything you've done. Even when you didn't know that's what you were doing, even when you were uncertain of yourself, you still showed up all the way." Her voice warmed further. "Oh, I'm *so* proud of you, honey."

It wasn't the sympathy I'd been looking for when I'd called her—quite the opposite! She agreed with Lisa!—and yet, by the time we hung up, I felt quite a bit better.

And I had a lot to think about.

CHAPTER 4

The next morning, I was finishing up breakfast when there was a knock on my door.

Oh good, I thought as I got up to open it, *Lisa's come to discuss today's tasks in person*—but it wasn't Lisa. JoJo Brixton stood there, lanky and gorgeous as ever, except for…

"What in the world are you wearing?" I asked.

"Technical gear," he said, as if that should be obvious. His signature feline shrug made the, uh, garment swish audibly.

"Technical…like, *outdoor* gear?"

"Got it in one!" he chirped.

I had no idea what to make of this.

The top part of his getup seemed to be a jacket of some kind, but the sheer number of pockets, straps, rivets, snaps, and little tabs that appeared to have no function at all was staggering. The lower part ("pants" seemed a grossly inadequate term) had the same sort of nonsense going on, and at least three pairs of horizontal zippers banding down the legs for quick conversion to anything from pedal pushers to booty shorts, presumably. The ensemble's full-spectrum mélange of earth tones made it look as if a whole REI catalogue had somehow been spray-painted onto a single outfit—creating basically the opposite of camouflage.

"Are you going to stand there and stare at me all day," he asked, "or are you going to let me in while you go get appropriately dressed?"

I am *appropriately dressed*, I thought, wondering if JoJo's usually acute sartorial sense had fallen on its head getting out of bed that morning, then sighed and stood aside. "Sure. Come in."

JoJo went to stand before my fire and warm his hands. Even that looked like a practiced gesture in such a costume. Only now did I notice his boots, if that's what those things on his feet were. They looked extremely "technical" too—and completely unscuffed. Had this whole regalia been airdropped in somehow just this morning? And, if so, for *what*?

"So!" he said brightly, turning around. "It's such a lovely day, I was thinking we might go for a hike."

I knew what all those words meant; but coming from the mouth of JoJo Brixton... "*You* are inviting *me* out for a *hike*? Where to, Alaska? Up Mount Everest?" There was not a hike on this whole island—or even clear around it—that required clothes like those.

"The secret to survival in the wild is preparation, darling! For the *unexpected*. Weren't you ever a boy scout?" He made a little shooing gesture. "Now, go on—you must have some outdoorsy clothing here somewhere; you've lived here long enough. I will avert my gaze while you change."

I shook my head. "JoJo, come on. You and I drink together, we banter, we work on this—"

He began shaking his head, too, but with an expression of urgent gravity completely at odds with his light and careless words. "It just struck me when I woke up to *such* a *beautiful* day, that I would *not* be satisfied until I had brought *you* out into this lovely morning for a hike with me. Oh Cam, do say you'll come. *Do!*" So bright, so cheery, but I almost raised my arms to fend off his commanding gaze.

I'm slow sometimes, but even I couldn't miss this. He had

something on his mind, apparently—not just the absurd idea of us starring in a play together—and he wasn't going to talk about unless I agreed to this hike for some reason. "All right. I'll get changed, but I need to call Lisa before we go." I turned to climb up the ladder to my sleeping loft as I asked, "So, where are we doing this 'hike?' How warmly do I need to dress?"

"Oh, I just thought we'd figure it out on the way," he said lightly. "I have a few different trails in mind. We can talk about it in the car. Bring a few layers, anyway. And do you have a backpack for drinks and snacks and stuff?"

So, he had the full metal jacket, but no backpack? "I'll be down in a minute," I told him.

As I started up the ladder, he pulled a chair up to the fire and sat down. James immediately jumped into his lap, and I was amused to see JoJo absently scratching my cat's ears. He'd never struck me as a pet-person either.

I didn't have any technical clothing per se. Certainly nothing to compete with JoJo's outlandish rig. I just changed into the comfy jeans and sweatshirt I liked to wear for walks of any kind outside, and decent trail shoes. I stifled a sigh, remembering the last time I'd gone hiking…with Colin.

I climbed back down the ladder and plunked my daypack onto the table. "I have a few bottles of water in the fridge. But I don't have much in the way of snacks."

"Water?" JoJo said with a faint note of horror. "Never mind then; just bring the pack. We'll stop at the market on our way."

On our way to where? I wondered. Probably not another helicopter ride to Seattle—not dressed like that. Were we going to another island? To the mainland? "How long will we be gone?" I asked, pulling out my phone.

He shrugged again—as beautifully as ever. "A few hours maybe?"

"So, I won't need a tent?" He gave me an unamused look as my call went to Lisa's voicemail. I left a message saying I'd check in later. "Ready," I said, grabbing up the empty pack, and taking a light jacket off a peg by the front door. He ushered me out, and I locked up.

When we reached Lisa's driveway, he held out the key fob to his Jag. "Want to drive again?"

"You don't have to ask me twice." I snatched the fob and hopped into the driver's seat before he could change his mind. "So, the market first?" I asked, starting up the car and clicking it into reverse the moment he'd fastened his seat belt.

"Yes ma'am."

He seemed cheerful on the drive to town, but didn't talk. He hummed and watched the scenery go by while I concentrated on not speeding in this wonderful car.

At the market, I followed him to the deli section and then to— you guessed it—the liquor department, where two four-packs of airplane-sized champagne bottles joined the pâté and brie cheese and elegant crackers and twelve-dollar-a-pound grapes already in his hand basket. On the off chance that we were actually going on anything resembling a real hike, I dropped a few bottles of water in there too.

JoJo rolled his eyes. "Don't expect me to drink any of that."

Back in the car, I started it up and said, "All right, where to now?"

"Moran State Park."

So, not off island then. That was a relief. I drove out of town and down Olga Road.

It really was a beautiful day. After we passed Cascade Lake, he directed me left up the road that led to the top of Mt. Constitution, but then told me to pull off only a mile up the hill. Signs indicated that this was the way to Mountain Lake, and too soon for me—I loved driving this car—we pulled into a parking lot by a picturesque lake.

When we'd parked, JoJo astonished me further by opening the glove box and pulling out a Discover Pass, which he hung from the rearview mirror. Since when did he have a state parks day pass? Had he done this before? JoJo, the *hiker!* Yet another new face.

"All set?" he asked.

Shaking my head in disbelief, I got out and grabbed my day-pack, then loaded the ridiculous groceries into it, since JoJo obviously wasn't going to carry them. He just watched as I shrugged the pack onto my shoulders. It would have been a lot lighter without all the champagne, but I wasn't about to suggest leaving any of *that* behind.

"This way," he said, setting out toward a trailhead.

We were apparently doing the Mountain Lake Loop, which, according to the signs, was not quite four miles. "You're actually serious," I said. "We're really going for a hike." I hadn't really believed it until that moment.

He cast a glance over his shoulder without slowing down. "Camilicious, have I ever not been serious with you?"

I wasn't even going to dignify that question with an answer.

⁓

After several ignored attempts at conversation, I fell silent and concentrated on enjoying the hike. It was a weekday in April, and the parking lot had been nearly empty, so we saw very few people on the trail. Though, during tourist season, I imagined this hike would be quite crowded. It hugged the lakeshore very scenically without being too strenuous, which made a nice change from the steep, sweaty Turtleback Mountain hike I was more familiar with.

About twenty minutes in, the trail widened, and JoJo slowed so we could walk side by side. "See?" he asked. "You didn't know you wanted to take a hike today, but isn't this nice?"

"It is, and I'm always up for a hike. I just never realized you were the hiking kind."

He laughed. "I'm full of surprises, Camikins; you must know

that by now. But I also had to get you away from your cabin; because, now that you're *on the team*, I can tell you a few things that neither of us is supposed to know." He gave me a sly glance.

"Oh," I said, hardly surprised. "So that whole speech the other day at the courthouse about rules and discretion—even with each other—was just…"

"Rules are made to be broken," he cut in with a lopsided grin. "And that was purely just *for the record*. I'd have thought that was obvious."

"What record? It's not like anyone could have been fooled by that snarky show. What was the point, when everyone must have known as well as I did that you were just going to turn around and do something like this the minute their backs were turned?"

"The point," he said, with almost paternal condescension, "is that when flipping off one's handlers, one mustn't make it easy for them to prove you did so, later. No one who's ever met me expects I'll be well behaved. I wouldn't want them to. But I've been careful to make sure *the record* shows nothing but me being compliant—well, compliant beyond the few attitude issues anyone should expect from an innocent bystander coerced into such unpleasant collaboration. They'll have a hard time pinning me down in court with no better evidence than that. *'And not one week later, Your Honor, he went* hiking *with her!* Hiking—*if you can believe it!'*" His imitation of Agent Veierra's voice was barely recognizable, but I got it. He gave me a smug smile. "It's not what you actually do that matters, Camikins, or what *they* know about you either; the whole game is about what they can punish you for. And the 'law and order' clan can only punish you for things they can prove from the verifiable record. They know that as well as I do."

Wow, I thought. Already planning for his own eventual indictment? I was seeing more and more what an empty act the "shallow and frivolous" JoJo face clearly was—not that this left me any more comfortable about him. "If you say so," I said aloud. "But why couldn't we just have this talk in my cabin?"

"Oh sweetie…" He put a hand on my arm, just for a second. "Are you really still that trusting—even now?"

"Who needed trusting? My cat? My rabbit?" I rolled my eyes. "Even Lisa is too far away to hear us scream there, JoJo."

"You're that certain no one has planted listening devices there? Darling, we've both been recruited to 'spy' for them—as you're so fond of calling it—and it *still* hasn't occurred to you that one or more of the players in our little drama might want to keep abreast of what *you* are up to as well: who you talk to, who comes and goes?" He chuckled softly. "Spying tends to beget more spying, in my limited experience."

"If it's the bad guys you're talking about, any interest they've had in me must have been there for quite a while now, but you never seemed afraid of talking at my place before."

He shook his head sadly. "Just to make sure we're on the same page here, Camikins, you do understand that we're not just trying to protect Lisa—and ourselves—from the 'bad guys,' right? That the 'good guys' don't mean her—or us—anything much better?"

"*No. Really?*" I said, amazed at the sheer ridiculousness of his implication. "So, you think my cabin's been bugged by Sheriff Clarke, or Agent Veierra? Right after they recruited me?"

He hunched his shoulders. "How long did Sheriff Clarke stand on your porch the other day?"

"I have no idea. Does it matter?"

"So, a while then maybe? And what would he have been doing out there, making friends with the rabbit? Did he ever go inside your house? And who else drops by—with or without your knowledge? What about Lisa?"

"Oh, seriously!" I laughed. "Now you think *Lisa's* bugged my cabin? Why would any of them even bother, JoJo? I've already agreed to report to all of them! What would they need to bug my home for?"

He just stood blinking at me. "How tragic, to watch such perfect innocence disfigured," he said mournfully. Or, mock-mournfully anyway.

Just then, a young couple approached us from the other direction. We fell silent as we passed them, except for the exchange of friendly hellos. They both eyed JoJo's getup with barely disguised amusement.

When they were well past, I said, "So, what are these things you wanted to tell me? Can we just get to that part, please?"

"Of course," he said, flippantly. "You're the one who's been holding us up with all these naïve questions." He responded to my scowl by saying, "The first and most important thing is that Marie woke up from her coma."

"Oh!" I cried. "That's wonderful news—how is she?"

"I only know that she's awake. My sources didn't get much more than that."

"Your sources," I echoed. "And…who would those be?"

He gave a small sigh. "I have…people…at the hospital, which no one is supposed to know about either. And that includes our 'good guys,' just to be clear."

"So our guys didn't tell you this? They don't trust their own confidential informants?"

"Trust," he said softly, uncertainly. "It's a complicated question, isn't it?" I wasn't sure what the question meant, so I just waited to see if he would go on. He did: "Trust is a kind of… novel experiment for most people, dearest. Not for you, it seems, but for the rest of us, at least. I hope you'll forgive me for taking it in baby steps."

Baby steps? Was JoJo unsure of trusting even *me* now? "So if it's all that cloak and dagger, then how do you know I'm not just helping them trap you, or even Lisa, and lying about it like everybody else?"

He looked at me sideways for a long moment, his grin growing. "Oh, Cam. You are just the cutest thing sometimes."

Oh, you still think I can't lie, huh? I thought, getting more irked with him by the moment. *Maybe I should just vanish on you right now and see what you think then, Mr. Zipperpants.* "I suppose you do expect me to lie to *them* now, though," I said aloud. "About everything you've just told me—your sources, all that."

He sighed. "I'd have no one but myself to blame if you told them everything I've said to you today, or ever," he conceded. Then he gave me a soulful look. "But that would be the end of my little trust experiment."

He actually sounded like he meant it. All this switching faces, back and forth, was making me crazy. "Well, I won't lie if I'm asked straight out, because if you're right about me, I probably couldn't pull it off anyway. But I won't volunteer anything either, or let on that there's things I'm not talking about. I'm better at that part, at least, than people think."

"Thank you," he said, simply—which seemed as weird as anything else that morning.

"You're welcome," I said carefully. "But—why is it a secret anyway: her waking up?"

"*That* is the best question you've asked all morning," he said, sounding more like his normal, cocky self again. "And the deeply disturbing answer is that I don't know. Nothing worries me more, ever, than what I don't know. I hear she's better guarded than the President now. When she's well enough to be released, they'll be keeping her in protective custody, I'm sure. Until then, according to my *sources*, the hospital staff has apparently been instructed that she's to have no visitors—very specifically including Lisa or me. Or so my sources tell me," he added, as if I might have missed that part somehow? "You see what that means, don't you?"

I shook my head, feeling long past any hope of figuring out what anything going on in my whole life these days might mean.

"Well," JoJo said, "at the very least, it means they've discovered that she knows something extremely important—and whatever it is has left them not trusting Lisa or me...which can't mean anything good that I can think of. Did they say anything about all this to you the other morning?"

"Me?" I asked, surprised. "Of course not. I haven't even been cleared to start working yet."

He nodded, and fell silent again as another group of hikers came along; four people with a dog on a leash this time. "Okay then," JoJo said when they'd passed out of earshot. "I didn't think they had, or you'd already have mentioned it to me, or to Lisa. But I wanted to be sure."

He knew what I might have mentioned recently to Lisa? How? I didn't ask. I didn't really want to know. They probably talked to each other even more often than either of them talked to me; I preferred just to settle for that explanation. For now, at least.

"So, when did you find this out?" I asked.

"A couple days ago," he said, nonchalantly. "Almost a week, I guess."

A week! "And you said *nothing* to me about it? Until now?"

He looked at me as if unsure whether I was serious. "And how could I have told you sooner? You didn't even know there *was* a team until a few days ago, much less that I was on it. And I certainly wasn't going to blather on about my sources at the hospital right there in the courthouse, was I?" He gave me a look of helpless indignation. "Here I am, telling you the first chance I had to spirit you away. Any sooner would have looked peculiar."

Well...maybe he had a point. "So, have you even got a guess about why they don't want any of us to see her? They can't seriously think we were involved in her poisoning...can they?"

"That requires a two-part answer. Part one is, yes, of course they can think any dang thing imaginable about us. There's no accounting for people's ludicrous assumptions. What do you think I've spent my whole life hiding from if not people's thoroughly insane ideas about who I am or what I deserve?" He looked away. "JoJo the charmingly obnoxious playboy was literally invented just to provide my dear family, and everyone else, with some decoy to punish for their dark assumptions instead of coming after me."

"Wait, what?" I asked, belatedly realizing that he might just have said something important.

He waved my question off, though. "We can get back to all that some other time. The second part of my answer is the most important one; it's not 'any of us' they're keeping her away from. It's just me and Lisa, apparently. My sources could not recall ever hearing your name raised, or seeing it on the blacklist." He gave me a weighty look. "Given your rather prominent involvement in all of these events, I doubt that such an omission could have been accidental."

"Well…what does it mean then?"

"Again, I don't know," he said with uncharacteristic discomfort. "It may just mean that, as you said, you're still not cleared for active duty and therefore not an actionable item on their inventory yet. Or…it could mean they don't see *you* as whatever kind of threat they imagine Lisa or I might be. But if they do happen to say anything about all this to you, I'd really like to hear about it…if you feel able to trust me that far. I know rules mean more to you than they do to me; but it's a lot easier for us to protect Lisa from things I can see coming than from things I can't."

I hadn't missed how carefully worded that veiled request had been: the implication that I was a rule-bound good girl, or that "our" efforts to protect Lisa depended on things *he* could see coming. I really wasn't as simple as he seemed to imagine. But I still couldn't believe that Lisa, or JoJo, could really be members of Team Bad-Guys. "I still don't see why they'd have pulled you into all this at all if they thought you might be one of the bad guys," I said. "Or, if they've just started to suspect you, why they'd keep you on board now. That makes no sense at all."

"Of course it does. Criminals are used as C.I.s all the time, because their own fear of incarceration gives the law such a fabulous handle to yank them around by, and because they're already so familiar to—and *trusted* by—the very people they're tattling on. And, before you ask," he said, as if reading my mind, "I still have no interest in discussing what their hold on me is—except to assure you it's all trivial, and unconnected to any of this." He made another sour face. "Minor lapses of attention to pointless bureaucratic niceties. I don't know how they can stand to look at themselves in the mirror every morning—especially Veierra, that fastidious bastion of performative scruples." He picked up the pace and hiked a little ahead of me, practically whistling in his effort to prove how little he cared. "Ooh, look, are those ducks out there on the lake?"

Okay, here was the annoying, obnoxious, irritating JoJo I'd known and loved. *Who trusts me. Riiiight.* "So, maybe if you didn't keep poking them in the eye every chance you get, they'd trust you a little more?" I tried. "Could that be worth trying, do you think?"

He just gazed out at the water for a while before turning to face me again. "You chose to do this, Cam. I didn't get to choose. I was coerced." His tone of voice was almost...severe? "And if I have to put up with that, so be it, but I'm going to do it on my own terms—not theirs. In case you haven't already figured it out, I'm not here to do their bidding. I'm here to steer—from inside—since they've left me no other option. I'm sure as heck not just going to leave my fate, or Lisa's, or *yours*, up to the Feds and their sanctimonious agendas—and that means making *sure* that I'm not blindsided again."

"When did they blindside you?"

He looked straight back at me, as if he'd forgotten JoJo the clown ever existed. "The day they yanked me into their little program."

I thought back to that day, in his parents' big unwelcoming kitchen, while the Feds searched upstairs. It was the first of JoJo's other faces I had ever seen: unsettled, frightened even. And here was that JoJo again. I hadn't understood what I was seeing back then, or had any reason to sympathize. But this time I did, and felt my heart soften, just a little, despite itself.

"I wasn't kidding about the ducks," he said, more softly, turning back to gaze out at the lake. "See?" He pointed. "There's a whole herd of them."

"I think it's 'flock,' not a herd, JoJo."

"No, it's only a flock if they're in the air."

I snorted. "I'm pretty sure a group of ducks is a group of ducks no matter where they are."

"All right. A flock, if you must."

I came to stand beside him and look. There they were, gathered around what was either an island or a small peninsula—it was hard to tell from such a distance. The late-morning sunlight glinted off the water where the ducks disturbed it. It was lovely.

We continued to watch for a while. "A place like this makes me realize how many opportunities I've wasted here," he said at last.

Surprised, I glanced over at him. "Opportunities?"

"My parents have owned the house here since Clary and I were teenagers. Mother had to buy on Orcas Island; her mind was set, and what she lacks in intelligence, she makes up for in persistence. But it was such torture to come out here. There was virtually no cell service on the island in those days, no internet, nothing. It was like traveling to the moon. We hated it. Clary and I never left our rooms unless forced to. We'd sneak out to steal booze and raid the fridge, and that was it." He kept his gaze firmly out over the water. I stayed silent. "As I may have mentioned, I've never much enjoyed the company of my family," he said quietly. "Being locked in a house with them all summer… what a hellish ordeal." He shook his head.

I thought about the only time I'd seen his whole family together, when they were out here for Thanksgiving. He and Clary had seemed to get along all right, but all that ridiculous drinking seemed…staged for effect. Like the teenagers they must have been.

"Poor little rich boy, I know," he said, his voice now sharp with self-mockery. "How terrible, to have to vacation in a palatial home in this beautiful place. Then I got to know Lisa. She had such a different way of seeing the island. Through her eyes, I finally began to understand what a spectacular place it could be for, well, *anyone* but a jaded teenage boy. She talked to me quite a lot about opportunities. *Life hands us opportunities, and it's our responsibility to make the most of them,* or some such bootstrap nonsense. You know how she is. She was trying to help me come to terms with my insanely privileged upbringing."

"Come to terms with it?" I asked.

"Rich kids don't understand privilege, Cam. Not at first. We don't really know until later on that everyone else isn't rich too. Then, as the truth begins to dawn, we start learning to hide our 'embarrassment of riches,' and defend ourselves from everybody else's envy and resentment. I was just starting to struggle with how much I had, and how little I'd done with it. Lisa tried her best to help me through that. Of course, I didn't listen to her. I didn't know how. It felt like it was already too late, and I should just lean in and get what I could from it. That's why Orcas will always feel like one more wasted opportunity among so many in my pointless life."

He'd actually put a lump in my throat—JoJo Brixton! "That has to be the most sincere thing you've ever said to me," I murmured.

"Ugh. Sorry about that. I *loathe* sincerity." I could almost literally hear the window snap shut as he patted my arm. "Don't worry, I won't make a habit of it. I see a nice downed log over there with a view of the water. Shall we explore the contents of your ragged little backpack, and talk about how much fun we're going to have doing your play?" That was the end of our *sincere* conversation.

But it was the beginning of the snacks.

CHAPTER 5

After JoJo's Jaguar roared back up the driveway, I retrieved Lisa's binder from the broom closet and went to check in with her as I'd promised to. But as I approached her house, the front door opened and she walked out with purse and keys in hand. "Oh!" She smiled when she saw me. "There you are!"

"Sorry, something came up," I said, holding out her binder. "Is it too late to meet?"

"Thank you for getting this!" She took it from me. "I'm just headed out, I'm afraid. But I'm sure the list of tasks we talked about yesterday will still keep you plenty busy for a while, won't it?"

"Oh, yes. For days, at least."

"Well, then we don't really need to talk now," she said cheerfully. "I'll just drop this inside the house and go. If I need you for anything else, I'll text. And, of course, feel free to text or call if you need anything from me, okay?"

"Thanks. That sounds good."

"Fine," she said. "I've actually cleared my schedule somewhat since we talked, so you'll probably see more of me than I led you to believe."

That was welcome news. "Great!"

"Have you reached out to Roland Markus again yet?"

"I left him another message yesterday afternoon."

"Good. He can be difficult to pin down, so you might have to camp on his doorstep. Well, I'd better be going. Don't worry about calling if anything comes up. I'm here for you."

"Thanks," I said. "I appreciate that."

With a wave, she started back inside with the binder, then stopped and turned back to me. "Oh! I almost forgot; Paige Berry has invited you to join her and some of the other boosters for lunch tomorrow at the senior center to discuss everything. She's fabulous about marshalling the volunteers around refreshments and everything. I hope you won't mind that I took the liberty of confirming, conditionally, that you'll be there?" she added with a wicked grin. "If that's not going to work, just—"

"Oh, no, that'll be fine," I rushed to assure her, suspecting she'd have consulted me to begin with if I hadn't been missing in action with JoJo.

"Oh good. You'll want to touch base with her tomorrow anyway, just to confirm the details, okay?"

"You bet."

"Well then," she said breezily, "I'll let you go, and be off myself."

I had barely let myself into my cabin when my phone rang. I pulled it out of my pocket and saw an unfamiliar number; but it was local. "Camille Tate," I said as I answered.

"Camilla? I'm glad I caught you," said a brusque male voice. "Roland Markus. You left a message about Eliza Cameron's play. I have a few minutes this afternoon at four, I could squeeze you in. Come by the shop." Then the line went dead.

I stood staring at the phone. *Camilla? Eliza Cameron?* Getting my name wrong was understandable, I supposed, but did he really not know Lisa's? He hadn't even waited for me to confirm that I'd be there. And where the heck was "the shop," anyway?

I guessed I knew the first item on my to-do list.

ɞ•ɔ

Roland Markus's shop was just outside of Eastsound in a small business park next to the airport, catty-corner from the sheriff substation. The addresses I'd found online seemed to indicate he had four contiguous storefronts there.

I parked out front of the first address at five minutes till four, then knocked on all four doors in turn, finally getting a response at the last one.

"Oh, there you are," he snapped. "Come in."

I followed the man into a disorganized office. There was no place to sit—at least, not for me; Markus sat behind a large desk overflowing with piles of paper and what appeared to be bits of trash and a strange assortment of toys. "Tell me about the play," he demanded.

I stared back, wondering if I'd already done something to offend this man somehow. He was middle-aged, and entirely unremarkable looking—brown hair, jeans and a sweatshirt, smallish eyes—and...some other quality above and beyond his brusque manner that just struck me as *wrong*. *Focus on the play*, I told myself. "Um, it takes place in a beauty salon—" I started.

"Oh, got it, you're doing *Steel Magnolias*. Right. So we'll need a Southern salon sensibility—soft fabrics, pastel décor, lighting, something very feminine—"

"No, not *Steel Magnolias*," I interrupted.

"You're not doing *Steel Magnolias*?"

"No, it's a different play about a salon in Seattle."

"*Seattle?*" he exclaimed, as if I'd told him the salon was in a leper colony.

"Yes. People in Seattle get their hair done, and we don't need a feminine sensibility because half the salon employees are men," I explained, refusing to be cowed by this creature, though it was hard not to be. "They do men's hair there, too."

"They don't *do* men's hair in *Steel Magnolias*," he said, as if *I* were missing some important point.

"Well, as I just said, this isn't *Steel Magnolias*. It's an older business, kind of retro—"

He waved a dismissive hand. "A salon is a salon is a salon. The visual language is all the same; only the details differ." He stared up at me gnomishly. "I'll have a better idea once I see the script—you *do* have a copy of the script for me, I assume?"

"I will soon. They're still being printed."

He exhaled impatiently through his nose. "Well, get it to me as quickly as possible. I'm quite busy, Callie; this is a terrible time of year to schedule new business. Eliza knows this, and yet, year after year, she sends her minions over here anyway."

"Her name is Lisa, and mine's Camille—Cam, actually, and—"

"Fine; Camilla then." He waved my objection away again. "A minion's a minion. I don't know where I'm supposed to find an entire *salon* at such short notice. Still, it's Cameron's budget, and if that's the way it has to be—"

"Mr. Markus, hasn't this play been on your schedule for, like, a year?" I just had no more patience to spare for such a pompous, self-absorbed twit. "My understanding is that *Lisa* plans out her season well over a year in advance."

He snorted and shook his head. "Oh, don't quibble details at me," he said as dismissively as ever, "you know very well what I mean."

I *didn't* know, but I saw no point in drawing this out one moment longer than I had to. "So, it's going to be held in the same place as usual—the barn at Madrona Farm—"

"Oh, that barn!" he cried. "I've told Liza any number of times, that musty old space is Just. All. Wrong. I have fabulous tents—we'll do the whole production outside, under canvas. It's the *summer* play, after all! The weather will be beautiful, and a tent *breathes* so people don't suffocate! I'll hang sensual draperies inside and out, so graceful in the breeze, *mesmerizing*," he rhapsodized. "The Farm has a wonderful field just behind that moldy barn; the mud will be mostly dry at that time of year. You'll see. Leave it all to me." He started scribbling illegible notes on a lined pad of yellow paper. I could see they were illegible, even viewing them upside down. Or maybe it was some kind of shorthand? I didn't know and didn't care.

"Mr. Markus," I managed through half-gritted teeth, "the play will be on the stage, in the barn. No tent needed."

He went right on scribbling. "I'll talk to Alice. Just leave the big decisions to grown-ups, okay?"

I felt my eyebrows climb about two feet; *grown-ups?* "The *big decisions* have already been made, Mr. Markus, and who on earth is *Alice?*"

He looked up, as if surprised and annoyed to find me still there, then rolled his eyes at the ceiling. "Right, Liza; whatever," and went back to scribbling hieroglyphics. "You're obviously *not* the decision maker here. It was a cowardly waste of my time to send you, I have to say. If Liza wants to ignore my expertise and make these decisions herself, she could at least find the courage to come down here and tell me herself. But that's how it is with these Seattle folks. So used to hiding behind functionaries. If I just—"

"The *barn*," I cut in with enough force to make him flinch as he looked up, glaring at me. I'd even startled me, to be honest. "You can call *Lisa* if you want," I said, a bit more civilly, hoping he most certainly would not, "but she will say the same. She made it perfectly clear to me that the play will be held in *the barn*."

He shrugged, looking very put out. "Fine. But you're making a terrible mistake. Outdoor theater is the wave of the future, particularly in a garden spot like this."

"Noted," I said. "Anyway: the setup, *in the barn*, should be quite simple. As I mentioned, it's a mid-century salon; old but not run-down. It's actually kind of cool again, in a retro way—"

"Leave the décor to me, Connie. That's my business, after all. I've been doing this for years and years and years—and not just in podunk little places like this one. I only came here for my nerves, actually, and I have to say, it hasn't worked out very well. This whole island is going to hell in a handbasket these days, and you know why? *New* people." He glared at me pointedly. "This deluge of *new people*, swarming over everything like locusts at a picnic, is ruining everything that was peaceful and sublime about Orcas Island when *I* came here."

I couldn't help myself. "It's ants. The saying is *ants* at a—"

"Don't foist your clichés on me." He shook his head wearily. "I know all about your kind; I worked on Broadway. In fact I've designed the set for *Steel Magnolias* numerous times, including St. Louis Rep's production. I'm not just another volunteer rube in this dismal backwater."

Wait, the dismal backwater he'd just described as peaceful and sublime? A garden spot? I was tempted to press that point too, but he just kept talking.

"I've worked with *real* celebrities with *real* talent, out in the *real* world, young lady. And I gave that all up to seek refuge and creative solitude out here, away from all that pointless noise and furor…"

"Right." I was *so* done here. "Well then, lovely meeting you, Mr. *Markles*. I'll be sure and get a copy of the script to you as soon as they're printed up, if you'll just confirm that we *are* on your calendar?" I stared down at him, suddenly grateful that he hadn't offered me a chair. I channeled all the force of my emotions, my inner Lisa Cannon, maybe even some inner Diana Brixton, into my unblinking glare.

That seemed to work, to my surprise. "Yes," he allowed.

"Great!" I sang. "I'm *so* happy to know this is all under control. Thank you *so much* for squeezing us into your busy schedule, and for agreeing to create a fantastic, retro-style salon set for us on the stage, inside the barn at Madrona Farm, for a play that is most definitely not *Steel Magnolias*. Bye now!" I turned on my heel and stomped the three steps to his door, which I barely refrained from slamming behind me. Then I went on stomping all the way back to my car, four doors down, telling myself that when this play was done, I was never, *ever* going to work with this horrid person again. If that meant doing the job *myself* next time, so be it. Learning to do stage sets couldn't possibly be any harder or more unpleasant than letting this idiot do it.

❧

I will neither confirm nor deny scurrilous rumors regarding therapeutic chocolate to help me through the rest of my afternoon. Sadly, the Brown Bear was already closed for the day, so my first choice—a giant chocolate muffin with crunchy sugar baked on top—was not available. But I made do. The grocery store had plenty of other options.

Unfortunately, not even chocolate stopped me from continuing to fume all the way back to West Sound. Seriously! What gave that man the right? He might be a legend in his own head, but back at the salon in Seattle, I'd read every celebrity tabloid that ever crossed our waiting area—cover to cover—and not one of them had *ever* mentioned Roland Markus.

Lisa had warned me, sort of. But nothing like loud enough. Some of my residual anger was leaking over onto her now too as I took the curves on Deer Harbor Road a bit faster than I should have. I even wondered, just a little, if maybe she *had* sent me over there to get out of dealing with him herself. But I couldn't imagine Lisa being cowed by *anyone*, least of all a creep like Markus. And besides, the mere idea that a single word he'd spoken—about anything—ever—could have been even a little bit right was a total non-starter for me.

"Well, I guess this is why people hire production assistants," I told James and Master Bun, crossly, as I stomped back into my A-frame and tossed my purse and jacket onto the table. After that, I paced around the room for a while, then dropped into the chair beside my stove.

Why had I let that useless, irrelevant man get *so* far under my skin, anyhow? And where on earth had I found the guts to throw his obnoxious insults back in his face that way? That wasn't... how I usually did things.

Okay, yes, Jen had congratulated me a couple times recently on standing up for myself—like the day JoJo showed up with all that crap about "taking care of me." But I'd gotten to know JoJo pretty well by then—or thought I had, anyway—and had stopped feeling careful around him ages ago. *Markus*, on the other hand, was a total stranger, and a business associate of Lisa's. He'd totally deserved everything I'd said, of course. I didn't feel sorry about any of it, and certainly didn't feel I owed him any apologies.

But I might owe Lisa one.

She had called him "the best there is," after all, and said we really needed to work with him. Would he make her pay for my tantrum now; refuse to work on her production, even? Would Lisa forgive me if he did? What would we do for a set then?

Would she be as shocked by my behavior as I felt now? Oh, I had to tell her about it, and right away. I'd be in even more trouble if he got to her first.

Maybe this new job was not going to be as exciting as I'd been imagining—if it even lasted long enough for me to find out. I wished that I'd just kept my big mouth shut—but he'd been such an utter monster that my brain had just vanished into a cloud of rage. I couldn't even remember feeling that angry at anyone since—

"Ohhhh!" I gasped, getting it at last... Since the last time I'd seen *Kevin*.

Self-absorbed, insensitive, dismissive, fake creative prima donna! Kevin and Roland Markus were like *twins!* That's what had happened. Markus had pushed every *Kevin* button I had! And I'd just let that warp my behavior and endanger my job. Oh, this mess needed cleaning up—right away.

I pulled the phone out and texted Lisa: *Hi. There's something I think we should talk about. Tonight when you get back, if you have time?*

I had barely pressed send before she replied. *I'm actually on my way over to see you right now, if that's all right?*

What? *You are?* I texted.

Within sight of your porch, she wrote. *Is this a bad time?* She'd put a happy face after the question. But I had a very non-happy face feeling about this unexpected visit.

No. This is fine.

Great, she texted back. *I'm bringing chocolate.*

Chocolate? Telling her that I'd just had chocolate didn't seem very strategic right now, so I sent a happy face back to her—not ten seconds before her knock.

I went to let her in, shoving the phone back in my pocket.

When I opened the door, she smiled and held the open box of candy out to me. There were already several pieces missing. "The triangular ones with red sugar crystals are especially good," she said. "It took a lot of self-control to save one for you."

"Well…thank you," I said nervously. "Um, are we celebrating something?"

She gazed at me. "You tell me."

I looked down and closed my eyes. "He already called you, didn't he?"

"Yes," she said. "About twenty minutes ago."

"I'm *so* sorry, Lisa. I don't have any idea what got into me."

"I don't know what got into you, either." She chuckled. "But I'm *very* impressed!"

My eyes flew open in surprise. "You're not…upset?" I blinked. "Wait, what did he tell you?"

"I'll spare you the excessive verbiage, but, basically, he said he'd never in his whole long and lofty career been treated with such disrespect and outright hostility by anyone before." For some reason, even this seemed to...delight her? "It's a lie, of course," she added.

"What is?" I asked in a daze.

She gave me a smirk. "I'm sure he's been treated that way lots of times. I've treated him that way myself, more than once. He really doesn't leave people much other choice, does he?"

"You...knew he would treat me like that? And you didn't warn me?"

"I'm sorry, Cam. Maybe I should have, but...I had a feeling you might handle him better unprepared." She shrugged, cheerfully. "And it seems you've proven me right!"

"What? How? I completely melted down." I couldn't catch up with my own confusion. Was there something I was missing here? A setup of some kind? Was I about to be fired after all—were these chocolates my severance pay? Or was it really safe to feel relieved?

"Cam," she said gently, "some people use advance warning to prepare themselves for success, but others use it to psych themselves out—worrying about what might go wrong, and whether they'll blow it, until it's a self-fulfilling prophecy." She gave me a quizzical look. "Does one of those traits sound more familiar than the other to you?"

I wasn't even sure what she was asking, or what I was supposed to say.

"You respond extremely well to *unexpected* surprises—even very unpleasant ones," she went on. "I've seen you do it again and again. You've handled so many really frightening experiences here with such remarkable courage, surprising calm, and practical sensibility. I've only ever seen you make trouble for yourself when you had time to anticipate some challenge, and think yourself into a panic about it." She smiled, knowingly. "Like writing a play script. Or accepting this job as my assistant... Am I wrong?"

Well...okay, I could kind of see her point. I guessed. I shook my head.

"So this time, I decided not to help you psych yourself out. I just trusted you to handle Markus as he happened to you—and it worked, didn't it? Brilliantly, I'd say!" Her beaming smile returned, and she thrust the box of chocolate box at me again. "Don't you want one? I really do think a celebration is in order."

"But…why?" I said, reaching blankly for a chocolate, because I'd been told to. "What's *brilliant* about melting down like that?" And speaking of brilliant, how long had I kept her standing there on my doorstep? "Sorry, I didn't mean to—would you like to come in?" I stood aside, and gestured for her to enter.

"Thanks, I'd love to! I've been meaning to come down and see how you're settling in. I've just been so busy."

She walked in, glancing around as I went to sweep my purse and jacket off the table.

"Okay," I said, "but…I still offended your set designer pretty badly, didn't I? I don't understand why that doesn't bother you. What if he refuses to work with us now?"

"Oh, not a chance," she scoffed. "His whole illusion of importance would vanish the minute people like me stopped needing what he does. He'd never seriously tell us to get lost, for fear we might oblige him and go." She turned to me, looking happy. "What a charming nest you've made here! It's…not too small for you?"

Why did *everyone* keep… "No, it's actually the just the right amount of space for everything I have. It doesn't feel empty, or cluttered… Does it?"

She glanced around again, seeming a little mystified. "No. You're right, it doesn't. Are you a decorating genius too, Cam? Maybe I should have you come do a consult about my place."

"Your house is completely perfect," I said, still a little weirded out that we were standing here making pleasant small talk after what I'd done. "And I'm too busy working as your production manager to consider any additional work." I gave her a nervous smile. "I mean, I am still your production manager? You're really not…disappointed in me?"

She gave me the closest thing to a cross look I'd seen so far. "You still don't believe me, do you? That's why I came straight over here—with chocolates. I knew you'd be beating yourself up now, and for nothing but handling him more perfectly than I'd ever have imagined you could."

"See, that's the part I still don't get," I said, quietly. "You're being so nice about this, but I don't see how I handled any of it *perfectly*."

"Well then, let me tell you what else he had to say just now, okay?"

Oh. "There was more?" Of course there was. How could there not be?

She nodded. "First, he told me that if I wanted to do my dang play in a grimy old barn instead of his luxurious tent under the open summer sky, he was perfectly happy just to let me—that he'd follow *every single one* of our 'idiotic instructions' to the last detail, and it would serve us right. And then he warned me that when we finally realized what a disaster we'd brought on ourselves, there'd be nothing he could do about it, even if he wanted to. We'd be stuck with what we'd insisted on." She raised her arms, and did a funny little victory dance. "We've dodged right past all *his* brilliant ideas for *our* play, and gotten everything we wanted to start with—in record time! It has *never* taken me less than six or seven weeks to wear him down the way it seems you've done in a single afternoon." Still beaming, she brought her hands together in a brief round of quiet applause. "Brava, Cam. You've surpassed my expectations—again."

Stunned, and weak with relief, I sat down before my legs gave out. But when she suggested I come back to her place for a glass of wine to "balance the chocolate," I found enough strength somewhere to accept her invitation.

CHAPTER 6

My next task was hopefully going to be less exasperating. The following day was my lunch appointment at the Orcas Island Senior Center with the "booster club" that supported Lisa's company.

Paige Berry, dressed in layered purple garments conspicuously free of goat nibblings, met me at the door. "Come in, come in." She ushered me through a large, attractive lobby into an equally spacious dining room. Many seniors were already seated at round tables there, with plates of food in front of them; a cafeteria line was arranged against the back wall. The air was heavy with soft conversation, the clink of silverware, and the distinctively pleasant aromas of food.

A smiling woman stopped us at a check-in table by the door. "So you're with Paige? Lunch is a dollar, dear."

A whole dollar! Well, with my new salary, I could afford that. I handed a single to the cashier, who thanked me and wished me a pleasant lunch.

Paige led me across the room to a large table where four elderly ladies were seated with full plates in front of them. "This is the young woman helping dear Lisa with her play!" she told them. "She's the production assistant." I made to sit down in an empty chair that had obviously been saved for me, but immediately Paige said, "Lunch! We need to get our lunch! Nothing can be decided on an empty stomach!" She started for the buffet line, beckoning me to follow before any of the other ladies even had a chance to introduce themselves.

I followed her to the buffet—a serve-yourself scenario. We got trays and cutlery and napkins, and there was plenty of everything, so I took small portions of several meat-in-sauce dishes and some fried shapes of…something. The green bean casserole at least looked *familiar*, so I took a fair amount of that while Paige piled her plate with lots of everything.

We had a choice of drinks from a machine that dispensed lemonade ("It's from a mix," Paige whispered), skim milk ("Very possibly powdered," she volunteered), or iced tea ("Decaf," Paige assured me). She helped herself to the tea. I opted for the lemonade.

Paige looked askance at my tray. "You didn't take any pretzel salad! I'll get you some. It's one of Agnes's specialties." She plopped a small plate on my tray that held a square of something that looked nothing at all like salad. There wasn't any lettuce—or even any pretzels that I could see. Feeling mildly anxious about how much of this would turn out to be edible, I followed her back to our table, while *Food snob, wine snob, car snob* sang in my head.

We rejoined the four women, who were now concentrating on their own plates. So, I tucked in too. To my relief, the green bean casserole tasted just right. So I braved some of the more questionable items. "Wow," I said after a bite of chicken-something-over-rice, and then *"Wow!"* after taking a big bite of hamburger-something over flat noodles. "This…stuff…is *delicious!*"

Paige's milky blue eyes twinkled at me over her own loaded fork. "What did I tell you?" She assessed my plate. "The hamburger stroganoff always goes quickly. You'll want to secure your seconds before it runs out."

I thought about refusing politely, but the other ladies were all still eating and I'd paid an entire dollar, hadn't I? "Okay," I said, and got up to refill my plate, going heavy on the stroganoff. When I'd polished all that off, I decided to dare giving the pretzel salad a try.

It wasn't a salad at all. It was a dessert, and it was delightful.

Some minutes later, rubbing my tummy and stifling a groan, I leaned back and looked up to a circle of smiling, expectant faces. Apparently they'd all been watching me eat.

"It's so nice to see you dig in with such *gusto*," said Paige.

"You youngsters can eat *so much!*" chimed the woman to my right.

"Enjoy it while it lasts, dear," said the impeccably dressed woman across from me. She had precisely cut white hair that matched her slightly frosty tone. "It all catches up with you eventually."

The ladies agreed in chorus, though they all looked pretty ropy and strong, to me. I realized, looking around, that I'd seen most of them power walking in town or along Crescent Beach whenever the weather was good. (And…they couldn't also be some of the witches on paddle boards at Halloween, could they? I'd only seen photos, but some of these profiles seemed rather familiar. I would certainly check that out in person this October.)

The prim woman across from me got up and swiftly gathered everyone's plates without a word. "You don't have to…" I protested, but Paige laid a hand on my arm as the woman took them to a bus tub.

"Nature abhors a vacuum, and Linda abhors a mess. Let her do it."

The other ladies nodded.

Well, if this was how it was done at the senior center, this was how it was done.

I dug through my bag and found a pen and my little notebook. Yes, I'd finally given in to the prevailing island custom and bought a notebook of my own. I may be a slow learner, but I do eventually get there. The trouble was, I still had a bunch of notes in my phone, so I opened that up, too, and set it by the notebook. I clicked my pen, looked up, and smiled. "As Paige said, I'm Camille Tate. And who do I have the pleasure of working with today?"

"Well, I'm Linda Meadows," said the woman with the nice haircut, back from the bus tubs. She turned to her companions. "And I'm sure we all appreciate what a busy schedule you must have today, so thank you for making time for us." Her tone was definitely frosty. Was that just her style? Or had I eaten more than a *polite* guest should have?

"Oh, no, I'm fine," I reassured them. "This is my only meeting today. So take all the time you need."

"Oh, we won't need that much time, Camille. We're all pros at this," said a woman with a playful smile, salt and pepper hair, and exceptionally penetrating eyes. "I'm Virginia Chisholm."

"And I'm Diana Crowe." She waved at me with a small, graceful hand. In fact, everything about her graceful and small, except for her large brown eyes.

"I'm Kathleen Silver," said a tall, slim woman with incredible bone structure and silky hair that matched her name.

Paige watched the introductions with approval. "All right, let's get down to business then." She turned to me. "Camille, I trust Lisa Cannon has explained how long we have enjoyed helping her and the rest of the island's live theater purveyors put on their shows?"

"Yes," I said, "and I really appreciate your help, as I get up to speed on things."

I read the list of tasks to be discussed that Lisa had given me: managing and distributing posters, notices and advertisements with the Chamber of Commerce and local media; arranging for the printing of programs and the "program folding party" a few days before opening night; procuring and selling intermission snacks; coordinating volunteer ushers—a whole host of essential duties that, for whatever reason, these women were willing to do without pay. "Have I missed anything?"

There were some headshakes around the table. "Everything seems accounted for," Linda said, "though other things always manage to come up."

"Like that set for *Amber Waves!*" said Virginia.

"Oh, yes!" Diana cried, and the whole table chuckled. She turned to me to explain: "Did you see it, dear?"

I shook my head, remembering how José spoke of it. "I haven't, but I've heard it's a little…depressing?"

Kathleen scoffed. "Depressing? No, no. It's an *incredible* play."

Virginia chimed in. "But whoever told you that must have seen the dreadful set we started with. It was supposed to be a bucolic country setting, with rolling hills in the background, and a bright blue sky overhead. But, er, *somebody* had *misunderstood* the instructions!"

"The set he made was straight out of *Wuthering Heights*," Kathleen said. "Bleak moors, dark and stormy sky, even a gloomy mansion brooding on the horizon."

Diana leaned in. "Lisa was *beside* herself!" Everyone laughed; Diana wiped her eyes with her napkin as their laughter faded.

I could guess who *somebody* had been. I wondered if he'd done it on purpose.

Who was I kidding? Of course he had.

"When the whole thing was finally revealed, there was only a day and a half till opening night," Virginia put in. "So we just went to the hardware store for paint and brushes, and had a set-brightening party!"

"We fixed it," Linda said proudly. "That's what we do. We just get to work and fix things."

Kathleen leaned forward. "But ever since then, Lisa inspects every scrap of the set design, and watches his work on it like a hawk."

Linda looked skeptical. "Oh yes. Here's hoping he can even get the set done on time. As production manager, I suppose you'll be in charge of that now, Camille." She sighed. "Roland Markus is downright impossible. So don't look away, dear. Not for a minute."

More sighs and a few nods echoed around the table.

I was in full agreement, of course, but it didn't seem exactly politic to say so. "Well, Lisa does say he does nice work…"

"Oh, his sets are usually beautiful. They're just…a little progressive at times, shall we say."

"Yes, but *beautiful*."

"There's no way she'd use *anyone* else."

"Of course not. Even though he's the *worst*."

"Because he's also the *best*."

"Completely impossible, yes, but his *results*."

"Absolute *best* results."

"Except when they're the worst, like that *Amber Waves* set."

They all nodded in agreement. "Well!" Paige said brightly. "Mustn't let this devolve into a gossip session. What else do you need from us, dear?" she asked me.

"That's probably good for now," I said. "The poster and program are still being designed, I think? They're with…" The name escaped me.

Linda supplied it. "Andrea Miller. Those will be on time and beautiful, have no worries."

Virginia raised a hand. "But I want to proofread them!"

"You'll get to proofread them," said Kathleen. "Andrea will email you a proof before she sends the files to the printer."

Virginia raised her brows. "Good. I loathe typos."

Linda raised a hand. "I'll ask her to let me know when they should be ready, and get them picked up and distributed. And I'll organize the folding party too."

"Linda loves a party," muttered Virginia.

Kathleen elbowed her and stage-whispered, "*I'll sneak in some wine*."

We talked through the remaining items, and in no time, all the responsibilities were assumed and my job was finished. Well, that

was easy. I looked at the list on my phone, and compared it to
everything in the notebook, and made a few more notes.

"Hm. That's an interesting system," remarked Linda. "Is there
a reason you do it that way?"

"Well!" I closed the notebook. "I think that's all I have for now.
So—thank you all for introducing me to the best lunch in town!"

Linda leaned in and looked me directly in the eyes, very gravely. "You *are* aware that youngsters are only welcome in the center
with an escort of the appropriate age, yes?"

"Oh, uh, yes," I assured her. "Paige made that perfectly clear." I
gathered up my bag and notebook and got to my feet. "All right,
I'll leave you all to the rest of your afternoon."

Paige Berry got up as well, giving Linda a glance. "As the party
responsible for your presence in the hallowed halls of the senior
center lunch, I'll *escort* you to the door. Wouldn't want you getting lost and stumbling across something here young eyes aren't
meant to see."

Everyone laughed again, except for Linda. But I found myself
wondering, for just a moment, if there could be some truth to the
jest… Orcas Island was a mysterious place, after all. Who was to
say the senior center wasn't a hub of—what? Life painting classes
with nude models? Cryptocurrency mining? Rare tropical macaw
smuggling?

Who could say what these women might be up to?

As we passed through the lobby, Paige paused and set a gentle
but firm hand on my arm.

"How are you *doing*, my dear?" she asked, gazing into my eyes.

It was not a casual question. This old lady and I had been
through so much turbulent water together, and I knew by now
that she understood me much more deeply than most other people did. But I had a whole host of things I couldn't tell even her
about now. "I'm all right," I said; which was honest—so far as
it went. "I'm completely freaked out about having to act in this
play, but mostly I try not to think about it, and keep myself busy

with the rest of it. Like this." I gestured toward the dining room. "Stuff like this is very nice. And distracting." I smiled.

"But that is not the *only* thing you need distracting from," she said, still studying me.

She *would* be the one to see right through my best efforts at secrecy and deception. I wouldn't even let myself wonder how she had found out I'd agreed to gather secrets for the Feds. But I wasn't going to give anything away, either. "What do you mean?"

Paige's gaze softened only a touch. Then she shook her head slowly. "Oh, you poor dear. It must be so very hard for you, but I have the utmost confidence that you can handle it."

"Handle...what?" My heart started to pound. Yet my arms weren't tingling. Paige's hand still rested on my forearm, and felt comforting somehow, in spite of what she was saying.

She gave me a small, tender smile. "This rough patch between you and Deputy Rankin."

Now I felt flooded with relief—and frustration. "Paige, it's not a rough patch, and there's no 'between' us. We're not a thing— never were. And never will be."

She just kept shaking her head and smiling at me. "Oh, Ca- mille. Do not let discouragement convince you to surrender. Time is the best healer. Have faith."

I shook my head too. "Paige, no, seriously. Listen to me. It wasn't a breakup; there wasn't anything to break. I'm truly fine. There was just a misunderstanding, and I cleared it up, and we're all—well, clear." I gave her a stellar smile. "So! I should really be getting off to..."

Her clutch tightened just a bit, still managing, somehow, to feel soothing, not controlling. She patted my arm with her other hand. "You call it a misunderstanding, and you're not wrong; but I think the misunderstanding is somewhere else in the equa- tion." She gave me a mysterious smile and squeezed tighter be- fore dropping both hands. "Little gestures, Cam. Little gestures are so much more effective than words. I know as a playwright, you are focused on words; but remember the gestures. And never, ever lose hope." She turned and started walking toward the front door once more.

I paused a moment, a bit nonplussed, then caught up to her with a confident smile. "Really, there's nothing to worry about with Kip. But thank you—again—for introducing me to your booster club, for all the help you ladies are going to be with the play, and for the delicious lunch!"

She eyed me with an unreadable look for a longer moment this time. "You've really grown, young lady," she said matter-of-factly, then turned and walked back to rejoin her friends.

❧

From the senior center, I drove to the Office Cupboard to relay some poster and program management details we had worked out over lunch. Then I drove down to Madrona Farms, and asked José if he would pass along—discreetly—anything he happened to learn about Markus's progress on the set. I didn't need to be told twice about watching Mr. Broadway like a hawk. From there, I went back up to the Island Market for a box of cereal and some cat food.

Through all of these errands, Paige's persistent obsession with what had—or hadn't—happened between Kip and me kept on percolating in the background; and as I left the market parking lot to drive home, I changed my mind and drove out of town in the other direction, toward Moran State Park and Mountain Lake, prodded by a vague desire for time to think without distractions. Driving had often been good at providing that; but the roads had been longer back in eastern Washington, and I was in the tiny town of Olga on the island's other side before I'd even really begun to process that whole mysterious conversation with Paige.

I was relieved that she hadn't figured out I was signed on as a confidential informant, of course; but her recurring assurances about my supposed love life were becoming…kind of baffling.

From anyone else, I'd just have shrugged it off. But this was Paige. Paige, who had repeatedly seemed to know things she shouldn't know, and kept turning up unsummoned at places just as things were happening there.

Paige who, while not vanishing like I did, could somehow become…unseen, or unregarded anyway.

Paige who grew the most astonishing vegetables, not to mention the goats.

She called herself "just a gardener."

Did she think I was one of her crops?

I drove past Olga and out toward Doe Bay where, on a whim, I turned off and down into the resort there. From the parking lot, it was a short walk past the massage and guest rooms, the little store and the restaurant, to an overlook of the bay. All this was so far from West Sound that I'd been here only once before, when Jen had insisted on taking me to dinner here. The meal had been spectacular, of course.

At the overlook, I availed myself of one of the weathered wooden chairs set out there, and stared off at the water—an open, airy vista nothing like the occluded scenery out my cabin's front windows. *And now you're a view snob too*, I thought, smiling at myself. How much longer before I became an entirely impossible human being?

I imagined Paige patting my arm with that tender, encouraging smile, and telling me that no human being is entirely impossible.

And, with that thought, the strange discomfort that had sent me here returned. Something about Paige's absurd but weirdly comforting remarks at the senior center had left me feeling… well, surprisingly uncomfortable. I wasn't sure why her misguided assumptions about Kip and me always bothered me so much, but they did—every time she brought them up. Was she meddling in my life—the way JoJo had? She did tend to meddle; she'd said so to my face the night she'd shown up so unexpectedly at my place and…somehow made me turn and face my birth mother's murder, and the fears I'd run from all my life. Had that been meddling? I didn't think so. JoJo definitely meddled at times, and so did Jen, however much I loved her. Even Lisa meddled, I supposed—though "mentoring" might be a nicer name for it. Becoming an *actor* sure hadn't been *my* idea. But meddling didn't seem like the right name for what Paige did. She'd never maneuvered me into doing anything. She was just…so freely outspoken about things.

Sure, Kip was gorgeous, of course, and very kind, and far too well behaved. But Colin had been nearly all those things too, and I was no more interested in dating a cop than I'd been in dating him—especially after all the trouble such baseless notions had caused Kip at work. No, however lucky Paige got at times, this time she was just chasing some "happily ever after" fairy tale she'd made up without my help. Did she think I needed some kind of handsome prince to be happy? That didn't seem like her. But…

I sighed and shook my head, deciding I had better not even object if she brought it up again. If I just ignored her matchmaking dispatches completely, then sooner or later she'd have to give them up, wouldn't she?

Who could say? Paige was a force of nature. There was no predicting or controlling her. And I had an endless list of tasks still waiting to be done, regardless of whatever I had told the ladies at lunch. So, I stood up and started walking back to my car.

As I passed the restaurant, I thought again of my amazing dinner there with Jen. Of course, she'd known all the servers, the cooks, and the bartender, so we'd been treated especially well. There wasn't anyone on the island Jen didn't know, it seemed. I was working my way up to something like that, I supposed. How many people had I met in just the last few days? Luckily, far more of them were like Paige's friends than like Roland Markus. But of all the people I had met here, I was sure that Jen would always be my favorite. As deeply as I admired, respected, and appreciated

Lisa, I just *loved* Jen.

I pulled out my phone to call and see what she was doing tonight.

Of course, I had no service. I'd gotten so spoiled with my new always-access, all-the-time reality that I'd forgotten how the other half lived. I shoved the phone back in my pocket and continued toward the car. The afternoon was stretching toward evening; I really had to get home and figure out dinner for me and the livestock.

But, as I drove back through town, I pulled up in front of the Barnacle anyway, on the off chance…and yes, there was her car. Score! I parked and went in through the propped-open door.

Jen was behind the bar, stocking the back shelves. "Sorry, we're not—" she called over her shoulder, then turned and saw me. "Oh hi! Come on in! I was just airing last night's liquor sweat out of this place before we open," she added with a mischievous grin.

"I'm not sure what liquor sweat is, but it smells nice in here now," I said, and took the barstool against the far wall.

"What's up?"

I shrugged. "I was going to ask if you were free for dinner tonight, but I can see you're not, so I just thought I'd say hi."

She leaned down to open a cardboard box at her feet, and started moving bottles of beer from it into an under-counter fridge. "If it's like a normal Tuesday night, we'll be pretty dead till a lot later—if it ever gets busy at all. You wanna hang out a while? I can make us a charcuterie plate."

Ooh, that sounded good. As tasty as lunch had been, it was a long time ago. "Sure, but don't interrupt your setup for me. I'm good to wait."

"Nothing to interrupt." She glanced at the clock on the wall. "Honestly, I'm about done, and we still have almost half an hour. Let's just hang out till a paying customer comes in."

"I'm a paying customer," I said, still feeling guilty over my ridiculous salary, like I always did whenever I saw Jen working so hard.

"La la la la I can't hear you." She stepped over to the tiny food-prep counter at the side of the bar.

A few minutes later, she set a beautifully laden board on the bar, and climbed onto the stool beside me. "This is great, actually," she said as she picked up a rolled slice of prosciutto and wedged the whole thing in her mouth. "I didn't get a chance to eat after I dropped all the dogs off. I thought I'd left enough time, but their owners are scattered all over the island, and I forgot to account for travel time."

"You have to drive them around, too? Their owners don't bring them to you?"

She laughed. "Of course not! Cam, people hire dog walkers because they don't have time to do it themselves. If they had to drive the dogs somewhere, they might as well just walk them."

"Huh." The whole notion was so foreign to me. Why have pets if you didn't have time to be with them? And then, my brain helpfully popped up to remind me that I'd been heading home to spend time with my pets before I stopped here. *Shut up*, I told it, popping another little wedge of delicious cheese into my mouth for distraction. Spending time with *friends* was important too.

"So what's new with you?" she asked. "How's rehearsal going?"

My turn to laugh. "We're not rehearsing yet—I'm still working on the jillion things that have to happen before that even gets started."

"Oh?" She tucked another piece of meat into her mouth. "Hey, I forgot drinks—some kind of lousy bartender I am." She hopped off her barstool. "I could make us the crazy cocktail special I've invented for tonight, but that would take way longer than a nice, simple glass of red wine."

"Red wine is great," I said, assuring my inner wine snob that whatever it was, it would be delicious.

Jen reached under the bar and pulled out a big bottle—double size, at least. The label was colorful and nearly illegible. She filled two glasses nearly to the brim and slid them over to our places, then left the bottle out on the bar back or the back bar or whatever it's called, before coming around to sit down again.

We lifted our glasses to toast, then drank, and sure enough, it was terrific.

"Anyway!" she said, setting her glass down. "You were telling me about the play prep."

I rolled my eyes. "Do you know Roland Markus?"

"Oh honey. Not *him*." She turned and gave me a very sympathetic look. "Is it bad? Already?"

"Afraid so. Why is he such a butt?"

"Well," she said, dramatically, "he used to work *on Broadway*. Or hadn't you heard?"

I snorted. "Believe it or not, he did mention it. A couple of times before his rant about how newcomers like me are ruining the island. Oh, and that I'm an idiot minion who should leave the real decision-making to the grown-ups."

"That sounds about right." She shook her head and took a generous gulp of her wine. "But don't take it personally—it's not about you."

"I didn't think it was," I assured her. "He started kvetching about the job as I walked through the door—before he could have known a thing about me."

We chomped and sipped in silence for a minute or two. Not many things can grab your attention like four different kinds of cured meats, house-made pickles, three kinds of mustard, a selection of strong cheeses, assorted nuts, and a big pile of super-tasty, super-salty crackers.

Oh and some squares of spectacular dark chocolate.

"Madrona Farms is great, though," I said, after a while. "José and Erin are *much* nicer."

"Aren't they wonderful? They offered me a job once."

"Of course they did. Doing what?"

"Managing events. But I'd have had to give up too much of the other things I do during the summer, and my hours would have been reduced to almost nothing in the winter. Still. They're great people; maybe someday."

I glanced around the tiny bar. "You could probably have kept this job, anyway."

"No, this is the one I'd have needed to drop first. Weddings run well into the evening, and the event manager has to stay on site till the last drunken guest has safely departed the premises. If I think it's a challenge to get them out of here, where ten people is a crowd, imagine clearing that huge barn."

"I hadn't thought about that."

"Good thing you have me around," she said with a grin. "I think of everything. So, what else?"

"Well, I had a delightful lunch at the senior center today."

She turned fully on her stool to stare at me head-on. "Wow," she said, after studying me. "I really need to get the name of your skin care specialist."

I snorted. "I was a guest of Paige Berry—and the island ladies' theatrical auxiliary booster club, or whatever they call themselves. We were going over all the stuff *they* do for each play. I had no idea so many people were involved in putting on a production."

Jen laid some cheese on one of her crackers and took a big bite. "It's like a little city," she said, around the mouthful. "I'm jealous. I've never gotten to eat at the senior center. I hear the food is really good."

"It was. And the price was certainly right. One dollar! If you play your cards right and stick with me, I might be able to get you in with me next time."

We both laughed. "So when *do* the rehearsals start?" she asked.

"We have to do the table read first. Go through the play together, but without acting, or so I'm told. Just to get familiar with it. So, after that, I guess. A week or two, maybe?"

"It's so exciting," Jen said with a happy sigh. "Your burgeoning new acting career!"

"It's not a career!" I said, perhaps a little shrilly. A couple walking by outside the Barnacle's open door glanced in, looking startled, before walking on.

Jen blinked at me. "It could be if you wanted it."

"I don't though!" I said, trying not to shriek this time. "It feels like some kind of, I don't know, punishment or something."

"I would have thought working with Roland Markus would cover that," she said, dryly.

"Hmph. That too." I took a swallow of wine before turning my attention to the last of those amazing crackers. "When this play is over, I am *never* acting again in my whole entire life!"

"Mmm-hmm," she purred, finishing her glass. She got down off her barstool and cleared our empty board and glass to the back bar. "You just keep telling yourself that." She sent a salacious look over one shoulder. "But I'm pretty sure not even Kip could resist the attentions of a famous actress."

"What attentions?!" I exclaimed in disbelief. *Jen too now?* "I have no *intentions* of paying *any attentions* to Kip—or anyone else here. Can I make that any clearer than I already have? Who is this crazy woman going after Deputy Rankin and an *acting career*? Everybody seems to know her but me!"

Jen had turned around by now to stare at me, open-mouthed. "Okay, not sure what I've just stepped in," she said playfully, "but I surrender, unconditionally."

"Sorry," I said. "I'm…overreacting, I guess. But I'm serious too. I—have—no—interest—in Kip Rankin. *Or* in acting. I became a caretaker for an empty house in the dead of winter on a remote island because I wanted to hide out. I wrote a play because I wanted to be a writer—alone all day with a keyboard. I took the job with Lisa because a personal assistant works *behind* the scenes. What part of *anything* you know about me or my life makes you think I'd be looking for an *acting career*?"

My voice had gotten louder and louder as I'd gone on, and then dang it, I was practically shouting again. Jen just gave me an

amused look. "Because you're so good at declaiming and emot-
ing. Isn't she, folks?" Her grin widened as she looked behind me.

I spun around and found, to my horror, that a group of customers had seated themselves at the banquette by the front windows. They all smiled, before bursting into applause.

I dropped my face into my hands. "Give me the bill," I said
to Jen without uncovering my face. "I need to get out of here. I
need to crawl into a hole and die. Right now."

"Nonsense," she said, and I heard the glug-glug as she refilled
my glass from that enormous bottle. "I already told you you're
not getting a bill here, and you can't leave before you're finished
eating."

"I *am* finished." I groaned, waving at the empty spot beside my
refilled glass where our charcuterie board had been. "You know
I'm driving, right?"

"Then I should probably grab you some dolmas and more
cheese or something," she said cheerily. "Just as soon as I get
these folks' order."

I stayed, and drank water (and ate food), until I was safe to
drive again. It would be just my luck to get pulled over by Kip.

Or by Larissa Sherman.

Or by any of the island's other deputies, frankly.

Oh, and I didn't want to crash my car and kill myself either, of
course. But at least then I would be dead, and not making a fool
of myself any longer.

In any event, I was legally sober by the time I left. I knew this
because Jen had a breathalyzer device behind the bar, for this very
reason.

"Point-oh-five," Jen said, after I'd breathed into the little black
box. "You're good."

"What's the limit?"

"Point-oh-eight," she told me. "So you're just barely over halfway there. How do you feel?"

"Fine. Full."

She grinned. "Good. Then my work is done here. Onward, budding actor!"

"I do not want to be an actor!"

"La la la la," she said again, as she cleared empty glasses from a table and wiped it down with a damp cloth. The place had gotten busy; a couple hovered in the doorway, clearly waiting for the table Jen was cleaning—the only open seats other than the barstool I'd just vacated. "Have a safe drive home," she said.

"Not going home," I answered sullenly. "Catching the ferry. Leaving Orcas and this play behind. Heading for the Tri-Cities, to sink back into obscurity. It's been nice knowing you." I pulled on my coat and picked up my purse, just to make the point clear.

"Well, bon voyage, I guess," she said, still grinning like a banshee. "Don't forget to send a postcard!" Then she turned to the newcomers. "Right this way! What can I get started for you? We have a special cocktail tonight…"

CHAPTER 7

I didn't see Lisa much over the next few days, though we checked in via text and hurried conversations when one of us was coming or going. I had plenty to do; I'd been back to the barn venue several times, checking on the progress of José's repairs behind the stage. I'd even had a reasonably productive follow-up visit with Roland Markus. He'd been no more pleasant to deal with, but at least he was staying on task. He kept calling me by the wrong name and starting every third sentence with, "But when I did *Steel Magnolias*..." But he didn't bring up the cow pasture again, thank goodness.

After about a week, Lisa called me over for a sit-down meeting. "How is everything going?" she asked, as we settled in her living room with coffee and tiny cookies.

"Surprisingly well. Except..." I told her about my latest horrible meeting with Markus.

"That man." She rolled her eyes and dunked a cookie in her coffee, somehow managing to keep her fingertips dry. And then she transferred the moist cookie to her mouth, leaving no drops or crumbs anywhere on her face or clothing. *When I grow up, I want to be Lisa Cannon*, I thought, and not for the first time.

I went on to report everything that had been accomplished

during my other various meetings and errands, careful to acknowledge how much more there was still to do. "I'm hoping that the ladies' auxiliary will be able to put up the posters next week," I finished. "And oh, I almost forgot: I picked up the play scripts this afternoon, and will send them to the cast tomorrow."

"Wonderful, wonderful," she said, reaching into a purse on the coffee table and pulling out a little day planner. After shuffling some pages, she said, "What about Monday then for the table read? We can do it here; we generally start casually, just in this house."

She wasn't seriously *asking me*, was she? "You're the director," I reminded her with a smile.

"Of course, but you're the playwright…and the star."

My heart thumped faster in my chest. Didn't I have enough to worry about with all the details of managing the play? "Lisa," I pleaded. "I know you think acting will be good for me, and all that—but I'm just not feeling any better about doing it, and I can't see that changing. We have enough time to find someone better, someone with experience. This island must be full of talent! I see posters for other shows everywhere. Don't you want someone who's going to be, well, *good?*"

Oh, her smile was always so kind. "Cam, Cam. I know this is frightening. But I have at least as much confidence in you as I did before—no, *more*. You've dived right into every task you've been given so far, and you're doing marvelously. You'll take to acting just fine. I know you will."

She would never believe me. I mean, yeah, it was great that she believed *in* me, but… "You're still going to be my understudy, and take the part if I can't do it, right?"

"I promise." Then she gazed at me another long moment, as if weighing some decision. "In fact, I'm going to share something with you that almost nobody else knows. I think you might find it helpful right now."

"All right," I said, trying not to sound as dubious as I felt.

"It's crucial to keep this bit of information to yourself," she went on. "If it were to get out, it would endanger not just me, but other people as well."

I nodded, wondering, *What in the world now?*

"As it happens, Derek wasn't the first person to think of stacking my troupe with, hmm, ringers. My own first attempt was disastrous but…" She frowned. "Well, let's just say I got better at it. Two of my current actors were hired to…keep an eye on things, and protect me, if necessary."

"So two of the actors are…bodyguards? Not actors?"

"They're both."

"Which ones?" I asked, astonished.

Lisa pursed her lips and then gave a tiny shake of her head. "For their protection, and my own, I can't tell you. And you really mustn't ever mention this—to anyone."

I felt on fire with curiosity. I'd met maybe six of the troupe's actors over the months I'd been here. Bella had made the strongest impression, by far: she was an outsized personality, loved to be the center of attention, and was beautiful. She exuded confidence. And Petey had seemed harmless.

Which showed what I knew. They'd turned out to be Derek's plants.

"I can't guess who they might be," I said, hoping she would give me at least a clue or two.

"Excellent." She smiled back at me. "And please don't try. I'm only telling you this because they came to me with no acting experience whatsoever, just years of experience in personal security. They couldn't just hang around the troupe without making their real business here conspicuous—and I didn't want even my other actors to guess that for a number of reasons; so I decided to integrate them into the troupe by casting them in a play. They weren't much happier with the idea than you are, but they agreed to give it a try. And guess what? They not only *enjoyed* the experience, they're *good*, Cam! They've come to love acting, and no one—in the community, in the troupe, anywhere—has any idea they're anything more than talented actors with rather scant theater résumés. And soon, we'll say the same of you." She leaned back and sipped her coffee with a satisfied expression.

I took another cookie. "Well," I said finally, "I really want to believe you're right. You've been right about so many things so far. But I still don't want to be an actor. I'm sure about that much."

She smiled again, and shook her head. "No, with respect, I don't think you are, Cam. We haven't even done the table read yet, and I don't see how you can be sure of anything about this without even having tried it yet."

I leaned back in defeat. "Okay. But if I do this play, can I just go back to being your assistant next time? That's keeping me plenty busy. I've driven around the island more times this past week than I have since I moved here."

Her little smile grew; now it seemed almost smug. She was enjoying this, dang her. She set her coffee cup down on the table and leaned forward. "That's actually an excellent segue to the next item on our agenda." She got to her feet, gesturing for me to get up too. "Come this way, please."

I followed her to the front hall, where she turned—not to the kitchen, as I'd expected, or to the front door straight ahead of us, but to the interior garage door. I'd kind of forgotten it was there, never having used it when I'd lived here.

She opened it and leaned in, blocking my way as she switched on the lights. "Ah, there we go," she murmured as the outer garage door rolled open on its tracks.

Then she turned around and stepped aside with a broad smile. "What do you think?"

I looked past her. There was a small, sleek mahogany-colored SUV in there, glinting in the sunlight that streamed through the open doorway. "Oh, that's gorgeous," I told her. "And probably more practical for the island." Her tiny bright-blue roadster was adorable, but not really a country car.

"I should think so," she said, still with that secret, proud smile. "That seems like a good idea, with all the driving I'm asking you to do here…" And she held out a key fob.

To me.

With a Porsche insignia on it.

"You're…letting me drive…your car?" I asked, confused.

She responded with a soft, quick chuckle, and shook her head. "Not my car," she said, grinning. "Your car."

My mind…stopped. I couldn't quite make my hand obey my brain, even though the words were running through my head: *She's giving you a Porsche.*

No, my mind answered. *She's…loaning it to me. She wants to let me drive it. For the day. For an hour. She's…what? What is she doing?*

"Your *company* car," Lisa added. "This was one of the things I was busy doing off-island a few weeks ago. I'd hoped to come home with it then, but they needed to have it transported from Portland, and I didn't want to wait for that." She was still holding out the fob. "Go on: see how she drives."

I managed to reach up and take the key, though I'm not quite sure how. "I…my company car…is a *Porsche?*" I finally stammered.

"Of course," she answered. "We can't have you driving all over the island in a twelve-year-old Honda. This is a Porsche Cayenne, to be precise. I did some research, and it should be just right for your needs."

I clung to the fob, blinking, looking between it and this gorgeous, gorgeous vehicle. "What if—what if I scratch it?"

Her smile broadened. "If you're using this vehicle the way it should be used, it's going to get scratched. That's what insurance is for! So—you have the key. Scratch away!"

☙

Lisa took pity on me and didn't stay to watch me back the

thing out of her garage and, hands trembling, try to figure out how to turn it around in her driveway and get it pointed toward the road. I was so nervous, my arms started to tingle.

Don't you dare chameleon, Camille Tate.

I inched up the hill, barely daring to push down on the accelerator; I could feel the power of this beauty, ready to surge away from me.

This is so much snazzier than JoJo's Jaguar, I thought, and smirked. Just in my own mind. Because the rest of me was still in shock.

The smell of it! I had always thought "new car smell" was a cliché, or at least an exaggeration; now I realized I had just never actually been in a brand new car before. I looked down at the odometer: less than two hundred miles on it! Crazy.

I stopped at the top of her driveway and put on my turn signal. It was in the same place as it would be in a normal car. Wait, should I figure out where the headlights and things were, before haring off on real roads—with other drivers?

A car drove past while I was sitting there dithering. A normal, non-Porsche car. *Poor thing,* I thought, and then, *I must never, ever ever lose this job, because I am now one hundred percent irretrievably spoiled. A rotten to the core car snob! For real!*

I finally got up the nerve to pull onto the road. I hadn't explored all the car's gizmos and gadgets and controls, but it was a car, after all; there's not a lot of variety in the basic setup. Pedals and wheels and shifting column and windshield wipers and all that.

Except it was all just…entirely different.

The thing purred like a kitten—a five-thousand-pound kitten, controlled entirely by my hands and my feet. Responding immediately to my every move—my mere thought of making a move.

I drove sedately at first, just taking it in. Not believing it. When I got to the stop sign, I went straight, so I could take those sweet curves right down by the water of the West Sound harbor. Oh, the car felt like an extension of my body…

I turned left at the next stop sign, on Orcas Road. I could have turned right and gone on down to the ferry, and beyond, but the road became dirt not long past there, and I didn't want to do that to such a shiny beast on her first outing…

Her. Oh, the car was already making herself known to me. I wondered what her name was?

I'd never named my Honda. Boring old machine, reliable and dull. But I had named my first car, a bright orange Dodge Dart that was fifteen years older than I was, when I got her in high school. She was Pumpkin, of course.

This Porsche would have a sleeker, cooler name. She would tell me what it was eventually.

And then suddenly I was approaching town—when had that happened? Had I been speeding, or dreaming? On a whim, I turned right and drove through the town, feeling both powerful and self-conscious as I looked at the pedestrians as surreptitiously as I could, wondering if I would see anyone I knew. Wondering if anyone would recognize me—if they would believe what they were seeing.

I sure wouldn't.

I was through town in a moment, then driving along Crescent Beach. The tide was out; people walked up and down the beach, and a few intrepid kayakers were out on the water, even though the day was crisp.

I passed the Country Corner, and the gas pumps there. Ooh, I bet this thing guzzled gas—and on the island, filling a tank was pricey indeed. I looked down at the gas gauge: full, of course.

But it wouldn't stay full if I kept driving around like this, un-necessarily.

Today, I would splurge. I turned right and headed down Olga Road, following my path of the other day, but in an entirely different vehicle.

It felt silly to love a car, but I didn't care.

❧

It had seemed so comfortably, survivably in the future, until, suddenly, this evening was our read-through of the play, all together, out loud. Lisa had called it a "table read," but when I got to her house, she had a lavish party set up in her big sunken living room.

The actors—the *real* actors—were all there when I arrived, drinking and talking and laughing. A stab of fight-or-flight terror hit me as I stood in the entryway. I could just flee! Run away, go back to my old life! Have nothing to do with any of this!

But then I'd have to give back the Porsche. And she hadn't even told me her name yet, though I was considering Tigress. We'd driven across the island four or five times by now, exploring every road we could find. What a clever trap Lisa had set for me. I sighed in resignation, and stepped down into the party.

"There you are, darling," JoJo said, sidling over to take my arm. "Drink?"

"Should we be drinking before we do this? Isn't this kind of like working?"

He laughed. "Camikins, really?" And then he led me to the long narrow table where Lisa had set out a full bar and seriously excellent munchies—shrimp cocktail and tiny toasts with caviar and those absurd grapes and mini-quiches that were obviously *not* from a big-box store. And nuts and cheeses and crackers and about a jillion more things I couldn't even focus on, because I was too nervous and JoJo was shoving a big glass of red wine into my hand.

"She had the *table read* professionally catered?"

"Of course she did," purred JoJo.

Of course. I sipped and then sipped some more, waiting for it to calm me down. Weirdly, my arms weren't tingling, but I still wanted to run and hide. Or, better yet, get into my beautiful car and drive to another planet where no one ever had to stand out on a stage in front of people and speak lines.

"Cam!" Lisa cried from across the room. She patted the arm of an actor she was talking to—a very tall, handsome man, I couldn't help but notice—and guided him toward me. "Now we're all here. You've met everyone, yes?"

"Um…I think so?"

"This is Charles," Lisa said, probably reading the panic on my face.

"Nice to see you again," Charles said warmly, shaking my hand. His brown eyes sparkled in that way that only brown eyes can when they catch the light, and his voice was lovely: smooth and elegant. As were his inky eyelashes. No, seriously, they were *elegant eyelashes*. "I *love* the play, it's just wonderful."

"Uh, thank you," I said, blushing, and not just from the compliment. He was so *handsome*.

"It really is!" said a woman I remembered from last winter… what was her name? "I love doing comedies, and yours is the best we've had our hands on in quite some time."

"This is Rebecca Marianas," Lisa said, seeing how tongue-tied I'd become, and helping me out again. "You know? Let's just go ahead and start with introductions all around." She raised her voice slightly. "Everyone? Let's gather round while I introduce you all to Cam, all right?"

In a moment, we were all standing in a semi-circle. I glanced around at all the sort-of-familiar faces. I'd seen these people off and on over the winter, but they ran in a pack, and I hadn't really gotten to know any of them.

"I think you all know me," Lisa said, smiling. "And, in addition to being producer and director of Cam's play, I'll also be under-studying the role of Felicia." Her eyes danced with amusement as she said this. "To my left, Cam, is Charles, who will be taking on the delightful role of Kristoff. Next to Charles is Rebecca, who will be doing the first track characters—mostly female roles, many of the salon's clients, as well as a few other little bits." Rebecca smiled and nodded at the group. "Then there's Hal," Lisa continued, referring to a slightly older man, maybe in his forties. "Doing the second track parts. Mostly male roles. He and Rebecca will be arguing over who has the better track, if history is any guide here."

Hal playfully elbowed Rebecca in the side. Rebecca pretended to be wounded badly by this, staggering and nearly falling to the floor (but not spilling a drop of her drink). Oh look, they were acting already. And having so much fun with it. What *was* I doing here?

"Next is Glory," Lisa said. "She'll be embodying Charlotte Winkleton, which I am *so* looking forward to seeing."

My eyes widened in surprise. Glory was perhaps in her late twenties, plain and average-looking. I vaguely remembered having seen her before, but couldn't recall having ever heard a peep out of her. Even now she just smiled shyly at the group, keeping her eyes slightly downcast.

This was our Charlotte? Dramatic, charismatic, *elderly* Charlotte Winkleton? Though I clearly didn't understand anything about putting on a play, I had heard the phrase "casting against type"—maybe that was what was going on here?

"Then, we have JoJo," Lisa said even more warmly, "who has agreed to take on the role of Martin, the second lead." JoJo, next to me, bowed extravagantly, but restrained his hamming to that.

"And, last but *certainly* not least, here on my right we have Camille—Cam—who is the playwright, and my production manager. She will also be playing the role of Felicia. The lead role. Now, let's all give ourselves a big hand and get this production off to a rousing start!"

Everyone applauded, and they were *all* looking at me, not at each other. I felt like such a pretender: embarrassed, incompetent, and ridiculous—and I didn't think any of that would be improving any time soon. Thanks to the wine, my arms still weren't tingling, but...I needed a distraction.

Girl Detective. That would do it. I looked around the circle, wondering which of them were the other two not-actors here? I could see no visible clues. Maybe it would become clearer once we got into the reading and rehearsals, though Lisa had told me they were as good at this as everyone else now.

"All right!" Lisa went on, when the applause had died down. "Let's have a five-minute break to gather ourselves, and get started."

That turned out to mean two things: full drink refills, and lines for both bathrooms. I vaguely noted that JoJo had refilled my wine glass. "I can't drink all this," I whispered to him. "I need to be able to see what's written in the script."

"You are just too adorable, Cam. Need I remind you that you *wrote* the script? The rest of us have to learn the lines; you can just improvise."

Not in a million years, I thought, and took a swallow. *I can't improvise my name, right now.*

Five minutes passed in an instant, and suddenly everyone was filing up the several steps and finding places around Lisa's big dining room table. The cast settled in with more whispers and giggles, and a rustle of papers as they got out their scripts—my script! I almost forgot to pull my own out. Because I was such a pro at this, obviously.

Lisa took the head of the table, watching with a gentle smile until everyone was quiet.

Now, my arms began to tingle in earnest, cascades and shivers all up and down, threatening to spread to my shoulders. *No, no!* I told myself, quite firmly, and took another sip of wine. Across from me, JoJo gave me an encouraging smile.

"All right, everyone," Lisa said. "This is just to get familiar with the play as a whole, and start finding all our characters' voices. Let's try and get through this with as few interruptions as possible. If anyone thinks we might want to make changes, Cam can make quick notes of that, but we'll work on them later."

Everyone was nodding; this was obviously old news for them. She was probably explaining all this for my benefit. I felt even smaller in my chair.

"I'll be reading the stage directions," Lisa went on. "And I believe everyone knows which parts are theirs, yes?" She looked at Rebecca and Hal, with their handful of small parts between them. They nodded.

Lisa pulled a small pair of reading glasses out of her shirt pocket, put them on, and opened her script. Then she started to read in a crisp, clear voice: "Lights up on an empty, retro-style beauty salon dimly lit by the blue light of a rainy Seattle dawn as someone outside fumbles with keys at the salon entrance, stage left."

"Um, sorry," I said timidly. Lisa looked up at me in surprise. "The entrance—it's on the right, isn't it?"

"Ah," Lisa smiled awkwardly, "yes. When we discussed stage directions, I forgot to explain that 'stage left' and 'right' refer to the *actors'* left and right, not the audience's. I fixed that in the last edit, but I forgot to mention it to you—for which I apologize."

"Oh," I said, mortified. Right out the gate: a demonstration of my absolute cluelessness. The real actors exchanged a few sneaky glances. "Sorry."

"No, no. That one's on me." She cleared her throat, looked down at her script, and continued reading the opening stage directions. "Felicia enters juggling boxes of salon supplies, a handful of mail, and a (rigged) umbrella, which blows inside out as she comes through the door, causing her to drop what she's carrying all over the floor. Felicia closes the door behind her, muttering to herself, and stoops to re-gather her parcels."

Lisa stopped reading and looked up. At me. Across from me, JoJo looked at me too. Actually, *everyone* was looking at me. Expectantly. Why were they—"Oh! Oh, sorry," I said again, because *duh*, the first line was Felicia's. *Mine.* "Darn it, the mail's soaked," I read, blushing so hard I thought my face might catch fire. My arms started tingling all over again. I rubbed them as surreptitiously as a person being stared at by a table full of people could.

Lisa went on to the next stage direction: "One package comes up trailing a long tangle of cut hair."

Down the table, Hal chuckled.

"Eeeewww," I read, shaking my hand as if to free it of a hank of hair. "Dang it, Kristoff! How complicated is a frigging broom? You just push it around until—"

Lisa read, "She is interrupted by the sound of someone stumbling beyond an interior doorway, stage right, and raises her broken umbrella like a sword."

"Who's there?!" I snarled. Okay, I was getting the hang of this now. It was good to have words printed right in front of me. Helped with the brain freeze. "I've got a gun! It's an automatic, and, and I know how to use it—so you better just leave! Right now! Just go! I'm serious!"

Lisa: "Martin's voice, from off stage right:"

JoJo/Martin: "Don't shoot, Felicia! I'm harmless!"

Me/Felicia: *"Martin?!"*

Lisa: "Martin stumbles through the doorway, stage right, looking disheveled, with his hands up, and gazes pointedly at Felicia's umbrella."

JoJo/Martin: "What are you? Mary Poppins gone gangsta?"

Lisa: "She lowers the umbrella and he lowers his arms."

Me/Felicia: "What are you doing here so early? And…why do you look like crap?"

JoJo/Martin: "Because I feel like crap? Should have slept in one of the salon chairs, but it's too bright out here with all those street lights."

Me/Felicia: "You slept *here*? Why?"

JoJo/Martin: "I had a date last night…it didn't end well. When she kicked me out, I couldn't think where else to go, so…I came here."

Me/Felicia: "Why didn't you go home?"

JoJo/Martin: "I just told you: she'd kicked me out."

Me/Felicia, after staring at him briefly: "Kicked you out of...
your own apartment?"

JoJo/Martin: "Yes, Felicia."

Me/Felicia: "Your *date* kicked you out of *your own home*?"

JoJo/Martin: "How many times do I need to explain this?"

Me/Felicia: "And you let her do that because...?"

JoJo/Martin: "She was *really* upset. Hysterical, even. I didn't
know what else to do!"

Me/Felicia: "Hysterical about what? What did you *do* to her?"

JoJo/Martin: "Nothing."

Me/Felicia: "Nothing?"

JoJo/Martin: "Nothing. I swear."

Me/Felicia: "You must have done *something*."

JoJo/Martin: "Well...she *wanted* me to do something. She
made that...pretty darn clear. But, for Pete's sake, we just met
last night! It was our *first date!*"

Me/Felicia: "Oh, Martin..."

Lisa: "Felicia turns away briefly, pursing her lips and shaking
her head in amusement."

Me/Felicia: "Okay, I get what happened now. But I don't get
how you ended up letting her kick you out of—"

JoJo/Martin: "I just wanted her to know I was a decent guy.
Not one of those animals who just wants...you know."

Me/Felicia: "And...that made her hysterical, because...?"

JoJo/Martin: "I'm not sure, actually. I told her the first date
was out of the question, and...well, I may have...expressed some
surprise that she thought otherwise."

Me/Felicia: "No... You implied that she was a bimbo—for
wanting you? Really?"

JoJo/Martin: "I said no such thing! She asked why I'd asked
her out if I didn't find her attractive, and I asked if dating wasn't
how people find out whether they're attracted or not, and out of
the blue, she just started hitting me with her shoe, Felicia! I've
got puncture wounds to prove it. They don't call 'em stilettos for

nothing."

Me/Felicia: "Martin…you are the most…"

JoJo/Martin: "What? What was I *supposed* to do?"

Me/Felicia, stifling laughter and giving him an incredulous look: "Well, to begin with, ask *her* to leave *your* home, maybe?"

JoJo/Martin: "I did! I mean, I *suggested* that. Several times. But she just kept saying, *Get out of here, you clueless neuter!*"

The entire cast cracked up, startling me. But, well, it also felt good.

JoJo/Martin: "Those shoes hurt. I'm not kidding about that. So I left! It's not like I could just pick her up and physically throw her out. That would've been assault, right? I'd be in jail right now."

Lisa: "Felicia turns away again in disbelief and crosses stage left, where she starts going through the damp mail in a cursory way. Martin rinses his hands and face at the shampoo sink, tucking in shirt, etc."

Me/Felicia: "How on earth have you worked in a salon for so many years without learning *anything* about women?"

JoJo/Martin: "What do you mean? I listen to you ladies talking all day about what sex-crazed, obnoxious animals men are. But when I try to be a *sensitive, respectful* guy, the kind of guy you all keep saying you want—"

Me/Felicia: "You're not sensitive, Martin. You're clueless. There's a difference. A *sensitive* man who *understood* women would know that when one comes back to a sensitive man's place after a nice date, and starts making it *pretty darn clear* to that sensitive man that she'd like some attention, and the sensitive man isn't feeling it, then that sensitive man knows how to say no—respectfully, regretfully—without making her feel like a…"

JoJo/Martin: "But—"

Me/Felicia: "You know what? I bet she kicked you out of your apartment because you'd made it so clear she could. That's your real problem, Martin. Not just last night, but with every one of these sob stories you keep bringing me. You're just way, way, way too nice to actually *be* nice. You're so nice, it's mean. You either need to find some woman who's as *too nice* as you are, or you need to give—it—up."

JoJo/Martin: "And where would I look for such a too-nice woman? 'Cause I've sure never found any of them online."

Me/Felicia: "Maybe you should try a convent."

JoJo/Martin: "A *convent?*"

Me/Felicia: "It's a place where they store nuns."

JoJo/Martin: "I know what a convent is. But come on, nuns don't *date*, Felicia—at all."

Me/Felicia: "Then you'd both be starting at about the same skill level. Which might help."

The whole table cracked up again, louder this time. I grinned and relaxed another tiny notch.

JoJo/Martin: "So, wait—you're *admitting* that, for all your talk, what you ladies really want is those wild, sex-crazed beasts you spend all day complaining about?"

Me/Felicia: "No. I'm not saying that at all. What we want are respectful, intelligent, caring men who turn into wild, sex-crazed beasts when they're invited to. Is that so hard to figure out?"

JoJo/Martin: "But…"

Me/Felicia: "Quit with the buts! Dating is not just about holding hands with the Little Prince, Martin. If you're asking women out in the first place, should I have to be telling you that?"

Lisa: "They are interrupted by the arrival of Kristoff, who parades through the salon entrance, stage left, wearing an outrageous costume, absurdly styled and colored hair, and platform shoes, under a feather-rimmed golfing umbrella."

Charles/Kristoff: "Salutations, effery-vun—on ziss *gloriouss* Zeattle zommer morgen!"

My eyes widened. That wasn't what I wrote…? Lisa looked confused too, and set down her script. "Charles—is that an accent of some kind you're doing?"

Charles nodded, grinning. "Ja! German. I've come up with some backstory for Kristoff that I think will enrich—"

"Well, you know I love that kind of creative initiative," Lisa interjected cheerfully, "and I deeply appreciate the effort and enthusiasm you're bringing to this role, but I think it may be just a bit early for…that…yet. Let's get familiar with the script first, and the writing itself."

Charles seemed to kind of shrink into himself. "Oh—sure. I… You bet. Sorry."

"No apologies needed," Lisa said, smoothly. "I really do want the sort of thing you're doing. Just, a little further on in the process. Let's go on then, everyone. Cam?" She looked to me with a bright smile.

"Right," I said, feeling embarrassed for Charles. Was he one of the not-actors? I cleared my throat and read Felicia's next line: "Well, aren't you cheery this morning." And then I winced at the awkward aptness of the line.

Lisa: "Felicia stoops to pick up the discarded hank of hair."

Me/Felicia: "Let's talk about this, Kristoff."

Lisa: "Kristoff raises a foot."

Charles/Kristoff (still flamboyant but no longer "German"): "I am wearing a brand-new pair of *Fluevogs* this morning—and the first thing you want to talk about is that ugly old scrap of hair?"

Me/Felicia: "There should *be* no scrap of *old* hair here to talk about, Kristoff; only scraps of *brand new* hair, and even those just briefly. How many times do I need to explain this to you? One of the fundamental tools of your trade here is a *broom*, and yet—"

Charles/Kristoff: "Oh! Is that the mail you're holding?"

Lisa: "Kristoff jumps up and snatches the mail from Felicia."

Charles/Kristoff: "If I'm not mistaken, opening the *mail* is part of my *job* here too, and I wouldn't want to start the day by *imposing* on you *twice* before I've been here even *five minutes*."

Lisa: "Kristoff sorts through the damp envelopes, pausing with concern halfway through."

Charles/Kristoff (dropping all affectation): "Why are we being written to by an attorney?"

Lisa: "Kristoff looks up at Martin with narrowed eyes and shakes his head."

Charles/Kristoff: "How many times have I said that one of your haircuts would get us sued someday?"

Lisa: "He opens and starts reading through the letter."

Charles/Kristoff: "What…?"

Me/Felicia: "What is it?"

Charles/Kristoff: "Oh…NOOO!"

Me/Felicia and JoJo/Martin, in unison: "WHAT?!"

Lisa: "Kristoff reaches up to tear at his hair, which comes off in his hand. He stares at it for a beat, as if he'd forgotten it was a wig, then hurls it to the floor."

Charles/Kristoff (basically screaming): *"We're SCREWED! Game over! No warning! No mercy! NO PAROLE!"*

Lisa: "In the middle of this outburst, the salon phone rings. Kristoff lunges to answer it, and in a profoundly calm voice, says…"

Charles/Kristoff: "Salon Contempo, how may I be of assistance?… We open at ten o'clock… Yes, for many years now; generations, in fact… That's right… I *know*, isn't time *amazing*? … I *understand*. Thank you *so* much for calling."

Nobody was even trying not to laugh now. Hal was trying to catch his breath; Rebecca was literally snorting. JoJo was giving me *such* a look. Even Lisa seemed like she was struggling to be the serious schoolmarm—I mean, she'd read these lines, more than once—but hearing them spoken…

Anyway, it was kind of the best moment of my entire life, is what I'm trying to say.

Lisa finally contained herself and read the next line of stage direction: "Kristoff hangs up, and looks back at the letter in his hand."

Charles/Kristoff: *"GENERATIONS! Oh, the humanity! Our*

glorious heritage and legendary reputation—snatched away in an
instant by the bitter winds of—"

Lisa: "Felicia darts in to snatch the letter away, and starts reading rapidly."

Me/Felicia: "*What?* Oh no… *Oh NO!*"

Lisa: "Martin grabs the letter from Felicia and starts reading."

JoJo made a pretend-grab across the table, nearly scaring me
out of my pants, but I managed to recover. Then he shrugged, as
if to say *Acting*, and read his line: "*What? No!*"

Lisa: "Martin looks up at the others."

JoJo/Martin: "Our landlord *died?*"

Charles/Kristoff: "Yes! He's gone! Forever! What are we going
to *do* now?"

Me/Felicia: "Kristoff…are you all right?"

Lisa: "Kristoff has begun to sob now."

Charles/Kristoff: "Do I *look* okay? How can you be *so insensi-*
tive at a moment like this?"

Me/Felicia: "I'm…I'm sorry. I didn't even know you knew
him."

Charles/Kristoff: "*I DOOOON'T!*"

Me/Felicia: "Then, what the… Why are you grieving for a
landlord you don't even know?"

Charles/Kristoff: "I'm not, you moron. Did you even read the
rest of it—about his ungrateful inbred children?"

Lisa: "Martin looks down and reads further, then looks up in
horror."

JoJo/Martin: "But they…why would they do that?"

Lisa: "Felicia grabs the letter, and reads in growing horror."

Me/Felicia: "They can't."

Charles/Kristoff (weeping): "*They can! They will! We're homeless!*
Cast into the street like penniless orphans! And less than a year before
Christmas!"

Lisa: "He gazes mournfully down at his discarded wig."

Charles/Kristoff: "We're as dead as he is now. Because…"

All three in unison: "They're going to sell the building."

Charles/Kristoff: "Where am I to go now? What am I to *do*? My whole wardrobe is entirely *calibrated* to *resonate* with this august establishment."

Everyone burst out laughing yet again, but stopped abruptly when JoJo dropped his script on the table with a thud. "This is unfair." We all turned to look at him. "Kristoff gets all the best lines, while I have to play this…*clueless neuter*." He threw me a beseeching look. "Camikins. I was born to play Kristoff. Please. Why can't I play Kristoff?"

"I didn't cast the play, JoJo."

Lisa narrowed her eyes at him. "Those 'clueless neuter' lines make your character what he is, JoJo—the perfect straight man—so be a good actor and *make* them *entertaining*—as written, please."

JoJo pouted at her, then at me with sad puppy-dog eyes. "Well can't we at least spice up *my* dialogue? Even just a wee smidgen? Or, I know, the salon has a back room. Couldn't Martin just take Felicia's excellent advice, and try seducing a few of the customers there or something?"

"You mean the room *offstage*, JoJo?" Lisa asked, with a slightly brittle smile. "Are you suggesting these seductions just be performed in sound effects, or that we build a whole second set just to showcase Martin's inexplicably sudden spasm of sexual prowess?" More chuckles around the table. "You've actually *read* the entire play, yes?"

"Of course I have," JoJo said, kind of unconvincingly.

Lisa exhaled through her nose, but held tight to her smile. "Don't be a pest, JoJo—not here, and not with me." There was an edge there. Everyone had stopped giggling and grown uncomfortably quiet. "You know," Lisa suddenly added, "I think we've lost the thread a little. So let's take a short break to breathe and reset, shall we? Then we can resume with greater focus."

She stood up without waiting for an answer and marched out

of the dining room, through the kitchen, and on down into the living room. As I got up, I caught a glimpse of her heading toward the back of her house...to her bedroom? Bathroom? Out the back door and down to the beach on Massacre Bay? I had no idea, but...boy, she was upset.

JoJo stood and stretched, looking both essentially JoJo-ish—insouciant, relaxed, uncaring—but also kind of...self-conscious. He grinned around at the other actors, who were all getting up and retreating as well, then, with a look of almost unguarded concern, headed off in the same direction Lisa had gone.

Everyone else drifted around the house in small groups, chatting quietly, stretched and smiled with pretended nonchalance, and renewed their drinks as if nothing were wrong; but their body language screamed *Oh please get us out of here...* Despite everybody's effort to hide it, this whole enterprise was so obviously spinning off the rails, already.

My play is doomed, I thought. There had been that one perfect moment, and then... *Lisa is furious with us—with JoJo, with everyone—right here, tonight, this is the end of my theater career, in any capacity...*

I was just trying to sidle out of the room when I felt a tap on my shoulder, and wheeled around, unable to hide my flinch.

It was Glory. "Sorry," she said, "didn't mean to sneak up on you."

"Oh, that's fine." I smiled at her. She hadn't even gotten to say a line yet. Sad, that she had spent so much time preparing only to have it all fall apart before it had even started.

She leaned in and murmured confidentially, "It's always a little tense on the first night. Getting such a big project off the ground." She shrugged and wrinkled her nose. "Don't let it get to you." She smiled, and her face lit up. She wasn't so plain after all.

"Um, thanks," I said. Nice of her to try to make me feel better, I supposed, but what was the point now?

"Your dialogue is fabulous," she said, "including every one of

Martin's lines, whatever Little Lord Brixton thinks."

I snickered at that, while also wishing for some way to fall gracefully through the floor.

Charles sidled up and joined us. "Yes, I was just going to say the same thing." All signs of flamboyant Kristoff were gone from his demeanor; his presence was…august, serious…almost Shakespearean. "It's all so pitch-perfect!"

I just stared at both of them. "Uh…thank you?"

Charles smiled. "You're welcome, and thank *you*. I can hardly believe this is your first script."

"Me either!" said Glory. "You have a great ear, Cam. It's some of the most natural dialogue I've read in ages. Well, aside from Kristoff, of course." She turned to Charles. "You slay, Kristoff!"

"Oh, I'm just chewing away at the scenery."

Glory looked at me, smiling. "And you're reading beautifully."

I just stood there with my mouth hanging open, unable to contain my disbelief. "Are you kidding? I was in shock the whole time. I'm still in shock. I feel like a complete—"

Charles raised a hand to stop me. "Everybody feels like that the first time. Am I wrong, Glory?"

She shook her head. "At my first table read, I felt like a complete fool." She smiled at me too. "That's what you were about to say, right? That you feel like a complete fool?"

I nodded, sheepishly.

"Well," Charles said, "Glory's absolutely right: you're a natural, and we're excited to have you onstage with us." He held my gaze. "We're all here to support each other through the curtain call on our final performance. Each of us feels alone up there—in the light, up on a stage before that darkened audience."

Glory *tsk*'d at him. "Now you're just scaring her."

He offered me an apologetic smile. "But none of us is ever really alone. That's all I mean to say. They don't call us a troupe for nothing."

I smiled at them, feeling somehow both reassured and unconvinced. If everyone felt so nervous before getting on stage, why didn't they just…not get on stage? That's what I would have done—if Lisa had let me. I could remember all the way back to elementary school, how there would always be the "hams"—kids who just loved to be in the limelight. Joking, fooling around, showing off; those were the kids who got into theater. People like JoJo. Not the shy invisible ones like me.

"All right, everybody," Lisa said. I'd noticed her come back into the dining room a minute or two ago, followed by JoJo, looking unusually subdued. "Let's give this another try, shall we?"

We all took our places back at the table again. I glanced over at JoJo, who carefully studied his script. He looked…downright meek. I'd never seen him look anything like meek before. What had she said to him?

"Cam?" Lisa said. "Would you pick up where we left off, please?"

Felicia, Martin, and Kristoff continued speculating about how much trouble they may actually be in, and what to do if the new owners shut down the salon and turned the building into condos, or five new Starbucks, or whatever. JoJo read his lines without hamming it up but also without further complaint. Kristoff did indeed steal the whole first scene—I'd had so much fun writing him, but had I gone a little overboard?

Even the cast members who were not in this scene seemed entirely engaged in the process—laughing at the right places, paying rapt attention—though I still felt trapped in a fog of mortification.

Weirdly, no one seemed to notice.

Were they just being nice? It didn't feel that way; it felt genuine—as if they couldn't see that I was faking it. It was as if I had already vanished…*had I?* But no, I was still here, not tingling; everyone was still interacting with me—well, with *Felicia*—hearing my lines, responding to them. That was silly; of course I hadn't vanished.

But there certainly *was* something dissociative about it.

And yet. We got through the first act somehow. Lisa called another break; I took the opportunity then to have another small sip of my wine, and a snack. We'd been going for over an hour. Sitting around a table reading a play out loud doesn't *sound* like intense work...but it was.

Act two went even more smoothly than our eventual run at act one. Even JoJo had finally eased out of his snit, and began seeming to enjoy Martin's character arc. (Martin was a fine character! Way more depth than Kristoff! Kristoff was comic relief!) I suspected Lisa had been right; JoJo hadn't read the script before tonight. He'd probably just counted on sailing in and dazzling everyone, then been surprised to be playing a "straight man," as Lisa had put it. Rebecca and Hal really got into all their various small parts, doing an amazing job of embodying vastly different people, sometimes of the opposite gender. And Glory was *amazing*. When she read Charlotte Winkleton's lines, she became that dramatic, elderly woman. It was like she grew taller, took up more space—all without leaving her seat at the table.

Nobody, nobody at all, seemed like a non-actor there. Just me.

Finally, the last line was read—and the whole table erupted in spontaneous, boisterous applause! A few actors even got to their feet! And then JoJo did too! It was really too much. A standing ovation! For me!

I looked helplessly at Lisa, who gave me a friendly wink, so I turned to JoJo. He was smiling down at me, and his smile seemed genuine. Nothing arch or performative about it.

I see you, his smile seemed to be saying, *and I like you.*

I smiled tentatively back up at him, and then around the table. I still felt nervous, but a kind of sweet warmth crept into me as well...could it be possible that this might actually work?

Yes, I was faking it. But after all, wasn't that what acting was? Faking it?

I got to my feet too then, at last, and applauded as well. I wasn't clapping for me: I was applauding this amazing company, these people who had worked so hard to bring characters to life—to turn the characters I'd imagined in my head into people. Real people, with opinions and jokes and personalities and—everything.

Oh my goodness. I'd written a play. *For real.*

CHAPTER 8

After that night, my life became an even busier blur—errands and follow-ups and meetings about the play, not to mention the beginning of actual rehearsals. We rented the Grange for those, because Madrona Farm was booked up until a few weeks before the performances started. And those last weeks would be a busy time of set construction, and technical rehearsals.

Despite continuing meetings with Roland Markus, some things went well. I was shocked by how quickly the cast learned their lines. Even JoJo was close to being "off book." (I'd started learning all sorts of new theater lingo now.) Maybe we were going to really pull this off.

I was washing my breakfast dishes in preparation for heading into town—in my *Porsche* (okay not mine but you know), to pick up some office supplies, when there was a knock on my door. I opened it, stopping short when I saw Deputy Larissa Sherman standing on the porch, holding her hat in both hands in front of her waist. I groaned inwardly.

"Good morning, Ms. Tate," she said. "I'm sorry to bother you at home. I hope I haven't come at an inconvenient time?"

I just stared at her, taken aback. There was not a trace of sarcasm or mockery in her voice. She sounded quite nearly…sincere? I'd never seen her so excessively courteous, well, ever. I wondered if she was mimicking Kip, but it didn't seem that way. If anything, she looked embarrassed.

"Um, no," I finally managed. "This is as good a time as any, I suppose."

"Good," she said, with a small nod. "I've been sent to ask you if it would be possible for you to come down to the substation to answer some more questions about our investigation of the Marie Tolliver incident."

"Oh," I said, still trying to figure out *what the heck.* "Like… right now?"

"If that would be convenient, yes." She glanced down at her hat, then back up at me. Was she…trying to smile? Could she know how?

I was completely baffled. Then it dawned on me that this might finally be my first confidential informant meeting? "Uh, yeah, I could come down. Sure."

"Thank you. If there's anything you'd like to take care of before we go, I'm happy to wait."

I just shook my head. "No—no, that's okay. I was just finishing my dishes; I'll grab a sweater."

"Take your time, Ms. Tate. I'll wait out here." She stepped down from the porch and went over to look at the view.

Beyond weird. I watched her a moment, then closed my door to keep at least some of the heat inside. I did the last dish, left it in the drainer, and grabbed a sweater and my purse. "Okay, James, you're in charge today," I told my cat. "But if you have another rockin' party like you did last week, I'm grounding you and leaving Master Bun in charge from now on. This is your last chance, you hear? I mean it."

He rubbed against my ankles and then went to peer into his food bowl again, in case all the nonsense noises I was making had something to do with a second breakfast. What I really wanted was to tell him what I was thinking—that always helped me work things through—but I didn't want to risk Sherman overhearing me tell my cat that Sheriff Clarke had told me that Sherman didn't know that JoJo and I were confidential informants, but had that changed, and was that why she was being so peculiar?

Well, only one way to find out. I stepped outside and locked up. "Okay, ready."

Sherman turned and walked back over. "It's so peaceful here."

I nodded. As we walked toward the cars, I asked, "Am I driving again, or are you?"

"You're welcome to drive. I'll just follow you there."

In front of Lisa's house, Sherman's patrol car was parked next to the Porsche. I'd moved the Honda to a spot behind the garage, cleaned it up and covered it with a tarp, which was all part of me trying to work up the nerve to sell it, but *anyway,* I clicked the fob to unlock my new ride.

"Nice car!" Sherman said. She still sounded entirely sincere. Even Kip wouldn't be this polite and cheerful.

"Thanks," I said, opening my driver-side door. "It's not mine, really. Just a company car. I...well, you know, I work for Lisa Cannon now. I mean, I already did, of course, but I've been promoted, I'm her assistant now..." I trailed off, awkwardly. *Why am I explaining things to her she knows already?*

"I thought I'd heard something about that. Congratulations, Ms. Tate." She looked over the Porsche with an appreciative eye; the eye of someone who knows her horsepower-flesh. "Looks like a real step up."

She sounded genuinely impressed, even pleased for me. Had I woken up on a different planet this morning? Some Bizarro World reversal? Was Jen going to be an angry monster, and Paige Berry an exotic dancer? Or maybe I hadn't woken up at all; maybe I was still dreaming.

Sherman followed me to town, staying a proper distance behind me, but still visible. I returned the favor, not even driving passive-aggressively, like I usually did when she was behind me. We parked in front of the substation; she hurried over and escorted me to the door, opening it for me and gesturing that I should go before her. She repeated these courtesies at the doorway of the small conference room. "Can I get you a cup of coffee? It's fresh."

"No, thank you," I said, wondering if I should ask her to run into town and buy me a latte somewhere. *Would* she?

Today, who knew?

She nodded. "All right. Sheriff Clarke will be with you in a moment."

"Ah," I said, pleased to see at least that piece of the puzzle drop into place. This clearly was part of my informant duties, so maybe Sherman was in on it now? Though of course, asking her about that would be indiscreet. "Thank you."

She gave one last mannerly nod and stepped out, closing the door behind her.

Wow. We were apparently going to polite each other to death.

She *must* have been brought into the loop. That was the only explanation I could come up with for this bizarre shift in her behavior. I marveled at how much she was controlling herself, though. It had always been so obvious that she hated me; even if she now knew that she might have to work with me, she should be seething with resentment.

Perhaps I'd underestimated her.

The door handle rattled, and Sheriff Clarke walked in. "Good morning, Ms. Tate," he said with a slightly distracted air, and sat down at the end of the table. He was actually sort of a kind-looking man, I decided; craggy and handsome, with a quiet strength to him. "Thank you for making time to come down and talk with me."

"No problem," I told him. "Is this…about my new duties?"

He nodded. "Yes. Your clearances all came back clean as a whistle. All questions about your character have been satisfactorily answered, and you're cleared to proceed. So, shall we get started?"

Questions about my character? What questions—and whose?

"Sure," I said, "but…can I just ask—does Deputy Sherman know about what I'm doing for you guys now?"

He cocked his head, looking confused. "No, ma'am. Why do you ask?"

I had no recourse but the truth. "Well, she was just so…*polite* to me this morning."

Sheriff Clarke gave a slight nod. "I'm glad to hear that. We strive for courtesy in all our public interactions. In fact, we insist upon it."

"Okay. But…" Should I just tell him she hated me? Probably not. "Well. I don't really think I have anything to report yet." Other than Lisa's confidential revelations about her husband, which I wasn't going to share. They'd said I didn't have to.

The sheriff chuckled softly. "Oh, that's fine. You weren't expected to. That orientation must've left you with an awful lot to remember. But as I told you then, we're planning to direct your attention to specific sources. It's never best for informants to act on their own initiative, Ms. Tate. So, don't worry, no one expected you to have reconnaissance for us at this point."

I smiled. "Thanks—I wasn't exactly clear how this was all going to start. So what's my first assignment?"

"After some consideration, we've decided we'd like you to visit Sheila Bukowski."

I just about fell out of my chair. Fear and near-panic shot through me. *"Sheila?"* I gasped. *"Where?"* Then my panic rose. *"Oh my gosh—is she out of jail already?"*

Oddly, though it took me a moment to realize this, my arms didn't tingle.

The sheriff raised his hands in placation and reassurance. "Whoa, no, sorry, Ms. Tate. It was clumsy of me to spring that on you. Ms. Bukowski is still in the Skagit County Jail, and if all goes as expected, she'll soon be incarcerated at a state or federal facility."

I rubbed my arms anyway. Lifelong habit. "I, um, whew. I'm relieved to hear that."

"My apologies. That was entirely my fault, ma'am. I should have prepared you."

"Yes," I said, still trying to catch my balance. "You should have. But I mean…you want me to visit her in *jail*? And *why*?" Before he could answer, another thing occurred to me. "I'm going to have to testify, right? Are witnesses supposed to go visit their attackers in *jail*—before the trial, I mean?"

The sheriff looked uncomfortable. "Those are good questions, Ms. Tate. Spot on the money. I didn't realize you had such legal expertise."

"Oh, I don't. I just remembered reading about that in, uh, a mystery book." I rubbed my forearms briskly. "But couldn't this visit be, like, tampering, or something?"

He looked slightly amused now. "Under some circumstances, it could be. But here's our plan." He leaned forward. "Federal authorities have worked out a plea bargain for Ms. Bukowski, in exchange for some key information. She's just awaiting sentencing at this point." He paused, watching my face, which must have given something away, like, how completely stunned I was. "I thought you'd been told. I'm guessing maybe not, huh?"

"Who would have *told* me?" I was suddenly furious. "I've been bracing myself to face her in court, and now you're telling me I don't have to? What wonderful news, except she *shot* me."

"I understand your…"

I cut him off. "What charges? What did she plead guilty to?"

He took a deep breath and let it out before answering me. "Murder in self-defense."

"You're *kidding*. Gregory Baines, right?" I would have laughed, if I weren't so incensed. "I *saw* it. What self-defense? He didn't have a gun."

"She says he did."

"But he didn't." My mind was racing, trying to make sense of it all. "I knew she killed him, but I was told it didn't happen. Everyone said it was a rehearsal for a play. Even Lisa said that. And no one's given me a straight answer since." I sat for a moment, thinking about that. And there had never been a body found, and Lisa said… I shook my head, trying to figure it out and failing. "And the charges about me? Kidnapping? Attempted murder?"

"Those have gone away. In exchange for…"

"For whatever *else* she told you. Which I assume you can't tell me."

"That's a fair assumption, Ms. Tate. But we'd still like you to talk to Ms. Bukowski."

"Why?"

He sighed, getting ready to tell me more terrible news no doubt. "As I said, she's awaiting sentencing. And she's hoping you'll speak on her behalf. In fact, we all are. Her sentence will be light, and we'd like to establish some credibility for that. For her protection, we don't want the deal to be too obvious."

"Let me get this straight. You want me, the person she kidnapped and shot, to speak on her behalf at her sentencing, to cover up the fact that she's made a deal with the Feds."

He looked grave and sympathetic. "This is a request we're making of you here. We're not in a position to give you orders. You are one hundred percent welcome to refuse. But we hope you'll agree." He paused, clearly gathering his own thoughts. "Ms. Bukowski has been closed up tight as a cider cork ever since she was arrested. She only gave us exactly what she had to, in order to get her deal. But we know there's more."

"She must have an awful lot of things to hide."

Clarke nodded. "The federal authorities like to understand all the aspects of a case, whether or not charges are involved. They want details, because details are like cracks. They look small, but they widen."

That made some sense to me, as I started to calm down a little. "So, details like…"

"The death of Megan Duquesne, for one thing. And that woman who was murdered on the would-be burglar's boat was Bukowski's cousin, as I believe you also know. Ms. Bukowski seemed stoic about her death—which suggests some connection to Bukowski. But she won't shed light on that either. We've recruited inmates at the county lockup to see if they could shake something loose. But she's not talking to anyone."

"Then why would she trust *me*?" I asked.

Sheriff Clarke nodded once more. "Because she wants something from you."

I stared at him. "But why would I *care* enough about her to speak on her behalf?"

"Hear me out. Didn't she give you a cat?"

Of course they would know this. "Well…yes. But that was before—"

"She gave you other gifts? Before that night, I mean?"

I thought about it. "A few things, maybe…strange things."

Clarke looked satisfied. "And when you were debriefed after the kidnap, you told Deputy Rankin that Bukowski had said and done things that suggested ambivalence, even regret about the fix she'd put you in. And the thing about trying to protect you—that night wasn't the first time she'd mentioned that."

True, she'd said that about James. As if an orange kitten was supposed to protect me. (Although, hadn't he?) "I guess so, yes," I said slowly.

"Understand, Ms. Tate," he drawled, "as small and strange as these actions may seem to you, they were meaningful to her. Enough so that she thinks you'll speak on her behalf."

"She…said that?"

"Yep. More than once, in fact, since her arrest. She repeatedly brings you up as a possible character witness. It's her idea."

I crossed my arms. "That's just creepy."

The sheriff nodded. "We think she's experiencing some distress. She always struck me as steady as a rock, until recently.

She's talking in her sleep, and she seems somewhat uneasy. That's a change. If she's off guard, and she sees you as sympathetic somehow, we're hoping you might jar something loose. The smallest thing—words, phrases—they can reveal quite a bit. If you know what I mean."

I nodded. "So I have to be *sympathetic*?"

"You do. You have to be ready to speak on her behalf, but only if she gives you some explanations. Filling in the gaps, so to speak." He seemed to be smiling under that lawman's mustache. Sheriff Clarke seemed less impatient with me; it almost felt like we were partners in this endeavor. What in the world had gone on around here, to effect such a change in everyone? I wondered if I should ask JoJo about this. "So, Ms. Tate," the sheriff said, after a moment, "is this something you'd be willing to try?"

I leaned back in my chair and opened my mouth to say no. "I have no idea how to visit someone in jail."

Wait, wasn't I going to say no?

"There's a procedure, of course." Clarke reached into a shirt pocket and handed me a slip of paper. Written on it in pencil were a non-local telephone number and, below that, a long string of digits. "Just call this number, tell them you want to visit a prisoner named Sheila Bukowski, and give them the inmate number written there. They'll grant your request. We'll see to that. But you have to make the appointment yourself—without any reference to us, of course. You understand?"

I nodded again. Still not saying no…

"Good," he went on. "You'll be given instructions on the phone about where to go and the rest of what you need to do. Once you get there, they'll walk you through every step of the way. They'll have no idea that you're anything but a private citizen wanting to visit a prisoner, so obey any rules or instructions you're given carefully."

"I'm the type who's usually pretty careful about instructions," I assured him, smiling ruefully.

Now he gave me the closest thing to a smirk I'd seen all morning. "*Usually.* That's what I'm talking about. Nothing *unusual* on this occasion, please."

"Right. I understand, Sheriff."

"I hope you do." He watched me another moment, then gave a small nod. "So, the last thing we need to work out here—and I'm going to need your help on this—is how to get you over to a mainland jail and back without Ms. Cannon knowing what you're doing over there. Because she can't suspect a thing about this in any way."

"Right, of course—oh, I'll need to get her permission to take the day off," I realized.

"And you'll need to explain why. And congratulations, by the way. Damn fine car out there. Deputy Sherman is very impressed."

I felt myself flush. "It's just a company car. I don't own it or anything." Then I allowed myself a small smile. "But yeah. It's pretty great."

"Yep." He leaned back. "So, you tell me. What plausible explanation can we give Ms. Cannon for this excursion?"

I thought about it. "I haven't been to the mainland since I moved here…I could just sort of be missing it there? Hmm. I haven't seen my parents since Thanksgiving. They're in Wenatchee. Maybe my mom's sick or something…"

Sheriff Clarke frowned. "Keep it simple and hard to verify. No sick parent or family emergency or anything." He rested his gaze on me. "The best lies contain as much truth as possible."

It hit me. "Oh!" I said, grinning. "I was talking to the set designer…"

"That Roland Markus fellow? Good grief. Sorry you had to do that."

"You know Roland Markus?"

"Not personally. But he's been hired from time to time to stage public events sponsored by the county, and…well, it's not my place to comment on such things. Please go on with what you were saying."

Wow. Even the sheriff knew what a pain Roland was. "Anyway, he wants photographs of my old salon, in Seattle. Not just the pretty ones they have on their website, but real photos of the place that show details. I don't have anything like that. I was going to call one of my former coworkers and ask her to email me some, but maybe I could tell Lisa I wanted to take them myself."

The sheriff nodded. "Now you've got it. You'll probably need to make it an overnight trip, with the ferries and the drive and all that. Plenty of time to pay a visit to Sheila Bukowski along the way."

I felt ridiculously proud of myself, for being so clever. Like I'd gotten a gold star from the teacher. And the more I thought about it, the more it sounded like a fun trip. I mean, the part about the cover story; not the visiting-Sheila part.

"Excellent," the sheriff was saying. "And then we'll debrief you after you get back."

"Sounds good."

"So, start with that phone call. They'll be expecting you, so just pick a few days in the next week that might work with your schedule. I know you have a lot to do, including meeting with Roland Markus." He shook his head. "Good at what he does, but he's not an easy customer."

"You could say that." *Everybody seems to.* I tucked the slip of paper in my purse.

The sheriff gave me one last smile. "I know this won't be easy."

"I'm happy to help." And strangely enough, I wasn't lying about that.

He got to his feet. I started to stand too, but he said, "Ms. Tate, one more thing—Deputy Sherman has informed me that there's something she'd like to discuss with you, if you have time. Would that be all right with you?"

Hmm. Maybe I'd get some answers about her sudden weird

politeness. "I can't see why not."

"Thank you. I'll send her in."

"Okay," I said, then had a sudden thought: "What if she asks why I'm here? What should I tell her?"

"She'll ask no such thing, I'm sure. But if she does for some reason, just tell her you're not sure yourself." He winked. "That's one of my favorite go-tos, by the way. Leaves the other guy to fill in his own answers with no *inadvertent* help from you, if you take my meaning."

"Smart."

"Thanks again, Ms. Tate," he said, with his hand on the door-knob. "Good hunting."

He left, and a minute later, Deputy Larissa Sherman came in, looking even more awkward than she had earlier. She closed the door behind her and turned to me. "Thank you for agreeing to talk with me, Ms. Tate."

Oh boy, she looked uncomfortable. "Um, sure, no problem."

She walked stiffly to the table and sat down across from me, removing her hat and setting it on the table in front of her, where she fidgeted with it before shoving it aside. Then, with the air of a kid about to take some unpleasant medicine, she raised her eyes to me.

"I need to apologize to you for my unprofessional attitude."

My mouth dropped open. What in the world to say? I mean, she wasn't wrong. "Well," I stammered, "I've been wondering what I did to make you hate me so much."

She nodded, looking grim. "I'm very sorry you've been given that impression." Then she stopped herself, and almost forcefully met my eyes again. "No, I'm very sorry that *I have given you* that impression. It's unprofessional of me, and I apologize."

"I…" Somehow, *I forgive you* didn't feel right. "Well, thank you for this. I appreciate it." We sat in exquisite discomfort for another moment, then I ventured, "May I ask why you're…doing this, right now?"

She shifted in her chair, and cleared her throat. "Well. It was brought to my attention, very recently—my behavior, I mean—and it was pointed out how inappropriate I was being. I've done some thinking, looking at how I might have let that unprofessionalism go on." She cleared her throat again, then folded her hands before her on the table. As if using them to hold each other still. "I apologize for handling myself so poorly. I hope we can move forward."

"Well, of course," I said—feeling so uncomfortable that I'd have actually *liked* to chameleon. But there was no danger here. "I'm sure it's…not easy, being in your position."

I wasn't even sure exactly what I meant by that, but she looked up at me, almost gratefully. "No, it isn't, not at all." She broke off and shook her head. "Anyway. That's not your problem. I'm an officer of the law and I need to treat everyone with respect and courtesy."

I wondered who put her up to this. I ran down the list; who had I even complained to about this? And then I remembered the conversation with Agent Veierra. Well, well; after all that talk about being confidential. Had Larissa been talked to? "Let's put it in the past and start fresh," I suggested.

"That would be awesome." She might even have relaxed a tiny bit. Then she looked down at her hands again. "So…I hope my attitude wasn't part of why you broke up with Deputy Rankin."

Oh, not *this* again. "There was no breakup," I said, firmly. "There was nothing to *break up* because we weren't ever *together*. I mean, we were friends, but nothing more than that. I came down here and made that embarrassing scene because too many people *thought* there was something between us, and it was hurting his career." That wasn't one hundred percent true, but I did have my dignity to consider. "And now, thanks to that, we're not even friends anymore."

She frowned. "Okay. But…I'm not sure he sees it quite the way you do."

My heart gave an unsettling little *thump*. I stared back at her, then quickly shook my head. "Then that would be his issue to work out," I finally managed.

Larissa shifted in her chair, then nodded briskly. "Of course." Then she smiled. "Well, thank you for agreeing to speak with me. I really do appreciate the opportunity to clear the air." She stood up.

Those cop shoes were awful. How did she stand it?

I got to my feet as well, emboldened to say, "The purple Fluevogs you wear when you're off duty…they're kind of to die for."

"They're not a patch on that car you're driving."

"Well, you *own* the 'vogs. I just *drive* the car." We shared an actual honest smile. Then she opened the door and ushered me out into the hallway.

"Drive safe now," she cautioned me at the front door. "I'd hate to have to pull you over for speeding in that beauty." And somehow, I understood that, fresh start or no, that's exactly what she'd do if I ever gave her the chance.

After all, it would be professional of her.

CHAPTER 9

I had a lot to do before my trip to "America."

I'd called the number the sheriff gave me, and my visit with Sheila at the Skagit County Jail was scheduled for the following week—an achievement I tried not to think about.

Lisa had been all in favor of my going to photograph the salon. She'd even suggested I buy a new outfit for it, and get my hair done at her stylist's in town. Then she'd carefully inquired whether I needed an advance on my salary for this, and I'd assured her I didn't.

"I barely spend the money you were paying me already," I told her. "And the assistant salary is even higher. I don't know what to *do* with it all."

She gave me a wry, almost unhappy look, then a quick smile. "Sadly, that won't last forever. One thing I've learned about money is that your lifestyle magically expands to overtake your income." And maybe she was right. I was getting a taste for fine foods and rare wines and fancy cars. And spendy stylists, my goodness! But my hair looked great after Priscilla was done with me. If I amortized my own self-inflicted haircuts over the last five months, I guess her rate wasn't too ridiculous.

Oh, who was I kidding. It was. But I did look great.

Now I stood at the rail of the MV *Chelan*, leaning into the bracingly cold wind as the ferry steamed toward the mainland. I didn't even worry about what the wind might be doing to my hair, the cut was that good. I'd taken the first boat off the island, hoping to get the whole trip done in one day. Lisa had encouraged me to rent a hotel room for the night—"Since this is official play business, you can expense it"—but I didn't want to. I wanted to sleep in my own bed, and I didn't want to have to arrange for someone to come by and see to my animals. Jen would have been perfectly happy to, of course, but she had enough on her plate.

I'm an early riser anyway, and the islands were beautiful in the dawning sunshine. This was the first time I'd really had a chance to enjoy more of this gorgeous scenery from a boat than the bit I'd passed during my short, very preoccupied ride to Friday Harbor with Sheriff Clarke a few weeks ago. The night last fall when I'd fled here from Seattle, in a heartbroken flurry, it had not only been pitch dark but pouring rain as well, while I was busy weeping my eyes out—as if more salt water had been called for by anyone.

Now I soaked in the beauty of *so many* islands around me. I knew there were more than the few the ferries served—I'd seen a handful of them on my way to San Juan Island—but wow, there must have been hundreds. Some were so tiny, I wondered if they even had names. That little rock sticking out of the water, big enough for one seagull: did it count as an island? Did it have a name too?

The first boat was also the slow boat, I'd discovered. Some crossings went straight from Orcas to Anacortes, but we'd already stopped at Shaw, and now we were pulling into Lopez. I'd heard…interesting things about Lopez Island, but I hadn't come here to check it out yet. It looked less populated than Orcas or San Juan, though there were plenty of cars lined up in the ferry line.

After we pulled out again, there was one last, long haul between some more islands, out across an open channel, and now I could see the *enormous* city of Anacortes looming on the horizon.

Well, it was pretty small and quaint, actually; but my goodness, I'd gotten used to rural life in a hurry, hadn't I?

The ferry's speakers blared an announcement: time to go back to our cars in preparation for offloading.

✂

Tigress had onboard navigation, which was good because I'd never gotten the hang of using any of those map apps on my phone. It guided me off the ferry and through Anacortes, to the feeder highway that led back to the interstate. At every step of the way, I felt more annoyed, frightened, even overwhelmed by— well, everything. So many people! So many cars! *Stoplights!* The pace out here was absurd; everyone seemed angry, in a hurry, blandly cutting one another off, honking, running yellow lights, turning without signaling—ugh.

How was I going to handle Seattle, I wondered. Would one of these road-ragers run my beautiful new Porsche clear off the road before I even got there?

I merged onto I-5, having a bit of a tussle with the traffic already there, but eventually found my knack again. When we left the congestion of Mount Vernon behind, the road opened up and the speed limit increased.

Ahh. Better. I finally began to relax and enjoy my drive. Because she was a sweet car, and she liked to go fast, I set the cruise control carefully; it would be the easiest thing in the world to let my foot sink down on that accelerator. And out here, I didn't know any friendly deputies.

My visit to the jail wasn't until three that afternoon, so the salon would be first. That had seemed a good plan when I'd set this up: in case the visit upset me so much that I had trouble driving, or acted weird in front of my friends. But now I wished it had been the other way around. My dread was already growing, and I was afraid now that I *would* act weird when I got to Seattle, just because I was so nervous.

Nothing to be done for it now, though.

Traffic thickened up through Everett, of course, and then again, much worse, as I got closer to Seattle. Tigress was very well behaved in traffic, as if she didn't mind slowing down and letting the other motorists get a good look at her. Some of them even shot me envious glances, despite all the other "big Seattle money" vehicles racing (or crawling) by. I didn't mind their attention at all.

I took the exit for the salon and wended my way through the city's streets, marveling yet again at the *crowds*. So much congestion! And construction *everywhere*. Four times I was diverted from the way I was familiar with onto streets I didn't know— only to have the new route get rerouted, or sent down dead-end or one-way-the-wrong-way streets. Thank goodness for that onboard navigation, which rescued me again and again. How did people live this way?

I had lived this way, of course. For years. How had I done it?

I was discovering new ways in which I'd become spoiled every single day lately. Now I was spoiled for cities?

Bizarrely, when I finally pulled onto the street in front of the salon, there was a parking space *right out front*. I pulled Tigress into it and parked, just sitting there a moment, gathering myself. I peered through the salon's front windows, but couldn't really tell who was in there. Brenda, for sure; no mistaking her tall platinum hairdo. Beyond that, I didn't know.

Okay. Time to go in.

I got out, then almost forgot about parking meters. Sheesh. They didn't take coins anymore, so I had to find a little kiosk halfway down the block, and buy a ticket with a credit card. Way to go, Seattle; always making things just that much more complicated.

Then I walked back to the salon, took a deep breath, and pushed open the door.

"Good morning," Brenda sang out, "how may I—ohmygosh, *Cam*?! Is that *you*??"

"Hi!" I squealed. "Yes!"

She dropped the comb she was holding onto her tray, whispered a quick word to her client, then rushed over to me, picking me up and spinning me around before dropping me back on my feet again. I giggled in happy surprise, gasping for a breath when she released me.

"You look amazing! Julie—get out here, it's Cam!"

Julie came out from the back room and cried, "Cam!" More hugs, more squeezing the breath out of me.

I glanced nervously back at Brenda's client, sitting neglected in her salon chair, but she was just grinning back at us. "Go ahead," she said, "I'm not in any hurry."

I turned back to my old friends, feeling suddenly bad that I'd never called or texted or anything. Well, the phone lines work both ways, I reminded myself; and I was here now. I looked around. "Is Ashley here?"

"Nah, she's off today," Brenda said. "Parent-teacher conferences."

"Well, tell her I said hi."

"Are you moving back?" Julie asked. When I shook my head, she said, "How long are you in town for?"

"Just the day."

"Ashley'll hate that she missed seeing you," Brenda said. Which kind of surprised me. I'd been the quiet one, here. "Especially 'cause you look so *good!*"

"I know, right?" Brenda said, reaching out to finger my hair. "Look at this! Who's doing your hair now?"

"A woman on the island—" I started, but Julie was already walking all around me, examining me from head to toe.

"Nice clothes," she said, when she finished her tour. "Island life clearly agrees with you."

"I think it does," I said, "and—"

"We sure have missed you around here!" Brenda cried. "We haven't found a permanent renter for your chair; we just get a load of temps running through."

"Ugh, sorry about that," I said.

Brenda shrugged. "You were always so steady. And so *good*. So, you're still caretaking for Diana Brixton?"

"Actually, that only lasted a month or so, and then—"

"She's clearly paying you very well!" Julie said, laughing.

Brenda swatted her on the arm. "Listen to her, would you? She just said that gig is over, which is obvious, I guess, judging by the hair and the clothes. Like, now she's selling real estate, or running a nonprofit or—oh, I know! You're front-of-house for some amazing, expensive restaurant, aren't you? With a hotel at-tached?" She turned to Julie. "Orcas Island has *such* good restau-rants, and I hear they're not cheap."

"No, I—" I started, but I also couldn't stop giggling. They hadn't changed a bit. No wonder I never said a word when I worked here.

"I've never been to any of the islands," Julie told Brenda, with a wistful sigh, then turned back to me. "So, what's it like? Tell us everything!"

I'm not sure they've run entirely down yet, I thought. "Sure, but first, you guys tell me everything! I must have missed so much around here. What's new, what's the latest?"

They looked at each other and shrugged. "Not much," Julie said. "Brenda already mentioned the temps."

"That cute little café on the corner is a Starbucks now," Brenda said.

That was too bad…and also no surprise. It was the Seattle way, after all.

"You guys look good," I told them. "And Ashley's good too?"

"She is," Brenda said. "That boy of hers keeps growing up. Seriously, she's gonna hate that she didn't get to see you. You should have warned us!"

"Hey, I could call her, see if she wants to come by," Julie offered.

I shook my head. "Not on her day off. I'll come back another time, I'm sure." I had no idea when, but…once I'd recovered from the shock of being back in urban chaos, I'd sure enjoyed driving that Porsche on the freeway. Hard to imagine I wouldn't find some reason to do it again. "So, what else is going on?" I asked them both.

"That's kind of it," Julie said, glancing at Brenda. "Rain, clients, construction, cost of living. Work, sleep, work some more. You know." She shrugged again. "Seattle."

"Yeah," I said, feeling the heaviness of it even as I also felt the sheer relief—glee, nearly—of not having to live here anymore.

"So: tell," Brenda ordered me. "But come over here, I'm gonna finish Celeste's hair while you talk."

"No, really, I'm good," Celeste called out.

"You may be good," Brenda told her, "but Sharee Butcher's coming in after you, and I don't want to have to make *her* wait."

We all laughed as I followed Brenda over to sit down in the empty chair next to hers, and caught sight of myself in the mirror. Yeah, they were right, the haircut was amazing; it tousled so well. The damp chilly wind on that ferry hadn't hurt it at all.

Julie leaned on the counter next to me while Brenda got back to working on Celeste.

"Well," I started. "So like I said, I only worked for the Brixtons for about a month."

Brenda met my eyes in the mirror, looking over Celeste's head as she combed the ends up and snipped. "What happened?"

"We…had a parting of the ways. It kind of wasn't pretty."

"Girlfriend," Julie said sympathetically, "I didn't want to say anything at the time, because you were obviously set on it, but I *so* saw this coming. That Diana Brixton is a piece of work."

"She is," Brenda agreed, and I just nodded.

"Is she still coming in here?" I asked them.

They both shook their heads. "Nope," Brenda said. "We gave it a try—"

"All three of us!" Julie laughed.

"—but…we also had a parting of the ways."

"At this rate, she's gonna run out of Seattle hairdressers," Julie said.

"I suppose she can get started on Bellevue," Brenda put in.

I watched them bat the conversation back and forth, waiting patiently. They'd remember me sooner or later.

"So what *are* you doing now?" Julie finally asked me.

"Well, after leaving the Brixtons', I went to work for their next-door neighbor. Caretaking her place at first, and now I'm her personal assistant." I stopped, not quite believing I'd gotten that all out without getting interrupted.

"Ahhh," Brenda said, giving Julie a significant look in the mirror. "*Personal assistant.* That's where the money is."

She wasn't wrong. "I'm really just getting started at that," I told them, "so I don't have a lot to tell about it yet. The other thing I did, and that's why I'm here today, is that I wrote a play."

They both stared at me, then Brenda nearly shrieked. "A *play*? You wrote a play? I didn't know you were a writer!"

"Me neither!" Julie cried. "That's fantastic!"

"What's it about?" Brenda asked.

"Actually…it's about this place. Working here."

Now they both shrieked, and not just nearly. Even Brenda's client, Celeste, yelped a happy cry, clearly caught up in the general excitement. I began to get a little worried about the scissors in Brenda's hand.

"That's amazing!" Brenda said, finally putting the scissors down and reaching over to ruffle up my hair. "About *this place*—about *us*?! Oh, tell us everything! Can we read the script?"

"Uh…" I hesitated, then blurted out the rest. "You can—um,

actually, it's being produced, on the island, this summer—" everyone gasped "—and I'm, well, playing the leading role in it!"

Then I slammed my hands over my ears so the shrieking wouldn't deafen me.

When the fireworks died down, they pumped me for information, and occasionally quieted down long enough for me to impart it. By the time I'd managed to tell them a sanitized version of how all this had come to pass ("the former lead had a personal emergency and been forced to drop out at the last minute"), Brenda had finished Celeste's hair. Now they were all sitting there listening to me tell them all about it.

"Cam, no offense, but that almost doesn't seem like you," Brenda said. "I mean, being on stage, starring in a play."

I was about to tell her how I felt—terrified, blank with panic, absolutely certain that it was going to be a complete disaster and that I couldn't believe I'd been railroaded into this—but when I opened my mouth, what came out was, "It's a bit daunting, I won't lie, but so far it's feeling like an interesting growth experience for me."

"I'll say. That is a*mazing*," Julie murmured, shaking her head appreciatively.

Where in the world had that take come from? I wondered, but it felt…right. True. Or at least, becoming true. "Yeah," I said, as it came clearer in my mind, "not just the rehearsing and all that, which is getting more comfortable every time we do it, but also the rest of what goes on behind the scenes to put on a play." I gave them a quick rundown of what I was doing for Lisa and her company—amazing myself when I listed everything I'd either done, or saw to getting done. "So many moving parts! And it's kind of…fun, I guess…to find out I'm able to handle it all. I mean," I quickly added, "Lisa's supervising me pretty closely—I'm still just learning—but, you know, I never knew I had anything like this in me." I stopped before I could say something regrettable about being *just a hairdresser.*

But they were still nodding sympathetically, still excited about my news. "I can't believe you wrote a play about us," Brenda marveled. "And it's actually going to be on a stage!"

"Can you get us tickets?" Julie asked.

Surprised, I said, "I'm sure I could. Do you think you'd be able to come up?"

"We would not miss it," Brenda said.

"We'll close the salon!" Julie said. "'Cause Ashley's not gonna let us go without her too."

"Road trip!" Brenda cried.

I smiled, my heart melting with affection for these old colleagues. "That would be wonderful," I told them. "I can probably even figure out a place for you guys to stay. I'd let you crash with me, but—my place is pretty small."

"Oh, no worries, we'll work something out," Julie assured me.

Then they asked me a million questions about Lisa and work as a personal assistant, most of which I was not able to answer because I hadn't done it that long yet, and the rest of which was off limits because of the NDA and discretion. "But seriously," I asked them, after all of that. "There's really no news from down here? No juicy gossip about anyone—or about one of you, even?" I teased.

"I'll cover my ears, if you've got hairdresser-only business," Celeste offered. "As long as it's not gossip about me."

Brenda patted her client on the shoulder. "No, you're good," she told her, then looked back at me. "Yeah, that's really kind of it."

"You haven't been gone that long," Julie added. "It probably just seems like it to you, because you've had a whole other life since then."

"And speaking of time…" Brenda glanced at the big wall clock over the mirrors. "Sharee will be here in a few minutes, I gotta get this station cleaned up."

"That's my cue," said Celeste. "I guess I should get on with things." She got up and grabbed her coat off the rack.

Julie brought the push broom out and started working on the floor while Brenda tidied up her instruments, putting her combs in the sterilizing solution and checking the levels in her bottles.

I got up to go too, and then said, "Oh! I almost forgot. I'm supposed to be taking pictures of the salon, for the set designer. Is that okay?"

Julie said, "You want me in your pictures or not?" She put a jaunty arm around the broom, as if it were a very skinny dance partner.

"I'll take some of each," I said, pulling out my phone and opening the camera app.

I photographed the salon from every angle, with the chairs both empty and occupied, and then took more photos of the back room with the sinks, and even the big closet where we stored the supplies and the gowns and all. I shot the weird stuff Roland had asked for: the power outlets, the way each stylist laid out the tools of her trade, the magazines clients read while waiting. The nail station, the polish racks, and the weird art on the walls. I shot it all.

Then my friends walked me out, which occasioned a new round of delighted shrieks when they saw Tigress.

No amount of assuring them that it wasn't *my* car was enough to dampen their enthusiasm. I'd probably never have left at all if it hadn't been nearly time for Brenda's next client to come in. Eventually, they both gave me several fierce hugs, and Brenda said, "I mean it, Cam: this is a complete makeover for you. No, more than that: you are a totally different person. No disrespect, girl, but you were…kind of a little mouse before."

I chuckled, only a little self-consciously. "Yeah, I can see that. I've…had a lot of time to think since then."

"It can't be just that," Julie insisted. "Your whole—I don't know, your presence, your whole being—it's different. Bigger, you know what I mean?" she asked Brenda.

"I do," she said. "I think you've got it. Cam, you take up more space now—psychically. It's magnificent." She glanced down the street. "Ah, and there's Sharee now."

They saw me off with another, final round of hugs after extracting solemn promises that I would get them every detail of the play and how to secure tickets.

"Opening night," Brenda insisted. "We want to be there for opening night."

"Amen," Julie agreed.

I got into the car, waved one last time, and drove off. Even Seattle's abominable traffic wasn't enough to dampen the warm glow of my mood after that visit.

It had been surprising. See the girls again had been as nice as I'd imagined it would be; but this had been...so much more. Several things were hitting me deeply as I wound my way back out of Seattle.

First of all, they'd been full of words—and gasps and shrieks and laughter and enthusiasm—but no real news. For all that noise, they'd said almost nothing about themselves. Hadn't they been the most charismatic, exciting, dramatic people in my life? I'd been a mouse; Brenda wasn't wrong about that. But only now was I starting to realize that being the louder ones didn't mean they were the ones with more to say.

I'd finally made it to the freeway to rejoin Seattle's signature brand of crawling traffic as the visit's second, and more unexpected, insight began to sink in.

Brenda and Julie were people who had known me better than almost anyone "before"—besides my parents, of course—whom I hadn't seen since Thanksgiving weekend—and Kevin, but the less said about him, the better. And, as such, these ladies were the only people I'd seen since my new life had begin to...*mature*, as it were, who could put actual "before" and "after" pictures of me together. Everyone else in my life these days was from the island. A few of the people I'd met early on there had begun to acknowledge a changing me, but even they had met a woman who had already decided to blow up her life and build a better one in its place.

Listening to two such *old* friends hold up those "before" and "after" pictures of me side by side that way had made it clearer to me than ever before that, apparently, I had actually built that better life! Or…more truthfully, that I was doing it; I certainly wasn't finished yet—with the construction of it, or with the cleanup. I cringed a little inside, thinking about breaking the hearts of two good men, just in the last month. And then I cringed again, thinking about all the things I hadn't been free to tell my old salon-mates…

Which led me right back to everything I'd pushed aside for the last few hours: I was driving north now, on my way to have a jailhouse interview with Sheila Bukowski.

Nervousness flooded back through me just as the traffic started opening up. I had to watch my speed now, and not push Tigress to her limit—blowing straight past Mount Vernon, and the highway 20 exit, and Bellingham, straight up into Canada where I could run away from all of it…

Nope, I told myself. My days of vanishing at the first sign of trouble were behind me now, weren't they? Hadn't that been what my friends had meant about me being bigger, taking up more space? Sure, I couldn't get a word in edgewise with them half the time, but when they *had* listened to me, I'd had something to say.

And I'd written a play. All my words. And I was going to stand on stage and say those words. In front of an audience.

That didn't sound half as scary as it once had. Was it just because the thought of facing Sheila was so much scarier? *She can't hurt you*, I assured myself. *She's behind bars, she won't get to touch you, there will be guards everywhere.*

I tried to make myself believe that.

I almost succeeded.

CHAPTER 10

I followed Tigress's directions to the Skagit County Community Justice Center in Mount Vernon, and parked in a "visitor" slot out front. I made myself take a few deep, calming breaths before I got out, and suffered a moment's absurd worry about leaving a Porsche here, in front of a jail. Then I laughed as I looked around at all the law enforcement vehicles surrounding me. There could hardly be a safer place to park an expensive car.

One more deep breath, and I squared my shoulders and walked to the front entrance, where I joined a short line of people passing through a metal detector before lining up at a check-in desk. When my turn at the counter came, the clerk seemed bored and businesslike, but my heart was pounding. I stated my business and handed over my ID and phone to be put in a locker. This left me without a thing to do in the waiting room. No Words with Friends with my brother, no texts with Jen, no strings of goofy emojis to Mom and Dad, no news sites to scan.

All around me were people who seemed to understand the assignment; families, husbands, boyfriends, girlfriends. They waited quietly—well, except for the kids, who *were* kids, after all. The grown-ups bought snacks from the vending machines, which

I noticed they didn't open, and worked on craft projects, read books or magazines, or just stared at the wall.

One by one, our last names were called, until at last I heard, "Tate."

It was time to face my fears.

I was escorted to one of a row of jailhouse phone booths, and seated there before a Plexiglas window. My arms were already tingling; I took off my jacket and sat on it so I could rub my skin directly. To my left and right, other visitors were chatting away on booth receivers. No one even seemed to notice me, or my fear, or my prickling arms.

Just when I was starting to wonder if I'd been forgotten, a guard appeared beyond the clear wall, leading Sheila in. Sheila's mean little eyes bored into me as she sat down, her mouth shaped into what passed for a smile. Then the guard turned and left us "alone"—or as alone as we could be in a room full of occupied phone booths. My arms were an electrical storm at this point. My heart threatened to race again; I took another calming breath and remembered what I was here for—and what I was *not* here for.

Sheila picked up the phone receiver on her end, and watched me scramble to pick up mine.

Her smile widened. "Did you *miss* me?"

I blinked and looked back at her. I'd been so nervous, but actually seeing her...she seemed diminished. She had always looked small and gray and thick, and she was still all those things, but she seemed even smaller now. Maybe it was because she was in those green scrubs, and had been led in by an armed woman in a crisp uniform. Not to mention being safely behind a pane of unbreakable glass.

"Um, not really," I started. "But, I mean," I stumbled on, "I understand you want my help. But I need some things cleared up first."

"Yeah, well." She glanced around pointedly. "This whole get-together's being recorded. You know that, right?"

"I assumed."

She nodded. "So there's stuff I can tell you and stuff I won't. No point in *helping* these turkeys hang me."

"Okay, so, what *can* you tell me, Sheila?" Because, suddenly, I was no longer playing a part. I really did need to know. "Can you tell me why you wanted to hurt me? What I ever did to make you do that?"

She shrugged her heavy shoulders and looked sour. "I never wanted to hurt you," she said gruffly. "You're kinda cute."

My hand went to my upper arm, protectively; I rubbed the old wound there. "You *shot* me."

"I was trying to protect you."

I shook my head. "How was kidnapping and then *shooting* me supposed to protect me?"

"You were *safe* where I had you!" she snapped. "No one knew where you were. You just had to stay put while I worked things out—not pull that damn vanishing act and run into the woods!"

"Excuse me," I said, pretending I hadn't heard her remark about vanishing, "but that's not how *protecting people* goes. You don't tie them up and lock them in a room with a bucket."

Her lips and eyes narrowed as she gazed back at me. Finally, she shook her head, and snorted. "I hear you work for Lisa now. What's she said to you about all this?"

My mouth dropped open. "How did you find *that* out?"

Sheila shrugged again. "Veierra and her stooges talk a lot for people who think they're in control of things."

The Feds were informing on *me*—to *Sheila*? What else had they told her, I wondered, and why? But I was here on a mission; I needed to stay focused. I had no idea how a mind like Sheila's worked, but…maybe, if I let her think I knew more than I did…?

"She's told me about Derek, and everything at their pharmaceutical company, if that's what you mean. She seems confused by what happened with Gregory though."

Sheila nodded, looking…relieved? It was hard to tell, especial-

ly through thick Plexiglas, but…why relief about that? "Good,"
she said. "Lisa was a good boss. Did me some pretty big favors.
I was tryin' to keep her out of trouble too, even that night when
you screwed it all up. I've told that to the cops who hauled me
in here, and to my no-good useless lawyer—but nobody takes a
thing I say seriously, do they? So mostly I just keep my mouth
shut. You tell Lisa I said that, okay? Including the *mostly* part."

I just nodded, trying to look sympathetic. *Keep talking, Sheila…*

But then her gaze sharpened. "So, what's Lisa told you about
me?"

"About you?" I asked, buying time to think. "Well…she praises
your loyalty."

"Yeah, I'll just bet she does."

Then, in a flash of intuition, some pieces fell together: actors
who weren't really actors. Hadn't Lisa told me that her first try at
hiding bodyguards in the troupe had been a failure? "But I guess
you mean, about your real job?" I asked, before I could second
guess myself.

To my enormous relief, Sheila nodded. "Okay. So you know
that part too, then. Good."

I exhaled slowly, hoping maybe I hadn't screwed this up completely yet.

Sheila went on. "I told her all that 'personal assistant' garbage
wasn't gonna fly. I'm not anybody's idea of a *secretary*. But Lisa
didn't want anyone out there knowing she needed protection,
'cause she didn't want any of those island fancy-pantses finding
out about all the crap she'd left back in Seattle. Tried to bury everything." She gave me a knowing grin. "Cannon's not even the
name she went by in the city. Didja know *that?*"

I shook my head, astonished.

Sheila's smile widened. She was clearly enjoying knowing more
than I did. But then she shrugged. "Well, she woulda told you
soon enough. You couldn't be workin' as her assistant for long

without finding *that* out."

So…Sheila not only knew I was working for Lisa, but what my new job was. Clarke had some explaining to do. Sheila was going on, though—delighted to fill me in on everything I didn't know.

"See, her first husband, right out of college, his name was Nelson."

"Her *first* husband?"

"Yeah, she doesn't talk about that one. But by the time she dropped him, their married name was all over her business, and she said it would've been a nightmare to change all those accounts and documents—confusing investors, that sort of thing. She didn't even change it when she married Derek." Sheila shook her head, as if this were the most astonishing part so far. "Wasn't till we moved operations to the island that she finally went back to her maiden name—Cannon—hopin' that'd make it harder for *old friends* to come find her."

So Cannon *was* her real name, at least—just not the one she'd used in Seattle. I was relieved to hear that; although, considering all the other things she'd trusted me with, I wondered why she hadn't mentioned it. "But…they found her anyway?" I prompted.

"Well, yeah! That's why Lisa hired me. You just said she told you that, didn't you?"

"Oh, yes; but she didn't tell me all the rest; only that you'd been a bodyguard."

"A bodyguard? That's what she said?" Sheila looked amused. "I was a little more than that."

"So, you were there to protect her from Derek?"

"*Derek!*" she scoffed. "That pathetic screw-up should'a hired someone to protect him from himself. Still can't see how somebody sharp as Lisa ever even gave that loser her number, much less married him. No. I was there to protect Lisa from much bigger fish, with much bigger teeth." She gave me a pained look. "Which is who I was trying to protect *both of you* from the night you sent the whole plan sideways."

I didn't waste time arguing about her definitions of "protection" this time. It seemed like we were getting somewhere more important. "So…bigger fish like who?"

She leaned back with a strange expression—part contempt, but sympathetic too. "Now, see that's your whole problem. Right there. You're like that dumb little girl in all those horror movies. The one who can't stop prying open basement doors and creeping down there to see where all the scary noises are comin' from." She leaned closer to the transparent wall between us. "And here you are doing it *again*, so set on ending up just like the other one."

"What do you mean?" I asked. "What other one?"

I could actually see Sheila's face shut down somehow. "*Such* a slow learner," she sighed.

Oh, no you don't. "Sheila, if you seriously expect me to stick up for you in court, I need to understand that night way better than I do now. And that means answers, not just more riddles. So, who was the *other one*?"

She shrugged indifferently. "Take your pick. How many dumb girls washed up on Lisa's beach since *you* got there?" She sounded almost bored. "Any of 'em oughta fit the bill."

This game, whatever it was, had me ticked off now. "One of those dumb girls was a relative of yours, wasn't she?" I tried to sound as bored as she did. "That really doesn't bother you?"

Sheila's expression hardly changed; in fact her face seemed almost frozen, but I saw her body tense. "Margaret would never have died at all, if it wasn't for you," she muttered into the receiver.

"*Me?*" I shot back. "You think *I* had something to do with… with *any* of those deaths?"

"If you hadn't been snooping around again, opening your big mouth," Sheila snapped, twitching forward, "no one would ever have known she was even there. That goes for poor, harmless Snooks too. They *both* died trying to help me out of messes caused by *your* big nose."

My head was swimming with questions now, but what had struck me first was who she'd left *off* that list of "my" victims. "What about Megan? You didn't mention her."

"Okay, so *she* wasn't your fault. How could she be, right? But she was *another snoop*—just like you."

"And she got killed for that?" I asked quietly, remembering Megan's pale, fraying body on the beach that morning.

"Well, you're the one who found her," Sheila said sarcastically. "Did she *look* killed to you?"

I ignored the barb. "By who?"

Sheila snorted again. "You're kidding me, right?"

I just gazed back at her, waiting.

"Well, I have no idea, of course," she said, as if the question were an insult. "I'm pretty sure Gregory Baines could have told you. But askin' him'll be awful hard now."

"Is that why you killed him? So no one could ask him what happened to Megan?"

"*No, Inspector Tate,*" she said crossly. "I did it because he meant to kill *me* next: it was *self-defense*, plain and simple, just like I already told Veierra and everybody else here. I freaking confessed to it, all right? That part's done! What more do you want?"

"I saw it all, Sheila. He didn't even have a gun."

"He always had a gun. He slept and showered and brushed his teeth with a gun. You just didn't see it."

"He wasn't even *pointing* at you when you shot him," I pushed—needing her to take me seriously—tell me the truth. Until I could make some kind of sense out of all this, I would never be able to set it down. I saw that now, so clearly. "Baines was still just talking to you when you pulled the trigger—about some deal you were *both* involved in. At least, that's how it sounded to me." I crossed my arms. "What deal *was* that?"

She leaned back and gave me an appraising look. "Maybe you should just put an ad in the papers: 'Hey, boys, come kill me!'

with a photo, your address and a phone number. What a waste of my whole life you were." She leaned in again, looking even more tired. "Baines was given one simple little task to do. And before you even ask, I'm not gonna tell you what it was. It doesn't matter. But he botched it—up one side and down the other—then came back to me full of sob stories and excuses, begging for a second chance. And, see, I understand some things about failing, okay? So I gave him a couple days to clean it up. But this time, he…screwed up beyond any forgiving! And when I told him he was done, he just told me it was my turn now."

"Okay. But a threat is still not a gun."

"Yeah, well here's another wake-up call, Inspector Tate. There's *lots* of ways to kill a person that don't take a gun—and it wasn't just me Baines threatened that morning. I was savin' Lisa's life too—probably even yours."

"Mine?" Was she actually delusional? "That was my first morning on the island, Sheila! Nobody but Diana Brixton even knew I existed yet. I was just out taking a walk. How did *my* life need protecting from Gregory Baines? And how would you even have known then if it did?"

"Just takin' a walk," she sneered. "Megan liked to take walks too. You ever walked beneath an owl's nest, sweet pea?"

What did that have to do with anything? "I have no idea. How would I even know that?"

"You wouldn't," she sighed.

"Is there a point here somewhere?" I asked impatiently.

"The point is the big white piles of owl poop under those nests, full of little bones. All the cute, clever little mice who used to own those bones were just out walking too—looking everywhere but *up*." She shook her head. "Just 'cause I didn't know you yet, doesn't mean your life wasn't in every bit as much danger from Gregory Baines, and others like him, as Megan's was." She paused, seeming to consider me again. "He'd gone all sweet on her. You found that out too, didn't you." It was not a question.

"I found…a letter." Why not say so? Sheila couldn't hurt me for it now. Not here.

She nodded. "I'm sure he'd have come sniffin' after the next pretty little thing living in her rooms. That's the kinda man he was. And as crazy about *sightseeing* as you are, you'd have ended up just like she did, soon as he got sloppy again." Her face was still pointed at mine, but I realized she wasn't looking at me anymore. Whatever she *was* seeing didn't seem to make her happy. "Very sloppy," she murmured, almost as if she'd forgotten I was there. "I never should've…" Then her eyes focused on me again, and she fell silent.

Never should have…what? She'd come that close to telling the truth—about something. "Are you saying Baines killed Megan?"

"Probably," she said. "Or had her killed; I didn't really get a chance to ask him."

"Why would he do that to someone he was in love with? What had she done?"

She peered at me again, from somewhere far behind that sad, closed face. "I have no idea," she said at last. "I want to make that very clear to whoever may be following along at home." She glanced up and around at the ceiling. "And just to fix the record, I said Gregory was *sweet on her*—which has nothing to do with love. Not for him, at least. Baines wasn't the loving type—except maybe when it came to liquor. And when he drank, he also loved to brag—about what a big man he was, and what *important* things he was doing—for *such* important people. Like I said, very sloppy." She hunched her shoulders. "If I had to make a bet, I'd say Megan died for knowing things she had no reason to—and all kinds of first rate reasons not to." Intensity narrowed Sheila's eyes. "Just like you've kept trying to ever since I *shot* one of the junkyard dogs you're *still* pokin' at. You turned me in for that! And I still tried to protect you! Don't you get it yet? I was just trying to get you off the freakin' island and under their radar that night, before one of those owls you never seem to think about flew down and ate you too. But you fixed that plan with your little magic trick, and now—*look where I am*—'cause of trying to help you!"

"No... No way." First JoJo, now Sheila? Didn't anybody I knew up here have lives besides mine to manage? "You were...trying to force me off the island?"

"*Yes!*" she nearly shouted into the phone. "*Haven't you been listening to anything?*" She glanced uncomfortably behind her, to where the guard had gone, then took a couple deep breaths, and went on more calmly. "Just help me get this mess carved down to size a little, okay? This place—these people—it's driving me nuts. I can't spend the rest of my life in here. Just tell 'em I was a good neighbor. That I took care of you and kept you safe. That I didn't ever hurt you on purpose." She raised her free hand in a plaintive gesture. "Then get your big fat nose *out* of this. All of it! You hearin' me yet? This is not a game! The people you're chasing aren't jokes like Derek. They're the real deal."

"But...why'd you shoot me, then? Who shoots someone they're trying to save?"

"Do I have to spell that out too?" She shook her head and leaned back with a huff. "It wasn't just *you* in danger, Miss Nosy! I put *my* butt completely on the line for you that night, tryin' to outsmart some very bad people; and I was scared, okay? I'll admit it. Is that what you need? I'm human too! Then you just disappear like that." She fell silent, staring at me. "I couldn't see how it was possible," she said, more to herself than to me, "unless someone else had taken you, right under my nose. And who could that have been except for them? I figured they'd caught up to us, and maybe you were dead somewhere already, and I was next. And then cops start pouring in from everywhere, and I can't see a thing, and...I panicked, okay? I panic sometimes! It happens." Her mean little eyes were round, kind of wild, and she pointed at me. "But it wasn't somebody else's magic trick, was it? It was you! So, how'd you do it?"

Oh, not this—not with her, and not here, of all places.

"How did I do…what?" I tried, lamely, praying she would just shut up. But, of course, she didn't.

"That vanishing act's what really screwed me over," she said, more pleading than angry with me now. "And I just…just keep turning it around in my head. But I can't figure it out. Tell me how you vanished that way."

My arms began to tingle again, naturally. I sat, half frozen—just from fear and indecision, not actual chameleoning—yet. But if I didn't manage to get hold of this quickly, I was afraid of giving her more than just an explanation. I forced myself not to look around for the security cameras trained on us. If someone was watching us right now, what were they making of her questions? They'd think she was crazy, wouldn't they? I mean, *I* thought she was crazy. If I just stayed calm—or *got* myself calm, and stayed that way… "I'm sorry, Sheila, but I really don't know what you're—"

"I need to know. Or I'll go crazy. I ain't kidding." She sounded caught between desperation and anger.

"Why didn't you just tell me all this? That night?" I asked, struggling to keep my voice.

"How did you do it?" she asked again, as if I hadn't spoken.

"Or explain it to the deputies who arrested you?" I pressed. "Or to Agent Veierra? After all this time, why are you just telling me all this now?" I was starting to feel myself come back, a little. "Did it just…take you this long to come up with some story you thought I might believe—because you need something from me now? How can I trust you? Why should I?"

"You are *so* ignorant," she said, fiercely. The pleading was gone. "Ignorant and *deaf!* Why didn't I just tell someone? Seriously?" She sneered at me above the receiver. "I've answered that question twenty times since we sat down here, and you're *still—not— listening!* Silence is the only protection I got now—not from the cops; *they're* no danger to me. I mean from the sharks I been trying to protect Lisa and all the rest of you guys from! I say the wrong thing now—even to you—and you think they'll just look the other way? I tell the cops what they want to know, I'm a dead woman. Just like Megan was—and Margaret. And you too, if you don't get a clue and cut it out."

"So now you're protecting them," I said, just frustrated enough to climb over my fear. "The same people you keep saying you've been protecting us from? What does that accomplish? If you *stopped* protecting them, they might end up where you are now—in jail. And then we might all finally be safe for real—including you. Tell them what you know, Sheila, and they'll protect you too."

"In here?" She looked at me as if *I* were nuts. "This place is like a...a warehouse of people they own! If I were stupid enough to talk, I'd be shanked before I had time to fill out the application form for *witness protection.*"

She leaned back again, and dropped her forehead onto her free hand. "I'll do the time it takes to live through this. But you at least gotta help me make it shorter, 'cause whether you believe it or not, I got here 'cause of *you.*" She looked up at me again. "I am not a murderer. I've killed some people, but it was never what I wanted. I hate hurting people. I hate even *seeing* people hurt. What happened to Megan, you have no idea how much I hated that—or how much I hated Baines for doing it!

"But people just keep leaving me no choice; you see that? I was never there to kill anybody; I was there to *protect Lisa*—'cause she was always good to me, always fair. She deserved to be protected! Baines was supposed to be there for the same reason, but he wasn't. He was a plant, workin' for the ugly side, and when I found it out, I gave him a chance to make it right—'cause I *really don't like hurting people!*" she snapped, making me flinch back, and reviving the tingle in my arms. She was breathing harder now and shaking her head. "But dumb girls washing up on beaches—that was never any part of it! That was all on Baines. I never wanted to hurt you, much less kill you. I like you! You're like Lisa! I gave you Megan's kitten, didn't I? 'Cause I cared—about you *and* the cat! I—am *not*—*a murderer*." She leaned forward again, gripping the receiver hard enough to make her knuckles whiten, and hissed, "Now *tell me how you did it!*"

The tingling spread up my arms and through my body before I could stop it.

"You were never gonna help me," she sneered when I didn't answer. "You don't believe me any more than they do. But *I* answered all *your* questions, and you owe me something for that! *One little answer's all I'm askin'!*" She dropped the receiver on the counter, surged to her feet, and screeched, "*Tell me how you DIS-APPEARED LIKE THAT!*"

And I was frozen in my chair. Helpless, in a room full of other people who were silent now in their phone booths, staring in our direction as the guard rushed out and half tackled Sheila, shoving her face-down onto the counter as a second guard arrived to help grapple Sheila's hands into a pair of cuffs behind her back.

"Oh! Look! *LOOK!*" Sheila yelled, her face still squashed against the table, but turned now, wide-eyed, toward me. "She's GONE! You see it? You all see it?"

But the guards were too busy dragging her away from the window and out of the room to look at anything but her. Everyone else, though, leaning out of all those phone booths…

With a massive effort, I managed, somehow, to yank myself back. My skin burned, my heart raced, I didn't dare try to stand, or even move yet; but I was there again.

I looked around me.

"What happened?" asked a young man leaning from the booth next to mine. "You all right?"

I looked back at him, not trusting myself to speak yet, and just nodded.

"She must be crazy, huh?" he said.

I saw nothing on his face but concern. No amazement. No

confusion—not about me, anyway. He didn't seem to realize that I'd been gone. Many of the others there had leaned back into their booths to continue their conversations. It seemed that, even after that, they hadn't noticed—or didn't remember—that I'd been gone. Just like it always seemed to work.

But Sheila had clearly noticed—and remembered, somehow. And, even if no one else here had, the cameras would too. Would my strange trick work on people who weren't in the room? People sitting somewhere else, watching video monitors?

Of all the places, and all the times…

It was past time to leave—if there weren't already people on the way to stop me.

ↄ৫

The clerk at the check-in counter seemed just as bored and businesslike when I collected my ID and phone again. But my fear didn't fade as I left the building, still expecting someone to run up and shout for me to stop. *It's not a crime to disappear!* I kept telling myself. *They can't arrest you for that! Can they?* All the way back to Anacortes, I had one eye on the rearview mirror, waiting to get pulled over and dragged back for…well, questioning. *Care to tell us what's* really *going on here, Ms. Tate?*

At the ferry landing, I had to sit in my car for half an hour, trapped in a line of other cars, surrounded on every side by more lines of cars, in the middle of a giant parking lot that seemed to stretch for miles in every direction. If they came for me now, I'd be a sitting duck with nowhere to run. *From what?* insisted some more reasonable corner of my mind. *It's—not—illegal to disappear!* No; it wasn't illegal to be a freak either. But no one trusts freaks—even ones who aren't tangled up in a bunch of unsolved murders. Would they just let a freak go on being a confidential informant—or would I become a suspect now? Would they think *I* had poisoned Marie—invisibly spiked her kombucha? And what about all those other victims? *All this did start the very morning you arrived, Ms. Tate. Isn't that right?* My imagination was going wild, the whole terrible story unfolding in my head. Would my next play be a crime drama—written in the creative solitude of my prison cell?

Even as the ferry finally approached the dock at Orcas landing, I still half expected to see sheriff SUVs parked across the loading ramp to block my escape. I imagined Kip gazing at me sadly as he put my handcuffs on. *I trusted you, Cam. We all did. What fools we've been.*

But there were no deputies waiting there either, which only made me wonder if those surveillance tapes night not even have been watched yet. Now that I thought about it, they probably didn't have enough staff to spare for just staring at video monitors all day. How long did I have before someone finally sat down to review them? Should I even bother going home? Canada was just a quick hop away—in several directions. I could turn around now and get back on another ferry to San Juan Island, then catch one from there to Sidney. But the day's last inter-island ferry had sailed hours ago, I realized. And...I could never just abandon James and Master Bun—not and live with myself, anyway.

When I finally got home, it was fully dark, and I was exhausted. The livestock wanted feeding, and boy howdy I needed a glass of wine. After that, I just lay in my loft staring at the darkened ceiling, wondering how many hours of freedom I had left. Eventually, exhaustion won out; but my dreams were all so terrible that even sleep wasn't restful.

And, of course, there was a knock on my door bright and early the next morning. I'd barely even gotten dressed. *Here it comes*, I thought, pulling the door open to find—sure enough—Deputy Sherman on my porch.

"Downtown?" I asked her, my heart sinking.

She nodded.

"All right, let me get some things together. Do you...want to come in?"

"No, thank you. In fact, I've got some other business out in Deer Harbor; you can just drive on down when you're ready. You're expected."

"I am?" Was that…a smile? From Deputy Sherman? Even now? "You're not…? I can just…drive myself?"

She gave me a polite nod and turned to leave, stopping at the bottom of the steps to add, "I'll radio in that you're on your way."

"Okay… I'll only be a few minutes."

"Right-o."

After closing the door behind her, I turned to my cat. "'Right-o?'" Had they just not told her yet that I was a freak now?

James rubbed against my legs, obviously aware that I was heading out, and not about to let me leave before I'd seen to breakfast. His, I mean; not mine.

"And she trusts me to get there without an escort," I added, shaking my head as I filled his bowl. Had they *still* not looked at those tapes? Then I had an alarming thought. Was Sheriff Clarke planning to watch them *with me*? Was that how our meeting would start—and end?

This whole line of thought had gotten ridiculous—a long time ago. I knew that. Well, part of me did, anyway. But my playwriting mind just wouldn't stop. I went ahead and packed a satchel with things I'd need for a number of play-related errands in town after I got done with the sheriff—if I wasn't taken straight from there to jail—or to some secret government laboratory, and tied to a table for "further study"—*Just stop it!* I told my playwright brain. *If you're right, we'll have years of time to write the dang play. But I have other things I need to think about right now.*

That seemed to do the trick—at least temporarily. I topped off Master Bun's food supply while I was at it, then headed off toward my car, even managing to consider whiling away an idle hour in town with a big latte and a crunchy-topped chocolate muffin, if the shops on my to-do list were still closed after Sheriff Clarke was done with me.

ࡔ

At the substation, I was shown into the usual conference room where Sheriff Clarke was already there, sitting at the table; he got to his feet as I walked in, beaming. "Well, Ms. Tate, it appears congratulations are in order."

I rocked back on my heels; I'd never seen this taciturn man so enthusiastic. Was that a good sign? Or was he just throwing me off guard before he brought the hammer down?

"Here, sit, sit down. Coffee?"

"No thank you," I answered automatically, before noticing that he had a takeout cup with "Brown Bear" on it in front of him. Oh well. Later maybe. Honestly, right now, I was wound too tight to handle even a swallow of anything.

He sat again and continued grinning at me. "We've reviewed transcripts of your visit with Ms. Bukowski, and the team is elated. You really loosened up the soil, so to speak."

"I did? The, uh, transcripts?" My throat felt almost too tight to get words through. "What about the videos? There *were* videos… weren't there? Has anybody looked at those?"

He looked a little nonplussed. "Well, yes. That's what the transcripts were taken from, I'm sure. I haven't seen the video myself, but others have." He gave me an uncertain smile. "Why do you ask? Did something happen between you two yesterday that only visuals would catch?"

"I…don't know. Don't you?" *Shut up, Cam! What are you doing?* "I mean, um, well, her weird outburst." I swallowed, trying to get some moisture back into my throat. "At the end—when they came to get her like that. I, uh, I'm still not sure what that… was about. I just wondered…if the videos might have…caught anything? To explain that?"

"Ah," he said, nodding as if there'd been some point to my babbling, which he'd just gotten. "I guess that must have been pretty traumatic for you—after everything you went through with her, before. We were all just so pleased with everything you accomplished that I hadn't thought about that part. I'm sorry."

Was he really unaware of what had happened? "Have you... talked with anyone who did watch those videos?" I couldn't keep myself from asking.

"Are you all right?" he asked, with visible concern. "I guess Ms. Bukowski's tantrum was kind of an assault on you, wasn't it? Would you like to...*process* that experience with someone? We have a psychologist on call for things like this, right in town here. If you'd like, I could—"

"No! No, that's okay. I just...I was wondering if..." *If you saw me vanish!* Would I blurt that out next? Something *very* weird was going on here. But until I managed, somehow, to get a better sense of what it was, I needed to calm down and stop giving him reasons to wonder about me—or to look harder at those videos.

Could the cameras just not been pointed at me when it happened? Sheila had been getting more and more upset, I remembered. Could her behavior have caused whoever controlled the cameras to...point them all at her? Should I even dare to hope I'd gotten that lucky? "I was just wondering if I did something— unintentional, I mean—to set her off that way," I said, impressed with myself for coming up with such a good explanation off the cuff like that. Was I getting better at this spy stuff?

Now Clarke gave me a sympathetic look. "I wouldn't worry about that, Ms. Tate. As I believe I mentioned last time we met, Ms. Bukowski has exhibited increasingly unstable behavior since her incarceration—which is not all that unusual for people in her situation. It's exceptionally kind of you to be concerned, but I doubt her tantrum at the end there was caused by anything you said or did. From what I recall of the transcripts—which were carefully compiled, and exhaustively detailed, I assure you—her accusations had clearly become more and more deranged. I'd guess she was just coming undone—momentarily at least. But, if you'll allow me to say so, Ms. Tate, you shouldn't let that become your concern. People like Sheila Bukowski have a natural genius for getting others to feel indebted to or responsible for them. You have no cause to feel either of those things."

"Well, no, of course not," I said, more mystified by the second. "I get that; but thank you."

"If anything," he continued, leaning back in his chair, "I have to say how impressed I am with your natural talent as an interviewer. You played her exceptionally well on a number of occasions during that conversation."

"I did?" I thought I'd just been trying to keep myself from panicking through most of it.

"Oh yes." His earlier grin returned. "That balancing act you managed between goading her about Megan, Baines, and her cousin, while still dangling a desire to understand her, and even a credible openness to the possibility of helping her in court was something to behold, I can tell you. If that did unsettle her, well, that's likely how you managed to get so much more out of her than we have. You handled it like a pro." He shook his head. "I've eaten quite a bit of crow for recommending against your induction to this investigation. Please feel free to take that as an apology, if you want. I believe I owe you one."

"Well…that's very nice of you," I said, more and more confused. How was it possible no one had seen me vanish? "Um… what did I get out of her? I mean, I can't really think of much that you guys hadn't already told me at some point."

"Oh, quite a bit," he said. "Ms. Bukowski has insisted all along that she simply had no idea who, exactly, she'd been protecting Ms. Cannon from. But her repeated warnings to you made it quite clear that she does know who at least a few of them are— which is one of the things we are counting on her to provide us with—eventually. She had already confessed to the murder of Mr. Baines too, of course, after he betrayed and threatened her. But she'd never hinted that the 'little task' she'd given him involved Megan Duquesne." His grin widened. "You goaded her into revealing that more clearly than I'm sure she realizes she did even now. She was almost certainly an accessory to that murder too—which was in no way 'self-defense.' That tip alone could prove very helpful in all sorts of ways—beyond giving us a lot more leverage with her than we had before. And the news that her cousin was up there specifically to dig Sheila out of some mess the night she died." He nodded appreciatively. "That may shed all kinds of helpful light on other matters too. You don't happen to know what mess she was referring to, do you?"

I had no intention of telling him about Lisa's binder. "Sorry. I have no idea, though I'm glad to know all that was helpful. But…if more leverage against Sheila was what you wanted, I'm still confused about why you guys bargained away the charges about my kidnapping."

"Ah…" He looked away uncomfortably. "Well, that's a difficult question to handle diplomatically. But, especially after yesterday, I suppose you're entitled to an answer."

I sure thought so.

He went on: "Our primary reason for using that charge as a bargaining chip was that we…weren't entirely confident we'd be able to get the charge to stick in court."

"Why not?" I asked, even more confused. "I was definitely kidnapped. Everybody knows that. You were all there to see it when I got shot. How much clearer can a crime get?"

"Well…" he said, "Ms. Bukowski does keep suggesting that you were in danger—but not from her—which is almost certainly untrue; but, under the circumstances, not half as ridiculous as many of her other claims seem. And then…" Now he looked almost painfully embarrassed. "We'd had testimony from someone that you might be…slightly unstable."

"What?" I just managed not to shriek. "Who said that?"

"I'm forbidden by law to tell you that, Ms. Tate. And I think it's quite clear to everyone by now that the testimony we received is…not likely as solid as some of us feared at first. But it seemed wiser to sacrifice an iffy charge to secure Ms. Bukowski's cooperation in regard to even more important matters."

"More important than me getting kidnapped—and shot?" I asked in disbelief.

"I'm afraid so," he said. "And, I'm not allowed to say more about that either. I should probably not even have told you as much as I have."

And there it was again—the loose lips of the law. Well, while I was complaining about things… "Actually, someone's told Sheila more than they should have too—about me. She knew that I've replaced her as Lisa's personal assistant. When I asked her how she'd found that out, she said Veierra and her staff had told her. I'm kind of wondering why you guys have been reporting on *me* to *Sheila*."

He considered me for a moment, looking more uncomfortable than ever. "I can assure you, Ms. Tate, that Agent Veierra, and everyone else associated with this investigation, has been extremely careful about every smallest aspect of the conduct of this case. No one has told Bukowski—or anyone else—a single thing of any potential importance about you or any other person not officially identified as a suspect. I am also entirely confident that any information about you that Agent Veierra did choose to divulge to Ms. Bukowski will have been trivial items of public record, without any potential for risk to you; and that they were shared for calculated effect, only after careful consideration."

I had never heard Clarke speak so carefully or so *formally* before. I wouldn't have guessed he could! But, whatever he was trying for, "innocent" was not what came across. "So how could telling Sheila the details of my current job help Veierra's investigation any?" I pressed.

"I think only she knows the answer to that; and I encourage you to ask her as soon as opportunity allows. But, if I were forced to hazard a guess, it may have been part of an effort to foster Ms. Bukowski's impression of you as a potentially sympathetic acquaintance? Someone who might understand her own situation prior to arrest better than most, and feel willing to consider her point of view in related matters?"

I thought of all Sheila's questions about what Lisa had told me—as her personal assistant—and the strange relief or regret my answers seemed to cause her. Had Veierra just been setting Sheila up to see me as an ally? Because we had so much in common?

"So," Clarke said, seeming eager for a change of subject, "now that we've seen how good you are at this, we'd like to try your magic out on another tight-lipped subject."

"Oh?" That…had to be a good sign; didn't it? Why would they be asking me to do this again if they'd seen what I was afraid they had in those videos? "Who is it this time?" I asked nervously. "Derek?"

I'd meant it for a joke, but Sheriff Clarke smiled politely, as if unsure whether I was serious. "No, ma'am. It's my earnest intention that Mr. Eccleston never so much as suspects your involvement as an informant—or even learns your name, if we can help it. However," he went on, "Marie Tolliver emerged from her coma a little while back."

I tried to feign surprise, grateful for the little bit of practice I'd been getting as an actor lately. "Oh my gosh! How *is* she?"

"Not great. And we haven't let anyone know she's awake yet, for strategic reasons, so please don't go spreading that around. She seems intact; but, for some reason, she's clammed up even tighter than Ms. Bukowski—which seems extremely odd for a victim of attempted murder…"

"She's probably afraid. I mean, *Sheila's* afraid, right? And Marie has always seemed terrified of nearly everything."

"Exactly." He leaned back in his chair and folded his arms across his chest. "She's still in the hospital now, under round-the-clock protective custody. But her doctors want to release her soon, though we've pressed them to hold onto her at least till we uncover more information."

"Release her—just out into the world?"

"No, of course not. She'll remain under protective custody until the investigation is concluded and any danger to her has been resolved. However, once she's been taken into hiding, there would be no feasible way for us to get you in to visit her without arousing both her suspicion, and who knows who else's."

My mouth dropped open. "Wait, you mean *I'm* supposed to try getting her to talk now?"

"Of course. I'm sorry; was that not clear?"

"But, why do you think she'd open up to *me*?"

"Aren't you two friends?"

I shook my head. "I wouldn't, it's not, um—I like her, sort of; but I wouldn't call us close."

"Hm," Clarke said. "We'd been led to believe you did frequent favors for her."

"Favors she asked for—not that I offered," I pointed out.

He waved that off. "But you cared about her enough to grant those requests—which is more than anyone else here seems to have done, yes?"

"Well, I guess so. And I *do* care. I've been really worried about her. I'm so glad to hear that she's gotten better, but—"

"And you're the one who saved her life," he cut in, "which must count for something, right?"

"I…never really thought about it."

"So if you found yourself in Seattle, it wouldn't seem out of character for you to visit her?"

"I guess not," I admitted.

"Good. This visit will have to seem in character, because sooner or later, Ms. Cannon is almost certain to find out about it."

"Right…" I began thinking about the implications too—and about JoJo's "sources" there. He wouldn't be fooled by any excuses I gave for going there—in character or not. Would his sources be? "Too bad I just *was* in Seattle. Yesterday."

"Yes," the sheriff said, "but I'm afraid this has to happen very soon. We need to know why she's not willing to talk with us about what happened, who she thinks did this to her, and why she thinks they did it. We have to find out what she's afraid of. Is she avoiding self-incrimination of some kind—or protecting someone else? Are loved ones in danger? Does her assailant have something on her? She's the potential key to all of this; and we need to pursue these questions before someone else biases her responses—or she's just taken into hiding, as I've mentioned. You'll be her first and likely *only* non-law-enforcement visitor since waking, Ms. Tate. And you'll probably get just this one chance at talking with her. Anything you can get out of her will be very helpful."

"But—how am I supposed to explain another trip like this to Lisa? I can't just turn around and leave again."

He leaned back and scratched his chin. "Is it possible you forgot to do something yesterday?"

"Like what? Most anything I wanted to buy in Seattle would be easier to order online and just have shipped here... Even if I'd left something of my own there, why spend all day going to get it instead of just asking my friends at the salon to put it in the mail?"

"Well, let's give it twenty-four hours, and finalize the details tomorrow," he said, waving the whole matter away. "I'll talk with the others and be in contact. Let me know if you come up with some solution of your own, of course." He pushed himself to his feet.

"Of course," I said, getting up as well.

The sheriff reached out to shake my hand. "Thank you as always for your help." Then he led me from the conference room and out to the front door.

I backed up and pulled out of the substation's lot, thinking, *How am I still free?* Had no one at the jail but Sheila seen me disappear? How could that be true? My "gift" had *never* worked that way. Either I was *there*—for everyone present—or I wasn't.

These questions just made me feel as if my head was being inflated. Over-inflated. I shoved them all away before they made me pop, and headed toward town without any plan beyond a vague but urgent wish to escape—from what, I didn't know, or *want* to know. I was still free somehow. That was enough for now.

The shops I needed to visit were all still closed, of course. Almost nothing on the island opened before ten o'clock—if at all—on weekdays. It was still barely eight-thirty now. But if I drove all the way back to Massacre Bay, I'd have all of thirty minutes before I had to come back here by ten. And I did want to get my errands seen to before the businesses were swamped with customers.

Ten minutes later, I was seated at a picnic table in Brown Bear Bakery's small street-side garden, with a latte and a crunchy-topped chocolate muffin in front of me. Because some things just run even deeper than dread—chocolate being at the top of that list—until five o'clock, at least, when wine bumped even chocolate down a notch. Sadly, it was nowhere near five o'clock.

My first sugar-crystal-crunchy bite of warm, gooey yet fluffy chocolate muffin was as delicious as ever. But I hadn't even swallowed it before the questions I had pushed away back at the substation began to sidle back. *Did you just imagine it?*

I closed my eyes, trying not to acknowledge what I was already too late to deny about the real question underneath that one. *If you'd really disappeared, the cameras would have seen it. People may "forget." But cameras don't. So…*

Did you really disappear, or just think you did?

Have you ever *really disappeared?*

Or—

No! I refused to hear it—even in my head; or tried to, anyway. That first bite of muffin felt like a hairball in my throat now.

Sheriff Clarke's transcripts had been made by people who had watched those videos very carefully—recording every potentially significant detail. He'd made that clear. And if they'd said anything about me disappearing, why would Clarke have just blithely sent me off on this new mission to squeeze information out of Marie, without a word about it?

So it must not have been there, in the video.

But if it hadn't happened even on film, then…had it happened at all? Or…

Or are you just crazy—

"Stop it!" I hissed, just quietly enough that no one else seemed to notice.

—like your mother?

Someone had told them I was *unstable*. Who had that been? Who had they talked to? Was it obvious to everyone around me? Were my supposed friends here just politely silent about it in my presence?

Whoa! Slow down there, girl!

It was Jen's voice I heard inside my head now, calling me back from the edge. My brain knew who to call, it seemed. *Are all the other people you've ever hidden yourself from "crazy" too then? Okay, maybe Sheila is. But Colin and his ex? Porter and his wife? Kevin, even! And how many others before him—over all those years since the night that man completely overlooked you right in front of him as he stood above your mother's body with blood on his hands? Don't you think he'd have killed you too if he'd known you were there? They all had important reasons to know you were there—and care about your presence. But they never did—then or later. So…crazy doesn't explain things any better, does it?*

I sat there, staring down at my all but untouched muffin, and barely breathing for what seemed a very long time. But she was right: the woman inside me with Jen's voice…

Me, of course. *I* was right.

If all those other people weren't crazy too, then what explained *their* behavior? Even if Sheila *was* crazy in other ways, she clearly hadn't been able to see me after I made myself vanish that night—or yesterday afternoon. Why would she have done that—to herself—if I'd just been *pretending* it was true? Why would Colin, or Porter and Verna—as sane as people get—have stood there pretending not to see me, if they could? *Something* had happened—all those times. Something that covered its tracks even on video, apparently. So…what did that mean? How could it possibly work? I didn't have any idea, and knew I wasn't likely to come up with one just by sitting here for a few more hours, staring at a muffin that was losing all that gooey warmth it had come off the oven rack with. What a pointless waste *that* would be.

I had figured out exactly nothing I could put my finger on, but I felt better now, for some reason. In fact, I felt surprisingly hungry. I'd never had time to eat breakfast that morning. I'd had nothing but a glass of wine or maybe two the night before. In fact, I could not remember eating anything since the breakfast sandwich I'd bought while I'd waited for the boat to come yesterday morning! Good grief! Why hadn't I passed out by now?

That muffin didn't last three minutes after that; and when I'd wolfed it down, I went right back inside for a big, thick slice of their silky quiche, and a large, creamy hot chocolate to wash my coffee down with. Life was full of mysteries, but as Paige Berry—who clearly knew more about mysteries than anyone else I'd ever met—had recently exclaimed, *Nothing can be decided on an empty stomach!* Wasn't that what she had said back at the senior center? I was nearly certain of it. That woman had so much wisdom!

CHAPTER 11

By that evening, I had put the whole business of my unfortunate disappearance at the jail pretty firmly aside—as much from exhaustion as anything else. I was just plum out of new ways to worry about it, or even to try explaining it. If they were going to come after me, they'd surely have done it by now, right? And I had something better—or more immediate, anyway—to worry about now.

I got to the barn a few minutes early, on purpose. Despite everything else I'd just been through, I was still feeling uneasy about my various roles in *this* whole endeavor. Tonight was our first real rehearsal in the barn itself, and I thought it might help to sort of ground myself in the space, alone, before it was time to begin *acting* for keeps.

But of course I wasn't alone in the room. Even before I opened the door, I heard hammering; and when I walked in, José was down on his hands and knees up on the stage. "Hey, Cam!" he called across the big space, when he noticed me. "Just shoring up the infrastructure! I'll be out of your hair in a minute."

"You're fine, I came early," I told him. "Just wanted to check it out."

He smiled at me again. "Don't let me stop you."

I walked slowly across the stage as José stood to pack up his tools and materials, then headed for the offices. It wasn't entirely empty; there were three chairs set where I imagined the salon chairs were supposed to be, and a couple of long folding tables at the back of the stage which probably represented the mirror counter. Another long table was on the right-hand side of the stage—no, *stage left*, I reminded myself; it was so hard to stop seeing things from the audience's orientation. The stage left table was set close to a square of tape on the floor, probably the salon's door? Exploring further, I saw there was actually lots of tape on the floor, marking things that weren't here yet—I wasn't even sure what they all were. I'd texted all my photos of the salon to the irreplaceable Roland Markus, but apparently he hadn't been paying close attention to the spatial stuff (well, of course he hadn't), because some of those markers seemed to be in the wrong places.

I paced around, then moved the chairs closer to the back tables. The operators were going to need to be able to reach the counter while they were working with clients, after all. Then I turned and looked out at the empty barn before me, once more imagining rows and rows of chairs. Chairs with people in them. People I knew. People I knew looking back at me...

Across the barn, the side door opened, and JoJo, Lisa, and Hal walked in, talking and laughing. I tried to look nonchalant, and not at all as though I had deliberately arrived early so that I could process yet another episode of anxiety and imposter syndrome.

They'd barely reached the stage before the door opened again and Glory came in. Within another minute or two, the rest of the cast had arrived.

"Cam!" Lisa greeted me as she stepped up onto the stage and glanced around. "What do you think?" Before I could answer, she narrowed her eyes a moment and added, "Those chairs are too far back; see? Off their markers." She pointed to three small squares in the middle of the floor. "Now who'd have done that?" she mused as she went to start correcting the problem.

"I moved them," I admitted. "The salon chairs can't be so far from the counter…"

"They won't be, when they're actual salon chairs." She gave me a kind smile as she tugged them back into their designated positions. "And besides, it doesn't need to function as a real salon; it just needs to *look* like a real salon. Or even to *indicate* a real salon as seen from out there." She waved at the empty room. "It's a very different perspective from the audience."

Okay, I could understand that, but some of the literal stage directions literally had the actors literally reaching over to pick up combs and scissors and stuff from that literal counter while they were literally supposedly working on clients sitting in the chairs, but…I wasn't going to begin our first real rehearsal by arguing with the director. I just nodded.

"Your photos were invaluable," Lisa went on. "I think Roland has really captured the essential layout of the space, don't you?"

I glanced around, trying to see what she was seeing. All I could see was tape and temporary furniture. "I guess?" I finally said. "It's a little hard to envision."

Lisa laughed. "I understand. You'll see, though." By now, everyone had gathered at the foot of the stage, chatting and…and what in the world? Hal was standing a little apart from the group, opening his mouth very wide, then closing it again, then opening it, then closing… Rebecca was making a series of noises—not words, just syllables, louder and then quieter again, up and down the scale. Glory and Charles were talking with JoJo, except they were also sort of play-slapping at each other? Play-sword fighting maybe?

I looked back at Lisa, very puzzled. Nobody had acted like this back at the Grange.

"Warm-ups," she told me quietly, and then clapped her hands and said more loudly, "All right, everyone, shall we get started?"

It took a few minutes for everyone to clomp up onto the stage. The noise was deafening. I wanted to ask Lisa about it—surely this couldn't be right, the audience was not going to be able to hear a word we were saying, would they?—but nobody else seemed to notice, and Lisa was busy getting us all situated, positioning us in our starting places, scripts in hand; and then all of a sudden we were…rehearsing!

ತಿ

It was kind of a blur at first. Yes, I'd written the lines, and we'd spoken them at great length around that table at Lisa's house and at the Grange, but standing on *the* stage—even holding a script—moving through the space that represented my imaginary salon, speaking my character's words to the other characters—it was truly unreal.

It was happening!

I didn't have time to feel nervous, after the first minute or two. I just stumbled along, trying to keep up. Wishing I didn't sound so hesitant, so unsure.

Then JoJo stumbled over a line. *Well, he's not an actor either*, I told myself, as I nailed my next line. Then *Charles* stumbled over a line. In fact, he had to say it, read it, and say it again. Nobody batted an eye.

And then there came the moment when I realized, almost in passing, that we'd done the whole first scene, fluidly. *Oh hey*, I thought. *That was cool.*

Lisa had been watching from a folding chair off the stage, about where the front row would be. Now she stood up and clapped. "Excellent, people! That was excellent." She beamed up at us. Charles gave a deep, dramatic bow; JoJo and I followed suit, and the other actors—who weren't in this scene, but who'd stood at the edges of the stage watching—also stepped out and bowed, laughing.

"Shall we run through it one more time before moving on to scene two?" Lisa asked.

"Sure," I said, as Charles and JoJo nodded.

Lisa walked around to the staircase on stage left. "One quick thing first," she said, stepping onto the stage.

I watched, surprised, as she went to the three folding chairs and moved them closer to the "counter" table. She glanced over at me, gave me a small smile, and said, "I just needed to see it to be certain." Then she went back to her audience chair and said, "All right, whenever you're ready."

❧

We got through four scenes that night—a little over half of the first act—restarting each scene as needed whenever we flubbed it too much. And I mean *we* flubbed it: even with scripts in hand, everyone got lines wrong, everyone looked the wrong way or moved the wrong way or stepped on each other's lines, or missed cues. I quickly stopped feeling self-conscious and really began to engage in what we were doing: making deliberate choices about how to deliver a particular line (often different from how it had sounded in my head as I wrote it!), or how to stand or move, what to do with body language. It was really, really kind of wonderful.

And mysterious.

"I still think Martin is a complete dud," JoJo complained to me during a break—but quietly, so Lisa wouldn't hear him.

I just smiled at him. "Once you really tune into your inner Martin-ness, *dahling*, I'm sure you'll find his spark."

JoJo tilted his head and looked at me quizzically. "You seem…"

"What?" I asked, when he didn't go on.

He shook his head. "Nothing—I mean, I don't know. I'm glad to see you looking so comfortable with all this."

I didn't ask what *all this* meant—the play, surely, but more than that? How much, if anything, did he know about my visit to Sheila? We hadn't had a private meeting since our hike around Mountain Lake; I really didn't know what might be going on behind the scenes. And then I wondered, could it have been him who had told them I was unstable—back when he'd still been trying to get me out of harm's way? I felt my eyes narrow, and looked away before he saw it, and started wanting to know why I'd looked at him that way.

"All right," Lisa said, "I know it's getting late, but I thought we might do one more run-through of the end of scene four, starting when the third new client of the day comes in. It's such a complicated bit, and it would be good to start getting it as anchored as possible. Is everyone up for that?"

"Sure," said Rebecca, looking at Hal, who also nodded. It was really their call: they carried the burden of this part of the scene, each playing several different characters.

"Good!" Lisa said, glancing down at her copy of the script. "Page forty-seven, then, and start with Trent. When you're ready!"

I stood by my "salon chair," pretending to cut someone's hair; JoJo stood by his, pretending to wait for his next client; Charles stood by the "front desk."

Rebecca tromped into the salon, embodying Trent, a suit-wearing businessman.

Charles/Kristoff: (looking surprised, talking very smoothly and fast) "Welcome-to-Salon-Contempo-how-may-I-help-you-if-you-even-have-an-*appointment-do-you*?"

Rebecca/Trent: "No, I don't, but I have an important meeting at the bank in fifteen minutes, and we both know you're never very busy in here."

Charles/Kristoff: (affronted, but pulling himself together) "Well as a matter of fact—"

Hal, playing Tiger, an insufferable hipster, sauntered into the salon.

Hal/Tiger: "Hey man. Sorry I'm late. Tiger—appointment at two."

Charles/Kristoff: (to Trent) "As I was just saying—"

Rebecca/Trent: (pointing to Martin's empty chair) "Whatever. *He* doesn't look busy right now." (He starts to walk over to the chair. JoJo, as Martin, looks panicked.)

Charles/Kristoff: (now clearly remembering that he cannot be a jerk to *anyone* right now because anyone might be the new owner) "Ah! Yes, oh, well, um, as you see sir, his appointment just walked in, but if you'd care to have a seat over here, I can bring you a glass of tea—a cup of wine even—I mean—"

Rebecca/Trent: "Was I unclear? I have a *meeting*. At the *bank*. In fifteen *minutes*." (All three salon staff exchange meaningful looks: *A "bank meeting" about taking over the building?*)

Hal/Tiger: "Hey, it's cool, man, I can go get a vegan chai whip down at the corner and come back in fifteen."

Without waiting for an answer, Tiger sauntered hipsterly back out of the salon.

Charles/Kristoff (looking relieved but still worried, mutters under his breath): "But we've still got the twins and…" (straightens up, smiling hugely) "Right this way, sir!"

Kristoff practically danced Trent over to Martin's chair, fussing over him elaborately as Martin draped and fastened the gown, again offering a muddle of beverages, all of which Trent declined. Martin barely managed to get rid of Kristoff so he could start the haircut, knowing he must do it quickly, perfectly—and cheerfully.

The salon door opened and Hal, now playing Jeanette, a middle-aged matron, sailed in.

Hal/Jeanette: (laying a heavily ringed paw on Kristoff's brocaded arm) "Oh my dear, I know you said there's nothing till later this week, but it's an emergency. Do you hear me? An *emergency!*" (She points to her hair.)

"Oh, hello, Mother," muttered JoJo, and I couldn't help it, I giggled, and that set JoJo off—and then, because laughter is contagious, all the actors broke out laughing. Just the sight of middle-aged Hal pointing to his own tousled mop, declaiming his lines in such a convincing matron's voice, had been enough to undo everyone.

"All right, all right," Lisa said, after a minute. "Let's focus."

"I'm sorry," I said, still trying to contain myself.

Hal stretched and took a deep breath, clearly trying to get himself back into character. "Was I too much?" he asked me. "I can tone it down a bit."

"No, you were perfect," I assured him. "The audience *should* laugh there—and they will. The cast—and I'm talking to *myself* here—just has to hold it together."

"When you're all ready?" Lisa prompted. "From Jeanette's entrance, please."

We moved forward without a hitch for several more lines, but it all fell apart again when Rebecca, playing twenty-something twins Jill and Jenny, came in.

Charles/Kristoff: (fawning over the smartly dressed twin) "Jenny, darling! Your ensemble is stunning! But where's your lovely sister?"

Rebecca/Jenny: "Locking up the car. She'll be along any minute."

Charles/Kristoff: "Well let's get you started then. It's a circus here today!"

We'd already been over this part of the scene, so I knew how capable Rebecca was of playing two people at once. She was really quite convincing. But Lisa's unbelievably brilliant staging of this feat was an almost mind-boggling miracle of choreography and timing, and Rebecca's concentration must have been off, because she tripped over JoJo's foot almost immediately, nearly landing on her butt before JoJo reached out and caught her, then eased her into his "salon chair."

"Ouch!" she cried, grinning widely for some reason, so what in the world…?

"My scissors!" JoJo yelled, in a tone of exaggerated panic, miming the imaginary scissors in his hand. "I was still holding them! I've stabbed Jenny's eye out!"

"And I'm sitting on Trent!" Rebecca exclaimed. "We skipped over the end of his haircut, so he must still be here!" Rebecca was nearly doubled over in laughter, and of course none of the rest of us could control ourselves after that. I snuck a look at Lisa in the front row, imagining her peeved expression of tried patience, her little gesture of bringing her slender fingertips to pinch the bridge of her perfect nose…I was relieved to see her stifling a smile as well.

When we'd all caught our breath again, Lisa said, "Perhaps I've pushed you too far for this evening. I think we've hit the point of diminishing returns."

"Happens every time in new space," Hal whispered to me.

"I'm afraid this is never going to work anyway, the way it is," Rebecca said to me, wiping tears from the corners of her eyes. "We only skipped like two lines—that's nowhere near enough time to get me out of here as Trent and back on as Jenny, even without the costume change. Should we maybe add a little more material in here to make time for the transition?"

I thought a moment. I'd never intended for one person to play a bunch of different roles—I hadn't even known casting worked that way—but she had a good point. "It's been a while since the audience has heard any mention about *why* the salon gang is being so anxious and weird with all these new clients," I said. "I mean, I doubt they'd have forgotten, but it wouldn't hurt to remind them. We could have Felicia and Martin stage-whisper to each other about which of these unfamiliar clients must be the new owner they have to impress?"

Charles put a hand on his hip and affected a cocky stance. "While Kristoff is *dying of boredom* there by the door, watching the circus go by without him."

"Speak for yourself," JoJo muttered.

I swatted his arm. "Hush, you." I looked at Lisa, who was watching us all with an unreadable expression. Because she was the *director*, after all. The person to whom these questions *should* be addressed. "What do you think?" I asked her. "Should we add some reminders in here? I know Felicia and Martin have already talked about it after Mabel and Clarence come in, but I could move that bit sooner—"

"Oh, I just don't know," she said, casually. Too casually? Was I stepping on her toes? I was just answering questions the cast was asking me... Were *they* stepping on her toes? "I'm going to let you folks work this through—but starting with our next rehearsal. I believe we should pack it up here." She closed her script and stood up. "Thank you, everyone, for your excellent work tonight. We've covered a lot of ground, and I'm quite pleased with what I'm seeing."

The "school's out" vibe that immediately erupted on the stage made it clear that she was right: we had indeed reached our limit for the night. The cast gathered their belongings and practically tripped over each other scrambling out. I got my things together too, and hurried off the stage, catching up to Lisa before she left too.

"Hey," I said to her, "do you have a moment?"

She turned to me and smiled. "Of course." She glanced around the large dark barn. "Are you going my way?"

"I...was planning to go home, yes."

Her smile grew. "Well, I had just been thinking it had been rather too long since I'd had a quiet glass of wine with my friend Cam. Shall we convene in my living room?"

"I'd be delighted."

ဆာ

I held the wine in my mouth, savoring it. Why was it so yummy? I still knew nothing about wine—and I wasn't going to learn, drinking from unlabeled bottles—but I tried to think about the experience happening on my tongue. The wine was full and juicy, without being sweet; there was a barely noticeable bite, though the general sensation was that of smoothness; it just...wanted to be tasted. I swallowed and smiled up at Lisa as she stepped down into the living room and set a small platter of chocolate truffles on the coffee table between us.

I reached down and took a truffle. Dainty enough to be eaten in one bite, so that's what I did. Okay, whatever else was true about this wine, it absolutely needed to be accompanied by rich chocolate.

Lisa sipped wine and savored chocolate as well. We both closed our eyes and let the experience wash over us for a minute. Then she set her glass down and said, "You had something you wanted to talk about?"

Oh yeah right. I set my own glass down and turned to her. "So, I thought tonight went pretty well—"

"It went *amazingly* well," she interjected, still smiling.

I nodded. "Well, it's a good cast."

"And a good play."

"Um. Thanks. So." I stifled the urge to reach for my wine-security blanket. "So I just wanted to check in with you about—well, you're the director, but it just seemed like—everyone was asking *me* for direction, and ignoring you?"

"Ah." She leaned back and thought a moment. "I can see why you would…they're excited about having the playwright onstage with them. And so am I. I'm delighted to see the growing rapport between you and the cast. It's all very organic."

"Well, it was fun," I allowed, remembering all the laughter. "But I kinda felt like…well, maybe it was *too* fun? We were acting like kids, and you kept having to get us to refocus."

"Because I'm the director."

"Right, and I'm *not*. They shouldn't be asking *me* about stuff like how they deliver their lines, and where they should be on the stage."

"I think it's all working out very well." She picked up another truffle and chewed it slowly, thoughtfully, chasing it with a sip of wine. "In fact, it's a nice break for me. I can be autocratic at times—and that never works well, organically."

I started to protest, but she held up a hand and went on.

"Don't bother arguing with me. I know myself, and I think that women should be more autocratic, more often. Certainly, some directors are that way. They know exactly how they want each line delivered, down to the syllable."

"But not you?"

"No. For me, a play is the ultimate in collaborative creativity. You wrote the play. I'm directing it. But the six of you are up there on the stage, bringing the magic to life *together*. The actors are living and breathing those characters, and the world of the salon. That requires communication and even experimentation—which end up getting squashed if everything is bound up in 'shoulds and shouldn'ts.'"

"Well, I can see that," I said.

"But it's not just the usual alchemy of working as a group of performers that I'm talking about. You're not the first writer to star in her own play, and you won't be the last. You're right there, experiencing what works and what doesn't, and able to make changes, because it's your play. My actors would have to be idiots to not take advantage of this opportunity—and they are *not* idiots."

"No, they're pretty brilliant, aren't they?"

Lisa's smile was one of pure delight. "I'm glad you think so! And I'll admit it, I was worried that whenever they questioned a line—and they will, believe me—that you'd be defensive and prickly. But you're not. You're open and thoughtful." She smiled again, and watched me take another wine-and-chocolate infusion to deal with my embarrassment at all these compliments. "Just don't let them railroad you. JoJo would like to. He tried at the table read. And you stood firm. That was just the right thing to do."

"No," I protested. "You straightened him out; I didn't."

"I have to do that fairly often. He's such a beautiful disaster." She frowned. "I was afraid you'd take out your pen and start making notes to 'fix' Martin, but, to my delight and relief, you didn't! And Martin is just exactly who he should be. You're vulnerable about acting, but you stand firm as a writer. I'm quite proud of you, Cam."

I nodded, wanting to bat the compliment away, but she'd laid it all out so convincingly.

"It is a lot, though, isn't it?" Lisa asked. Her concern seemed real. "Working on so many things at once. The production, the script, your own role. Is it too much?"

I started to do my usual thing, minimizing everything I did and pretending everything was just fine. But I sensed an opening here, and stopped myself. "I am…feeling pretty worn out."

"Well then, speak up, Cam! If you wear yourself too thin, it impacts everything else. You absolutely must commit to a regular regime of self-care." She began to tell me about her masseuse, and an acupuncturist she liked on the island. "I mean it. Self-care is crucial."

I studied Lisa, and thought about how much invisible time and money went into maintaining her glowing appearance. As a former salon worker, I knew it wasn't as effortless as it looked. "I'm just not…I just don't think about that, I guess," I admitted. "Self-care, I mean."

"Well, it's time to start." She raised her glass and gave me an encouraging smile. "Start when you're young. Drink water, take walks, care for your beautiful young skin like it's the only thing standing between you and this hostile world, because it is. And always get a good night's sleep, especially now, because we're going to need to do this four times a week till opening night—on top of everything else on our plates. Cheers."

"Cheers," I replied. I'd been wondering how on earth to tell her I needed to go back to Seattle for a day, and here she was, practically pushing me onto the ferry. How amazing was that? Maybe some things really did just work out. Could luck be as real as trouble—sometimes? "I think you're right," I told her. "I could find a day with no commitments and go spend some time pampering myself…back in Seattle again? Would that be okay?"

"That sounds fabulous!"

I went home that night, fed the menagerie, and followed the boss lady's marching orders—the good night's sleep part, at least. If the powers-that-be wanted to watch over me, I was going to let them, for once.

☙

The next morning, I left a voicemail message for Sheriff Clarke about Lisa's unwitting answer to our problem; and the day after that, I was called in to the station at the crack of dawn again to finalize the details. Once again, there was no sign that he or anyone else had noticed my brief "absence" at the end of my brilliant interview with Sheila. I left the substation still anxious and confused about how that could be. I might never know the answer, but clearly I'd been given a free pass somehow. Was I going to keep pushing at it until I *made* them notice? *Just put it down, Cam.*

Since then, the play had kept my mind occupied, and tired enough to sleep at night. Rehearsals were still going really well. Tonight, as we all stood around afterward, complimenting each other on how amazing we were and how much fun this was, I realized that I was too wound up to just go home to bed.

"Hey JoJo," I said, tugging his sleeve as the group broke up. "Wanna go get a cup of coffee or something?"

He raised an eyebrow. "Do you know of a café open on the island at this time of night?"

"Well, actually, no."

"Lower Tavern always has a pot on," Glory remarked, over-hearing us.

JoJo made a face. "Or we could skip the coffee nonsense and find a beverage more appropriate to the time of day."

"The Barnacle it is," I agreed, and turned back to Glory. "Wanna come?"

"I can't tonight," she said. "Some other time?"

"Absolutely."

JoJo took my arm. "Looks like you're stuck with me, darling."

"Ugh, how terrible."

"Likewise. But we shall endure."

We drove separately; JoJo's Jaguar didn't fascinate me quite so much since I'd been given such a luxurious ride of my own. I parked Tigress behind his car in front of the small bar, and followed him in.

"Hey!" Jen cried. "My two favorite people!"

The Barnacle was nearly half-full, which meant there was exactly one open table, by the front window. We took it, and Jen walked over, grinning. "What'll it be? No, wait—let me just bring you tonight's special cocktail, you're both gonna love it."

JoJo peered up at her. "What's in it?"

Jen looked mysterious. "I think I'm going to let you guess. You game?"

"You'll have to tell us what it's called, at least," I said.

"Sure. It's a Ruby Sipper."

JoJo chuckled. "Oh, that's clever. By all means: barkeep, bring us two Ruby Sippers, stat!"

"You bet!" She sailed back behind the bar, where she set up two martini glasses, then started concocting something down on the counter below, where we couldn't see what she was doing.

"This should be fun," I said.

"I suppose. As long as it isn't insipid. I despise insipid cocktails." JoJo gave a heavy sigh, put his elbows on the table, and rested his chin in his palms. He looked up at me with big sad puppy-dog eyes. "If nothing else, it'll help me drown my sorrows, I suppose."

"What sorrows?"

He batted his lovely eyelashes at me. "Martin. He is the biggest sorrow of my life. You promised it would get better, but that man has zero charm, zero charisma, zero appeal!"

I rolled my eyes. "Sounds like the actor's problem to me!" I gave him a mock-punch in the arm. "In fact, it's kind of amazing, how dull you're playing him; if I didn't know better, I would almost think you're doing it on purpose, to punish me for not making him the star."

He brought his hand to his chest in a pearls-clutching motion. "Cammybear! You cannot be serious!"

"As the grave." I snickered.

From behind the bar came the sound of a cocktail being shaken vigorously over ice. We both glanced up at Jen, who winked and kept shaking the drink over her head, wiggling her whole body in the process. Everyone at the bar watched this little dance with vivid interest.

I smiled at her, and turned back to JoJo. "Martin has his charms. You just have to find them."

"Great. I'll find his charms somewhere in all those hangdog, lonesome-loser lines. *Maybe I'm just not cut out for romance. Women are as confusing as chess.* Come on, Camilove, throw a guy a bone."

"Everyone laughs when you say those lines."

"I prefer to be laughed *with*—not *at*," he said petulantly. "And they laugh way more at Kristoff. You don't want me to have to start *improvising*, do you?"

"If you change one precious word of my magnum opus, I swear I will—"

I was interrupted by Jen's bringing two lovely, ice-cold, brim-full, ruby-colored drinks to the table and setting them before us—as ever, without spilling a drop. "There you are! Two Ruby Sippers." She stood back, folded her arms across her chest, and watched us.

"Hmmmm…" JoJo pondered, studying the drink. "Garnished with lime peel *and* a cucumber slice—interesting." He leaned forward and sniffed. "I do detect the cucumber, but is that just the garnish or also…Hendrick's?" He sniffed again, more deeply this time. "I don't smell gin though, so it's not that."

I glanced up at Jen, who looked amused. "You gonna taste it or just talk to it all night?"

"Tsk, tsk," he chided, not removing his gaze from the drink. "My reputation is at stake here: I cannot miss an element. And if I just begin to guzzle it, I'll lose all the wisdom my nose brings to bear." He took another whiff. "Is that…grenadine? No, too obvious. And too sweet. Jen Darling doesn't mix overly-sweet cocktails. Perhaps…Campari? No, wrong direction, I don't smell anything herbal."

"All right," Jen said with a laugh, "you have fun with that. I have work to do."

I grabbed my glass and took a sip. Whatever it was, it was delicious. "Yum!" I called to my friend's retreating back.

"Well?" JoJo asked me.

"Raspberry?"

He snorted. "Don't be silly. I smell something citrusy…"

"Well there's a big ole piece of lime peel here," I pointed out as I took another sip. Sweet but not too sweet; well balanced. Yum indeed.

"No, not just that." He finally picked up his glass and took a tentative sip, swirled it around on his tongue, and swallowed.

"I never thought I'd be rooting for you to go ahead and drink already, but…"

JoJo laughed. "Yes," he said after another moment. "Lime definitely, but also orange. The red color is throwing me off—maybe blood orange?" He sipped again. "But what's tart?"

"Raspberry is tart."

"Nobody puts raspberry with cucumber, that would just be—"

Jen passed by our table again on her way to the banquette on the wall. "Figure it out yet?"

"No!" JoJo cried. "You devilish woman, I need more time."
She laughed.

"We can just look on the chalkboard by the door," I said. "She lists the ingredients there."

"And ruin the game? Perish the thought!" He covered his eyes with a palm and lifted his drink with his other hand, taking a bigger sip this time. "All right," he said, setting the glass back down but keeping his eyes covered. "Cucumber, lime, orange, and something tart."

"This game is becoming tiresome," I said loftily, as Jen headed past again on her way back to the bar. "I just want to enjoy this delicious concoction."

"She picked an intriguing name," JoJo said, uncovering his eyes. "A little sexy, a little mysterious."

"Sexy?"

"Oh sure. Ruby Sipper? Conjures up images of sipping some delectable elixir out of a woman's elegant red shoe…after slipping her elegant slender foot out of it…"

"Huh, I only thought about *The Wizard of Oz*," I said.

JoJo snorted a laugh. "Oh, my innocent, innocent Cam…"

I glared back at him. "I'll have you know, I'm not all that innocent."

"Have you ever had a lover drink champagne out of one of your shoes?"

"Ugh, no! I wouldn't want that—for him *or* for me. Would you? Seriously?"

He took another long sip, nearly emptying his glass. "I'd much rather pour the champagne into a lover's belly button and sip it from there, or…"

I felt my face heating up as I pondered the image. Or no, no it was just the drink. Whatever was in it packed a punch. I covered my sudden embarrassment with another sip.

JoJo's eyes sparkled with merriment. "Cam! I've unsettled you!" He looked delighted.

I forced the absurd feelings down. "You wish!" I parried, grinning back at him.

JoJo started to say something, then stopped, giving me the

oddest look. It was almost…real. As real as when he'd dropped his guard on that hike and told me how he really felt as a child; except this time, there was a whole extra layer of…fraught-ness?

He cleared his throat and tossed back the last of his drink. "Barkeep!" he called out. "Another of these mysterious concoctions, my good woman!"

I glanced down at my drink. Oh what the heck. "Two!" I called to Jen, who laughed at us from behind the bar, pulled out a cocktail shaker, and filled it with ice.

When I finally dragged my gaze back to JoJo, he still looked discomfited, and even weirder, he was still silent! Because what was there to say, right? I mean, sure, he was gorgeous and charming and rich and all that, but he was *JoJo*. And I knew he wasn't attracted to me. (I'd still never even one hundred percent determined whether he liked girls *that* way.) But…what had just happened there?

All at once, he gave me a bright, quick smile. "Cam, acting agrees with you."

"What?" I asked, surprised by the sudden subject change. "What do you mean?"

He leaned back in his chair, looking much more himself. "I've been meaning to tell you. I noticed it again in rehearsal this evening. You're opening up—seeming more and more self-possessed—even displaying flashes of charisma, dare I say it!"

I waited for the inevitable sarcastic zinger. Another complaint about Martin, no doubt; or a dig at my mousiness; or whatever. But it didn't come. He seemed…almost sincere. Twice in one evening!

Wow.

"Well, you're changing too," I ventured. "I keep getting the feeling that we're actually…talking to each other these days. You keep displaying these flashes of sincerity, *dare I say it.*"

"Sincerity? My god, tell me you're joking, or I'll jump off Lisa's dock." JoJo rolled his eyes.

And here was Jen with our second drinks. "Come on, no guesses?" she asked, setting them down.

"Cucumber vodka, Cointreau, lime juice, and a splash of Campari," Jojo decreed.

"Close! But not quite right." She just grinned and turned away.

"Wait," JoJo called after her. "You're not going to tell us?"

"You're not giving up when you're so close, are you?" she called over her shoulder.

"I thought for sure that was it," he grumbled, sipping his new drink. "You're not even going to tell me which part I got wrong?"

Jen just winked.

I finished my first drink and picked up my second. Whoo, had this been a mistake? I suddenly started feeling the rest of the kick from the cocktail. "I may need you to help me with this one," I told JoJo.

"My darling Camillini, I am ever at your disposal." He flashed his wicked smile. "Particularly when it comes to *disposal* of adult beverages."

"I knew I could rely on you."

He put a gentle hand on mine. It was cool from his drink. "Always."

Flirtatious banter? Sincerity? "Actually, I do need your help with something," I said, without quite having decided I was going to.

"Oh?"

I glanced around. Jen was keeping an eye on us from behind the bar—probably just curious if we were going to solve her riddle—and it was very noisy in here, but… "I can't talk about it here. When we leave, okay?"

JoJo's eyebrows raised. "Oh! Secrets! My favorite." He downed half his drink. "Just say the word."

I did the best I could with the second drink but, especially given that I would need to drive home, I poured more than half of it into JoJo's glass. He had no trouble with it, of course. Jen came back when she saw our glasses empty. "Another try? Or more research?"

JoJo leaned back in his chair and blinked his lovely lashes up at her. These men and their eyelashes. Was it fair, I wondered? "My dear Miss Darling, I'm afraid we must repair to an undisclosed location to continue our deliberations on this crucial matter." A credit card appeared in his hand. "So we shall settle up here and bring you the correct answer…later."

"We close in forty-five minutes," she said, taking the card.

"Technically, tomorrow is also 'later,'" JoJo pointed out.

Jen laughed. "Ha, I knew I could stump you!" She went off to run his card.

"Except she said I was close," JoJo murmured to me. "Probably the Cointreau was wrong; that's too mainstream for her. Artisanal orange liqueur…ah!" he said, smiling up at Jen as she brought back the bill and his card. He signed with a flourish after adding, I noticed, a very generous tip. "Until later!"

"I look forward to it." Jen grinned at us both as I got somewhat unsteadily to my feet. "Take care, you two!"

JoJo extended an arm, and I took it, as we walked outside. "Could we, like, walk around the block or something?" I asked.

"Are you drunk? After one drink?"

"One and a half. And no. I'm not drunk. I'm still wound up, and sick of being inside all the time. A little fresh air and exercise would do me some good."

"Well, then, let's go, Camikins."

We walked up the street, away from the grocery store, to the darker and quieter part of our already dark and quiet little town. After passing the "escape room" with its cute faux-boarded-up windows and mysterious sign, JoJo said, "Well? What's so secret?"

"They asked me to go visit Maric in her hospital room, and see if I can get info out of her," I said as softly as I could. "I guess she's refusing to say anything to anyone about what happened, or who did it."

"Really," JoJo said, in a way that suggested his *sources* hadn't told him this.

"I had to pretend I didn't know she'd come out of her coma," I added, mostly just to let him know I'd kept *his* secret.

It was a little too dark to see his expression. "Did they believe you?"

"I think so."

"And who is 'they'—Veierra and McMichaels?"

"No, Clarke. And yes, I think he thought I was surprised."

"What else have they had you doing?"

"Am I supposed to tell you that?"

He snorted softly. "No, probably not... You probably weren't supposed to tell me about visiting Marie either. But forget I said it." We reached the corner and turned down North Beach Road, heading into town again.

"Anyway," I said, "Lisa's not supposed to know about the visit with Marie—and I'm assuming you won't tell on me."

"Moi?" he said, sounding scandalized. "Are you seriously questioning my integrity? I am a man of honor to the core, as you must surely know by now."

"Yeah. That's why I'm asking. You won't make me sorry I told you this, right?"

He sighed. "Pulling things over on our company handlers causes me not the tiniest pang of regret. But my few ill-advised attempts to deceive you have proved surprisingly painful—for me too, I mean." He shook his head. "And so. On several recent occasions, I've trusted you with more of my own secrets than I have ever divulged to anyone before. You can safely do the same with me."

I supposed that would have to do. "Okay. Thanks."

"So...is that it?"

"No. We had no idea how to hide my visit to the hospital from Lisa. But, by some stroke of good luck, she started urging me to think more about 'self care' the other night—which is why I'm supposed to be going back to Seattle soon to spend a day 'pampering myself.'"

"*Excellent!* Oh, my dear little Camikins, you are growing up so fast!"

I gave him a sideways look. "If you say so. The problem is, I'll need to come home with lots of stories about all the pampering I did, and some kind of evidence to prove it, I suppose. But I really don't have any idea what pampering involves—or where to go for it. I mean, it's got to be something more than a really nice haircut, right? So, I was hoping you—"

"*That's* what all this cloak and dagger was about? My poor deprived little waif, you have come to precisely the right concierge! Hot stone massage and green tea facial at Belltown. I have the number in my phone, if you actually want to make and then break an appointment." He spit all this out with the confidence of a Jeopardy contestant. "Though honestly," he went on, "I'd find some way to keep the appointment, and arrange your visit with Marie around it—because Lisa is as right as rain about this, and she *will* be able to tell whether you were really there or not. The results are *so* obvious—trust me."

"You're brilliant."

"Aren't I? And when you get back, go straight to Lisa and tell her about how you dropped by the hospital and *Oh My Gosh! Marie was awake! Can you believe it?* Let Lisa do whatever she wants about it from there."

"I can't," I sighed. "They don't want anyone knowing she's awake—for security reasons, and as soon as she can handle it, she's apparently off to some hidden location for her own protection till the trial's over."

"Oh!" He was silent for a moment. "Well...that's good to know."

Sources falling down on their jobs a little? I thought.

We were nearly at the corner by Darvill's now; I turned us left, to go toward Prune Alley and our cars. We walked in silence for a minute. How quickly and easily he always came up with answers, or some plan. "You're a very good liar, aren't you, JoJo?"

"You're not just figuring *that* out too."

I'd been determined to say nothing. Just keep my nose out of it, and my mouth shut for once—like Sheila had begged me to do. But... "Was it you who told them I'm *unstable*?"

He stopped walking, abruptly, and stared at me. "Have we... skipped a page somewhere?"

"The Feds are dropping the kidnapping charges against Sheila as part of a bargain to get her cooperation, because someone told them I was unstable—and they weren't sure they could get the charges to stick if that came out in court. Was that part of your little campaign to get me safely out of harm's way? Because—"

"Cam, stop!" he said, with surprising ferocity. I heard no humor or sarcasm in his voice at all. "I can't believe you'd even think—"

"I don't know what to think!" I told him, almost as fiercely. "I wouldn't have thought *this* if you hadn't done so many other things I'd never have thought you could. If I'm wrong, I am so sorry. But...I had to ask. And don't pretend you can't see why."

He drew a long, deep breath, and let it out a second later in an even longer sigh. "No. Of course I see why. But I didn't. Trust me or don't." He began to walk again, and I followed suit.

We continued in silence for a while after that, passing the co-op on the left and the grocery store on the right, until I couldn't stand the silence anymore. "I do," I said. "Trust you. Or...I would never have asked you to begin with."

He stopped again, and turned to face me, taking my hand in his this time. "I do have a code of honor, Cam. It's not one anybody else is ever likely to crack. But it's in there. And there's no room anywhere in it for betraying you *that* way. What I set in motion between you my mother... That was a terrible mistake. But I learn from my mistakes—especially ones that painful."

Now it was my turn to breathe more deeply. "I'm glad it wasn't you."

"I'm…glad you risked asking." We started to walk again.

A minute later, we were approaching our cars. "Do we need another circuit?" he asked.

I took another deep breath. "No, that's enough trauma for one night, I think. Thank you for the talk…and for helping me deal with the drinks."

He chuckled. "Who knew you were such a lightweight? Drive carefully, Camilicious. If you like, I'll follow you back."

"That's probably a good idea." I was stone cold sober, but I felt strange, and vulnerable. As I drove home, with JoJo's annoyingly bright but still comforting headlights in my rearview mirror, I thought about the whole encounter. We'd flirted in the bar; very definitely flirtation. But that was what JoJo did, almost as reflexively as breathing. Except there was that moment…had there been something of a spark there, something more *real*?

I thought about it, and realized that in the entire time I'd known him, I'd never seen him do anything but flirt. With everyone. Always.

But nothing more.

I was probably just lonely. A grown woman, untouched for months, aside from that lovely but regrettable interlude with Colin in my cabin—which hadn't improved anything for either of us. I knew I wasn't ready, but this solitude was getting old.

Everything had been moving so fast lately. So much to process, so much to manage, both out in the open and behind the scenes. The play. My busy life as a CI. My own…inner personal growth, wherever the heck that was going.

No wonder I was longing for someone's arms.

But, were there any arms but my own to find on this little island? I was beginning to doubt it.

CHAPTER 12

Lisa had been delighted about my plans to go have a hot stone massage and green tea facial at some fancy city spa; and all too soon, here I was—after so many months of unbroken island solitude—on a ferry to the mainland for the second time in one week. There were so many kinds of whiplash at work in my life these days!

I'd been informed by Sheriff Clarke that my clearance with security staff at the hospital had been arranged, but that I was *not* to let Marie know *at all* that law enforcement had had anything to do with my visit. "Just tell her you've been very deeply concerned ever since you found her that day and called for rescue," he'd told me. "Then take it from there."

So simple! As if.

I still had no idea how or where I was supposed to "take it," of course. I'd certainly have no problem walking into her room and expressing my very real relief at seeing her alive; but after that… my imagination failed me.

The ferry didn't stop at Shaw this time, or at Lopez; just steamed away toward America as I paced around and sighed on the outside passenger deck. I hardly even noticed the scenery as my mind went on gnawing at the puzzle. Knowing that Clarke had started thinking of me as some kind of miracle worker didn't make anything easier. I was just me, groping around in the dark—about everything.

Maybe if I just…let Marie take the lead, some path would become obvious, and—

I was so lost in thought that I almost ran into someone. I stopped short, turning to apologize and—oh crap! "Colin!" I gasped, looking up at him…and then at the lovely young, dark-haired woman beside him.

"Cam," he said, seeming almost as surprised as I was. "It's, uh, good to see you?"

I gave him an unsure smile. "Is it?"

"It is!" His companion sort of nudged him. "Oh! And this is Priya." His smile broadened.

"Priya!" I exclaimed, smiling at them as I reached to shake her hand. "I'm Camille Tate."

Her hand was small and slender, but I sensed its strength. "Pleased to meet you," she said, studying me carefully. "I think Colin may have mentioned you."

I was sure he had. This was just a little awkward.

"So…" Colin said, after Priya had released my hand.

"Nice morning—isn't it?" I offered, glancing at the scenic islands I had been ignoring.

"It is," Priya agreed. "I bet all this is lovely in pretty much any kind of weather, huh?"

"What…brings you guys here?" I asked. "Just getting off-island for a day?"

"Priya lives in Anacortes," Colin said. "I've been giving her the grand tour. Turtleback, Rosario, Orcas Pottery—you know."

"Ah, yes." All the places he'd shown me. My smile felt suddenly a little tight; but I had the good sense to keep my mouth shut. "That's a lot to see in one day."

"It was two days! We stayed on his boat!" Priya sounded so excited. "It was so much fun—and a lot more comfortable than

I had expected."

Colin looked a little nervous then. Which was ridiculous, because come on. There had been a few kisses—wonderful, lingering, meaningless kisses—and a lot of hikes. But we'd never actually been *dating*. I had made that…well, *painfully* clear, in the end.

So then, why did I feel so weird, seeing him standing there with another woman tucked into his arm, who liked hikes and thought his boat was charming?

Was I…*completely* sure his arms *weren't* the ones I had been wishing for the other night, after the Barnacle, and JoJo?

Yes, I told myself. I was.

I really *had* made that decision—too permanently and too many times to pretend confusion now. "So, why aren't you two on the boat today? It's such gorgeous sailing weather."

"Priya has to go back home," he said. "I'm just keeping her company on the return trip."

"And he wants to see my place," she added, gazing at him fondly.

Ugh, this was making me so uncomfortable, no matter what I had decided. "How did you guys meet?" I asked.

"Through friends!" Colin said, even as Priya said, "Nauticalove-dot-com!"

I bit back a smile. "Is that…a dating site?"

"Sure is," Colin said, struggling, almost successfully, not to look abashed.

Priya nudged him with her elbow. "Oh, come on, everyone meets online these days. And I'm sure glad *I* gave it a try." She patted his arm, then glanced back and forth between us, before giving me an almost…sympathetic smile? "Anyway, I need a cup of coffee. Do you want one?" she asked Colin. He shook his head no. "How about you?" she asked me cheerfully. "My treat."

Oh, she was smoother than I'd thought. "No, thank you," I said. "I'm good."

"Then I'll just leave you two to chat while I go get myself a pick-me-up." She beamed at me again. "It's been very nice to meet you."

"You too," I said, realizing that she was almost certainly leaving just to give us a chance to talk alone, which seemed surprisingly kind—and trusting.

I really *wanted* Colin to be happy. And she seemed, well, nicer than I'd wanted to admit at first. They even *looked* nice together, standing there, holding hands: a happy couple.

Colin bent down and kissed her on the cheek. Then she headed off, still smiling. When she'd vanished back into the boat, I turned to Colin. "She's *very* nice."

He nodded, giving me an embarrassed smile. "Yes, she is."

"I'm happy for you, and I'm…I'm really sorry for the way I mishandled everything…you know…"

He held up a hand and shook his head. "Got it, Cam. Nothing to be sorry about." He looked rueful. "You'd been trying to get me the message for a while, but you were too nice. Sorry I needed a clue-by-four to get it."

"Oh please. I sent so many mixed messages—"

"You did." He looked away, seeming to struggle for words. Then he turned back. "But if you hadn't tossed me overboard, I'd never have gotten mad and taken Jen's dare to sign up for that stupid website. So, uh, thank you."

"For ticking you off?"

"Did the trick," he said with a shrug. We both burst out laughing.

Priya returned at that moment, bearing two cups of coffee. "What's so funny?"

Colin, despite having declined earlier, took the cup she offered, and brought it straight to his lips, probably to get out of answering her question.

"Oh, just island stuff," I said, wishing I'd asked for a cup after all.

Priya gave me another of those smiles. "So, where are *you* headed this fine morning, Cam?"

Excellent! A chance to practice my story. I gushed on about just needing a day *off* after being so *busy* with everything going on in my life lately. I treated them to a blow-by-blow of my most mundane tasks, some of which had actually been done by the Booster Club ladies. By the time I wandered off into self-care, and needing to get the company car out on a freeway now and then, they were glancing over my shoulder, clearly looking for reasons to get moving again.

Well, that was one way to shut down an awkward encounter. Just bore them to pieces.

℘

After managing to drive my fancy—and *still unscratched*—car down a narrow, curvy little ramp, and safely off the ferry in Anacortes, I spent an hour and a half not-quite-speeding Tigress down I-5, still thinking about Colin, and these little stabs of loneliness I kept doing nothing about back on the island. Why was that? There were lots of hunky pairs of arms waiting to be asked out there. I saw them almost everywhere I went—with their tool belts and their pickup trucks; muscling things around on the docks or in their fishing boats; out on tractors in the fields, at the grocery store, or outside of the Lower Tavern every day at quitting time. But, seriously…where would I have *put* the man of my dreams, these days, even if I found him? Between lurching from job to ever more daunting job, writing—and now managing and *acting* in—a play, and, oh yes, navigating a seemingly endless string of mysterious crime stories on my way to becoming an actual *secret agent*—not to mention struggling to come to terms with a whole lifetime of inner demons—where would I have found space to squeeze in a relationship?

What did I actually want? Some man to kiss and comfort me and listen while I poured my heart out during the few minutes every couple weeks when I found time to even notice I was lonely? What if the man of my dreams needed *me* to listen to *him*? Perish the thought. More likely I would rush out in the middle of our heart-to-heart to go report to Sheriff Clarke, or meet the booster club, or Roland Markus. Colin had spent half a day repairing my broken rabbit hutch, and I'd forgotten he was even there! He was a terrific, *very* sexy man—who had very clearly wanted me. So why *hadn't* I wanted him? Was it…just because… my life was already too full to fit anything even half as large as love into?

When had *that* happened? How had I become too busy for love?

As I reached the outskirts of Seattle, traffic started to back up ahead of me. I glanced down at the speedometer. *Whoa there!* I looked up at the rearview mirror as I backed off the accelerator. No flashing lights. Whew! My imagination shot me a vivid image of Kip writing me a speeding ticket.

And, weirdly, that's when it struck me that I wasn't just too *busy* to find love. The tender arms I longed for couldn't belong to a cop…*obviously.* Or to a hunky boat-builder. Or even to a rich, charismatic, flirtatious playboy. No, every time a hint of romantic possibility so much as reared its head, there was instantly some reason why any such idea was *impossible.* He can't really mean… He's probably just… Don't even bother going there!

I hadn't just become too busy. I'd been willfully shutting down every chance that came along, hadn't I? Was I too scared? Still?

But scared of what?

I looked in the rearview mirror again, just to be sure, then put Tigress on cruise control *(Sorry sweetie!)*, and reminded myself that I should be working out a plan for getting Marie to open up, not writing scenes in my head for some sappy romance novel.

According to Tigress's onboard navigation, I was just a few miles from my exit for the spa, anyway. I shoved all the mopey clutter in my head aside, and started paying attention.

And here's what I learned during the next hour and a half about hot stone massage and green tea facials:

The massage part was beyond amazing! Now I knew exactly where the arms I had been longing for were located—or the hands, at least. Too bad there was a three-hour trip—each way—between them and me. *That* relationship was not one I would ever find a way to fit into my current schedule. As for laying hot stones all over my body afterward, that time would have been better spent on more rubbing from those unforgettable hands.

The green tea facial, however, felt…well, weird, honestly, and really cold, and it made me itch something fierce. I decided that it must be intended for people with oily skin, which wasn't me. I was so glad when it was over. But it did leave my face glowing amazingly. JoJo had been right about that part at least; if I hadn't gotten that facial, one look would have told Lisa I'd never really been to the spa.

So, all in all, I'd probably have claimed not to know what everyone's excitement was about, except that actually I did, and his name was Elliot—or that's who it had been on that particular morning, at least. I was very sure that I'd be dreaming about his hands for many nights to come.

After that, I got dim sum for lunch. Orcas Island may have many wonderful things, but a dim sum restaurant is not one of them. And then, well, all good things must come to an end. It was finally time to do what I'd actually come here for. I charged yet another eye-popping bill to my credit card—Lisa had made me promise to expense everything I did that day, of course—and then I headed off to the hospital.

ᏨᎧ

After parking in the hospital's multi-story garage, I found my way through the building's glass and metal maze of hallways and waiting rooms to the main check-in desk. When I gave the receptionist my name, and inquired about visiting Marie, she tapped away for a moment at her keyboard, then looked back up at me. "I'm sorry, Ms. Tate. Ms. Tolliver is not allowed to have visitors at this time."

"I...what?" Hadn't Clarke set all this up? "Can you check again? I was told I could see her."

She dutifully tapped at her keyboard again, and shook her head. "I'm sorry, Ms. Tate."

"But I..." What to do? "I'm a very close friend... Is there maybe someone else I can talk to? About how she's doing, at least?"

"You can take those elevators to the ICU," she gestured, "and try talking with someone at the nursing station there. But I don't think you'll get a different answer."

A line was forming behind me, so I thanked her and headed for the elevators.

On the ICU floor, the duty nurse gave me the same answer as soon as he heard Marie's name.

"Are you sure?" I pleaded. "I'm Camille Tate. Is there nothing about me in your, uh, database or whatever?" I couldn't just tell him that the Feds were supposed to have set all this up. Sheriff Clarke had made that part very clear. "I really thought I had an appointment." Was I going to have to call Clarke? How awkward was this? And very not-subtle.

The nurse sighed, and typed on his keyboard. Then his eyes widened. "Oh! So sorry, I just came on, and no one told me. But you're still going to have to talk to the officer down that hall there." He pointed; I followed his gaze to a guard leaning against the wall beside a doorway.

"Thank you." Flooded with nerves now, I headed down the hall.

The guard watched me approach, then pushed himself up off the wall, taking a posture that basically screamed, *Nope*.

I was screaming *Nope* right back—on the inside, anyway. Outwardly, I smiled. "I'm Camille Tate, and I was told to see you about visiting Marie Tolliver."

He blinked and caught himself, then nodded. "Yes, Ms. Tate. And ah, I'm sorry, but I'll need to see some ID, and do a quick search of your bag and your…person."

"That's fine." I dug through my purse and handed him my driver's license, which he glanced over and handed back. Then he made quick and professional work of the rest, even inspecting my shoes. I felt ready to board an airplane.

"All right, you're good."

He opened the door, and I stepped into the dimly lit room. Marie was lying there, half swallowed in a hospital bed that seemed unusually large, until I realized that it was just because she was even smaller than she'd been before. Numerous IV tubes ran into her arms, attached to several monitors at the head of her bed—all of them blinking, but, happily, not beeping.

I remained standing just inside the door after the guard closed it behind me. Marie seemed to be asleep, and I wasn't sure I should wake her. But as I took a step forward, she opened her eyes. A look of confusion covered her face. "Cam?" she asked in a hoarse voice. "Are you really here?"

"I am."

She surprised me with a tentative smile. Oh, her teeth were looking dreadful.

I made myself smile back—*remember your story!*—and walked over to the bed. "Hi!" I said lightly. "I was in town, and…I just thought I'd come ask them how you were doing. I hadn't heard you were awake—that's so great! Are you…feeling better?"

She just stared back at me. Was this a mistake? Was she just not up to conversation yet? But then she said, in a quieter voice, "There are guards out there, aren't there? How did you get in?"

I nodded. "It was really weird. They had to call someone, and it took forever." I shrugged. "But I guess they decided I wasn't anyone they needed to worry about."

She gave me another weak smile, then sighed. "No, I guess you're not." She sure did seem…slow. But then, she'd been in a coma. "They said you found me," she went on after a minute. "That night? They said you saved my life."

Was this a question? I wasn't sure, but I nodded. "You sent me that unfinished text, so I went over to check on you. And I'm glad I did." I glanced around the room and found a guest chair by the far wall, which I pulled over to her bedside and sat.

Marie was still gazing at me, looking very confused. "What text?"

"You said you'd heard something, but then the text stopped. In the middle of a sentence."

She looked away. "I don't remember that." Then she looked back at me. "My phone is gone. I can't call or text anyone… They say it's to keep me safe."

"Safe from who? Do…they know who did this to you?"

Marie just gazed back at me, as if trying to figure me out. "Do you?"

"Do I what? You mean, do I know who did this to you?"

She stared at me, punctuating her silence with the occasional slow blink.

I cleared my throat. "Marie, I saw someone prowling around your house that evening. I told the deputies, but…I don't think anyone believes me. I guess they didn't find any footprints or anything." She just watched me, wide-eyed. "It was scary," I went on. "And we've all been so worried about you. Lisa was half out of her mind about it."

She gave that slow blink again. It took me a moment to realize that she was tearing up. "I'm sorry," she whispered.

Had I misheard her? "What?"

"I'm so sorry." Her voice was a little clearer, but her eyes were brimming.

"For what, Marie?"

"For getting you into all this. For what I've done to Lisa…" She trailed off, blinking harder.

I leaned forward and laid my hand gently on her arm, careful to avoid all the tubes. "What have you done to Lisa? She doesn't think you've done anything to her. In fact, she feels like this is her fault. She feels terrible—for you."

"Oh?" Marie sounded surprised. "She told you...what did she say?"

I paused, suddenly uncertain whether I should have opened that can. Well, too late now. "She told me she sent you to work for Derek, and something happened there to make you sick. She doesn't know what, but she thinks it was her fault." I stopped there to see what she would say.

She furrowed her brow. "Why did she tell you that?"

I shrugged. "Well, now that I'm her assistant, she's been telling me a lot of private things about her business."

"Her assistant?" Marie sounded even more confused. "I thought... Weren't you her caretaker? I was her caretaker too, once..."

Oh dear. Maybe the reason no one was getting anything useful out of her was because she wasn't really all there yet. "You caretake for the Brixtons now," I told her, gently. "Next door. Do you remember that?"

She nodded, looking sad. "But you're Lisa's assistant now? Not just her caretaker?"

"Yes."

She exhaled, a sad little almost-laugh, and looked away. "Of course you are."

I wasn't sure what to make of that. Hadn't anyone told her? I honestly couldn't remember. I hadn't wanted to rub her face in my promotion after the way she'd been packed off to the Brixtons; and I *had* still been functioning as Lisa's caretaker when Marie was...taken away. Had Lisa told her? Probably not, I realized—for the same reasons.

"I was you, once," said Marie.

"What?" I was lost again. "Her assistant?"

She shook her head, still looking away from me. "Her favorite."

I kept silent, waiting to find out where this was going.

"I know you think I'm stupid," she went on, softly, "and silly, and—well, helpless, Cam, but I was so smart once. And so... good at everything. I was Lisa's favorite then." She finally looked back at me with a sharp, almost frightening focus—her previous vagueness suddenly gone. "I don't blame you. Not at all. I like you—a lot. But, it was hard to watch you all that time. Being me. Who I used to be. Lisa, taking you under her wing, and grooming you for—"

"No, Marie," I broke in, unable to help myself. "She told me how smart you were. *Are.* She said you were the most brilliant and capable young woman she'd ever met, and whatever happened to you with Derek broke her heart. You're still her favorite, and she's devastated that she put you in harm's way—that she hasn't been able to find out what happened, or how to—"

"She didn't," Marie interrupted. "She didn't put me in harm's way. I did. I did this to her. And now..." She bit her lip, and her eyes welled with tears again.

"Marie, we don't have to talk about this right now—or ever," I rushed to say, afraid this might be more than she could handle yet. "I just came to see how you were. I didn't mean to—"

"I've put you in danger too," she cut in quietly, struggling to hold back tears. "I know what it means to be where you are now. These are not safe people. Their attention, any bit of it—it's not good. You need to get away from them. Get off that island, and... hide. Anywhere you can."

"What do you mean?" I asked, as calmly as I could. "What kind of danger are you talking about? From who? Is that why you're being guarded here?" I was trying not to sound like I'd known any of this. But she went silent again, just staring at me, like the proverbial deer in the headlights. "Have you told the authorities about any of this?"

"I can't," she moaned. "I can't do that to—" She seemed to collapse into herself then, closing her eyes. Tears dripped down her cheeks. She looked exhausted, and sicker than ever.

My heart broke. "I don't want to make you worse," I said. "Let's just drop this, okay?"

She sniffled, then whispered, "No." So I waited, and after a minute, she opened her eyes again. "The police can never know, or anybody else. I've hurt Lisa enough already. But there are things I wish I'd…things I need to tell her before…" She bit her lip and paused again, then turned to me. "You always seemed like someone I could trust, Cam. I need a favor. A very big favor, and I'm sorry, but there's no one else I can ask."

"I'll do it if I can," I promised. "I care about you, Marie. We all do."

"I need you to tell Lisa…what happened. But no one else. Especially not the deputies, the police, the FBI, anybody like that. If I give you a message for Lisa, will you promise never to tell anyone what I said?"

I had no idea what to say. Marie was watching me avidly, her bloodshot eyes wide in her sallow face. I'd come here precisely to report everything she said to law enforcement. But I *needed* to hear anything she could tell me about danger to me or Lisa. I didn't want to betray her trust, especially after everyone else in her life had obviously done so; but if I answered her honestly now, she wouldn't tell me anything. That seemed obvious. And it seemed clearer than ever now that lots of people might really need to know.

There was no right answer. So which wrong answer should I choose?

"Will keeping this from everyone else put other people in danger?" I asked, realizing that my best way out would be to change her mind about insisting on my silence.

She shook her head. "If you guys think other people need to know, Lisa can tell anyone she wants to. But I have to let her decide that. I've kept too much from her already—I can't do that anymore. So promise me you'll tell no one but her."

I couldn't hesitate or she'd clam up again. "Okay," I said, hoping I was making the right choice. "I promise."

"Thank you." Marie sighed, closing her eyes again for a moment. "I know I'm putting you in a bind, but...well, you're already there. And I'm sorry for that too. That's the first thing I want you to tell Lisa—that I'm more sorry than she'll ever understand. I know she would have gone to the authorities right away, if I'd just given her what she needed to do it. But I was... so confused, and so stupid already. And Derek had twisted my mind around so badly. I had everything backwards then. I didn't see..." She shook her head.

I put a hand on her arm again. "Don't beat yourself up," I urged, gently. "Just tell me."

She blinked at me. "Okay...I'll try." She looked away, and started nodding to herself, as if working through whatever she was about to say. Then she closed her eyes again. "It was a longevity drug; what Derek was working on. Or, that's what it was supposed to be. But it wasn't working. And he...wasn't handling anything the way he should have." Her eyes opened, but she still didn't look at me. I realized that she was struggling not to cry again. "If I'd just gone back and told all this to Lisa, she'd have shut him down right then, maybe even turned him over to the law. We would all be safe now. But I decided to wait until I had gathered more to tell her. And then...I realized what his new drug really was, and..." She broke down, and began to shake with nearly silent sobs as I stroked her arm softly.

What had Derek done to her? Images from my own childhood, *very* unwanted—especially now—began rising up in my mind, and I felt almost afraid to know what she'd say next.

"Oh, Cam," she wept. "I was so smart—and so stupid. I thought... I thought I could fix it. And Derek... He seemed so grateful—so relieved—like he'd just gotten caught up in a bunch of terrible mistakes he didn't know how to get himself untangled from. He said how brilliant I was—how I could save him and

Lisa's whole company, if I could just…" She buried her face in her hands, then pulled herself back under control. "He told me how grateful everyone would be, and what a brilliant future I would have…if I could…pull this off." She shook her head. "And I believed him." Now she turned and looked me at last. Straight in the eye. "Because I *wanted* to. So badly."

And then she told me.

CHAPTER 13

I didn't even get out of my car during the ferry ride home; just sat there behind the steering wheel, on the parking deck in a double line of other, mostly empty cars. I was on the late boat, so there were no views to miss. But, mostly, I just didn't want to deal with anyone right now—even passing strangers. I couldn't imagine putting on a social face and making nice—maybe ever again.

I kept wiping tears away as I thought about everything Marie had told me; so brave, and stoic as she'd unburdened herself—to a *trusted friend*. To think that *I* was all she had for that.

Well…I would be going straight to Lisa's house when I got home. No matter how late it was—or what Clarke had said about keeping all this from her. I could not even imagine sleeping with this still locked up in my head. And the only way my legal handlers were ever going to hear what I'd learned was when Lisa passed it on to them—as I was sure she would. I had promised Marie, and I had no intention of being the next person to betray her trust.

When I finally got back, Lisa's house looked darkened for the night; only the motion-detecting lights outside responded to my arrival. Hoping she hadn't used my big day off to go away somewhere too, I climbed out of Tigress and walked to her front door, where the motion-sensitive porch light came on as well. I knocked as softly as I could and still hope that Lisa would hear it. To my relief, she answered almost right away.

"Cam!" she said, looking confused. "Is…everything all right?"

After a brief hesitation, I said, "No."

She frowned. "Come in." She pulled the door wider, and stood aside as I entered.

"Sorry to bother you so late," I said, relieved to see a few dim lights still on in both the kitchen and the sunken living room.

"That doesn't matter. What's happened?"

I wondered how to even start as Lisa headed for the kitchen, beckoning me along after her as she led us through it to the dining room. There were more lights on there, and her usual pile of papers on the table, next to a half-full cup of coffee. She sat down behind her work, looking at me expectantly as I took a chair across from her.

"After my, um…spa session this morning," I began, still trying to organize my thoughts, "I realized I wasn't far from Marie's hospital." Lisa grew very still. "So, I decided to go see if they would tell me anything about how she's been doing." The emotions I'd been shoving down all evening welled back up, making my eyes brim again, and Lisa didn't miss that.

"Has…she died?" she asked quietly.

I shook my head. "She's awake," I managed over the lump in my throat.

"She is?"

"Yes. And she told me what happened—all of it. She made me promise to tell you everything—but no one else unless you decide they should know."

I had never even imagined seeing Lisa so close to naked alarm before. She seemed almost frozen for a moment. *"Tell me then,"* she said at last.

Now came the part I still had no idea how to do—how to even

keep straight in my head. "The thing she asked me to tell you first is that she's sorrier than you will ever know."

Lisa's mouth fell open, slightly. "What for?"

"That's just what I said. And, well…this is where it all gets…much more complicated." I decided to just stick as close as I could to the order Marie had said things in. "She told me Derek was working on a longevity drug."

Lisa's eyes widened briefly. Then she closed them and shook her head. "That idiot," she growled, more to herself than to me. "The *fountain of youth*? How could even he have been that stupid?" She opened her eyes again. "It wasn't working out, I assume."

I shook my head. "Marie said the mice weren't living any longer than normal mice, or even getting any healthier. And Derek had been making…a lot of *bad decisions*; that's how she put it. His team hadn't been following any of the proper…" What had she said? "Protocols? And there were a bunch of legal hoops he should have been jumping through too; she told me about those, but I didn't really understand a lot of it. He'd been ignoring them as well, though, and—"

"Why didn't she come tell *me* all this?" Lisa demanded. "That's exactly what I sent here over to him to find out! If I'd known, I'd have—"

"I know," I cut her off. "Marie knows too. That's…part of what she's so sorry for."

Lisa gazed back at me, clearly trying to get her own feelings under control. "I'm sorry. I should just let you tell me. Please, go on."

I re-gathered my thoughts. "She says Derek also seemed pretty frightened of some investors that she thinks he'd made promises to. Promises he couldn't keep."

Lisa brought a hand up to massage her forehead. "Well, that confirms a lot of my worst fears. But I'd guessed that, actually… Quite a while ago."

"The more Marie found out," I went on, "the more she thought there must be even worse things for her to uncover; and…she says she was afraid you'd react so quickly that Derek would be scared into hiding the rest before she'd discovered any of it. So… she put off reporting to you. She knows now what a mistake that was." Lisa looked down and shook her head, but remained silent. "That's when she convinced Derek to give her some hands-on time with the actual research experiments, and discovered that, although the mice weren't living any longer, they were all geniuses now." Lisa raised her face slowly, wide-eyed. "Smart as dogs. That's what she told me. She called it…cognitive enhancement, I think, and said it was off the charts."

"Well…" Lisa sounded stunned. "I did not see that one coming. But…she's *sure* those results weren't just something Derek's team had faked somehow?"

"Oh, no. I mean, yes; she's…completely sure." Another wave of grief thickened my throat. "I'll get to that part in a minute; but when she told Derek what she'd discovered, she says he became ecstatic, gushing about what a genius she was, and filling her head with promises of a future beyond her wildest dreams— worldwide fame and Nobel Prizes." I sighed, remembering Marie's disgust as she'd explained all this. "He said she had not only just saved his life, but yours too, though she still isn't sure whether he meant it literally or not. He admitted he had made mistakes— bad ones—that he hadn't known how to undo, but told her he'd been desperate to keep those mistakes from taking you and the whole company down with him. Then he said that what she'd just discovered could be the answer to all of it. He just needed her to make it work—the *right* way. He promised her there'd be no corners cut this time."

With every word I spoke, Lisa's face looked more like a thundercloud about to break loose. *The faster this goes, the better*, I thought. "But he also warned her that you'd just shut the whole project down without listening to anything they had to say, unless they could present the new drug to you completely finished and ready for all those official tests and permit processes and everything. He told Marie he was afraid you'd just get mad and destroy everyone and everything, including yourself, inches from the finish line without thinking it through first."

The look on Lisa's face was terrifying now. I was glad to know such anger wasn't aimed at me. But I didn't know whether it was just meant for Derek, or for Marie too. "He gaslit her, Lisa; all the way. Tricked her into thinking she was the hero who could either save everybody or just let them all crash. And she's so ashamed she didn't see through that now, and so sorry about it. She doesn't just blame Derek either. She admits she got caught up in her own dreams of achieving something…historical. She hates herself, and nothing I said to her seemed to change that. But the scientist in her just couldn't stand to think of letting such a miracle get wasted because of Derek's stupidity before she even got a chance to prove it really worked. Derek had twisted her mind around so far that she thought you wouldn't even let her try to—"

"You don't have to keep defending her," Lisa snapped, looking away from me. "I know very well what that lying, narcissistic snake is capable of doing to anybody's mind. I *married* him, didn't I?" She spent a moment staring at the darkened windows by the table. "I mistook Marie's brilliance and youthful confidence for seasoned experience and self-possession…and sent her into the adder's den completely unprepared. That's indefensible." She looked back at me. "So, what else? There's more, I presume."

"Yes," I said. "So, she got lost in that dream. But…she's such a good and honest person, Lisa, at heart… She knew all kinds of things could come apart at any minute, and decided that the chance had to be grabbed quickly, before something shut it down for good. But she wasn't willing to put anybody else in danger, so—"

"No, no, *no, NO!*" Lisa shoved her chair back and stood up. The anger on her face turned to horror as she stalked off toward the windows. "I don't want to hear this!"

I wished I *could* not say any of the rest. Just walk out of here. But I had promised Marie that I would tell Lisa all of it. I nodded, not brave enough to even look at her as I said, "She used it on herself. The drug."

When the words were out, I looked up to see the calmest, most unflappable, self-assured, and powerful woman I had ever met bring her hands up to her ears as if to squeeze her head with them, then wrap her arms tightly around herself, then swing them halfway outward in some kind of appeal before wrapping them around herself again—as if she had no idea what to do with any of her body. She wasn't looking at me anymore. She hadn't even glanced at me since I'd said it.

And there were even worse things I still had to tell her. "That's how she knows the drug is real," I went on. "She became a genius too. A super-genius. For a while." I kept my eyes on Lisa now. I owed us all that much. "Then the mice all died—*total cognitive and autonomic collapse,* she called it."

"But…I don't understand!" Lisa's voice trembled with frustration. "Why didn't she just come to me for help? I'm the one who'd sent her there. She was too smart not to see what was at stake—for *herself!* Derek never sees the truth—about himself or anything—just his fantasies; but she had to know she was in way too far over her head!"

"She was afraid, Lisa. She knew how foolish she'd been—how badly she'd messed up; and your respect meant *everything* to her." Could Lisa really not get that? "She thinks…she has maybe one or two months left, now that the antidote's cut off."

Lisa stared. "What antidote?" she asked with sudden, quiet intensity. "Cut off *how?*"

"Oh…" I said, realizing I'd left that whole part out in my rush to get this over with. "The mice had been on this stuff a lot longer than she had, so they started going long enough before she did that she had time to use her mental superpowers to work on a cure—or at least some way to slow down her brain's failure as much as possible. And she found a kind of temporary treatment before her declining mental health stopped her from going any farther."

"So, there's a cure!" Lisa said, sounding more like her usual self again.

"No, not a cure," I said, sadly. "Just a way to slow the symptoms down some."

"Well, then at least the promise of one! What's happened, then? Has her supply run out?"

I shook my head again. "Once Marie's mind started going, she had no idea how she'd made the antidote; and, anyway, it required all kinds of equipment and supplies she had no access to anymore. But Derek still had all that, and told her he would keep her supplied with all she needed—as long as she kept everything from you."

I thought Lisa would explode when she heard that. But she just wilted, visibly. Her skin looked almost gray now as she walked back to the table and sat down again. "So, why did she fall into the coma? Has this treatment of hers lost its effectiveness somehow?"

I sighed…wishing… There was no way out but through. "No. Derek just stopped sending it to her."

"What? Why? That's *murder!"*

And here comes the next shoe, I thought. "Derek…sent Marie up here to spy on you. Just like Bella and Petey. But once she got up here, she realized she couldn't do that to you. So she just stopped sending him reports; broke off all communication and hoped she was too far away and too…well looked after here for him to do anything about it." I hunched my shoulders. "Derek had been sending her the antidote in all those cases of kombucha and supplement drinks she always said she ordered online, and…I guess she didn't think he'd really stoop to killing her either, because it wasn't till she got so sick that she finally figured out he'd just been sending her cases of plain old kombucha—with no antidote at all." I bowed my head, remembering again the mean things I'd said about her while that was going on. "She told me this afternoon that she just…gave up then, and stayed in her house, waiting to die."

Lisa sat staring at her hands now, folded on the table in front of her.

"I think she believes she deserves to die," I said, "for what she's done to you—or thinks she has. She seems so resigned to it; almost like it's the last escape she's got left to hope for."

"Well, that's absurd," said Lisa, looking up. "She didn't really think I'd hear all this and just stand by and watch her die while there's an antidote out there to stop it, did she? Neither will the authorities, I'm sure. I assume she's told *them* all this, at least?"

"No. I already told you; she said no one was to know but you— and me, of course—unless *you* decide to tell them."

"Why on earth?" Lisa exclaimed.

"Because she doesn't want to ruin you. She thinks she kept things from you that you needed to protect yourself, and would have used to prevent all this. All she seems to want is to make that right before she dies. Almost the minute I walked in there today, she told me you and I were in danger, and then refused to tell me anything more unless I promised to tell no one, for any reason, but you. So…I promised—because we needed to know. And I don't want to betray Marie's trust again; but, Lisa, we have to tell the authorities, at least, don't we?"

Lisa didn't just look gray anymore. She looked older than I'd thought she could. "Yes. We absolutely do." Then she gave me a wan smile, with a trace of the reassurance I had always seen in her face before. "Thank you, Cam. You just keep…" She fell silent, and drew a long, deep breath. "I'll leave a message for the sheriff as soon as we're done here tonight. Thank goodness you decided to stop by and check on her." She shook her head. "And I'll tell you right now, Cam: I have no intention of letting Marie die. If anyone in the world should have the resources to figure out how to recreate that antidote, and make it work even better, it's the people I employ, and my many other connections in the industry. Derek's crossed all the lines there are; and given everything you've just told me, I'm pretty sure the law will have little trouble finding my despicable ex-husband, and squeezing what we need to know out of him quickly enough." She gave me a grim smile. "Which means I need to get to work now, setting a few things in motion."

At my confused expression, she went on.

"I've been expecting something like this; for years, actually. Not this particular horror story, certainly, but…well, let's just say that I've made plenty of plans, and now it's time to put them into action."

I could see her marshaling her strength and determination, transforming herself back into the Lisa Cannon I'd known before—though I wasn't going to be able to forget the Lisa I'd seen here tonight. This day had transformed so many things for me—and not in easy ways: my picture of Marie, and of myself, and of Lisa too. Watching her collect herself now, after her earlier despair, and start rising to the task of dealing with all this so quickly… That was—

"In fact," said Lisa, with something much more like the kind of full-blown smile I was used to, "there are opportunities here that I intend to make the most of."

"Opportunities?"

"Yes. Life is always full of them." She reached down, opened her planner, and began to make notes, just as calm as could be. After a minute, she looked up and fixed me with her clear, cool gaze. "I hope you've been paying attention to everything I've shown you, Cam. About the theater company, and the house, and what it takes to keep it all going. Orcas is the heart of my life, in so many ways, and I'm going to need you to keep it beating while I'm busy with other things now." She gave me a long, considering look. "If you thought I was busy before, you'd better brace yourself, because dealing with all of this is going to put way more on my plate. I'm afraid you're really going to earn that salary now. I'll need you to, well, more or less *be me* in some ways. For a while, at least."

"Be you how?" I asked, feeling more and more alarmed. "I've hardly even started to figure all this out yet. I can't—nobody can *be you!*"

"This why you're paid the big bucks," she said cheerfully, going back to making her notes.

"What will you need me to do?"

With a small laugh, she said, "Nothing beyond your capacity. I'm quite sure of that by now." She set her pen down and smiled up at me again. "But we'll talk more about it soon, okay? Right now, I need to make some calls—beginning with that message for the sheriff. Why don't you go get some sleep? I'm certain you'll need it."

"Are you sure? Will you be all right?"

"Oh Cam." Her smile grew even warmer. "Yes, I'm fine. Life has thrown plenty of troubles my way before, as you're aware. It just takes a little time to adjust, that's all. And a little preparation. Like I said, there are always opportunities—even in the darkest situations."

I was clearly being dismissed, and she was right; I did need to sleep—very badly. And I just might, now that my promises to Marie were kept. "Well, okay." I stood up. "And, thank you."

"For what?" she asked, seeming genuinely puzzled.

"For taking this to the authorities. I know this could damage your company's reputation; Marie made that clear too. But she said you had to be the one to decide, and…maybe now that you have, she'll be willing to talk with them, and you, about all of this herself."

Lisa gazed at me with the strangest expression…something almost like regret. "No Cam; thank *you*. For so many things. Meeting you is the best thing that's happened for me here, I think.

Now, go get some sleep; I'm serious. This was supposed to be a self-care day, remember? Go take care of *yourself*—for a few hours, at least. That's an executive order."

❧

I woke up with the sun, as usual, and was surprised to feel so well rested. Could that have something to do with yesterday's massage? I couldn't think of any other explanation after such an awful day. My bed felt so good, though, that I stayed beneath the covers, thinking about everything.

Lisa and I had talked until well after eleven; had she even been able to leave a message for the sheriff that late? I hoped so. Clarke hadn't wasted any time coming to get my report after the visit with Sheila, and if Lisa hadn't made that call before he showed up to ask about Marie, I'd just end up betraying her trust after all.

I wondered how ticked off he'd be about my ignoring his orders, and telling Lisa. As if I'd had any other choice. I wasn't here to help them catch a bunch of vicious liars and cheats by becoming one myself. If the sheriff took that out on me, well... Marie had lived through way worse, hadn't she? And so had I sometimes.

Lisa's claim that people she knew could figure out that antidote and keep Marie alive made me feel especially hopeful. If that was true, it would make it all a lot less painful—for everyone but Derek, maybe. What a monster that man must be!

I wondered again about Lisa's mention of *opportunities*. I'd been afraid Marie's story would just make her feel even worse than I felt, since she'd sent Marie to Derek. But, no; Lisa had just proved once again that...she was Lisa Cannon! I stretched deliciously, and turned on my side. Yes, it had been an awful day—except for that massage, of course—but there'd also been way more cause for relief than I'd ever expected by the time I'd finally gotten into bed last night—and all because of Lisa.

What an amazing woman!

And today…would she be expecting me to start *being her*, somehow?

Well, whatever that turned out to mean…maybe I would just stay in bed a little longer.

Minutes later—or so it seemed—I was startled awake by someone knocking at my cabin door. I groped for my phone, and brought it up to see the time. Good grief, eight-thirty—I'd gone back to sleep! I scrambled out of bed, grabbing my robe off the floor and pulling it on as I peered down over the loft railing to see who was there. But, of course, that spot just outside my doorway was the one part of my porch hidden from view inside the house. I started down the ladder, thinking, *How Orcas Island was it to build a glass-fronted house without any concern about knowing who might be at your door?* Well, the island's worst predators were raccoons, I supposed—or they had been, anyway, till Derek and his crime wave had shown up.

"Coming!" I called as I reached the floor; the knocking stopped. I tightened my robe and went to pull the door ajar, and there was Sheriff Clarke, of course.

"Oh good," he said, without a smile. "I was afraid you might have got away already."

Was that…a strange choice of words? Or was my guilty conscience just coloring things? Had someone had finally noticed how I'd disappeared on a security video?

I looked down—as much to hide my famously bad poker face as for any other reason. "Sorry I'm not dressed, Sheriff, but…I had a very long day yesterday."

"So I've heard," he said, still not smiling. "Went right to Lisa Cannon with it—without even talking to me first?"

Oh, thank goodness! I thought. *It's just that.*

"I thought I'd made that part especially clear," he went on.

"She's called you then?" I pulled the door wider, and looked up at him. "I'm the one who asked her to."

"Yes, I know. I've just come from her place, in fact. We had a nice long chat. It seems you've once again exceeded almost every expectation I had—except for one. Which, I must admit, surprises and disappoints me, just a little."

"I see… Did Lisa tell you why I went to her first?"

"Ms. Cannon did happen to mention the promise Ms. Tolliver extracted from you. And I could hardly complain to Ms. Cannon herself about how she knew any of that in the first place, since doing so would likely have tipped her off to the fact that you're workin' for us. You didn't feel moved to tell her all about that part too for some reason, did you?"

"No, Sheriff; I did not," I said, a little surprised to find myself feeling more irritated than intimidated. "But, if Lisa told you that, then can't you see I had no other choice? Except for lying to Marie, of course—after she's been betrayed by everybody else, and left to *die* because of it—just to find out what you wanted to know? If I were the kind of person who'd do that, you should never have trusted me to start with." He cocked an eyebrow at this, but remained silent. So, naturally, I just kept digging my grave deeper. "I know Lisa Cannon pretty well by now. And I don't think I would have told her any of it if I hadn't been completely sure she'd do just what she did: turn around and call you—like *I asked* her to. But after my promise to Marie, I'm not sure I could have made myself tell you any of it either. This way, you got what you wanted without making a back-stabber out of me, or crushing Marie's trusting heart one more time before she *dies*." I crossed my arms, and jutted my chin out. "So, win, win, win, right?"

He went on staring at me. I stared right back—though, inside, I was running around with my hair on fire, shouting, *Who ARE you, and what have you done with Camille Tate!?*

Finally, a corner of his mouth crept up, just slightly. "Ms. Tate, you are a truly remarkable person." I still heard no hint of humor—or forgiveness—in his voice, but he wasn't pulling out his handcuffs either. He looked away for a moment. "As I believe

I've mentioned before, you have been an almost constant master's course for me in the art of rethinking biased assumptions; and I thank you for that—again." He turned back to me. "But I'd like to point out that you *did* have other choices. Better ones."

"Like what?" I asked, a little less, well…belligerently.

"Like just coming to me first, and saying, 'Sheriff, I cannot, in good conscience, violate my promise to Ms. Tolliver. So I'd like to do as she requested, convey her message to Lisa Cannon first, and ask Ms. Cannon to pass it all along to you.'"

"You'd have gone for that?" I asked, doubtfully.

He tilted his head. "Or, you could just have come told *me* that Tolliver was staying silent for fear of hurting Ms. Cannon, and suggested that we send Ms. Cannon to talk with her directly—which is what we're arranging for right now, in fact. Ms. Cannon will be on a boat tomorrow to go relieve Ms. Tolliver's fears of talking with us."

I could feel my cheeks growing warm, despite the crisp morning chill. "I…didn't think of that…" I looked down again, feeling foolish.

Clarke released a grumpy huff of laughter, then pushed back his hat and sighed. "Ms. Tate," he said wearily, "one of the classic hazards of my profession is that we spend so much time rubbing shoulders with the worst kinds of people. It's easy to forget that there are people like you in the world too—or see them coming in time to head off misunderstandings like this one." He shrugged. "But we don't just make up instructions like the ones I've given you for no reason. There are a million tiny ways to derail an investigation like this one. And some of my instructions are crucial to *your* safety, or the safety of others, like Ms. Cannon."

"I'm sorry," I said. "It was an awful day, and…I wasn't thinking straight by last night. But, it seems pretty clear Derek's known where Lisa was for, well, years at least, hasn't he? Letting Lisa know more about what he's done… How can that put her in any greater danger?"

Clarke's smile vanished again. "Derek Eccleston is a nasty little piece of work, all right. But he's the least of Ms. Cannon's concerns in all this, or yours, quite honestly."

"But...Marie..." I stammered. "Derek's not the guy you're after?"

Clarke shook his head. "He's never been much more than a fish hook to us, Ms. Tate. What the pike we're really angling for know—or care—about Ms. Cannon, is still unclear. Eccleston is probably in greater danger from them than she is, at this point. And it's my sincere hope that you are still entirely invisible to them; or seem too trivial, at least, to draw their attention. But keep making command decisions on the fly like you did yesterday, and that equation could change in a flash—for you or Ms. Cannon, or others you don't even know about. You hearing me now?"

So, Sheila had been telling me the truth. About that part anyway. I nodded, and just managed not to rub my arms from sheer habit, though I realized with mild surprise that nothing was tingling—anywhere—which seemed strange after such a scary warning.

"Now, if we've flogged this topic enough," Clarke said, "I would be extremely grateful for an opportunity to hear about yesterday's remarkable harvest straight from the horse's mouth." He smiled. "If you'll forgive the mangled metaphor. Would you have time for that?"

"Now?" I asked, glancing down at my robe.

"I'm happy to wait here while you dress, of course." He turned away, as if to admire the view. "But I've got too many other things to tend to, in light of your success, to arrange a substation interview at such short notice—inconspicuously, anyway. And inconspicuous is *particularly* important just now. So, here would be best, if you don't mind?"

"Well, just come in then, that's fine." I held the door open for him, and he entered, tipping his hat, while I climbed back up to the loft to change out of my robe. I did look behind me once as I climbed, belatedly realizing what an immodest choice of climbing gear the bathrobe was; but he'd taken a chair with his back to me, and sat gazing through my cabin's wall of glass.

When I was dressed, I climbed back down, offered him a cup of coffee as I got one for myself, and sat down to repeat Marie's horrible tale all over again. He listened thoughtfully, shaking his head or sighing from time to time, as any human being with a heart would have. He occasionally interrupted to ask for clarification, but otherwise said nothing.

When I was done, he just sat gazing into some middle distance, then said, "Well, that's remarkable, Ms. Tate. A truly astonishing haul." His eyes focused on me again. "Those investors she says Eccleston seemed scared of; did she mention any specific names—persons or companies? Or say anything to suggest that she might be in possession of more information about any of them?"

I shook my head.

He mirrored the gesture, smiling faintly. "Ms. Tate, you've turned out to be perhaps the most productive asset I have ever worked with. I'm going to miss you. I truly am."

"Miss me?" *Wait, what?* "Am I…going somewhere?" What *were* the penalties for CIs who disobeyed their instructions? Were Sheila and I about to become roommates?

"Oh!" He leaned back and chuckled. "No. I'm sorry. You're not *going* anywhere. But I believe your work as an informant is finished."

"Finished?" I said, caught completely by surprise. "Because of going to Lisa?"

He looked bemused. "No, ma'am. Because I believe you've brought us all we needed. If Ms. Cannon can persuade Ms. Tolliver to work with us now, I'm pretty sure she'll provide enough evidence to tie this investigation up, and move on to indictments and prosecution. You have our lasting gratitude, Ms. Tate," he said soberly. "If we should discover some further need of you, we'll let you know. But, unless you hear from us, you're free to get back to your normal life—which, from what I hear, is plenty busy without us in it."

I could not believe it. I was *done*? No more morning interrogations? No more unscheduled trips to America? "That's...fantastic!" I'd never wanted this job to start with—and even without having to *be Lisa*, I really needed the extra time until the play's run finished.

"But, one last thing, Ms. Tate," Clarke said, leaning forward. "From this moment forward, you really must *not* discuss a word of this with anyone. Not a single word. Really. I've asked Ms. Cannon to say nothing more to anyone, including you; and made it clear to her that you'd be asked to do the same—even in private." He leaned back again. "I'll be making the same request of your free-spirited friend, JoJo Brixton. You're not to discuss any of this even with him now. It's *over*, Ms. Tate—for you, at least—until this has all played out in the courts, and sentencing has come and gone—which will likely take years. And, if you're wise, not even after that. I wasn't exaggerating about caution for your own safety. You want *no one* associating you with any of this business—ever—if it can be helped. So, can I count on you, *this time*?"

"Yes," I said, careful to sound chastened. "I understand."

"Good." He stood up. "And now, I've got a million things to see to. This is where things finally start getting interesting in *our* neck of these woods." He tipped his hat to me. "Thank you again, Ms. Tate. For *everything*." Then he turned and headed for the door.

As he reached for the handle, though, he stopped and turned back to me. "And best of luck with this play of yours! I've heard very good things about it. I'm hoping to come catch a performance myself some night. It'll go wonderfully, I'm sure."

"Thank you. But, I think you're not actually supposed to wish me luck."

"I'm not?" He looked puzzled.

"No, you're apparently supposed to wish me a broken leg." Charles had explained it all to me in great detail, as gravely and eloquently as Charles explained everything.

Clarke's brows furrowed. "A *broken leg?*"

"It's some law of theater that says the unexpected will always happen, so we're supposed to *expect* something awful—so that… awful things won't happen?" I made a helpless gesture.

He gave me a skeptical look, then grinned again. "Sounds like a good rule for law enforcement too. Well then, Ms. Tate, break a few bones, and I hope the theater falls down too." He gave me a wink. "Better?"

"More than enough," I said.

"See you at the theater, then."

A few seconds later, even the crunch of his boots on the gravel path outside was gone—and I was done! Just like that! What a much better day this already was.

I'd hardly turned around to gather the coffee cups when a text dinged in. I pulled my phone out, saw Jen's name on the screen, and opened the message.

Heya—walking the puppers on Crescent Beach in about a half hour. Wanna join me? Would love the chance to talk.

I stared at the phone. *The chance to talk.* About what? That didn't sound…completely casual.

Sure! I texted back.

Great! Wear crummy pants. Tides way out. Wet muddy dog alert. :)

I sent her a winking emoji, and clicked the phone off. Of course, the crappy thing was that I wouldn't be able to say a single word to her about my awesome new demotion.

CHAPTER 14

Jen and six dogs were already on rocky Crescent Beach when I got there. She held all the leashes in one hand and waved at me across the road after I parked.

I joined her, smiling at the ridiculous picture they made. "I guess I imagined them better...coordinated."

"Huh?"

"In size." I pointed at the tiny terrier trotting hard to keep up with a big loping shepherd of some kind. "That little guy's gonna get twice as much exercise as everyone else."

She laughed. "A dog is a dog. Anyway, these are from four different owners. Those two goobers are owned by a woman out in Olga," she pointed to nearly matching border collies, "and Rufus and Roger are littermates." Hearing their names, two very pretty Goldens stopped and smiled up at her. "Yes, yes, you are very good dogs!" She patted their heads and got everyone moving again.

I fell into step beside her. "You do a good job keeping their leashes all straight," I said, after a minute.

"Thanks! It didn't take them long to realize I'm the alpha." She glanced over at me; we both chuckled. "Dogs just want to know who's boss. Then they all fall into line."

"You make a very good alpha," I assured her.

"Don't I know it. Do you want to hold a leash or two?"

I shook my head. I mean, I love dogs, but I was unable to muster much enthusiasm…my head was still too full of everything I wished I could tell Jen. All these giant bottled up secrets made me feel awkward. And lonely.

We walked in silence for a minute. "So," she said, "seen Kip lately?"

Now why was she asking me *that*? "*This* is what you wanted to talk about?"

"Just answer my question."

"No, I haven't," I said, after probably too long a pause. The way this topic kept just…erupting was beginning to freak me out. Like people were *purposely* not listening to me.

My mood sank even lower.

"So…why do you want to talk about that?"

Jen looked over at me, oddly. "Why *don't* you want to talk about that?"

What the…?

We just looked at each other for a moment, then Jen shrugged. "So, how's the play going?"

"It's going great," I said, still trying to figure her out. I turned to look at the beach ahead of us. "We have tech rehearsals next week; I'm not really looking forward to that as much, though."

"What are tech rehearsals?"

"Lights and sound cues, and effects; stuff like that. From what I've heard, it's just hours of standing around saying cue lines while they adjust things."

"Oh. Well…that doesn't sound so fun."

"But it really is going great, in general," I said, trying to sound more enthusiastic.

"That's what I've heard! I can't wait for opening night—unless you're gonna let me come to the dress rehearsal?"

"Oh, um, sure," I said. "If you want. But if you come on opening night, there's a reception."

"I want to come to both."

"Okay." I did try to sound excited, but I couldn't shake the feeling that there was some agenda I was missing here. *Would love the chance to talk.* So here we were; and she just seemed to be... asking random questions? Was she stalling for time? Just how serious was this thing she wanted to talk about?

A breeze picked up, blowing in the fresh-yet-briny smell of the sea water beside us. The tide was low indeed; we had a lot of damp beach at our disposal. And here we were, trudging along in silence, watching all the wagging tails ahead of us—waiting for...what?

"Did JoJo ever guess what was in my cocktail?" Jen asked.

I had to think for a moment to even remember what she was talking about. "I don't know."

She gave me a brief glance and pursed her lips. "Huh. Well, I heard Colin has a new girlfriend."

"Yeah, I met her on the ferry the other day," I said. "She seemed really nice, actually."

"And you didn't *tell* me that?" She stopped walking. "You didn't even *call* me?" I stopped too and turned to her; she clicked at the dogs and they all halted, waiting for their alpha's next command. But she was looking at me, and she seemed...sad? Hurt?

"What...?" I asked. "What's going on? What did you want to talk about—really?"

She looked as confused as I felt now. "I didn't want to talk about any *thing*. I just wanted to *talk*." She put a hand on my arm, looking concerned. "Cam, are you okay?"

I shook my head, and put my hand over hers and gave it a squeeze. "Nope."

"Oh, I knew it," she said. "I heard they called you in for questioning again."

"Yep." And there was nothing I could tell her about *that*, either.

"You'd tell me if you were in serious trouble, right? 'Cause...

people are starting to wonder…"

I stifled an unhappy laugh. That had been sort of the plan, after all: let people think I was a suspect, so they wouldn't wonder if I was an informant. Had the plan worked too well? "They've asked me a lot of questions," I told her, as honestly as I could manage. "I have zero answers, but they've made it really clear I'm not allowed to talk to anyone about it. *Anyone*." I held her gaze. "I'm sorry."

She shook her head. "I'm sorry too, and I don't mean to pry. It's just…" She stopped, now looking at the dogs, all still waiting expectantly. "We used to talk about *everything*, Cam."

She was right. And then I got it.

Who would have thought that Jen Darling, with her finger on the pulse of everything and everyone on this island, would feel left behind by me? But that had to be it. She was no fool. She knew I was holding secrets—but had no way of knowing how badly I wanted to tell her everything. About my trip to see Sheila, and what I knew about Marie, and how worried I was about Lisa. I wanted to tell her every scrap of it!

"I'm sorry I've been scarce," I said. "There's just—so many things going on lately. You know. All this stuff with the investigation, and then the play, Lisa—everything. It's overwhelming. But I'm not trying to push you away, Jen. You'll *always* be my bestie—just in case that isn't clear."

She smiled at me. "And you're mine, hon. I know that. I do. Come on—let's walk. And talk. Because there are lots of other things to talk about besides the crazy stuff that's been going on this year. Right?"

"Right." We started up again, to the dogs' great relief and delight. Jen chattered while we walked, and I relaxed a little, just listening. There was gossip about who'd been into the Barnacle together, and some random anecdotes about the people she walked dogs for, and a wild weekend of college students at the B&B that had the exhausted owners ready to throw up their hands and sell.

I nodded and smiled, soothed by the normalcy of it all.

"Oh!" she said a minute later. "Have you heard the latest about the ex-boyfriend?"

For just a minute, I thought that she'd had some boyfriend I hadn't known about. And then I realized what she was asking. "Kevin?"

"Yeah." She laughed. "Oh, that nutjob."

"What now? I haven't heard anything. I told you, I'm drowning in rehearsals and all the rest of it. You're my only source of gossip anymore. So—spill."

"Oh, this is rich. Okay, so apparently the market *did* get tired of having his Intruder squatting in their parking lot, siphoning off their deli sales, and sending his customers off to their bathrooms. So the store manager went out to make him go…and he asked her out!"

I rolled my eyes. "Of course he did."

"She told him no, of course. So he drove off in a huff—which is what she wanted anyway, so that all worked out. But it goes on!" Jen's face was all wicked amusement. "Then he apparently drove to the freakin' top of Mount Constitution and parked *there*."

"You're not serious."

"I'm dead serious. He propped open his little side door and put out his sign and started selling sandwiches right there in front of the gift shop—in a state park! Well it didn't take long for a park ranger to come tell him, *No way, dude*. And you'll never guess what he did then."

I shook my head.

"He came on to the park ranger! She was a little weirded out by it, but she sent him packing."

"Wow, desperate much?"

"And then!"

I stopped again and turned to her. "There can't be *more!*"

"I haven't even gotten to the best part!"

"Okay…"

"He lumbered that big tub down to the ferry landing, and took up like eight parking spots in that lot just above the hotel. Propped open his window and…"

"No!" I both did and didn't want to hear where this was going.

"And of course one of the ferry workers called the sheriff's department…"

"*No.*"

"And who should answer the call but Deputy Sherman…"

"No! He did *not* come on to *Larissa Sherman*?!"

"He most certainly did! And apparently they're getting married." She couldn't even get the sentence out before snorting with laughter, and now I was laughing too. "Kidding! But, oh Cam, what is the *matter* with that guy?"

"I wish I knew. But these overtures seem kind of strategic, don't they?"

"Yes, you're right, these are definitely parking-based overtures."

"How romantic. I wonder where he'll turn up next? Is he going to park in the senior center driveway and try to pick Paige Berry up?"

Jen snorted again. "Good point, actually—that's a really long driveway. And if Paige turns him down, there are lots of other ladies there who don't drive anymore, and would love to be chauffeured around in his great big *love*mobile!"

I thought about the group of theater boosters… "I don't think so. Those women would have *him* for lunch." I wiped my eyes. "Oh Jen. I've missed this so much."

Jen smiled. "Same here. I miss our Trixie Belden days."

"So do I. I miss *you* so dang much."

"Then stop being so busy and *call* me, Cam. Okay, I know our girl detective days are over," she had no idea *how* over now, not that I could tell her, "but we'll get drinks, or just hang out, or maybe some other bunch of weird stuff will start happening and we can snoop into that."

"Okay. I'll be around more. I promise."

"Good." She pulled her phone out of her pocket and glanced at it. "Anyway, I gotta wrap this up and get off to the next gig. Thanks for meeting me."

"Of course." I gave her a wry smile. "Serene island life, eh?"

"You know it, hon." We shared a hug before we parted, which involved a lot of mutual relief—and leashes, and a few happy, jumping dogs.

☙

And, suddenly, it was just a week before opening night! How had *that* happened? I was busier than ever with a swarm of endless rehearsals and play-related errands that somehow only I could handle. Right now, for instance, I was walking around Eastsound to make sure all the businesses selling our tickets still had enough stock.

Because, of course, the residents of Orcas Island wanted nice, physical tickets, not just scan-codes on their smartphones.

I didn't mind. It was a lovely day, and so much fun to chat with everyone, and see how *well* sales were going!

I pushed open the door to Porter's wine shop with a big grin on my face, but was disappointed to see a stranger behind the counter.

"Can I help you find something?" the young man asked.

"Oh, I…no…is Porter here?"

He offered me the patient smile of someone who's been asked the same question too many times. "He's not, but I'd be happy to help with anything."

"Thanks," I said, smiling back at him, "but I'm not here to buy wine. My name's Camille Tate, and I've come to check on your supply of tickets for *Salon Confes*—uh, *Confidential*." I still stumbled over the name; I'd called it *Salon Confessional* for all the months when I was writing it, but Lisa had decided *Confidential* sounded more intriguing.

His smile widened. "Oh yeah! We do need more, especially for opening night." Then he looked hard at me. "Did you say you're Camille Tate?"

I nodded.

"The star? And the playwright!"

"Yes."

"Wow!" he said, looking star-struck. "Right here in our shop!"

I managed to get him back to how many more tickets they needed for which dates—though I could only give him a few for opening night. "Sorry," I told him. "That's a popular one."

"Everyone loves opening night."

At this rate, we'd have to break out every single chair in the venue. I'd been feeling okay, but now *that* freaked me out.

By the time I left the wine shop, after autographing the play's poster for the nice fellow, I decided I'd give the rest of my supply to Darvill's bookstore. They were one of my favorite places in town, and had been selling more tickets than any other business.

I smiled at people I passed on my way there, surprised at how many of them I recognized. Was I…finally fitting in here? I would never be Jen, of course, or Paige Berry—who'd lived here for decades, and was eccentric as only true islanders can be. Paige and I had had a—well, not a clash exactly, but a *disagreement*, I guess, about the intermission refreshments. I'd had to convince her that goat cheese kale chip cookies were *not* the same thing as white chocolate macadamia nut, and insist that she give the crowd what they wanted, not what she thought they needed. She'd huffed a little in disapproval, of course, and wandered off muttering about dealing with divas. But later that day she'd brought me some *very* delicious cookies to taste—with zero kale content. That I could detect, anyway.

And that was just one of the many, many things I'd handled in recent weeks. Part of me still couldn't believe the complexity of all this—how much sweat and suffering, how much work, how many *people* were involved in staging a simple little play. In just a week, it would all be real! And then, a few short weeks later…

it would all be over.

Lisa had said this would be good for me—and she'd been right. Hardly anything frightened me anymore. I hadn't chameleoned since that time with Sheila, or even tingled—much. I was starting to feel...well, confident. In charge.

Capable.

I hadn't heard from anyone in law enforcement since Clarke's last visit a few weeks ago; and, honestly, I didn't miss them—though I was still bothered now and then by a nagging uncertainty about whether I'd really been set free for succeeding, or fired for breaking the rules.

I also wondered sometimes whether Marie was working with the authorities now, and still at the hospital, or in protective custody somewhere—as well as whether there'd been any progress on getting her antidote back. I hadn't been able to ask Lisa about any of this, obviously. She seemed more or less her same old self still, and had said nothing else about me having to *be her*—which I was *very* thankful for. It did bug me some to see JoJo almost every day and not be able to talk about any of this, or even ask if he'd been let go too.

I walked up to Darvill's entrance and stepped inside, ready to greet my friends behind the counter; but stopped in my tracks. A *very familiar* figure was just concluding a purchase there.

Kevin? In a bookstore? All he ever read was cookbooks—and only so he could complain about how incompetent other chefs were, or brag about how much better his book would be when he finally got a publishing deal (oh and got around to actually writing a book).

He finished his purchase and turned around. A moment of surprise crossed his face, and then he grinned. "Well, look who it is!" He held up—*no I am not seeing this*—a ticket to my play!

"What are you *doing*?" I blurted.

"What does it look like?" he asked, still grinning. "Buying a ticket to my girlfriend's play!"

"Your girlfriend? You've finally found someone who'll *date you* here?" In my amazement, I hadn't fully processed his remark.

His grin faltered. "Don't be that way, Cam. I know we've had our little misunderstandings, but you know as well as I do that we're still—"

No, wait! "You mean *me?*" I cut in. "*Seriously?* I left you the night I left Seattle!"

He scowled at me now. "Well, this is not the best place to have this conversation, maybe?"

Oh, brother. I really, really did not want Kevin coming to my play. Just his being there would ruin it, and he knew it. Probably the only reason he wanted to come. How could I get that ticket away from him? "Okay. Let's have it outside, then."

"Sure. If you really want to!" He looked hopeful, the idiot.

I turned and stomped out the door, not even checking to see if he was following. But he was.

On the sidewalk, I turned and faced him, hands on my hips. "Since when do you go to plays?"

"Since when were you *in* plays?"

Oh no you don't. "It's *my* play, Kevin. I wrote it. I'm in it. And you have no right to go to it."

"It's a public event." He gave me that look. The look of gentle patient weariness worn by every martyred man who ever had to put up with an *irrational* woman. "And you're selling tickets to the public—which is me. So what's the problem, Cam?"

I walked right up and got in his face—which actually made him flinch! Home team scores! "The *problem*, Kevin, is that I came all the way up here to live *my* life away from *you*—and yet here you are again, somehow, sticking your giant ego, in that giant *Intruder*—because of course you would drive something called an *Intruder!*—who even names an RV that? But of course you homed right in on it! That's *so you!*"

"What the...what?" he stammered, taking a half-step back. But I could see his anger growing now: his lovely green eyes narrowed, and his luscious lips thinned. "This is about my *RV* now? What on earth has gotten into you?"

"A spine has gotten into me, that's what!" I shouted. "And no, this isn't about your stupid Intruder, you moron."

He crossed his arms and narrowed his eyes. "I'm worried about you, Cam. You're not yourself. You've changed; you don't seem... well."

Oh, that did it. I'd had more than enough of this from him to last forever. "I'm just *fine*. It's you! You *followed* me here and you won't go away because *you* weren't done with me yet but guess what? I'm done with you. I want you out of *my* life—and *my* play—and *my* circle of friends. I came here to get away from you. So, *leave!*"

He just gaped at me, like he was talking to someone he'd never met before. Which he was, I realized. He absolutely was. The realization filled me with fierce delight. But then he spoke again. "I only stayed here because I was worried about you, after those cops came around."

"After...what cops?"

"You know what cops," he growled. "I guess someone told them about us. They came and asked me how well we knew each other—which is *pretty well*, in case you've really forgotten—and said you were tangled up in some kind of investigation. They wanted to know if I thought you were..." He caught himself. "I just answered their questions."

Oh...WOW! "It was *you!*" *Kevin* had told them I was unstable—because of course he had!

"No, it was *you!*" he said, looking caught between embarrassment and anger. "They asked me who you were, and I told them the truth. What else was I supposed to do?"

I clamped my mouth shut for a minute—and breathed. Because the last thing I wanted was to blow up now, and let him claim I'd proved his point. When I had myself under control, I spoke slowly, so it would be perfectly clear. "I want you off this island, Kevin."

"Don't you tell me what to do." The anger was starting to slip out around the edges of his concerned act. "This isn't *your* island."

"Well it's sure more mine than yours, Mr. Intruder." I dug into my purse and pulled out a twenty. "I don't want you in the audience at my play. So give me that ticket." I thrust the bill at his face.

He slapped it away, and it fluttered off down the sidewalk on the breeze. *"Are you losing your mind?"* he snapped.

"I'm fine, Kevin. *I'm* just *fine.*"

He shook his head. "No you're not. You need *help*. These delusions you have... You've needed help for a long time."

Months, no, *years* of anger flared up inside me. And even self-absorbed Kevin must have noticed, because his jaw clenched, and he took an abrupt step toward me.

I backed up, and my skin tingled... *Oh no.* I clenched reflexively to stifle the chameleoning, but Kevin stepped into me again, his eyes cold with anger. My mind lurched back to our confrontation on the night I'd fled Seattle, six months and a lifetime ago. He shoved his face at mine, and hissed, "You belong in an *asylum!*"

And at that moment, a door slid open in my mind. I stepped through it, as if I were stepping onto stage, and this was just a play. *You called me* crazy—*for trusting you with the truth.* Just weeks ago, I had vanished in a prison visiting room filled with people, and video cameras pointed right at me. And nothing had happened. So why not here? *You think I'm* crazy, *Kevin?*

I let it happen. I just blinked out of existence, right in front of him.

As my gift's grip froze me in place, I felt a brief wave of self-doubt—who else was out here on the sidewalk? How stupid had this been? But...I didn't...really care somehow. To my dawning amazement, I didn't feel afraid at all. I was seeing myself from some new place in my brain, where I had control of things like fear…and stage fright and anxiety. It was the most wonderful feeling! And the frozen grip of my strange gift just *dissolved!*

I shrugged out of the tingling and pain as if I was stepping out of a dress, and I was visible again. My anger washed away with the rest of it; now I felt only power. I blinked up at Kevin, who stared at me in shock.

"What… What the hell did you…" he stammered.

I gave him a smile. "What's wrong, Kevin?"

"What did you just… How…" he stammered, taking a step back, looking more and more frightened. "What kind of trick was *that?*"

"Trick?" I purred, dripping with concern. "I have no idea what you mean." My smile widened. "Are you okay? You're acting a little…*crazy*. Are you *crazy*, Kevin?"

He stumbled backward, looking horrified, then turned and bolted out into the street. Fortunately for him, there wasn't any traffic on Eastsound's main drag just then. He headed at a dead run for his Intruder, parked half a block away.

"Should I get someone to *help* you?" I called after him, thoroughly enjoying myself. "You look like you need some *help!*"

At the RV, he jammed his hand into a pocket and yanked out his keys. The theater ticket came out with them and fluttered to the ground. If he noticed, he didn't care. He just fumbled at the lock, yanked the Intruder's door open, and leapt inside. A moment later, the engine roared to life, and the monstrous vehicle lurched squealing into the street, tearing off toward the west exit from town, toward Orcas Road—and, with any luck, the ferry landing.

I hope Sherman doesn't pull him over for speeding, I thought. If I really had scared him off my island, I didn't want anything standing in his way.

Not even a deputy sheriff in purple Fluevogs.

I glanced around then, wondering if anybody else was gaping at me. But there was almost no one around, and none of those

I saw seemed like they'd noticed anything. Because, that's how it worked, apparently. People didn't notice…unless…I wanted them to?

ᏨᎧ

I bowed again, feeling giddy. Applause rang in my ears.

Okay, only a dozen people were at the dress rehearsal, but they'd given us a standing ovation; and the reviewer for the *Island Times* had popped to his feet with the rest of them, clapping and cheering!

I couldn't help grinning, first with a bit of restraint, then as if my face would break from it. I'd never, in all my life, felt anything like this.

Jen was there; and Paige Berry, who had laughed and stomped and cheered, clearly not offended by anything in Charlotte Winkelton's character—or even by our cookie debate. There were two men I didn't recognize, one of whom checked his watch before they made for the door. Were they mainland reviewers? Maybe we'd even get some Seattle business!

Oh, this was the *best!*

We trailed off the stage, thanking the high school kids who served as our invaluable stage crew, and congratulating each other on our way to the dressing rooms. "That was perfect!" Glory said. "You're a natural, Cam."

I beamed back at her, enjoying the contrast between her old-lady makeup and her youth. "You too! You inhabit Charlotte so completely!"

"Well, she's such a wonderful character to inhabit, thanks to you!"

Halfway down the hallway, Lisa stood, seeming preoccupied. But she gave me a quick smile as I approached. "There you are. Still mad at me for making you act?"

I laughed. "No. I am very, very not mad at you, Lisa."

"Hm." She was smiling, but she still seemed only half there.

"Lisa? Is something wrong?"

She pressed her lips together in a tight line. "Not with you, Cam. I am just so proud of you."

I wanted to pull her into a hug, but that would get stage makeup on her elegant black sweater.

In the dressing room, I let myself slip back into a happy trance, hardly aware of taking off all that makeup or putting on my normal clothes.

Back out in the now largely deserted hallway, I saw JoJo a ways off talking quietly to Lisa. They both looked...tense. When Lisa slipped away, he turned, saw me and immediately brightened. "Camarooni! You were *fabulous* tonight!" He came and hugged me.

"Thanks! You too!"

"Who knew I could play a clueless neuter with such veracity!" We both laughed. "I'm too pumped to go home. You want to go get 'coffee' somewhere?"

"Sure. I don't know if I can ever sleep again anyway."

"Same. I'll drive."

He surprised me by parking in front of the White Horse Pub, rather than going on to the Barnacle. At my questioning glance, he shrugged. "I hate ruts."

Since when was the Barnacle a *rut*?

We found a quiet table in the corner and were quickly served. Even at night, our view of the huge saltwater sound that filled the center of our horseshoe-shaped island was spectacular through the pub's wall of picture windows.

"A toast to you, Camikins. To your play, and your courage, and your generally sweet self." We lifted our drinks, red wine for me, a gin-and-tonic for him. "I mean it," he said, after we'd sipped. "You were incredible. I would never have known you hadn't been acting all your life."

I gave a small snort. Because I *had*, of course; just not like he meant. Though, ironically, maybe less so these days?

"Which would be amazing enough," he went on, after a generous quaff of his drink, "except that you also wrote the play! You're a multi-talented woman."

I was suppressing the urge to squirm, but also, well, kind of proud of myself. "JoJo, seriously, that's… Okay, thank you." I could do this. If vanishing didn't scare me so much anymore, why should praise? "Thank you very much."

He cocked his head and looked at me. "Very good," he murmured. "You're not deflecting my compliments. You've really changed."

I shrugged. "I've been…working on it."

"Working!" he said theatrically. "How dreary." He gave me an indulgent smile, then gazed thoughtfully down at his drink. "I… don't think I want to play this part anymore."

"Seriously?" I gasped. "JoJo, tomorrow's opening night! You can't—I know you hate your character, but it's *way* too late to find someone else, or even rewrite—"

He laughed softly. "No, Cam, sorry. I don't mean the play. I'll see stodgy, boring Martin all the way through to his stodgy, boring end. I'm talking about…" He spread his arms and gestured at—everything? "I need to leave."

"Leave what?"

"Me. *This* me. Here. This life." He glanced around the room. Most of the tables were empty; a baseball game played on the TV over the bar, the sound muted. "That's why I brought us here, honestly. So there'd be no one to perform for."

"Well, except me," I pointed out.

He smiled softly. "I don't have to perform for you, Cam. I've been realizing that, for a while now. That's partly what made me see how much I want…something better." He gave me a meaningful look. "When all of *this* is finally done, at least."

This…? Meaning the play? The investigation? They'd all be wrapping up soon, I guessed, which would free him from his coerced roles as both Martin and an informant. But…with all that over anyway, couldn't he just... "Well, for how long? Are you coming back? Ever?"

"Details, details." He shrugged. "I'm just ready for a change, Cam." He took a hearty sip and set his glass down. "You've shown me it's possible, after all." Then he gave me a teasing smile. "And anything you can do, darling, I can do better, right?"

"So, where will you go? Who do you want to be instead of JoJo Brixton, international thief of hearts?"

He blinked. "I don't know." He turned to gaze out at the moonlit view—or maybe at his own reflection in the window. "That's the problem, isn't it? He's been so easy, that JoJo. Swimming through life on a warm current of sleazy charm and booze and money." He turned back to me. "If I stay here, or any familiar place, I'll just keep diving back in. You know?"

"I do know. Sometimes you have to shake up everything." I'd come here for the same reason, hadn't I? But still, I was crushed at the thought of losing him.

"I feel like doing...something creative. I mean, *you* did, so how hard could it really be?"

"It might be nice if you didn't insult me every time you complimented me. Just a thought."

"Oh, you know you love it." He winked. Same old JoJo. "I think I want to travel, but not the way I've done it before."

"What way was that?"

"Traveling while rich." He gave me a rueful smile. "You leave everything behind that way except your whole stupid world." Then he winced. "You can slap me anytime. I know how obnoxious it is when rich people complain about their money."

"He says to the woman who's driving a Porsche," I countered with a smile.

"Which she is quick to inform everyone that she does not own," he parried.

I nodded. "So that's all you know? Somewhere far away, doing something creative—as if you weren't rich?"

He rolled his eyes. "I'll figure it out. The money will buy me enough time to get things sorted out, at least."

"Or you could *really* jump ship and just leave the money behind right now," I said, giving him a *Who knows?* shrug. "See what happens on its own once the money isn't there. I came here with nothing, you know. I had to take a job caretaking for your mother just to buy food."

He gave a dramatic shudder. "Oh that I should *ever* have to stoop so low…" But then he grew serious again. "I'll think about it, though. Sometimes poor people say smart things."

"More high praise. Watch me blush."

He wagged his head apologetically.

"Seriously, try it. See what happens."

"I just might." We sipped in silence for another few minutes. When he spoke again, he sounded even more thoughtful. "Maybe it's not such a bad thing that my past caught up with me. I might have gone on like I was forever, you know. Money…insulates people; makes them feel invincible. Lisa warned me about that—more than once. Kept telling me everything has a cost, and everyone has to pay, eventually. I should have listened to her."

"She does seem to end up being right about things." I thought about how glad I was she'd won our argument about me acting.

"I'm really going to miss her," JoJo said quietly.

"Is that…what you two were talking about, after the rehearsal? You leaving?"

He looked up at me, serious and fond. "The *old* JoJo would just have answered that question, wouldn't he? Without thinking twice."

So…was that a no? What *had* they been discussing then? Had I caught JoJo disregarding Clarke's instructions again? "Well," I said, finishing my wine, "I'll miss *you*. This sincere and thoughtful you, I mean; though I absolutely adore the other you, too."

"Don't worry," he said sadly. "He'll always be there, like a comfortable suit of clothes, ready to be slipped on at any time. Probably nothing I can do about *that*."

"Good. Because as much as I like this JoJo, I love that JoJo."

"Everyone loves that JoJo. Everyone but me." He got out his limitless credit card, and signaled for the check.

CHAPTER 15

The audience was a murmuring mass of dark shapes. The stage was beautifully lit, and a perfectly realized salon had magically risen up from that bunch of folding furniture and tape marks on the floor—miraculously on time, after all those stupid meetings with Roland Markus, which was all beside the point now because—

It was *opening night!*

I stood listening from the wings, in my costume and makeup, as the audience settled into their seats. My parents! My Seattle friends! And all my island friends too, of course. Paige Berry had even found me in the dressing room to say that *Kip* was here—which surprised me, considering all our awkwardness these days. But I'd just smiled, and told her, "That's nice," wanting nothing to distract me from enjoying tonight. Now, though, I was nearly breathless with nerves and anticipation…

I felt a gentle hand on my arm, and turned to find JoJo all done up as Martin.

"Oh good," I said, "you haven't run away yet."

He indulged me with a smile. "I told you, Camikins, I'm not going anywhere till I've put Martin to bed. Because *someone* has to put him to bed."

I patted his hand. "Thank you… But I still wish you weren't going anywhere at all."

"Oh, don't worry; I'll be back to visit you. Lots."

I gave him a skeptical look.

"I swear it!" he protested. "You'll hardly be able to get rid of me. Of course, I'll be living poor by then, so I'll have to sleep on the floor in your tiny cabin; and I'll snore so loud you can't sleep, and clutter the place up with empty bottles of wine that you'll have paid for, and I'll invite all my poor and tasteless new friends over to eat up all your eggs, and maybe even your cat food, because I won't be able to afford pâté anymore. And then we'll probably use up your antacid supply too, and you'll wish you'd never even—"

My eyes widened as the house lights began to fade. "JoJo! We're starting!"

"Oops!" he whispered. "Where was the call to places?"

"And you're *over here!* Your entrance is over—"

"I know!" He darted off as total darkness covered everything.

Seconds later, the stage lights began fading up for scene one. They were almost to full strength when I heard a loud *BANG* and JoJo's exclamation, "OUCH! *Crap!*"—as the set's entire back wall lurched forward and waffled like we were having an earthquake. I stared in wide-eyed horror as props fell from the counters and clattered across the stage. A hanging product shelf plunged to the floor, sending empty prop bottles of conditioner and shampoo bouncing in all directions. Kristoff's broom fell over with a loud *smack!*, and a prop trash can rolled loudly toward the audience.

Then the stage lights faded back down, leaving everything in darkness again.

Ladies and gentlemen, thank you for coming to our play, I thought in miserable disbelief. What were we supposed to do now? Someone touched my shoulder in the dark, and I nearly shrieked, spinning around to find Charles this time, in his Kristoff drag, leaning away in the ghostly glow of backstage safety lights with both hands raised to reassure me.

"Sorry!" he whispered. "Didn't mean to scare you."

"What just happened?" I hissed, listening to the audience's growing murmur of confusion.

"I think JoJo tripped over one of the support struts holding up the set flats. I just saw him running behind them along the back edge of the stage, though I have no idea what he was doing up there."

"We were talking—here," I moaned, "and didn't hear them call places."

"I didn't hear places called either. Lisa may have forgotten in all the first-night chaos."

Lisa? *Forgotten?* That seemed unlikely. "Or maybe we were all just not paying attention."

"Well…the gods of theater are clearly giving you an extra special welcome," Charles said, as if it were nothing but a funny lark. "You must really matter to them."

I turned to peer back out at the darkened stage, where I could hear, and sort of see, black-clad stage crew scurrying around after fallen props and re-dressing the set. Whispers and quiet laughter were growing louder in the audience. What a *disaster!* "Where is *Lisa?*" I asked.

Charles shrugged. "Maybe in the tech booth; I don't know. She's dealing with this, somewhere, I'm sure." He patted me on the shoulder. "Cam, just take a few breaths, and let this go. We'll start again in a minute or two, and this will just be everybody's favorite story about the whole production. Trust me on that."

I drew a shuddering breath. "If you say so."

"I do. And FYI, nothing makes for a better performance than a big surge of adrenaline right at the start. That's what opening nights are *always* about. Now, find your happy place—and get ready to go out there and knock them dead."

"Okay, okay. Thanks," I sighed, realizing that there was a giant difference between performing for twelve people—most of them good friends—at a dress rehearsal, and a packed opening night house full of strangers! All my confidence from last night was gone.

I kept taking deep breaths, and mentally rehearsing my lines, until the lights began to rise again. Then, after one more even deeper breath, I stooped to get Felicia's stack of packages and mail—we'd cut the rigged umbrella weeks ago—and tucked them under an arm. Then I pulled my "salon keys" out of a pocket with my other hand, and stepped out into the wash of blue light behind the set's main door—in sight, now, of a giant audience I could barely see. As I jingled the keys for effect, and started to mime unlocking the door, my whole brain slid into autopilot.

There were benefits to functioning in a state of shock, which is absolutely where I was for those first few minutes onstage. It narrowed my focus to a little space around me, my fellow actors, and the lines we had rehearsed almost to tears of boredom. I had no other thoughts at all, or even any real feelings. The audience had—well, not exactly vanished; I still sensed them there—but they were surprisingly well hidden by the darkness they sat in; and I had no brain left to think about them anyway. I was focused, fiercely, on trying to get each line and movement out on time, pitched just as we had practiced them. This, I would realize later, was why we had rehearsed and rehearsed until each of us could do my whole play in our sleep—because that's exactly what I was doing now. And…to my slowly increasing relief, it seemed to work!

By the end of scene one, I was starting to inhabit Felicia more consciously, and even to notice the audience more. They were certainly out there, gasping at one moment, tittering at another, and even laughing out loud sometimes—right when they were supposed to! In fact, it all seemed to be going perfectly—except for that earthquake at the beginning, which I was ignoring now that things were clearly going so well again. I was beginning to believe that *maybe* this was going to work out after all.

When the lights went down, the stage crew scurried through their tasks updating the set, and then we moved carefully through the gloom to our new places. A minute later, the lights came back up for scene two. We were all on our proper marks this time. And nobody tripped over anything as Hal entered in the first of his "tracks" roles, playing the attorney for the deceased owner's family. He was wonderfully stuffy and officious in his fussy suit and fake mustache as he informed us all that the new owner might come by to look at the building in the next few days, but that he'd recommended selling it, so we should start looking for other jobs. Kristoff overreacted as hilariously as ever, and the audience was totally lapping us up!

When Hal's "lawyer" left the stage, Felicia, Martin and Kristoff huddled to process his doomsday message while Hal did a rapid costume change in the wings, and reentered in the next of his tracks roles, as the elderly matron Jeanette.

But I must not have been the only one fighting opening night jitters, because, in their rush and the backstage gloom, Hal and his costume assistant had forgotten one very important detail.

When he sashayed back onstage as an elegantly dressed older woman—still wearing the lawyer's *mustache*—the audience roared louder than ever. I almost threw a hand across my own mouth to stop a bark of laughter.

Charles, always a fast thinker, flounced Kristoff right up to Jeanette, ripped her mustache off in a huff, and held it up between them. "I don't know who convinced you to wear *this*, madam. But as a *fashion professional*, I am *compelled* to inform you that it is *not* a *good look*—especially on *mature* women!" He tossed the mustache over his shoulder as the audience laughed even harder. "Not since the sixties, anyway," he added dryly. "Whoever convinced you *otherwise* should be *reported* to the fashion *police*."

Jeanette donned a horrified expression, and brought a hand to her cheek in distress as another wave of laughter passed—while I bit both lips in my continuing effort to keep from laughing too.

JoJo looked like someone struggling not to pee. We were both working so hard to control ourselves, that, for a minute, neither of us could speak; so Charles went on covering for us by flouncing over to get his broom and dustpan, then coming back to very officiously sweep up the discarded mustache, glaring daggers at Felicia the whole time. The audience was almost falling out of their chairs by now—probably thinking I'd written it this way on purpose. The man really was a genius. He went to tilt the dustpan into a salon trash can—still glaring at Felicia—then turned back to Jeanette, and said, "Fear not, dear lady. I believe we can remedy your *fashion debacle*—*if* you have an *appointment?*"

"Oh…dear," said Jeanette. "When I called, you told me there was nothing till later this week, but it's an *emergency*. Do you hear me?" Hal reached up to touch his well-coiffed wig. "An absolute emergency!"

"*Clearly!*" Kristoff drawled. "Well, we've already given you a shave; might as well toss in a haircut too. This way, please." He led her to my salon chair as a last ripple of laughter faded.

By then, JoJo and I were able to go on. Our planned dialogue resumed, and before long, it began feeling almost as if we knew what we were doing again.

Which was a good thing, because in scene three, just after Rebecca left the stage as the self-important businessman, "Trent," she came back on as the twin sisters "Jill" and "Jenny." This was the most demanding bit of business in the show, and we'd worked hard on it in rehearsal, tweaking the original lines and some of the staging to make it work.

Rebecca entered the salon dressed as Jenny, wearing a fuchsia-colored hat and jacket.

"Jenny, darling!" Kristoff cried. "What a stunning ensemble! But where's your lovely twin?"

"Oh, just locking up the car," said Jenny, breezily. "She'll be along any minute."

"Well, let's get you started then." Kristoff said. "It's a circus here today!"

He led Jenny to Martin's chair, where she started to sit down, but popped right back up again. "Oh! Could I use your restroom first?"

"Sure," said Martin, pointing to the set's stage-right exit. "Right back there. If it's got a toilet, you're in the restroom. If not, it's the storage room; don't use that one, please."

"That's where he *sleeps*," Felicia told Jenny, clearly ribbing Martin.

Jenny gave them a puzzled look, and headed off stage-right.

While Martin, Kristoff, and I talked about why neither the old matron nor the twins could possibly be the new owners, Jenny was offstage changing her coat and hat before running around behind the stage platform—*not* up behind the scenery flats like JoJo had, of course, but safely down on the barn floor—to come up the stage-left stairs again as her own twin sister.

Our hushed conversation onstage was interrupted by Jill's entrance wearing the very same outfit as Jenny, but with a yellow coat and hat.

"Jill, darling!" Kristoff gushed. "What a fabulous outfit—it's so *you!*"

Jill gave him a puzzled look just like the one her sister had given Martin and me, and looked around the room. "Where's Jenny? I thought she'd be here already."

"She's in the restroom," Martin said.

"Oh no!" Jill exclaimed. "*I* need to use the restroom! And she always hogs it for hours at home! I'd better go pry her out of there before she gets too settled. Where is it?"

Martin pointed again. "Back there. If you don't see Jenny, you're in the storage room."

Jill flounced through the stage-right exit just as her sister had.

While the audience heard Jill bang on the door, loudly ordering her sister to get on with it, Rebecca was actually exchanging her yellow coat and hat for the fuchsia ones, while Martin and

Kristoff talked onstage about how much more backed up things would get if *someone's* appointment didn't actually start soon. They were supposed to be interrupted by the sound of Rebecca yelling something rude at her sister, then reentering the stage—in fuchsia—as Jenny. But as the guys ran out of dialogue…nothing happened.

The three of us looked at each other.

"You don't think they're…in there together, do you?" JoJo ad-libbed suggestively.

"Well, there's only one toilet," Kristoff replied with raised brows. "Is this some kind of twin thing I haven't heard about?" There was a titter here and there, but the audience seemed awfully quiet now.

"Felicia, dear?" called one of the twins from offstage. "We seem to have, um, a fashion emergency back here. Would you come help us, please?"

Oh, what now? "Of course!" I said brightly, giving Martin and Charles a meaningful smile as I headed for the stage-right exit—where I found Rebecca standing with a panicked member of our stage crew, and holding out the *pieces* of her fuchsia-colored jacket, and no sign at all of her costume assistant, Petra.

"I stuck my arm into the sleeve and it ripped right off!" Rebecca whispered frantically. "And I don't know where Petra's gone."

I had no idea what to do. So I stuck my head back out from behind the "hallway" flats and said, "Kristoff? I think this may require *your expertise*, please?"

"Oh dear! Is it a color clash crisis? I was afraid of that!" Charles gave JoJo a desperate look, and rushed offstage to join me.

I waved at Rebecca's ruined jacket and whispered, "Can you two ad-lib for a minute?"

"About *what*?" he asked, staring at Rebecca's coat.

"I don't know—ask Martin if he's been on any more disastrous dates?"

He rolled his eyes and ran back onstage just as Glory, in her

Winkleton getup, came running up the backstage stairs to see what was happening—followed closely by Hal.

"We need pins!" I told them. "From the dressing room."

"You'll never believe it, Martin," I heard Charles say onstage. *"Jill ripped Jenny's jacket to pieces while they were tussling over the bathroom! Now it seems they want a tailor! I guess I'd better go cancel some appointments!"* Clever.

"Should Rebecca just go out with it like this then?" I asked the others. "And *where* is *Lisa?*" Why should *I* be making these decisions?

"Yeah." Rebecca looked at Hal. "Why isn't she here?"

"I can't find her," Hal said.

"What?" Rebecca exclaimed, as if this was worse news than her jacket. "Since when?"

"Not since the show started." Hal seemed…excessively distressed. "You seen her?"

Rebecca shook her head, seeming as weirdly alarmed as Hal now.

"So, I ordered Chateaubriand for two—which sure wasn't cheap," I heard JoJo saying onstage. *"But when it comes, she tells me she's a vegetarian—so I* have *to eat mine, and hers!"*

"I'll go get the pins!" said Glory, already turning to hurry back down the stage-right stairs with the young stage crew member at her heels.

"I'll go look for Lisa," Hal said, rushing off too.

"So then, I asked her if she'd like to dance," JoJo said, *"but she says she's a Baptist, and that dancing is a sin—which is when I got the* hiccups, *from eating all that Chateaubriand."*

What on *earth* were they talking about out there? What was happening to my play? Did these gods of theater hate me? And where the heck was our *director* when we needed her? "I'm going back out to help them cover," I told Rebecca. "If you're not pinned up in…I don't know, a minute or two? Just come out with the torn coat, and…follow our lead, okay?"

She nodded, looking more and more freaked out.

I walked back onstage and said, cheerfully, "They're patching things up. How bad is the schedule looking, Kristoff?"

"Somewhere between eight and nine on the Richter scale," he said, ominously.

I sighed, and looked at JoJo. "Let's get them done fast, okay?" I glanced back into the stage-right hallway only to discover that Rebecca had now vanished too! Turning back to JoJo in growing panic, I said, "So, what was I just hearing about *vegetarian Baptists?*"

"Oh, Martin's been regaling me with tales of his junior prom," Charles drawled.

"Your *prom?*" I asked, not needing to *act* surprised.

A wild shout came from somewhere farther off behind the stage, followed by the slamming of a door, and then a loud and lengthy crash. All three of us whirled to look, before I swiveled toward the audience, hoping to see Lisa coming to our rescue from—*anywhere*. But all I saw was José rushing down the tech booth's scaffold ladder to sprint down a darkened side aisle toward the barn's back hallway. The audience began to mutter just as "Charlotte Winkleton" ran in through the salon entrance and grabbed JoJo by the arm. "I know I'm early for my appointment," she exclaimed, "but I need a strong young man to help me…with my car! Can you come, dear?" Charles and I could only gape as Glory dragged a bewildered "Martin" back through the salon door and offstage.

The audience was silent as the grave now—making it possible to hear the sound of urgent but muffled conversation, and several sets of running feet, from somewhere well back in the barn, quickly followed by a loud pounding even farther off, and JoJo's voice yelling, *"Open this door!"* There was a pause—not quite long enough for me to move or think—before we all heard JoJo yell, *"Come on, Derek! We all know you're in there now! This can't get anything but worse for you! Let her go!"*

Derek? The audience began murmuring in confusion and alarm as we heard Rebecca yelling too. I gaped at Charles, then gasped, *"Derek's here!"* I spun to face the darkened audience again and called out, "Kip? If you're out there, we need your help!"

I saw him stand before I'd finished speaking, and start shuffling—with courteous apologies, of course, because he was Kip—past the others in his row before dashing down the side aisle José had used, and vanishing behind the stage as well.

The audience was buzzing like an angry beehive now. Without another thought for the play or anything else, I ran through the salon entrance and down the stage-left stairs, rushing right by Glory, who stood alone with a phone pressed to her ear. "Yes, please hurry!" she told someone as I passed. "I think he's hurt some people!"

The man who had *poisoned Marie* was...*right here in this building!* And Lisa had been missing—all evening! I veered into the backstage hallway and saw Kip already standing with JoJo, José, and Rebecca, in front of the closed door to the women's dressing room. Running to join them, I heard JoJo tell Kip, "He's got Lisa in there. And Hal, I guess. Glory's calling 911."

"Hal must be hurt," Rebecca added. "He isn't answering me. And Petra's gone, so she could be in there too!"

Kip said, "Okay, listen: I need you all away from here. I want those people in the theater as far from this as we can get them too—but *not* outside the building, or we'll have a crowd out there before this is dealt with." Kip turned to me. "Cam, go make an announcement from the stage. Be *reassuring*, and ask them to move *calmly* to the lobby and stay there until a deputy informs them it's okay to leave." He turned back to the others. "While she's doing that, get all the theater doors propped open, so we don't have people getting stuck or panicked. Help keep them calm. And make sure they know they're not to leave the lobby. Now go, please."

I glanced at the closed door, hardly able to believe that the boogeyman I'd heard so much about was just inside it—with Lisa! Then I turned, and started back with everybody else.

"Sir?" Kip called calmly behind us. "This is Deputy Sheriff Kip Rankin. Multiple units are already underway to this location, and any further resistance will just make matters much, much worse for you. Do you understand?" He got no answer, but I could already hear sirens in the distance, which was reassuring. "Who's in there with you?" he asked, casually. When no answer came, he asked, "May I speak with Lisa Cannon, please?"

Then it struck me that Kip had no weapon, no uniform or badge. I'd called for his help as a deputy, but he'd been off duty tonight. And here he was now, as defenseless as any of us—except for his experience and training. What would he do if Derek came out and attacked him? Somehow...I had never thought of Kip as *brave* before. In spite of all the crimes we'd been tangled up in together, I'd never really taken the side of him I was seeing now seriously.

"What's Derek doing here?" I asked JoJo as we picked up speed. "Is Lisa all right?"

"I have no idea what's up with Derek," he said grimly. "But I heard Lisa talk to him through the door, so she's conscious, at least. Glory said he dragged Hal inside while they were fighting, just before the door slammed shut and all that crashing, so I have no idea about him either."

I saw Rebecca's lips purse. "I haven't seen Petra since she helped me dress for the twins."

"We gotta stay focused on what Deputy Rankin told us to do," said José. "I already sent the stage crew kids to the lobby, out of harm's way. They can help there." As we neared the stage, he leaned toward me and said, "Tell the crowd it's intermission now."

"No one's going to believe that. It's not even time for intermission; their programs make that pretty clear."

"So it's an *extra* intermission." He shrugged. "Doesn't matter.

Food just makes things feel more normal." He held up two fingers. "And twice as much cookie sales now, right?"

I'm pretty sure my mouth fell open. "Are you *serious*? Cookie sales? *Now?*"

"Hey, you get lemons; you make lemonade!" He threw his hands up as they all veered off toward the now very noisy audience. "Lemonade and *cookies!*" he called over his shoulder.

Wow, I thought, climbing back onto the stage. Talk about focus!

I came back through the salon entrance to find Charles at the edge of the stage, apparently in conversation of some kind with the audience. He glanced at me with obvious relief. "And here she is now, folks!" he announced. "The star and playwright of tonight's, uh, *spectacle*, to fill us in on what's happening," he turned back to me, "I hope?"

"That's right!" I said brightly, giving him a grateful look and trying to figure out what the heck to say and how to say it without panicking them all. "As, uh, most of you probably guessed by now, this is…not the play we'd planned to do. We're experiencing…" I sure wasn't going to get away with *technical difficulties*, "a…sort of domestic dispute backstage." In the sudden quiet of everyone's attention, we could all hear those approaching sirens getting louder by the second. "But I want to assure you that everything is completely under control now," I rushed to add, hoping that it *was*—or would be soon, at least. "So, uh, while Orcas Island's finest get all this, um, mopped up backstage, we're going to have…an extra intermission!" I was relieved to see the last few lobby doors being propped open. "Our fabulous Booster Club has baked an amazing collection of mouthwatering cookies and desserts for your dining pleasure," *Sorry to spring this on you early, ladies!* "and there is plenty of wine and other beverages for sale, which we hope you'll all enjoy out in the lobby for a while. *But I have also been asked, by Deputy Kip Rankin—who some of you may have noticed swinging into action just a minute ago—*"

I was briefly interrupted by a scattered but fervent round of applause, "to ask that no one goes outside, or leaves the lobby, until we're all officially notified that it's okay to. They don't need us underfoot out there, right?" Oh boy, I hoped these people weren't just going to stampede when all those sheriff cars screeched into the parking lot! "So now, let's all go *calmly* and *safely* to the lobby just behind you, please, and enjoy some delicious treats! There are restrooms out there too, of course." Then one last thought hit me. "And as soon as this is all cleared up—" I was half yelling now, to be heard over the growing hubbub as people rose and started shuffling out "—we will make an announcement about what's happening with the rest of tonight's play!" *Which I hope anyone will ever see now; thank you so much for that too, Derek, you giant turd!*

The sirens died—maybe to keep from panicking people? I had no real idea, but *my* job was definitely finished here. I turned to leave the stage, and found Charles staring at me, wide-eyed.

"What's wrong?" I asked him.

He shook his head. "Good job," he said, slowly, glancing back at our retreating audience. "They totally believe you—look at them going to have cookies while this all just gets cleaned up. You just *did* that!"

"Huh." I looked back toward the dressing room hallway, hidden from view now by the stage set, praying that Lisa, and Kip, and everybody else would be okay. "I guess we'd better go before we end up in the mix too."

"So, what *is* happening?" he asked as we started down the steps. "Is everyone all right?"

"I don't know," I said, suddenly miserable. "Kip's back there… handling it. But even Derek can't be dumb enough to go on hurting people with this giant crowd out here watching, and every deputy on Orcas Island pulling up out in the parking lot—can he?"

"Who is Derek?"

Realizing with a jolt how *indiscreet* I'd just been, I shrugged. "I have no idea. It's just what I heard JoJo call him."

As we headed up an aisle toward the lobby doors, Charles said, "Weird, and scary. But seriously, good job on crowd control there. You seemed totally calm."

And that was when I realized…that not one part of me had tingled all night long. Not when the set had almost fallen down; or when Hal had come on as Jeanette with a mustache, and we'd all lost our lines; or when the *whole play* had come apart around Rebecca's coat; or even when I'd run off down that hallway, knowing *Derek the monster* was somewhere just ahead of me.

Where *had* this woman I'd been all night come from? And what had happened to the one I'd been before?

☙

When Charles and I reached the lobby doors, we were pulled aside by José, who wanted us actors to wait in Erin's office instead—on the other side of the building. He felt that rubbing shoulders with the audience, while in our makeup and costumes, would ruin the "magical illusion" when the play resumed. I thought it was very sweet of him to imagine the play would resume at all, but Charles seemed sure Lisa would have agreed. So we followed him.

The others were already there—except for Lisa, Hal and Petra, of course—crammed in a space never intended for so many people. Despite the open window, it was warm and stuffy; and our costumes and makeup did nothing to make us more comfortable—especially poor Charles and Glory, who were more tarted up than anyone.

Fifteen minutes into our captivity, Erin showed up with a giant platter of cookies and pastries from the booster ladies. She apologized for the tiny space, but said the lobby wasn't that much better. They'd closed all the big double doors onto the parking lot—for obvious reasons—so things had gotten pretty stuffy there too, she said.

As everyone dug into the treats, Erin told us that the parking lot was bursting with sheriff SUVs—which had arrived very quietly, despite all those sirens we'd heard earlier—and that there were lots of deputies in the building now. But no one had offered any information yet about what was happening back at the dressing room.

JoJo asked her what the mood was like back in the lobby. She surprised us by saying that the audience seemed to be having a ball, then turned to smile at me. "That speech you gave was amazing, Cam. You really defused what could have been a much more unpleasant situation."

"Hear, hear!" said Glory. "I agree!"

"Honestly, this may be the biggest adventure most of them have ever experienced," Erin said. "They know they're going to be local celebrities tomorrow just for being here, so a lot of them are pretty pumped! And, of course, the eats aren't hurting anybody's feelings either. José's running himself ragged helping the ladies keep those concession tables stocked. You guys are going to make a fortune feeding all these captive appetites tonight."

It still kind of boggled my mind that *cookie sales* were even on the radar now. I understood that Erin was just trying to keep our spirits up. But didn't she, or anyone, understand that people we cared about might be hurt—or even dead by now? That Lisa Cannon was still in there with that *creature*? I glanced across at JoJo, who, despite Erin's cheerful report, didn't look any happier than I felt—and I felt grateful to him for that.

After Erin left, JoJo peered out through the office door, then sidled from the room without a word. No one even commented on this; we all knew JoJo by now.

He was back minutes later to report that something was definitely happening, because he'd just seen several deputies rushing from the parking lot toward the far side of the building; and two SUVs had driven off with lights flashing, but no sirens.

"You went into the *parking lot?*" Glory sounded scandalized.

"Of course not," he said, batting his lashes. "You know we're not allowed out there."

"Then how—" Charles began.

"There's a little door just down this hallway," JoJo sighed, "that opens right into the parking lot. I cracked it open just a tiny bit, and peeked outside for a while."

"Well, I'm glad you weren't caught—or hurt," I said, a bit irritated at the way he was teasing everyone for not scoffing at our instructions the way he had.

"Caught doing what?" he said cheerfully. "Peeking out a door?"

"We're supposed to stay—"

"—in the *lobby!* But we're *here*, so." He shrugged, and looked around as if this logic was too obvious to challenge.

"Sorry," I said. "I'm just...feeling pretty helpless."

Erin poked her head in to say they'd just been told that Lisa, Hal, and Petra were all free—news greeted with gasps of relief and delight by all of us—but that the guy in the dressing room had locked himself in, and the deputies were negotiating with him.

"So, how are they all?" I asked.

"I don't know. That's everything they told us." She glanced at our now-empty cookie tray. "You guys want another plate?"

After half an hour more without any further word, I began to feel that JoJo may actually have been right about...well, a number of things. I stood up and went to the door. "I volunteer for the next round of spying."

JoJo's brows climbed, but his smile was triumphant.

I cracked the door and peered out. "What can they do to me? Lock me up in some tiny cell all night?"

Charles rewarded that with a little huff of laughter.

By the glow of small safety lights along the hallway floor, I made my way down to the doorway, pushed it gently ajar an inch or two, and brought my eye up to the crack. I saw only three

SUVs now, and no deputies at all. I was about to pull the door closed again when I heard a voice growl, "Do these have to be so *tight?*"

I eased the door open a couple inches more. Two deputies entered my field of vision, holding a third man between them with hands cuffed behind his back. "*Oh…wow…*" I murmured. Was this Derek?

Who else could it have been?

I had imagined someone more…striking; taller, and more, I don't know, "criminal?" But he just looked like…any man. It was too dark to see him clearly, but he seemed of average height and average build—except for a slight potbelly—in jeans and a dark T-shirt, with short-cropped brown hair. What an unimpressive boogeyman!

As they neared a sheriff vehicle, one of the officers went to open its back door, and Derek twisted in his remaining handler's grip to look back over one shoulder. *"You're not hangin' all this on me, Lisa!"* he yelled. *"Better call your lawyer, 'cause we're goin' down together, babe!"* Before he'd even finished yelling, the deputy at his side wrenched him around to face the vehicle again, shoved his head down as he guided him roughly into the back seat, and shut the door. As he climbed behind the wheel, the other deputy swept the parking lot with his eyes, looking for…what? More bad guys? As his gaze moved toward my doorway, I pulled it gently shut, and turned to hurry back to the office—only to yelp aloud at the sight of Deputy Sherman standing not eight feet behind me wearing a crooked smile.

Dang it! I'd been caught!

"Ms. Tate," she said pleasantly, "would you mind coming with me?" She gestured down the hallway toward the backstage area. "Ms. Cannon would like to have a word with you before we release everyone."

"Oh! Sure!" I exclaimed, washed with relief. I caught up with her and asked, "So, what was Derek doing here?"

"I'm not permitted to speculate about any of this."

"Oh. Right."

"From everything I've heard, though, you guys handled all this exceptionally well." She turned to give me a kinder smile. "And Kip says the *play* was really something too."

"Yeah, well…" I said sadly. "I guess we'll just try again tomorrow."

She glanced at her watch. "It's still plenty early." Her expression softened. "Unless…you don't feel up to finishing it now?"

"Oh! No, I'm okay. I just… I mean, are people who've just gone through a hostage crisis really going to sit back down and go on laughing at a play now?"

Her smile became a little sly. "I'm pretty sure that Kip wants to see the rest, and I don't see why everybody else won't too. They're all saying it's really funny!"

As we rounded the next corner, I saw Lisa standing not far from the dressing room, gazing at the stage back. At our approach, she turned and smiled, reaching out to take my hands in hers. "Cam! How *are you*, dear?"

"How am *I*? I'm fine, of course! How are *you*? What happened in there?"

Lisa shot a glance at Sherman. "I've been asked not to talk about that yet—not even with you, I'm afraid."

I rolled my eyes and sighed. "Of course. *Discretion.* It's everywhere all of a sudden."

She gave me a knowing smile. "I'm really so sorry that all this happened in the middle of your big night!"

"Oh, please, Lisa! What does that matter next to everything you've just been—"

"It matters *tremendously*," she said. "We've both worked so hard for this. And from everything I've heard, it was going splendidly—despite a couple hiccups."

"You didn't…see any of it?"

She shook her head. "Derek knew right when everyone would

be most distracted, and didn't even wait for the opening lights to—"

Deputy Sherman cleared her throat, and gave us another apologetic look.

"Right," said Lisa. "So, anyway, now that…everything is safe again, I believe they're going to let our audience come see the rest of your play, if they wish to—but only if you and the others feel up to going on with it after all of this… Do you?"

She kept making it sound as if it had been *us* who'd had it rough tonight! "I'm fine. But shouldn't we be asking everybody, not just—Oh!" I gasped. *"How's Hal?"*

"Hal's fine now," Lisa said. "He's sporting a butterfly bandage on his forehead, quite invisible behind a slab of gauze covered in foundation, and says he's ready to go right on with the play. They let Petra out of the closet Derek locked her into some time ago, and she's game too. So, if *you're* still up for it, would you mind going back to get everyone else's opinions before we tell our audience what the plan is?"

"Okay… But, shouldn't the *director* be asking them that? They'll all want to see you, Lisa."

Lisa gave me a small, strange smile. "While they were stitching him up, Hal told me about all the little surprises you've already handled very well without me tonight. I believe you're fully capable of stepping in for me at this point. And I'd really like the chance to sit out there and just bask in your triumph, without having to run around backstage paying attention to nothing but the problems. Is that dreadful of me?"

"No, of course not!" I said, realizing how much of this ordeal's real impact she was probably hiding from me and everyone else. How like her. "I'd be happy to let you have a rest."

"Thank you," Lisa said, warmly. "Now, believe it or not, I still have some further details to tend to with the deputies, so, I'll let you marshal the troops from here, if you don't mind. Let Kip or José know what you've all decided, and—either way—I'll see everyone at the opening gala afterward, okay?"

"Okay." I leaned in, forgetting all about my makeup, and gave her a hug—gently, in case she was also hiding injuries from me. Then, I left her with Sherman, and went back to the others, who'd been going crazy wondering whether something terrible had happened to me. Even JoJo looked relieved when I walked in. When I told them about my talk with Lisa, and asked if they felt up to finishing the play, they just looked at me like I was crazy for imagining they might not. And virtually all those people in the lobby decided to stay too, and watch us do it!

So, here are a few things I learned that night about finishing a play just after a hostage stand-off. First, it is *so much easier* than performing a normal play! When our set had self-destructed just as opening lights came up, or JoJo had been left to tell old prom stories in the middle of a scene, I'd been so worried about what the audience must be thinking. But after your play has been invaded by an actual criminal and a giant swarm of deputies flashing lights and sirens, people will forgive you *anything*—and we knew it up there! That audience was ready to celebrate any and every funny thing we did—or even tried to do. They loved us just for going on again; and nothing happening onstage could scare us at all now.

What a party!

Not that I recommend this approach to anyone else, of course. I should say that too, I guess.

The rest of act one seemed almost effortless—with just one noticeable hitch in the last scene. The adhesive holding that makeup-covered slab of gauze onto Hal's forehead lost its grip under the hot lights. And, as the scene progressed, the family's snooty lawyer was forced to tilt his head farther and farther back, talking down his nose to everyone, while what looked just like a patch of his forehead to the audience slid lower and lower, until Hal's brow line looked more like a gorilla's than a man's. He finally improvised a hilarious exit line, allowing him to rush offstage earlier than planned. Most of the audience had figured out what was going on well before then, and just howled for half a minute after he left.

When the lights were lowered and raised again to signal our originally scheduled intermission, I walked to the front of the stage and asked the audience to vote on whether to have a second intermission, or just skip it and go on. They'd all been trapped in the lobby for close to an hour already, and I didn't even know for sure if there were any cookies or wine left. As they unanimously voted down the second intermission, José made a disparaging noise up in the tech booth and threw his hands up in disgust. But the rest of us were happy not to break the play's momentum.

In act two, the salon staff kept treating every unfamiliar customer as if they might be the new owner incognito—except for poor old Mrs. Winkleton, who looked to Kristoff like a "bag lady," and acted like…well, Paige Berry—not that I was ever going to admit that to anyone. She and her endlessly howling (thanks to our sound crew!) dog, Beauregard, were always shoved aside or pushed back in line for other, more "respectable" customers who might turn out to hold the salon staff's fate in their hands.

Only too-nice Martin refused to treat Winkleton that way, sneaking her into his chair when Kristoff was distracted, complimenting her, and finally even shaming Felicia into treating Winkleton and her intrusive dog like people too. So, in the final scene, it was poor old Martin who'd saved everybody's jobs when Charlotte Winkleton threw off her disguise and revealed *herself* to be the new owner.

In the play's last moments, she turned to pinch Martin's cheek affectionately. "I could never face myself in any salon mirror again, knowing I'd put such a sweet lad out on the streets." Then she turned to Kristoff. "Even you can stay, in spite of what a pill you've been. But I must insist that you stop dressing like a circus clown—unless, of course, you'd really rather be one." Kristoff shook his head in obvious distress, and she looked gravely around, then beckoned us all closer to stage-whisper, "*Confidentially*—and you really mustn't tell a soul, especially the family's dreadful lawyer—I hope to *expand* this delightful little business into the building's whole ground floor." She turned to Kristoff. "So let's start thinking *big*—instead of merely *loud*—shall we, dear?" Kristoff turned to smile wide-eyed up into the spotlight, clearly dreaming now of fame and fortune—as the lights went out to thunderous applause.

We'd done it!

As the lights came up again on our first official curtain call, the applause-filled air echoed with cries of "Brava!" "Author!" and "Encore!"—though I had no idea what *encore* they expected us to have left after everything else that night. Flowers and bouquets were tossed onto the stage from many directions. JoJo bent to grab a large bundle of white roses and blue irises, which he handed to me as we beamed at each other. I had never felt so happy—ever in my life.

CHAPTER 16

When we'd finally taken our last bow, I forgot all about changing out of my costume and makeup, because there were my parents standing in front of the first row! I hopped down and tumbled into Mom's arms for a huge hug. "You were amazing, sweetie!" she said, giving me another squeeze before handing me off to Dad.

"Knocked it right out of the park!" he said, nearly crushing the breath from me.

"Thank you!" I was almost jumping up and down from excitement and relief and delight and—everything. "I'm so glad you guys could make it! Even with…all that other stuff. "

"As if we would miss this?" Mom exclaimed. "I can't wait to hear more about all that kerfuffle in the middle; but you were *so brave*, dear! I was so proud of you!"

"And you got right back out there on the field and finished it!" Dad beamed at me. "I had my doubts about this place, honey." He glanced at Mom. "We both did. But it's been good for you!"

There was so much more I wanted to tell them, but we were interrupted by Brenda and Julie and Ashley from the salon in Seattle, who all had to hug me too, and squeal about how *unbelievable* the play was and how *amazing* my acting had been, and how blown away everyone back in town would be to hear about the cops and everything—just before they were interrupted by Jen, who barely had time to tell me how *awesome* I was—and how *much* we had to talk about all this *later*—before she was nudged aside by Porter and Verna Wendergrast, who were followed by I don't even remember who, until I saw José and the stage crew kids starting to set up for the opening night gala, and told everyone we really had to move this to the lobby now.

The hugs and congratulations just increased out there, until it all became a blur—did I really know this many people? And then, I was shaking hands with someone I was sure I'd never met—though he had Lisa on his arm.

"Cam," she said, "this is *Leonard Prix*." The way she emphasized his name made me wonder if I was supposed to recognize the guy.

"Nice to meet you," I said, hoping he wasn't someone I'd worked with while setting all this up, and then forgotten along the way.

"Lisa tells me you're not just the star, but the playwright too!" he said. "Can that be true?"

"Well, yes…"

"Astonishing!" He gave me a delighted grin.

Who *was* this?

Lisa, grinning too, rescued me. "Leonard is the artistic director of Emerald City Rep."

Ohhhh… Just Seattle's biggest repertory theater! Even *I* knew *that*.

"I *loved it*," he said, his eyes twinkling. "So fresh! So entertaining! And I don't just mean all that excitement in the middle—which you handled like a pro, I have to say. You were right, my dear," he said to Lisa, then turned back to me. "What an ear for dialogue! And you clearly know the city. I'd really love to talk with you about securing the rights."

"I…uh… The rights to…" I stammered.

"Produce your play, of course!" he laughed. "For our next season."

I gave Lisa a helpless look. Did my play have *rights*? Or…did I need to get those somehow?

"You two can talk more about this at the gala," Lisa said. "I'm sure Cam needs to get out of that dress and makeup before it starts. Shall we get a drink, Leonard?" She steered him away as I just stood there, stunned.

Emerald City Rep wanted…my play! I felt light-headed.

Mercifully, the people who'd been mobbing me had moved on now, so I turned and started toward the lobby doors in a daze—vaguely remembering the dressing room.

How much did a repertory company like Emerald City pay for the rights to a play?

I was so lost in thought as I walked back into the barn that I didn't even notice Kip coming toward me until he spoke.

"Ms. Tate! I was afraid I'd missed you."

"Kip! Hi! Uh…have you been waiting at the dressing room all this time?"

He shook his head. "No, just still helping clear things up back there. They let me have a break to come see the rest of your wonderful play, but it looks like I'm a witness now; and there are a lot of other, well, *administrative* things to deal with—or I'd have been out in the lobby to congratulate you with everybody else."

"Oh—it's way better we're meeting here. That was just…a mob scene out there."

"I'd expect it was. You were unbelievable tonight."

"What, *I* was unbelievable?" I laughed. "Kip, I don't even know how to *begin* thanking you for…everything you did. I've been dying to know what happened after we left you there, alone like that—" he raised a hand, preparing to tell me what I already knew "—but I know you can't talk about it, and I wasn't even going to ask. I just wanted to say that…that we all owe you *so much* for taking charge like that—on your night off! You were…

heroic."

He looked down, seeming embarrassed. "Well, thank you too. For such an entertaining and, well…enlightening evening."

"And thank you just for coming!" I exclaimed. "It's so lucky you were here, but…I hadn't really expected you to be."

He nodded, still looking down. "I guess I can understand your surprise. And, honestly…I might not have come if JoJo hadn't told me how good it was, and…how much he thought I really shouldn't miss it."

"JoJo…said that?" Why would he have done that?

Kip finally raised his eyes to meet mine. "And I'm glad he did. It sure was an amazing piece of writing, Ms. Tate. And you were…well, I had no idea how *funny* you could be," he said, not sounding all that amused. He looked down again, briefly, then off at nothing I could see across the room. "But, I get it," he said, at last. "I really do." He inhaled deeply and turned back to me.

"You get what?" I asked, suddenly nervous. I was clearly missing something big here. Something set in motion by *JoJo*, apparently…which wasn't comforting either.

"Ms. Tate, I just want to say, that…well, I'm sorry. For the way I mishandled…so many things." He was looking straight at me now—like I were the barrel of some gun.

"What are you talking about? What have you mishandled? Nothing *tonight*, obviously."

"Oh, come on, Cam," he sighed. "Let's not…pretend we both don't know who Martin is."

"*What?*" I blinked. "Martin—the character in my play? What has *that* got to do with—"

"Clueless idiot too *nice* to know how he should handle the attentions of a woman?" He gave me a pained look. "Too fumbling and tongue-tied to make his own intentions clear before he just…" He looked away again. "…insults her, and…runs off, feeling hurt, as if…"

I felt my painted brows soar as I finally understood what he was…what he thought I… "Oh, Kip, no! You don't really… think I wrote Martin about you? Don't be silly! I would *never*… do that…"

Kip gazed back at me, looking puzzled now.

But I really hadn't… *Had I?*

I mean, sure; I *had* been writing from my own experience—of working in a Seattle salon! Not of anything to do with anybody *here!* Well, except for Paige Berry, maybe. But she had been the only one—and that was completely different!

Or, okay, I might have tossed a tiny bit of JoJo into Kristoff too, I supposed, but… "Kip, I'm so sorry you thought that! Because it's *not true!* Where did you… Was it JoJo? Did he say that? Because, I didn't! I would *never*… Not to *anyone*, much less *you!*"

But the more I protested, the more Kip just looked at me. I couldn't un-hear what he had said. It couldn't be true!

It *wasn't.*

I was *absolutely* going to murder JoJo—with my bare hands—right in the middle of the gala, no matter how many deputies might still be wandering around this barn.

"Kip," I said, forcing a calm I did not feel, "I am *so glad* you told me about this. Because Martin wasn't ever you! You're the very opposite of him! You're a brave, capable, kind, heroic man—who just proved all of that again right here tonight! So, please, let's just…" I put on the best smile I could find in a hurry. "Listen, I'm so glad we talked. And so grateful for everything you did tonight—but I have *got* to get out of this costume and this awful makeup. The opening night gala is in—any minute now, right here in this room, and I'm already going to be late, and there's a man here from Emerald City—I mean the repertory company, not the one in Oz—but I have to talk to him, and…" I'd started edging away from Kip without really being aware of it. "I am *so* sorry to run off like this, but thank you! I mean it!" I was backing away faster now. "And let's definitely talk again. When all this other stuff is over. Okay? That would be so great." I'd backed halfway down the aisle now, while Kip just stood staring at me. "Thanks so much for coming—and for everything! See you soon!"

Then I just turned and ran past the stage and out of the theater without slowing down until I reached the dressing room, where I stood breathing hard, and stared around the place where Derek had held Lisa and Hal prisoner just a couple hours ago. Hadn't I been put through enough tonight—without this insanity too? I stood there, as all the night's adrenaline seemed to drain from me at once, wishing there were anyplace that I could just go hide, instead of having to attend some giant party now.

❧

Lisa's opening night gala was in full roar by the time I came out in my pretty new dress and a lot less makeup. I had regained, well, *most* of my balance—and decided not to murder JoJo right here in front of everybody after all. That could wait till later, when we were alone—someplace where his body could be quickly and *discreetly* disposed of.

I still wasn't thrilled to be putting a pretty starlet's face on for a crowd of people gushing praise and congratulations that I just… didn't feel up for anymore. But what was one more brief performance after all the others? And it *would* be brief. After everything we'd just gone through, no one here was going to find it weird if I left early.

The barn was done up in a whole extra set of lights and decorations now, supplied and overseen by the obnoxious—*"but talented"*—Roland Markus, who I could see gesturing grandly before a cluster of captive listeners over in a corner of the room that I intended to steer clear of. The space's party makeover did look very pretty, though, I had to admit. And *everyone* was there—the entire cast, of course, the stage crew, all the vendors and helpers and volunteers and generous donors we had worked with all these months to put the play together, along with José and Erin, obviously.

And Lisa, of course—with her distinguished guest. She must have been watching for me, because she led him on a beeline through the crowd right toward me hardly seconds after I walked in. Deputy Sherman, still in uniform, trailed behind them—which seemed odd, until I realized that she must be there to guard Lisa through the rest of the evening. I still had no idea, of course, what Derek had hoped to do by taking Lisa prisoner that way; but who could say there weren't other bad guys lurking around here somewhere, wanting to finish whatever job he'd failed at? Derek was, as I'd been told, just the low guy on this totem pole.

And…that was a spookier thought than I needed to be processing right now.

"There you are!" Lisa cried, happily, waving her drink at me. "You look stunning, dear!" She released Mr. Prix's arm and came to give me a hug while he looked on. "Thank you so much for letting me sit out there and watch," she said quietly, as we embraced. "It was the happiest experience I've had in ages. You were beyond words wonderful, Cam. Everybody was. I don't expect to see another performance that fabulous for…well, a very long time, if ever." She leaned back to beam at me. "Are you happy?"

"Yes," I said. Or I had been, anyway, before that awful talk with Kip. Looking at the expression of pure delight and pride on Lisa's face, I realized that I really should still be that happy as well. I owed her that much—and myself too. I'd been a fool to let JoJo Brixton or anything else ruin what ought to be the happiest night of my life. I smiled at Lisa. "You're always right. About everything. You've changed my life! And…" I shook my head, at a loss for words. "I will never doubt you again."

Her bright smile faltered. "That's…very kind. But it's also a pretty high bar, don't you think? Cam, it's *you* who've changed your life; not me. I just cheered you on from the stands—and maybe gave you a little shove when you seemed to need one." She glanced back at Mr. Prix. "Leonard, I believe you wanted another word with Cam before you go?"

"Yes, thank you." He stepped forward to join us. "I'm sorry to be leaving so early, Ms. Tate; but I have a plane waiting up in Eastsound, and the pilot has a wife and family who were expecting to see him home a bit earlier than, ah, this has turned out be."

"Oh, no need to apologize, Mr. Prix!" I said. "I'm just so honored that you came; and it was very nice of you to stay—well, at all."

He gave me a charming smile. "Actually, I hope to come back before the run is over and see your marvelous play again—as the author *intended* to present it." He reached into his pocket and handed me a business card. "I hope that when your life calms down a bit, you'll give me a call, Ms. Tate. I'd love to have you down to the city for lunch sometime soon, and discuss both the staging of *Salon Confidential* in Seattle next year, and the possibility of having you write something exclusively for our company's subsequent season—if that's anything you'd be open to exploring with us?"

For the second time that night, I stood gaping at him. "You want me to write a play—a new one? For Emerald City Rep?"

Lisa looked just like a proud parent, as Prix nodded. "Possibly even perform in it! We can discuss that too. Your work in the play was lovely. But your performance during the crisis... That said something even more important about your real potential."

I...had no words. All thoughts of Kip, or JoJo, or any of the night's other little setbacks were now completely swept away. This was...*impossible!* "I would be so delighted to have that talk, Mr. Prix!" I said, struggling not to literally bounce on my toes.

"Wonderful! I look forward to it too. But now, sadly, I must go catch that plane." He grinned at me. "It's been a *profound* pleasure, Ms. Tate. Break a leg, tomorrow evening—but, a bit more gently, eh?" He winked, and took Lisa's arm again. She blew me a kiss as they left, still trailed by Deputy Sherman, while I stood trying to convince myself that I hadn't just hit my head somewhere backstage, and hallucinated all this in the back of some ambulance.

"Who was *that*?" whispered a voice at my ear.

I whirled around. "Jen!" I threw my arms around her in a giant hug, which she returned with equal gusto. "Oh, I'm so glad you're here!"

"Well of course silly! Where else would I be tonight?" She glanced back toward the doorway Lisa and Prix had just disappeared through. "So... What did I just miss?"

"Oh! You are never in a million years going to believe this, Jen! That was the creative director of Emerald City Rep in Seattle!"

"Wow!" Jen said, mirroring my glee. "Is that, like, another theater company?"

I gaped at her. But, of course, she'd never lived in Seattle, so why would she know? "No, Jen; it's the *biggest* repertory company in Seattle! They have a whole theater of their very own downtown! And they want to do my play there next season!"

Jen's eyes grew round. "Oh, Cam! That's HUGE!" She threw her arms around me again, and we did bounce up and down together.

"But that's not even all!" I cried. "They might want me to write a *new* play, just for them!"

Jen pumped her fists up in the air and literally screamed— which drew quite a lot of attention around the room—not all of it happy. We'd just had one criminal attack that night already, after all. When she threw her arms around me again, everyone relaxed and smiled, probably thinking it was just some "girl thing." "You aren't just *exploding*, Cam! You've gone *SUPERNOVA!*"

"Okay, what's going on over here?" I heard my mom ask, and turned around to find my parents grinning with obvious curiosity. "You didn't just get engaged or something, did you, sweetie?" Mom asked, sounding *almost* sure that she was joking.

"No, of course not," I said.

"Oh, good," Dad said.

"Dad!" I gave him a disbelieving look. "You didn't really think I'd get engaged without even telling you I had a boyfriend first!"

He shrugged. "Things start moving pretty fast when people get famous. You gotta be careful about that sort of thing now."

As if to illustrate his point, JoJo wandered up just then—drink in hand, as always—smiling as if he could just barge right in and join our conversation.

I very pointedly turned my back on him, and rolled my eyes—earning an odd look from Jen. "Don't worry, Dad," I said, loudly enough to make sure JoJo could hear. "I can spot a loser from many miles away."

"That's my girl," Dad said with a smile.

"That's a gorgeous dress, Cam!" Mom chimed in, probably just wanting a change of subject.

"Thanks!"

JoJo sidled back into my field of vision.

I turned my back to him again. "So, should we all go get a drink?"

Jen glanced over my shoulder at him, then gave me another curious look. "Well, dang it," she said. "We have more to talk about than ever, don't we? But I gotta go—I have to be in Kangaroo Point in an hour."

"What? *Why?*" Not work; it was like ten o'clock at night.

"Dog emergency." She grimaced. "Its owners are taking their boat to deal with some family thing on Crane and can't bring Phoenix with them. I need to go dog sit."

"Wow. That's one spoiled dog."

"Spoiled dogs are my new specialty. But I need to go."

"Then you'd better go." I leaned in to give her another hug. "Thanks for coming."

"Oh, I was never going to miss this, Cam! I knew you'd be amazing—but, oh my gosh, who knew *how amazing*? We *gotta* talk tomorrow, or we'll have too much to catch up on ever!"

"Right. I'll call you!"

"You better, or I'll be calling *you*." She glanced over my shoulder again—so he must still be there, that stalker—then wriggled her fingers at me and walked away.

I turned back to my parents, careful to keep my back to JoJo. "So, how about you guys; want to come get a drink with me?"

"Oh, that sounds fun," Mom sighed, "but us old folks don't have the stamina you young show-biz types do. We really only stayed to say goodnight and congratulations again before going back to our B&B."

"You must be pretty tired too, after all that," said my dad. "Are you still up for brunch tomorrow, or should we just make it lunch, so you can sleep in a little longer?"

"Oh, no," I said. "I'll be fine, and New Leaf's brunch is not to be missed." I stepped in to give each of them a hug. "See you in the morning."

"Love you, honey," said Mom. "Don't you stay up too late either. Over brunch tomorrow, I want to hear all the gory details about whatever happened in the middle of Act One—and I doubt some tired zombie's going to do that story as much justice as my famous daughter will."

"Don't worry," I said. "I'll be going soon too."

I waved goodbye as they started toward the lobby, then turned around and almost flinched to find JoJo *still* standing right behind me, looking very puzzled.

"You're still here?" I asked, unsmiling. "Don't you have any *friends* to talk to?"

He leaned back, as if I'd taken a swing at him. "I *thought* I did. Are you...angry at me for something, Camikins?"

I sighed and looked up at the ceiling. I wished I could simply walk away, but he would just keep bugging me all evening with "witty" attempts at getting me to talk, and those predictable sad-puppy eyes, if I didn't deal with this now.

"Come with me," I said severely, heading for the barn's back hallway and...anywhere that I could stuff his body while there were still so many other people around to blame his murder on. It wasn't a half bad plan, really. Everyone knew what great friends JoJo and I had become these days. No one would suspect *me*... They might even end up accusing Roland Markus of the crime! Talk about karma!

Amazingly, JoJo followed me in utter silence. I must really have unnerved him—a thought that made me smile. In the hallway, several outdoor exits were propped open. I headed for one of them without even looking back to see if JoJo was still there.

"Where are we going, Cami?"

I stepped outside without answering, glancing around to make sure we weren't walking into someone's make-out session, or the stage crew kids' beer party or something. I saw nothing but a lovely view of starry sky over the fields of Crow Valley, and two empty sheriff vehicles still parked off near the corner of the building. One of them Larissa's, probably, and who else's? Wasn't the storm over now?

I leaned back against the barn wall, and waited while JoJo came to rest a few feet away. For a moment, we just stared at each other. Finally, he leaned forward. "So, are you going to speak? Or was I supposed to bring my telepath's handbook and secret decoder ring?"

Oh, no, none of that. Not this time. "I thought you were *tired* of playing that role, JoJo?"

He squinted at me, then slumped further back against the wall. "What have I done *this* time?"

"Are you *ever* going to stop meddling in my life?"

He just looked back, still seeming genuinely baffled.

"Wasn't it a lucky thing that Kip was here tonight?" I tried. "After all the, um, *awkwardness* between us lately, I was surprised he came." When JoJo just kept staring, I asked, "So, why do you think he did?"

"Mmmbecause...you two are friends? Or were once, anyway, before you read him that riot act at the substation? Maybe he just wanted to be supportive of your latest hobby."

"My *hobby?*" I snapped.

He shrugged. "Well, you're not being nice. Why should I?"

I was itching to tell him that Emerald City Rep had just expressed a lot of very serious interest in my *hobby*. But he would just belittle that news too, and I was so done handing him opportunities like that. "Kip told me that *you asked him* to come tonight!"

JoJo looked astonished. "*That's* why I'm out here getting switched behind the barn? Really?" He shook his head. "Okay, well, I did run into Kip the other day. And when he asked me how the play was going, I did tell him it was going great, and that you were terrific. And—yes—I even told him that he ought to come see it—because this was going to be the best thing Lisa's troupe had done in years!" He hunched his shoulders. "For *that*, you hate me now?"

"Oh, cut it out!" I was tired of these cat and mouse games. "Why was it so important to make sure Kip came to the play, except that even *you* are out there now, trying to make sure that he and I get 'back together'? You were the *only one* of my friends—well, except for Lisa—who wasn't jumping on that stupid bandwagon, except that now you're doing it too! Why won't anybody just believe me when I tell them there was *never—anything—between us?*"

"Oh well, no! Of course not!" He waved his arms in the air. "How could anyone think it?"

"*That—right there,*" I nearly screeched, "*is what I'm talking about!* You all know so much better than I do! Well, if I were interested in anyone on this island—which I am *not*—it sure wouldn't be a cop!"

"Why not?" he asked—as if he'd heard nothing I'd just said.

"*None of your business why not!*" I yelled. "The last person on this planet I need running my *love life* is *you*, JoJo Brixton! Who could *be* less qualified?" I pushed myself up off the wall and stuck my face right up in his. "But what I *really* don't get is *where on earth* you get off telling *Kip* that I wrote Martin about *him!*"

JoJo's face looked just like Jen's had when I'd told her about Emerald City Rep—only, without any of the joy this time; just slack incomprehension.

"I did no such thing," he said in hushed amazement. And then, just like Jen, his eyes got rounder. "But…what an *interesting* observation." The beginnings of a disbelieving smile joined his look of shock. *"Did you?* Am I playing *Kip?"*

"NO!" I screamed, and turned to slam both my fists against the barn wall. *"Just tell me what you said to make him think that!"*

"Me?" He sounded outraged now. "No such idea's ever even crossed my mind, until just—" He fell abruptly silent, looking up in concern at something beyond me.

I turned around to see Deputy Sherman and Sheriff Clarke walking across the field toward the two official vehicles. Between them was *Lisa*. As they reached the SUVs, Lisa turned to talk with Sheriff Clarke as Sherman went to open one of the closer vehicle's back doors. They were too far away for me to hear what was being said, but Clarke was talking to Lisa now, who stood looking down into the shin-high grass between them. And not happily.

I turned back to look at JoJo, who just gazed past me at the trio in the field, with a look of such terrible sadness. I turned back around. "Lisa?" I called softly.

"Don't," JoJo said behind me.

But all three of them were looking at us now. Lisa stared across the darkened field at me for a moment, then turned and said something to Clarke, who looked at me too, shrugged, and nodded at Lisa. As she started walking toward us, Clarke called out to her, "But let's keep it quick, please, Ms. Cannon."

She nodded without looking back at him as she drew closer and stopped.

"Well, Cam," she said wistfully. "You do have a knack for being in just the wrong places at just the right times, don't you." She looked past me at JoJo, who looked like a man at his own funeral. He said nothing; just raised a hand as if saying hi—or goodbye.

"Lisa, what's going on?" I asked. "Has something else happened?"

She seemed unsure of what to say. After glancing back at Sheriff Clarke, she said, "When you came to talk about your visit with Marie, remember how I mentioned I'd be busier than ever soon, and would need you to step up fully to your position as my assistant?"

"Yes…" I said, feeling worse by the moment. "Are you going off somewhere again?"

She nodded. "Pretty soon, I think. Now that Derek's been arrested, there are things for me to deal with that will require my full attention for…quite a while. But that's a much longer conversation than I can have now. We can sit down and discuss it all tomorrow, I'm sure; or Sunday, if that's more convenient for you."

My throat felt clogged with questions. "Okay, but…can't you tell me *anything*? Are they taking you into protective custody? Has someone threatened you? Someone worse than Derek?"

"Ms. Cannon?" Clarke called out. "We do need to be going."

Lisa gave me such a *not-like-Lisa* look. "I'm sorry, Cam. I really have to go. But I'll be in touch—I promise—just as soon as I'm able." She looked up and blew JoJo a sad kiss, leaned in to peck me quickly on the cheek, then turned around and walked back to Clarke and Sherman.

JoJo and I watched in silence as Deputy Sherman politely waved Lisa into the back seat of her vehicle, while Clarke got into the other one. Their engines rumbled to life, their headlights flared, and they drove slowly from the field, without any whirling lights or sirens.

When they'd passed behind the barn and out of sight, I looked back at JoJo, who looked nothing like himself at all anymore.

"They're not...*arresting* her, are they?"

He didn't even look at me, just kept his eyes on the field. I thought he wasn't going to answer—which seemed an answer in itself. But as I opened my mouth to ask again, he said, "Yup."

There was no surprise in his voice or on his face.

"You *knew* this."

He nodded.

"How long have you known?"

"Quite a while." His answer was barely loud enough for me to hear.

I didn't bother asking why he hadn't told me. "But why *her?*" I asked instead. "It was Derek, all this time; wasn't it? Or whoever all those other people he's tied up with are? What's *Lisa* done?"

JoJo finally looked at me, his expression bleak. "There really are things it's just better not to know." He turned, and started back toward the barn door. "Intermission's over, Camikins. You're the star of this show; you'll be missed if we don't get back soon."

CHAPTER 17

It was a night of very little sleep, of course. I barely managed to crawl out of bed the next morning in time to feed my zoo and get to brunch with my parents in town. The food at New Leaf was as amazing as ever, but despite my assurances the night before, I mostly *was* that "zombie" Mom had worried about. They'd actually gotten away last night without ever even hearing about Leonard Prix and Emerald City Rep. Now they were *so excited*—my father nearly busting at his seams with exclamations about triple plays and World Series wins—and I tried to act as excited about it for them as I'd been the night before. But I was *so tired*, and unable to stop thinking about Lisa.

Then, of course, they wanted to hear all about the "game-delaying crime wave," but there was no topic I wanted to discuss less than that one now. I just told them that "some man" had taken Lisa Cannon hostage in the dressing room, but that no one could tell us any more than that about an active investigation. What a useful answer *that* had become—for almost anything!

After hugging them goodbye outside the restaurant, and blowing them kisses as they drove off to catch their ferry, I dragged myself home, planning to just curl up and go to sleep again. But my phone began to ring almost before I'd gotten in the door.

I grabbed it out of my pocket, thinking it might be Lisa, but saw Jen's name on the screen instead. I knew how high energy she'd be after last night...I almost let it go to voicemail.

But...it was *Jen*. I answered it.

"Hi, Jen!" I said, trying to sound perky.

"Oh... Did I wake you up?"

So much for perky. "No, actually, I just got back from brunch with Mom and Dad."

"Ah... How did that go?" She sounded...strange. Almost like she was talking to someone at a funeral. I was halfway tempted to ask if I'd woken *her* up.

"It went fine," I said. "Are you okay?"

"Are you?" she said gently.

"Jen, what's going on?"

There was a pause. Then, "I heard something this morning... that I'm *positive* cannot be true, but... Lisa Cannon wasn't really arrested last night, was she?"

I rolled my eyes up at the ceiling. Did *anything* happen on this island, *ever*, that wasn't spread from shore to shore in less than half an hour? "How is it even *possible* that you know this already? Was it that hunky deputy's girlfriend again?"

"Oh no! It's *true?* Oh, Cam! How terrible! Why was she arrested? Are you going to lose your job now," she groaned, "and that gorgeous car? *Oh, hon! Will you have to move?* You can stay with me, of course."

"No, Jen; I'm still—"

"I'll get my ninja network on it, and we'll find you another place in no time! In fact, you know I just heard about this sweet little—"

"Jen, stop!" Silence, at last. "I *really* appreciate the offer. You are the best. But I think Lisa's going to want me here, at least for a while still, to caretake her house again, and manage the play until our run is finished. So I'm probably okay for now. I don't know much yet myself. But she said we'd be talking about it. Sometime

soon. Maybe even today."

"I'm sorry," Jen said. "But...how are you, really? Were you there when it happened?"

"I'm...sleep-deprived, and kind of...over my head. But otherwise fine, I guess. And yes; I was there—by accident."

"You sure have a lot more accidents like that than anyone else I ever met."

"That's what Lisa said." I sighed. "They did it very discreetly, behind the barn, near the end of the party. So no one would see, I guess. I only saw it because JoJo and I happened to be out there talking about—"

"Oh, I knew it!" she cut in again.

"You knew *what*?" What else was coursing through the grapevine now?

"Whatever was going on with you and JoJo last night, it wasn't very subtle. Was that something to do with Lisa's arrest too?"

"No." I brought a hand up to massage my forehead... *Kip*. I had almost forgotten that part. "It was about...something else," which I would *not* be getting into again, least of all with a grapevine nexus like Jen. Unfortunately, my answer only produced an expectant hush on her end of the line. "Which I don't want to talk about," I clarified.

"Oh, hon," she said sympathetically. "You really went through the wringer yesterday, didn't you... Well, I understand. But if you change your mind, I'm all ears, okay?"

"I know. Thanks. But, honestly, what I really need most right now is just to go get some more sleep, okay?"

"Oh, you bet! I could tell the minute you answered, actually. We can talk later about how over the moon you and your play were. I'm in and out all day, of course. But you just call whenever you're ready, and I'll pick right up. I'm here for you, Cam. You know that, right?"

"Thanks, Jen. You really are the best."

"No, *you are*—obviously! Now get some sleep!"

"Bye," I said, but she'd already ended the call before I could touch the button. And I was upstairs and asleep again almost before I'd pulled the covers up.

☙

I was awakened some time later by James: an alarm clock not even the dead could sleep through. Sadly, you couldn't set him for the time you wanted; James only went off when he was hungry—or bored—which could be any time of day or night. Right now he was head-butting my shoulder, so I scritched him and asked, "What am I supposed to do, huh?"

Continue scritching till it's time to fill up my food bowl, duh, he seemed to say. Or at least that's how I interpreted his continued purring and head-butting.

"No, I mean what should I do about *Lisa*?" I sighed. "She told me she would be in touch, but…do I just wait for her to call?" He purred. I kept scritching. "Do they even let arrested people keep their phones? I could try calling her; but she shouldn't have to deal with me in the middle of everything else she's going through, right?"

James hopped up onto my chest, and purred very gravely, right in my face.

"You're right. First, I should go see if someone at the substation knows whether calling her is even possible. Good thinking."

I lifted him off of me and set him on the floor, then got up to pull my brunch outfit back on. Downstairs, I put a little extra food in James's bowl—he had helped me figure out a plan, after all—and told him that if anyone but me came to the door while I was gone, he was *not* to let them in. "Are you listening to me?" I said severely. "There could still be very bad men lurking around here. So no heroic cat tricks while I'm out, got it? Not even for raccoons!"

He gazed up at me very attentively, and twitched his tail—which I took for a yes. Then I left the cabin to walk up to my company Porsche, hoping Jen hadn't been right to worry about how much longer it and the rest of my wonderful new life might last now.

Lisa's car was parked in front of her house right beside mine, but I'd seen it there on my way to brunch that morning, and gone to knock lightly on her front door. When there'd been no answer, I'd just figured that someone else must have brought her car back here last night.

I was halfway into the Porsche when I noticed that Lisa's front door was wide open.

It sure hadn't been that way this morning.

Could there be deputies in there—looking for something? But if so, where were their vehicles?

Or… Was it one of those bad guys I had just warned James about, here to finish some business that Derek had failed at? I still had no idea what he had even come here to do.

I stepped back out of the car and softly closed the door, my skin prickling for the first time since I'd scared Kevin off—only lightly, but definitely in the chameleoning way. I shoved back at the urge to vanish as I all but tiptoed down to Lisa's porch. To my mild surprise, the tingling faded. Was I really getting control of this thing somehow—after all these years?

I couldn't think about that now.

I walked silently to the open doorway and peeked inside, leaning one way, then the other, trying to make sure that no one was waiting to leap out and attack me. But there was no sign of anyone there. I cleared my throat, kind of loudly. No good could come of surprising anyone—good guy or bad, or even raccoon. Then I tapped lightly on the door frame. "Hello?" I called softly. "Is anybody in here?"

I heard footsteps coming from the dining room, and Lisa appeared in the doorway.

"Hello, Cam!" she said, smiling just as warmly as always. "Are you recovered from last night?"

"Yes! You're here! I mean, I'm so glad to see you, but…JoJo… told me you were being arrested last night…"

"Did he?" She looked less cheerful. "What *else* did he tell you?"

"Nothing. But, was he mistaken? I thought it had to be a mistake, right?"

Her smile faded as she looked down and turned an ankle out stylishly to show me the thick, blocky band fastened around it. "House arrest. Do you like it?" I tried not to look horrified, but my expression seemed to amuse her anyway. "It's the chic-est ankle bracelet Sheriff Clarke could come up with on short notice. I'll get something more fashionable, I'm sure, as soon as I find time to peruse the catalogues."

"I still don't understand. I know you can't talk about it, but—"

"I can, though," she cut in. "With you, at least. Would you like to come in?"

I nodded, and followed her through her kitchen to the dining room, where her table was as cluttered with work as ever. She sat in her usual chair, and I sat across from her. "Is it *okay* to talk with me about this?" I asked. "I don't want to get you in any more trouble than…I guess you're already in?"

"Don't worry. We have Sheriff Clarke's permission. I told him I'd need you to take care of my home and a good deal of my business while," she made an uncertain gesture, "all this plays out. He conceded that since you'd already been an informant for so long, you would know most of what…" She fell silent, probably in reaction to my mortified expression. My cheeks felt like hot pads.

"They told you that?" I barely found enough breath to speak. "Lisa, I never reported anything about you to them. I swear it. I told them I wouldn't do that when they talked me into this; and they said I didn't have to, so I never—"

"Oh, Cam, I know!" She looked almost as embarrassed now as I felt. "Clarke told me all of that too—while explaining his decision to let me talk with you. I'm so sorry, dear; what a stupid…" She rolled her eyes. "You might as well know that I've been one of their informants practically since Sheila killed Gregory Baines."

For a minute, all I could do was stare back at her. "Wait! So...
you knew about me? What I was doing—the whole time we sat
here in those meetings about *discretion* and—"

"No!" She looked ready to laugh now. "Any more than you
knew I was working for them too! Clarke only told me last
night—defending your honor every inch of the way, if that helps
any." She leaned back again. "They're *very* keen on compartmen-
talizing, aren't they? But Cam, if I'd had *any* doubts left about
your ability to be discreet—and I didn't, just so you know—
they'd be entirely erased now."

So, JoJo really hadn't told her either? That seemed...surprising.
If it was true.

"So, as I was saying," Lisa continued, "I told Clarke that there
was simply no way to equip my assistant for all these tasks if we
couldn't discuss at least *relevant* aspects of what's going on. In the
end, he agreed to let me, for the reasons I've mentioned—but
also because, as of last night, things have been set in motion that
make any risks posed by loose lips fairly moot now. Happily, the
sheriff seems to have left defining the term 'relevant' up to me—
which gives us a pretty wide latitude of permissible topics. So, if
you have questions, go right ahead and ask them."

"Okay." I had so *many*—including a few new ones now. "Who
were *you* reporting to them about?"

"That," she said, "is *not* a question relevant to any of your duties as my assistant, and therefore, not one I can justify answering." She gave me an apologetic look. "Try again?"

I shrugged, and sorted through the other possibilities. "Then
what are all these things that have been set in motion since last
night?"

"Oh dear." She looked even more chagrined. "I don't even
know much of the answer to that myself." She gave me a pained
smile. "Want to try for a third strike?"

I thought about asking if she knew JoJo was a CI too, just to see how she'd react. But if she *didn't* know… Well, I was still mad at JoJo, but not enough to do *that* to him, or to Lisa. So, all right; I supposed I should just get to the scary part. "If you were an informant for them too, then I *really* don't understand why they're arresting *you* now."

"Ah…" She looked down, steepling her hands on the table in front of her. "Well, that one is extremely relevant, I guess—since I'm going to be asking so much of you now." She looked up again. "I guess I should start by saying that Sheila wasn't my personal assistant at all, really."

"I know. She ran security for you; against Derek and whoever else all this is really about. She told me that when I went to visit her."

Lisa gazed at me, seeming daunted for the first time since I'd arrived. "You went to visit Sheila? In jail?"

Oh. So Clarke hadn't told her everything. "They sent me to talk with her—when I went to take those pictures of the salon in Seattle."

Lisa's brows rose. "I see. So, you really do have a better poker face than I thought, don't you. And what about that visit with Marie?"

I nodded. "They arranged that too."

She gave me a rueful smile. "Well. Just stop me then, if I'm telling you things you already know." I nodded again, and she went on. "Being the CEO of a pharmaceutical company hadn't taught me anything about managing security operations or personnel, and I wasn't very good at it. I hired Sheila for all of the wrong reasons—as if she were just another mentoring project. She did have experience; in fact, she'd worked for Derek. And, like so many others, she'd been mistreated and had become extremely disenchanted with him. I wanted to help her. Or help her avenge herself on my loathsome ex-husband, maybe. I thought her disgust with Derek would give her deeper incentive to protect me, even make her more effective."

Lisa gave a huff of grim laughter, then grew serious again. "But I certainly never instructed her to kill anyone—or ever even dreamed she might. So the morning she came to tell me she'd just had to shoot Gregory Baines—to protect *me*..." She made a helpless gesture. "I panicked. I was horrified. But Sheila didn't even seem to know she'd done anything wrong. She just seemed surprised I was so upset, and kept explaining how she'd discovered Baines had been sent by Derek to spy on me, and then killed the Brixtons' former *caretaker*—and who knew how many others! Imagine what it was like to just...hear this."

The poise and self-assurance I'd always seen in Lisa's face were gone now, making me sorry I'd asked the question. "From her point of view," Lisa continued, "she'd just done the dirty, distasteful work of protecting me from an imminent threat, and seemed to think I should be grateful! But I had no idea who Sheila even was, suddenly, and just grew furious, and terrified. I think she felt...betrayed by that."

I'd dismissed so much of what Sheila had said to me that afternoon as self-justifying nonsense. But now... I'd clearly sold her short.

"I had no idea what to do," Lisa went on. "Criminal penalties barely occurred to me at first. All I could think about was what such scandal would do to everything I'd spent my whole life building: the complete collapse of my company's viability, and of my legitimacy. And before I could think any of it through, there was a deputy at my door, asking about a reported shooting on my property."

My work.

"The minute I saw that SUV pulling up to the house, I sent Sheila out the back way into hiding—desperate to cover it all up any way I could." Lisa shook her head. "Then, I just...tossed up that disastrous story about a *play rehearsal.*" She looked disgusted with herself. "Not just a criminal lie, but such a stupid one— impossible to support for more than hours, if anybody looked into it—which Rankin certainly did." Her eyes focused on me. "I knew what a dreadful mistake I'd just made—and so, of course, I immediately made another even worse one."

She bit her lip, and looked away from me, out one of the windows—just the way Kip had looked everywhere but at me last night.

"I quickly modified my idiotic tale," she said, "by telling Deputy Rankin that, actually, Sheila had told me she'd be running lines out on the property with one of my actors that morning, but that, on second thought, I wasn't aware of anything in our current play involving a gun. I suggested he might want to talk with her about that." She looked down, clearly ashamed. "Sheila was the one who'd done this, after all—both to Baines, and to *me*. Let *her* explain it to this deputy. Then it would look like *she'd* been the one lying—to both of us.

"When Rankin asked to talk with her, I pretended I wasn't sure where Sheila was…and pulled out my phone to call her—in the very hiding place I'd sent her to. She answered, probably expecting an 'all clear,' and I asked her to come back to the house. Then…I claimed to be late for an appointment in town, and asked Rankin if it would be all right for me to go." Lisa shrugged as if her shoulders weighed a hundred pounds each. "I left poor, stupid, trusting Sheila to walk alone into the trap I'd laid—or the one we'd laid together, I suppose." She fell silent and gazed at me, clearly braced.

But if she expected me to despise her now, I couldn't. I knew too much else about her, and still had too many reasons to be grateful. I thought back on my visits with Sheila and Marie: how each of them had stories I had never understood, or even guessed at. And now, here was Lisa's. I couldn't look down on any of them; I just…wanted to cry. For all of us.

"But, none of that worked," I said, bleakly.

"No. The whole disaster fell apart in days, and I was suddenly facing an accessory to murder charge. The rest, I assume you've already guessed. I confessed to everything I've just told you—and to everything that I knew then about my ex-husband's conduct at our company, and his harassment ever since. Clarke called the FBI, the FBI called the Mounties, and when Veierra and Mc-Michaels were finished grilling me, they explained that Derek might be the chance they'd been waiting for to access much more important targets. They offered to adjust my potential penalties if I'd help them get to Derek and a few others in my orbit—which I was happy to do—and assist them as a confidential informant. Most of my time away this winter was actually spent on business for them. But that arrangement ended last night, of course, when Derek surprised us all, and triggered the investigation's end game." She gave me a lopsided smile. "So… Am I still 'right about everything,' Cam? Never going to doubt me again?"

I thought about how much had changed—for me, at least—between the time I'd said that to her last night, and today. And what it must have been like for Lisa to have floated through that huge party, celebrating my success and still trying to enlarge it, even then, knowing the whole time what was about to happen to her.

"I'm still grateful for everything you've done for me," I said at last. "And I still don't think you deserve what so many other people have just kept doing to your life."

Her smile vanished, and her eyes grew visibly moist. *Please don't cry now*, I thought, doubting I could see that without crying too—and not just for her.

"That's very sweet," she said, softly. "Much kinder than I think it would ever occur to most people to be. You're one of a kind, you know."

I thought again of all she'd done for me. "I've had good teachers—like you."

"And there you go again." She sighed. "So…while I'm confessing things, I also need to admit that I only ever befriended you at first because damage control seemed to require that. But…

you took me by surprise, Cam. And you've never stopped—ever since."

"So you knew…all this time, that you were going to be arrested in the end?"

She nodded, sadly.

"Will it all be like this now? House arrest, I mean?"

She shrugged. "I don't know yet, but probably not. The people they're really trying to take down here will have the best attorneys in the world and more money than God. Accusations of testimony influenced by excessive lenience would just be used as a path to mistrial. So I'll probably be doing a Martha Stewart stint in some real prison."

I could think of nothing to say that wouldn't just sound… naive. I couldn't imagine Lisa Cannon in jail. "So, why did Derek…do that to you, last night?"

"Well… Believe it or not, he thought he could convince me to bail *him* out of all the trouble he's left the rest of us in."

"*What?*" I exclaimed. "By taking you *hostage* in the middle of a play, with hundreds of people just outside the room?"

She gave me a mildly reproachful look. "Has anything you've heard about him made him seem bright?"

"No. But what could you have done for him? And why would you have done it?"

"When you convinced Marie to talk, the dam he'd been hiding behind broke. And it seems he was well enough informed to know his rope had reached an end. I guess he's been living off of credit or plain old swindling and theft for quite a while now—the dark powers he'd gone to for money have run quite out of patience with him. So, he thought he could frighten me into using my resources here to get him 'safely to Canada.'" She gave me another weary smile. "Apparently, he *wasn't* well enough informed to know that Canadian authorities have been right here working alongside the FBI. Even if the parties he's running from would blink at obstacles like national borders."

"Huh. But why did he even think you'd do it?"

"Oh, you'll be able to appreciate the humor in this one," she said. "Ready?"

I nodded, thinking, *Humor? In any of this?*

"He told me that if I refused to help him, he would just go tell the authorities about everything I'd done wrong. *He* was going to rat on *me*."

Okay... That *was* funny, if you knew... "Didn't you tell him they already knew all that?"

"Of course not. If I had, I'm sure he'd just have tried hurting me physically to get what he wanted—for all the good it might have done him." She shook her head. "I merely played dumb and stubborn, as we ladies are expected to, and kept him arguing and threatening and insulting me until someone finally noticed I was missing, and came to find us—as I knew they would." She gave me a slight grin. "If only you guys hadn't managed all those little fiascos on stage so well without me, it might have happened sooner, though I was horrified when Derek managed to take Hal by surprise, and knocked him out like that."

I thought about his and Rebecca's weird behavior when Lisa hadn't showed up to deal with "Jenny's" costume problem. "Hal and Rebecca were your bodyguards, I take it?"

"Yes. I guess that must have been pretty obvious too, by the time all this was done."

"And...what about all those bigger, scarier bad guys?" I asked. "I don't suppose you can tell me who all of this has really been about."

She shook her head. "My own attempts to get to the bottom of it, and to protect both my company's assets and my own from Derek, led me to conclude a long time ago that he was probably in bed with some pretty scary creditors; but even now, no one's telling me exactly who they are—for all sorts of obvious reasons."

I nodded. "So, do you know how long you'll be here then, before...you have to go?"

"I don't, actually. But I'm given the impression I'll be here for at least a week—which brings us to the question of *your* involvement from here—unless you have more to ask first?"

"No. Let's talk about what you need me to do."

She looked down at the orderly stacks of paper spread before her, then up at me again, almost anxiously. "Given everything I just told you, I guess the first question has to be, do you still even want to be my personal assistant?"

"Well, yes!" I said, startled. "Why wouldn't I?"

Lisa blinked at me, swallowed, and looked down at her papers again. When she finally looked up, her eyes were brimming above a grateful smile. "Thank you." She gathered herself, then said, "The play's clearly in great shape now. It should be pretty smooth sailing for the rest of the run. I'll just need you to keep managing things as you've done so beautifully all along—and settle up with everyone and get things all sorted out and put away afterward. The booster club ladies can help with that. They do most of it anyway, and understand the rest at least as well as I do. Tonight, however, we'll need to explain my absence to the cast. I'm hoping you can help with that too."

"Oh—right!" That hadn't even occurred to me yet. "So, you're not even allowed to attend performances now?"

"I'm afraid not. The sheriff was kind enough to let me finish enjoying last night's opening. But house arrest means exactly that. I won't be leaving this building again until I leave Orcas altogether for wherever I am required to be next."

Sitting there in her home as we had done so many times before made it easy to forget that she was already a prisoner. "So…what do you want me to tell the cast?"

"Well first, I'd like you to convey my tremendous delight in last night's amazing performance—and all the even more amazing heroism everyone showed during the, uh, unscheduled intermission. Then, I think it would be best for now just to say that last night's ordeal has left me in need of some rest and recuperation, and that the sheriff has asked me to stay at home under protective surveillance while they make sure no one else was involved in last night's adventure beyond the man they arrested. Tell them I've appointed you to cover my responsibilities for now." She shrugged. "They'll obviously have to be told the rest soon, so I'll prepare a letter explaining things, and have it mailed to everyone before next weekend. This weekend, however, I don't want them any more distracted than they already are from the task of getting more settled into their roles and the normal flow of performance. Questions?"

"Not about that part," I said. "But what about your life here? Will you need me to take care of things like mail and groceries now?"

"Well…yes, I suppose I will." She gave me a wry smile. "You see? Opportunities, just like I said the other night. You're finally going to get to shop for me, Cam!"

"I, uh, hope there are bigger opportunities somewhere here for you than that one."

"Oh, there definitely are," she said mysteriously. "They'll become clearer later." Before I could react, she went on. "I'll also need you to watch over the house again once I'm gone, of course." She waved again at all the paperwork between us. "I'm getting my affairs in order here, so that you'll have clear, well-organized files on everything you could possibly need to know. I'll leave you a manila envelope containing essential documents and instructions, as well as an easy index of where to look, under what file headings—or who to call—for any of the rest; along with a full set of keys for the house and outbuildings, of course. So there really shouldn't be any big riddles for you to navigate—about anything.

"I have no doubt whatsoever that you are completely ready for this," she added. "And I'm never wrong, about anything—not even that, remember?" She gave me a rueful smile. "I know it's a lot to ask of you, Cam." She looked down and shook her head.

"No, not a lot; *everything*—and you *are* allowed to tell me no—now or at any other time. I want to make that clear. What I've done...to place myself in these circumstances is not your responsibility to bail me out of in any way."

"Lisa, I'm so sorry all this is happening, but I'm not bailing you out of anything. The mistakes you made don't just cancel out the rest of who you are—all the people you've helped, or tried to, at least. And I *want* to be here for you like you've been there for me in so many ways since I showed up here."

Lisa smiled at me softly. "I could almost thank Sheila just for bringing you into my life. You're a treasure, Cam." She straightened her papers again, then looked back up with something almost believably like her usual smile. "And, just to be clear, your salary is already set up for automatic payment, and I've taken the liberty of giving you a raise. I'm not sure how often or easily we will be able to talk for a while; but finances, at least, shouldn't pose any trouble for you."

"That's... Thank you." Then something else occurred to me. "I'm not going to have to...do anything about your company in Seattle, am I? Because, I am so not qualified to—"

She waved the question aside. "I'd have appointed others to manage anything like that, Cam. But there's no need, because I've already resigned as CEO, and begun arranging for my complete separation from the company. I had hoped once that the authorities would come after Derek and his friends in some way that left me and my company seeming more deceived and victimized than...*involved* in what happened there. But the truth is, that business with Sheila and Baines was far from the first thing I botched along this road..." She fell silent for a moment. "My further connection to the company I built—in any way at all—would only risk taking everything I've accomplished there down with me. I won't do that to all the people who've worked so hard and well there for so many years."

Every time I thought we'd reached the bottom of this terrible well, it just got a little deeper. "How badly off is that going to leave you?"

"Oh..." She made a dismissive gesture. "Don't worry about that either. I still have plenty of resources, and friends on the board who are grateful I'm not making them fight me over this. Our separation agreement will leave me well enough provided for, I assure you. And, well, honestly, all this has made me see that...I'm actually ready to set all that down, I think." She paused, looking pensive. "For so long now, I've thought of that place as my biggest achievement and my primary purpose in life. But...if I hadn't been so consumed by concern for all of that, I don't think I'd ever have made the horrible decisions that brought me to this. I think my business has actually come to own me more than I own it, and that's been producing bad decisions on my part for a while, really; not just since everything blew up with Gregory Baines."

"Aren't you being, maybe, kind of hard on yourself?" I asked, wondering if I had any business giving Lisa Cannon advice.

"No. If anything, I'm finally realizing that it's time to be *easier* on myself. Whether you want to believe it or not, Cam, you've actually been mentoring me. Having you in my life has, well, reminded me of things—about what life used to mean—how it used to work, a long, long time ago, without all this." She gestured vaguely around herself. "That life, so long ago, is what created the woman who created my company; and, when all this unpleasantness is done, I'd like to find some of that life again somewhere in all the space I hope setting my company down will open up."

"Well, thank you. But I can't see how I've had anything to do with that."

"No, of course you can't," she said cheerfully. "You were just being you—which is why it worked so well." She stood up. "So, let's talk again as soon as all this information is properly organized; but right now I should get back to that task, and you should go do something to clear your head of all this before to-night's performance. The bar got set pretty high last night. You don't want slump tonight!"

"We won't," I promised her. "But we're really going to miss you."

"Not as much as I'll miss you guys," she said sadly. "P. T. Bar-num liked to say, 'Always leave 'em wanting more.' Well, you all certainly did that. I wish I could watch you all again—over and over. Thanks to you, I've gone out with a real bang here. There are worse fates."

"You're not *going out*. You're just…stepping away for a while, right? This is an intermission, not a curtain call."

"Well…" she said. "I'll be delighted if that turns out to be true."

CHAPTER 18

By the time I left Lisa's house it was after two-thirty. In less than four hours, I was supposed to be back at the barn to get things ready for our second, hopefully far less eventful performance. But she'd been right about doing something to clear my head. I could hardly imagine performing that whole play again with my mind in such a jumble. As I headed back to my cabin, I texted Jen to say I'd have to call her tomorrow; then I checked in with the critters, changed out of my brunch clothes into something more outdoorsy, and headed a short ways down Deer Harbor Road for a quick hike up the south end of Turtleback Mountain.

The trail is steep and sunny, with spectacular views of everything from the Olympic Peninsula to Canada. But I noticed hardly any of it as my thoughts went around and around—from last night's hostage crisis, our triumphant performance, and that amazing offer from Emerald City Rep, to Kip's belief that I'd written Martin's part about *him*, and JoJo's endless meddling in the background, even as he got ready to leave the island for who knew where or how long—and now Lisa's arrest for trying to cover up the murder I'd witnessed on my first morning here. All that—in a single day! *Twenty-four hours!* How was anyone supposed to cope with that?

I understood Lisa's panicked misjudgments—and I sympathized. I really did. If there was one thing I'd understood pretty much my whole life, it was panic. But…she'd lied to me, and to everyone, not just about what Sheila had done, but about…well, even liking me—at first, anyway. And what bothered me most, really, was how *many* secrets had been hidden, all around me, all this time, without my ever guessing any of it. Since the Feds had recruited me as an informer, even *I* had started keeping secrets. Everything just kept turning into something else in this "safe, peaceful, quiet" place!

I'd come to feel so at home here, with my new friends, and even with myself. But now, I wondered if I really knew any of us— even me—as well as I'd thought I did. Did I really want to be living in Lisa's house, running her theater troupe—"being her," even though I wasn't, and never would be? Even dear, reliable Jen had started acting like she was afraid *I* might leave *her* behind. I had just come here to hide, hadn't I? Hardly six months ago! And now, here I was: about as far from hidden as a person could get. Wasn't that crazy? Who would I be in six *more* months—and doing what? With JoJo gone somewhere, and Lisa in prison maybe? It all just made me feel like going home to lie down.

The hike helped, though. I was breathing hard before I reached the Ship Peak lookout, and tired enough to feel a little more relaxed by the time I'd hiked down again.

Back at the cabin, I was feeding the animals before heading back to the theater, wondering what it would be like to perform all those scenes with "Martin" again tonight. Could I do it without just getting him all tangled up in my head with Kip—or JoJo even—again and again for two more weekends after this—without even a director now?

There was a knock at my door. Well, it wouldn't be Lisa, I thought, and it wasn't, of course. It was Paige Berry, with her usual giant bag of produce—huge dark greens poking from the top.

She thrust it at me and marched in. "First crop of the year! Beets and green onions—with that deliciously hardy zing that being first up out of the winter ground always gives them!"

What I couldn't eat, Bun would. "Um, thanks," I said, setting the bag on my table while she went to warm herself in front of the fire I'd lit, hoping for a little cozy warmth.

"Roasted beets are *wonderful* in a salad," Paige went on, seemingly oblivious to—well, anything, "with chopped dates and goat cheese, of course—I threw some of that in as well. And a splash of orange balsamic shrub—easiest thing in the world to make. Balsamic vinegar, sugar, macerated oranges. Keeps forever."

"Thank you," I said again, wondering why she'd come just when she must know we would both need to leave for the theater soon. "So, um, were you just out for a walk again?"

"Oh no, I came quite specifically to congratulate you on last night's triumph, dear! No one on this island will ever forget that marvelous performance—and carried off despite such drama!"

I stared back at her, amazed at how...well, *tone-deaf* this seemed. Unless... Had she not heard yet about Lisa? Paige Berry, who knew about everything on the island—before almost anyone?

As if hearing my thought, her cheerful expression gave way to one of deep sympathy. "Oh, my dear, are you just miserable?" she asked sadly. "Of course you are. I've just talked with Lisa. I'm so sorry." Of course she'd known. Had she just been feeling out my mood before commiserating? She stepped over and wrapped me in a hug, which I surrendered to. It was more than a hug, really—more an enfolding, a holding, a deep soothing. As she murmured reassurances in my ear, I realized that this was just what I had needed—all day.

I drew out of her arms gently and looked her in the eye, remembering the last time she had come here without warning, on that terrible night...and the conversation we had...never really finished. Could all these timely appearances really just be happy coincidences?

And what about her absurdly gigantic vegetables at all times of year? Just the result of "water, sun and a dash of fertilizer"? I still didn't think so... *I will answer your question when you can answer mine.* That's what she had said.

James nudged her ankles, rubbing his whiskers against her tattered pant leg. She bent down to stroke his waving tail. James had always trusted her, and, with a small jolt of surprise, I realized that I had come to trust her too—and maybe even myself a little more as well.

I'd betrayed my secret in front of all those video cameras in the county jail, after all—and what had it cost me? Nothing I could point to, yet. I'd *chosen* to show Kevin the truth outside of Darvill's the day I'd run him off the island. If I'd taken such a risk with him, why not with Paige? Seriously, *why not?* If she was... something like whatever I was, I needed to know—even more than that marvelous hug she'd just seemed to know I needed too.

"Paige...can we talk for a minute?" I asked. "Before we have to go, I mean?"

She gave me a smile. "Well, of course, my dear. Why shouldn't we?" She went over to my little table and sat down. James wasted no time leaping up into her lap to start kneading a soft place for himself. "That lovely jar of mint tea might be just the thing right now," she said. "Shall we heat it up?"

"Jar of tea?"

"The one I had you put aside for later. Last time I was here; remember?"

"Oh!" *For heaven's sake.* That had been months ago! Had she really expected me to... Well, yes, of course she had—and now I didn't want to admit I'd just thrown it out the very next morning. "I'm so sorry. I, uh...drank it, I'm afraid. Some time ago. I could put a new pot on."

"Oh, don't bother then," she said with a dismissive gesture. "We do have to leave soon. I just thought if it was all ready to go… But no matter. What shall we talk about?"

I sat down across from her. "Do you remember our talk? That night?"

"Well, of course." She looked surprised. "I'd be unlikely to forget a conversation like that." She gave me a probing look, then leaned back slightly. "You had questions, I believe—as did I."

"Yes," I said, feeling chills across my skin again—that had nothing to do with chameleoning. "You don't…already know, do you? About me?"

"I would not presume to *know* anything you haven't chosen to tell me." She waited. Expectantly. And, suddenly, I *was* afraid again.

What if I was wrong? What if she just gaped at me, like Kevin had back on the awful night that sent me running here? What if she bolted out of my cabin and told everyone I was crazy?

"Nothing you can say will shock me, dear." She gave me a reassuring smile. "And nothing said here, however strange, will ever leave this room. You're safe. I promise."

James tilted his head and peered up at me almost as if to second her claim.

Take the leaps that come… She'd said that too. *Okay…* "I can't explain what I'm about to tell you," I said in a rush, afraid of losing my nerve. "I don't know how it works or what it means. But…when something frightens me… When I feel threatened, I…I disappear sometimes." I fell silent, despite the flood of qualifiers and disclaimers clambering to be added. I couldn't find the breath to say them. Paige just gazed at me, smiling, waiting for me to say more. She seemed unsurprised. "I mean…literally," I croaked. "No one sees me, or…or even remembers I'm there. I just…blend in and vanish. Like a chameleon."

"Oh yes. Like camouflage," Paige said, nodding as if some expectation had just been confirmed. "That makes sense."

"It does?" Even though I had suspected for so long that she might understand, it was still hard to believe. "How? Why?"

"Well, it explains a few things that seemed to make no sense in any other way."

"Like…what things?" I wondered now how many people besides Paige I'd tipped my hand to—and how badly.

"Oh…to start with, how so many things seem to happen right in front of you that would certainly not have happened if others had known you were there to see them. But most of all, I believe you because, as you clearly already suspect, I have some strange gifts of my own."

"I knew it." The words were out before I could stop them.

"Of course you did. People like us recognize each other."

"People…*like us?*" I said, as all the implications of that phrase began tumbling out.

Paige nodded. "People like you and I are rare, but we are by no means alone, dear."

I brought both hands to my mouth, as if that might hold back the half-disbelieving sob of relief forming in my chest. There were *others*—like me—like *us!* Until that moment, I had been so afraid, no matter what I'd told myself, that I *must* be crazy—like my mother. If…if she *had* been crazy. Had she been? Or just… "Do you…vanish too, then?" I managed.

"Oh no, though that sounds fascinating." Paige shook her head. "I…enliven, and…repair things. Or should I say…" She glanced down. "Things are enlivened and repaired *around me.* I'm not sure how much I really have to say about it."

"I've never…really had any control either. But I think maybe I'm starting to."

"How very useful that would be. But be careful. I find that things sometimes go awry when I try to make things happen with my gift. I'm sure you'll recall how that worked out for Porter and me." She shook her head. "It may be best just to…let your gift take the lead. Such abilities…know what they are for, and when they're needed, far better than we do, I think. A thing I wish *I* had understood earlier."

It was hard to imagine how letting my "gift" go on deciding when I should disappear could be better than learning how to have some choice about it. But I just said, "Well, at least your *gift* helps people. Disappearing seems to cause more trouble—for me, at least—than anything else; and, well, for other people too sometimes."

She gave me a sympathetic nod. "I can see how it must have seemed that way. But hasn't it protected you too?"

"Well, yes. But…it's also kept me…hiding all my life. Running from people." *And from myself,* I added silently.

"I really am trying to be much more careful about intruding lately," Paige said, "but many of us—most of us, really—are afraid of our gifts at first. And it's hard to discover much about something one is always hiding from, you know. Do you think your gift could be about more than just vanishing when you're afraid?"

"More…like what? Disappearing is the only thing it's ever seemed to do."

"Are you sure?" She gave me a wry smile. "This island is a very lovely place, full of lovely people, Cam. But it is also very insular. Outsiders are kept very much *outside* here, as I'm sure you must have noticed." Well, yes, of course I had, long before Jen had pointed the fact out to me. "Yet look at how you've come to be included here," she continued, "after what—not even a whole year among us?"

Much less time than that, actually. "Okay. Yes, I guess I have… But what does that have to do with—"

"You said it yourself, just minutes ago," Paige interjected cheerfully. "You *blend in*, like a chameleon." She spread her hands, as if her point were obvious, though it still wasn't. Not to me. "Couldn't your gift have something to do with blending in more broadly, dear? An ability to foster belonging and connection perhaps? Look at all the ways you have become an important part of so many people's lives here. Maybe blending in visibly is just the only expression of this gift that's caught your attention yet."

"Belonging and connection?" I blurted, almost laughing. "I've been an awkward freak all my life! I told you about...what my childhood was like."

"Your mother's death, and your terrible brush with foster care. Yes." She nodded sadly. "I have not forgotten, dear."

"My friends back in Seattle thought I was just a frightened little mouse. My...my boyfriend, back then... He thought I was *crazy*. How was any of that *belonging* or *connection*?"

"But you were *running* from your gift then, weren't you? Now, however—*here*... Well, you have not just fit in, but changed the very lives of nearly everyone you connect with. I can't think of anyone here who would even imagine you an 'awkward freak.'"

"I have no idea whose life you think I've changed—unless you mean...getting Lisa arrested."

"I wouldn't be so hasty to assume even that change is entirely bad for her," said Paige.

"*What?* How can going to prison not be bad? How can you say such a thing?"

"Well, I'm not the one who said it, actually." Paige shrugged pleasantly. "Lisa did. She seems well aware that this sad event has served to interrupt a life already going in all sorts of wrong directions. Didn't she say as much to you this morning?" Paige gave me a quizzical look. "She seemed to think she had, when we talked just now."

I thought back...well, yes. I'd just thought she was trying to put a positive spin on things. *Cam, you've actually been mentoring me...* Could she have been serious?

"Oh, really, dear," Paige chided. "Open your eyes and dare to have a look! You've changed *my* outlook on all sorts of things— not to mention Porter's! Don't you see that? You've changed not only Lisa's view of things, but even JoJo Brixton's, which I'd certainly never have expected to see. You've made your friend Jen think twice about her gleeful career as a busybody, and Sheriff

Clarke rethink all sorts of sad assumptions. Even Colin finally seems to have found a woman worth staying with." She leaned back, looking smug. "And then there's Kip, of course. I'd say you've changed his life quite profoundly."

Kip *again*? After all of this? I wasn't even going to take the bait this time. But she'd certainly been keeping a close eye on *my* life, hadn't she? "Well, I guess my *gift* may have helped get all those people into one kind of trouble or another too, if that's what you mean."

She rolled her eyes, looking exasperated. "Are you really so determined to keep running from yourself this way? Cam, in one way or another, your ability to go *unseen* has ended up forcing all of us to *see ourselves* more clearly, and changed us in the process. A complete outsider. In less than a year. I'd say your gift may be a great deal larger and more useful than you've ever guessed, my dear—if you will just stop hiding so hard from it, and pay it a bit more attention than you've...wanted to before."

As what she had been trying to tell me, so patiently and persistently, finally started to sink in, the tumblers of some lock, deep inside, began to turn... *Running from yourself...hiding from your gift...* Hadn't Lisa been telling me the same thing, in her different way, for months now? And Jen too. They'd all seen it. They'd all said so—in so many ways... But I'd been so frightened, for so long...of being *seen!*

I just sat gaping at Paige, hardly able to believe I might have missed so much...all this time. "Were you afraid?" I asked her. "When you discovered what you were, I mean?"

"Oh, not really. My gift was never so noticeable, or so frightening, as yours must have seemed. I was in my early twenties before I even really started guessing it was there." She shrugged. "I'd always just thought I had a *green thumb*, and a caring way with animals—and even that much didn't occur to me until well into my teens."

Lucky woman.

My mind was welling with questions now. "Are there others like us here? On the island?"

"None—that I know of, anyway. It's been just me, I think. Until you came along. But I have run into a few others, elsewhere in the world. We…stay in touch. Most of us, anyway, though some trust no one; which is why I am so honored that you've been brave enough to trust me, dear. Have no fear, I will not betray that trust in any way."

I shook my head, still barely able to absorb the fact that there were *others*. Like me. And one of them was sitting right here in this room! I was not alone. I was not crazy, or a freak. I was just… what, exactly? What *were* people like Paige and me? "Do you… know what these gifts are? How this kind of thing works?"

She leaned back and chuckled. "Heavens no, dear. Does it matter? They just do. What more does one need to know?"

But there were all sorts of things. I had more questions now than ever—and, finally, someone I could ask. "There is one thing that…well, it worries me, a little."

"Oh? And what is that?"

"I…uh… I had to visit someone in jail a while ago."

"Ah," she said. "Sheila, perhaps?"

I leaned back in surprise. "How can you know *that*?"

She gave me another of her little shrugs. "It just makes sense; that's all. Who else do you know here who'd be in jail right now? And…it would fit well with how all the rest of this has tumbled out so suddenly…"

"Does anything happen on this island that you *don't* know about?"

"Of course. Countless things." She gave me a strangely apologetic smile. "But I have a knack for speculation; and things do tend to come to my attention. Another aspect of my gift, I suppose. I have no idea what your visit with Sheila has to do with this discussion, though—beyond the fact that her life would seem to be another one your gift has changed."

Right, I thought, tempted to ask her how getting *Sheila* arrested could have been a good change—for her anyway; but I had a much more urgent question. "Right at the end of our visit, she got really upset and started acting…well, scary the way Sheila can. And, of course, my gift took over and made me disappear—just for a minute—right there in a prison visiting room full of other people and video cameras." The memory still made me shiver. "I have never been so scared of getting caught. I didn't even think I'd get out of the building before someone stopped me to demand some explanation. But no one's ever said a thing." If Paige didn't already know somehow that I'd been reporting to Sheriff Clarke, I wasn't going to tell her. I knew how *that* trap worked by now. "And I can't figure out why they wouldn't have, unless my disappearance that day didn't show up on the security videos…"

Paige went on gazing at me, as if waiting for something more. "And this worries you…how?" she asked at last.

"Well… If I didn't vanish on any of those security cameras, then…what does that mean?"

She went on looking puzzled for a moment, then her brows rose. "Oh! You're afraid it didn't really happen? That you've just been making it up in your head after all?"

"No. Not exactly," I said, suddenly unsure what I *was* trying to ask. "I mean, Sheila had seen me do it before—and unlike most people, she'd remembered somehow too. She was trying to make me tell her how I did it—like it was a magic trick or something—when she got so angry that the guards came to take her away, and I vanished. She was screaming at everyone to look at how I'd disappeared again—so something must have happened, right? But…no one else there seemed to notice I'd been gone… or to care, at least. And…that's not how I've always thought it worked. I've either been invisible to everyone, or I haven't. But if that's true, then…why not on the cameras too—or for anyone else there that day?"

"Ah…" she said sympathetically. "So, you still need to know how it works. Or if it's *real*, maybe? Is that what worries you?"

"I don't know," I admitted. "I just…need to understand what's been happening all this time. What I really *am*."

"Well." She sighed. "Now I am torn by a difficult choice. I could speculate about what *might* be happening. Or, I could advise you about why such speculation might not be wise or helpful. But either of those will be meddling, of one kind or another—which I keep trying not to do so often anymore." She turned her hands up, as if hoping I'd solve the problem for her.

"At least I'm *asking* you to meddle this time, which is different, isn't it, than just meddling without being asked to?"

She smiled, and nodded. "An interesting distinction. And not a bad point, really."

"Then, couldn't you just…do both? Speculate a little, then tell me why that's a bad idea—and let me figure it out from there?"

Paige began to chuckle, silently, making her body bounce slightly in the chair, to James's clear annoyance on her lap. "Oh, you are quite the handful, aren't you, young lady? Very well, then. Perhaps you're asking the wrong question. People often do. Should you be asking *where* it works, instead of *how*?"

"Where it works?" I was completely confused. "You mean, where I *am* when it happens?"

"No, I mean where your gift itself actually happens," she said, as if that should have been obvious. "If video cameras don't see you vanish, maybe it's because you don't vanish out here where such cameras are made to see things happen."

This was so not helping. "Where would I be vanishing except 'out here'?"

She tapped at the side of her head. "In here, of course."

Now my confusion was turning to frustration. "Didn't you just say I wasn't making it up?"

She rolled her eyes again. "Not in *your* head, dear; in *theirs!* Your gift might act on their minds, rather than on the physical world—which, before you ask, would certainly make it no less *real*." She tapped at her head again. "*In here* is actually where almost everything happens to any of us. And that's a completely different conversation which we must save for some other time. But, here's one last piece of advice, young lady, before I really do attempt to stop intervening in what absolutely must be *your* process of discovery." She leaned forward, gazing at me very gravely. "Are you listening?"

I nodded, wondering if this conversation could possibly get any weirder.

"When you don't know the answer to a question—especially a question like this one, don't rush to invent one. Fill such spaces with hasty speculation, and there won't be any room left for the actual answers, should any ever happen to show up."

She stood, slowly, giving James time to leap from her lap, under audible protest. "Now, while I'm sure you have a million other questions, we will have to address them later, I fear. Isn't it past time we were headed for the barn?"

"Oh!" I said, twisting around to look at the clock. I'd completely forgotten the play!

CHAPTER 19

Isn't it amazing how things we've expected all along can still take us so completely by surprise? Closing night had always been right there on the calendar, getting nearer, day by day. But as we stood on that stage for the last time, taking our final, final bows before a riotous standing ovation, I just could not believe that it was really over—the play we'd worked on for so long…and so much else besides.

News of Lisa's arrest had been a huge shock to the cast, of course. But her letter to us had so clearly and honestly expressed ownership of her poor if panicked choices, that our commitment to making her last production *shine* had just increased. I'd worried that enthusiasm for the play might shrink as news of her fate spread—which there was no way to prevent on this gossipy island—but, to my relief, our audiences had just grown larger and more excited as *Salon Confidential* became every bit as hot a local topic as its "criminal" backstory was by now.

They'd taken Lisa off the island several days ago—not to prison, she'd explained during our final in-person meeting. Not yet. Just into protective custody "someplace safer" for a while. When I'd asked why they'd suddenly decided that was needed, she'd just moved breezily on to other final instructions regarding my upcoming role as her caretaker and local representative.

I'd left that meeting feeling really, really sad, and more than a little shaky—a condition not helped any by Sheriff Clarke's phone call less than an hour later to tell me that the investigation had entered its "terminal phase," during which I was advised to exercise "additional caution, vigilance, and discretion." He'd given me a special phone number to call "immediately and without any hesitation if *anything* or *anyone* seems at all suspicious *anywhere* in your proximity during the next few weeks"—none of which had been comforting.

When I'd asked him if I was in actual danger of some kind, he'd said, "Oh no, Ms. Tate! This is just a routine call made to CIs at this point in any such investigation. No cause for alarm—though we do want you to use that number if anything at all seems *strange* to you, okay?"

His effort to make all that sound routine had just made it even more alarming, of course. I'd hung up wondering how I was even supposed to *know* whether something in my "proximity" seemed strange, when *everything* in my proximity had just been getting stranger since my literal first day on the island! I'd been half tempted to call that special number right away, and tell them that one of my dearest friends and best mentors *ever* was being carted off to prison while another was leaving town for good—to escape himself—and that I was starring in a play three nights a week now, before a whole roomful of strangers in the dark, any of whom might be a serial killer, I supposed—which all seemed pretty strange to me; *should I be concerned?*

But I hadn't, of course. I might be a star now, but I hadn't become a *prima donna* yet.

And nothing odder than usual had happened to me since then. Except that JoJo was leaving now. As in really leaving—and on the very morning after our last performance! He'd left a note in the women's dressing room informing me of that earlier this evening, which had hurt more than I'd have guessed it could. I mean, a *note? Really?*

We'd been talking far less since our argument at the opening gala; though, honestly, with me running Lisa's whole island kingdom by proxy now, there hadn't been much opportunity for us to hang out anyway. We'd only seen each other at performances—which were always rushed and full of distractions—and he'd gone right on seeming pretty much his usual outrageous self there. Our few interactions, onstage or off, had all seemed pleasant enough; though I guess I might have wondered at times, in a semi-conscious way, if we were all right.

Well, his little "FYI—goodbye" note this evening seemed to answer that all too clearly. Cornering him to hash all that out was now pretty much item one on my to-do list at tonight's cast party, which would be starting soon out in the field behind the barn—where Lisa had been arrested, and where Roland Markus was finally getting to use one of his *fabulous tents.*

But first, I was giving myself this one last moment to stand alone on the darkened stage before a now-empty theater, and think about how far I'd come.

These past eight months had been both the scariest and the most fun of my life. Who'd have guessed last November that this place would be too small to hide in? Being forced to stand on a stage and learn to perform in front of people had been even scarier for me than all those murders were in some ways. Yet, after a lifetime of being frightened into literal invisibility, here I was, center stage! The only vanishing thing about me now was my fear of being seen. I hadn't tingled once since that talk with Paige two weeks ago—not even during Clarke's alarming phone call. Maybe even more telling was my new comfort with praise. I'd bowed low to that clamoring audience tonight, and again, even lower, feeling nothing but pleasure. Then I'd gestured in thanks to my fellow actors, and the tech and stage crew, as if sharing the light with others was something I'd done all my life. All because of this amazing place, and my kind, quirky, sometimes troubled new family of friends here.

Who'd have guessed on the night I'd fled here in the rain and darkness?

Outside, I heard the jazz band plunge into a rousing kick-off tune, and knew my moment alone was over. I looked down and smiled at the ridiculously glamorous dress I'd bought for tonight—crimson, sequined, and form-fitting with a plunging neckline and an even lower back. The woman I'd been eight months ago would never have been caught alive or dead in a dress like this—even if she could have afforded it—not that she was gone now. No, she would always be inside me, cringing, blushing and apologizing; and I wouldn't have erased her even if I could have. She was me too—and responsible for everything else I had become. She'd sent me running here, hadn't she? I would always owe her for that, and for so much more.

I walked down the stage-right stairs one last time, then along the hallway to the barn's large back exit, and stepped out into a warm summer twilight festooned with a thousand Italian party lights. Rows of tall white banners dramatically lit in tasteful pastel colors swayed and belled softly on the gentle evening breeze. There were already lots of people on the brightly lit outdoor dance floor Roland Markus had installed; and behind the bandstand, his giant party tent glowed from within like a Mongol palace built of amber candlelight. The field was transformed, and the air was rich with the mouthwatering scents of all those wonderful appetizers Lisa's caterer had made. I'd done the legwork to arrange all these things, of course; but Lisa had called in all her favors, and spared no expense for this party—saying she wanted to thank her cast and crew for all the years of hard work and delight they'd given to her and the community.

My first responsibility tonight had not been assigned by her, though. I started toward the tent to get a drink, so that I could intercept the jazz singer's mic before the next number started, and raise a toast to the gone-but-not-at-all-forgotten founder of our feast.

Before I'd gone ten feet, however, a long, low whistle came from somewhere to my left, and I turned to find Charles looking me over appreciatively with an upraised thumb. Beside him, Glory nodded her approval with a wide smile. I struck a suggestive pose and gave them a seductive wink—drawing more whistles, and a quick scattering of laughter and applause from others in the crowd. The woman I'd so recently been just winced and blushed inside, reminding me that tomorrow I'd be back to life in the *real* world. And that was fine.

I continued toward the tent at a more businesslike pace. But just inside the doorway, I pulled up short in real if begrudging appreciation. An even greater abundance of silky drapery, dramatic lighting, and several large, lovely flower arrangements had it looking very Hollywood in here!

Unfortunately, the man responsible was there too, standing right in my path.

"Ms. Tate!" Markus exclaimed—getting my name right for once, surprisingly. He glided toward me with upraised hands. "What a stunning dress! And, if I may say so, what a stunning *play!* I'm so sorry not to have found some earlier chance to say this, but I think your delightful comedy would give *Steel Magnolias* a run for its money!"

I just stood blinking at him. What on earth was this about? Had he banged his head on a lighting fixture while setting all this up?

He halted in front of me, looking slightly abashed now. "I must also apologize for... Well, we got off on something of the wrong foot, I'm afraid. But I trust we can...start fresh, perhaps?"

And then I got it. Of course! *I* was Lisa Cannon now—for at least a couple years, anyway... And decisions about whether to hire him again—*or not*—might be up to me? It took all my new acting discipline not to laugh out loud. "Well, Mr. Markus," I said, smiling courteously, "I have to say that this tent of yours looks awfully nice too. And, while you were, in fact…a *little* obnoxious for a while there at the start, your set was pretty much everything I'd hoped for. So, thank you for all of that; and yes, by all means, let's just get off on a whole new foot next time!" I brightened my smile a bit more and cast an appreciative glance around the tent. "*Everyone* talks about how talented you are, and they're right!" I wriggled my fingers at him as I started toward the bar where my friend Porter was busily serving up the fabulous wines he'd provided at a breathtaking discount.

"Ohhhh, Ms. Tate!" he said as he looked up and saw me coming. "You are a vision!"

"Thank you, Porter! And thank you so much for doing all this for us!" I made a sweeping gesture at the bar.

"The pleasure's all mine," he said with a wry smile. "Verna and I have plenty to be grateful to you for. And any association with this terrific production can only be good for my business. What can I pour for you? On the house, of course."

"Well…have you got a decent Cabernet?"

"Certainly not!" he said, severely. "I do not carry *decent* wines, Ms. Tate." His theatrical frown dissolved into a grin again. "I carry only the *best* wines!" He pulled a dark, heavy bottle with wide, beautifully embossed shoulders from underneath the linen-covered counter, and poured my glass with a flourish.

"Mmmm!" I said, after my first swallow. It was rich and complicated; smooth on my tongue, and warm all the way down to my belly. And it left lovely legs in the glass. "I'll be in to get a case of this tomorrow."

"That," he said, wiggling his eyebrows at me, "was my wicked plan all along. Anything to lure more of your delightful company, my dear. And since this is probably my last chance to say so before you're mobbed all night, thank you for the best fun we've had around here in years. Verna and I loved your play to heaven and back."

Despite my new resolve, I felt my cheeks flame. "Thank you,

Porter. That means so much coming from you, and makes me even sorrier to rush off now; but I've got a toast to give up on the bandstand—and probably only seconds to get there."

"Run then! But carefully!" he chuckled, hiding the bottle away under the counter again. "You don't want to spill a drop of that."

"I always run carefully," I called back. "Especially when I'm drinking!" I was thrilled to see that Markus had vanished. But then I practically collided with Jen at the doorway. I managed not to spill a drop of Porter's amazing wine on either of us, but, weirdly, Jen just stood there, blocking my exit and gaping at me.

"Oh…*Cam*…" she breathed. "My *goodness!*"

"Are you okay?"

"You look…like a movie star." She sounded dazed. "I mean a *real* movie star."

If this had come from anybody else, the woman I was now might just have played it off with a snappy comeback. But this was Jen. And Jen did not act this way—not *ever* since I'd met her. She'd always been very encouraging and complimentary, of course, but not…in this weird *groupie* way. "Jen…?" I asked again, unsure what to think.

Her eyes rose to mine, and the dazed look vanished. "But if you're gonna wear a dress like *that*, hon, you gotta lean into it!" Her usual grin was back as she stepped in, glancing quickly around for effect, then reached straight up for my cleavage.

I took an involuntary step back, eyes wide—still without spilling the wine. "What…?"

Jen laughed. "Sorry. Just wanna make a quick adjustment." She made a *may I?* gesture.

I looked around too now, but Porter was busy with another customer, and no one else seemed to be paying us any attention. "Uh, sure?"

She stepped in quickly, gave my bodice a rapid downward tug, then stuck her hands inside my architecturally fortified neckline to either side of the girls, and shoved them gently but firmly in and upward, causing my cleavage to, um…announce itself more, uh, forcefully. 'The whole maneuver took less than five seconds, and I'm virtually certain that no one saw a thing, but my face was practically as red as my dress when she was done.

Jen took one more glance around, then gave me a self-satisfied grin. "There. Now you're *wearing* that dress."

"I've got to give a toast now, Jen! And I want them to remember what my *face* said, not—"

"—Then you should *never* have chosen this dress," she cut in happily. "But trust me, you should *definitely* have chosen this dress! Ooh-la-la, hon! If only Kip—"

"Do *not* say it!" I cut her off. "I don't want to hear that again—ever—from anybody." Just then, the band's first song finally ended. "Oh crap, now I have to run for real! That's my cue."

"I'll be right here listening—to your face!" Jen laughed as I dashed away toward the bandstand with a hand pressed over the top of my glass. If I'd just had my cleavage adjusted in the main tent without anyone noticing, there'd be some inconspicuous way to lick wine off my palm on a bandstand, right?

As it turned out, though, running with wine seemed to be another of my superpowers. I got there as the band leader was still chatting up the crowd between numbers, a little breathless, but without more than a drop or two on my hand. I didn't have to call my arrival to anyone's attention, because the lead guitarist made a lurid *wa-wa* sound with his guitar while grinning at my…presentation, which got *everyone* looking my way. "Before you guys go on," I asked, stepping up onto their low platform, "can I borrow a mic and make a toast to Lisa Cannon?"

"You bet, Ms. Tate!" said the vocalist. "But make it a long one, please. I'm pretty sure people will be in no hurry to look at *us* again when you're done." This got him a few chuckles from those close enough to hear.

Oh Jen, I so *did not need your help with this*, I thought, taking the mic from him with what I hoped was a gracious smile. I turned quickly to the crowd and raised my glass. "Ladies and gentlemen—" For some reason I was drowned out by a rousing wave of applause before I could say anything more, but pausing for applause was an automatic reflex by now. "Thank you!" I said when they were done. "Especially all of you who supported this production as donors, production partners, volunteer support staff—I'm talking to you, booster club—and, of course, our amazing cast and crew." I paused for another round of applause. "I especially want to thank Erin and José Salazar for all their labor and support hosting both this play and tonight's party!" I waited out more applause. "And, of course, I'd also like to thank the family members of our cast and crew. I know we turned many of you into widows, widowers or orphans for weeks before opening night, but we deeply appreciate your sacrifice."

"You can have him longer, if you want!" cackled a woman near the back. "Sure was a whole lot quieter at home!" This brought another wave of laughter.

"Yes, well, I'm sure our next production will be around before you know it," I assured her. "But I think there's no one who deserves our thanks tonight more than the founder of this theatrical company, and the primary sponsor and driving creative force behind so many great plays enjoyed by this community over the years. And she's the sole host of this lovely party too!" That drew plenty of applause. "I'm sure that most of us, so closely involved in this production, are aware of why Lisa can't be with us this evening, as she would so much like to be, and that we'll be deprived of her generous company for a while longer now. But she's done more for me in the past months than I will ever know how to say, and more for so many people on this island than I can begin to guess. So, if you have a drink in hand, I hope you'll raise your glass with me now. And if you don't have a drink, just act like you do—because we're all about theater here, right?" I lifted my glass to another smattering of laughter. "To Lisa Cannon!" I said. "Until she's back with us again."

"Lisa Cannon!" they roared back, raising their drinks—real or imagined.

"Thank you! Now, let's enjoy the party! I think we've earned it!" As they clapped and shouted agreement, I gave them a grateful wave, handed my mic back to the singer, and beat it off that platform as quickly as I could, still trying not to splash a precious drop of Porter's really very tasty wine on any of the well-wishers jostling forward to compliment my toast, the play, my performance—or my dress.

As the band swung into their next number, I found Jen waiting at the margins of the crowd. I just had time to thrust my glass safely to one side as she wrapped me in a big hug. "You are *unbelievable!*"

"Why?" I laughed. "What have I done now?"

"You were...so eloquent and in command up there! They were eating from your hand, Cam!" She shook her head in amazement. "I'm gonna have to start calling you Madam President!"

"Try it, and we're finished." I chuckled. And speaking of eating... "I can't actually remember when I ate last, but this wine is already going to my head. Wanna go find some food? I know the menu by heart, and believe me, we want some of *everything* before it's gone."

"Lead on!" she said cheerfully, as we started toward a smaller, open-sided tent where food was being served on tiny little paper plates to keep it from disappearing as quickly as I used to. I was not surprised to find Paige Berry working right beside the catering staff to serve things up and keep the line stocked—even though this party was supposed to be as much for her as anyone.

She glanced over as Jen and I reached the table, and leaned back, looking wowed. "Well! There you *are*, dear—at last!"

"At last?" I asked. "Was I expected earlier?" She hadn't imagined I was going to work the food line tonight...had she?

Her smile grew impish. "I suppose not. But it's such a pleasure to *see* you like this now."

Okay…I was clearly missing something. "Well, it's a pleasure to see you too—and so nice of you to be helping with the food still. Are you going to come out and celebrate with the rest of us sometime tonight, or just go on being heroic back here?"

This drew hopeful glances from some of the catering staff. I tried not to let them see I'd noticed, though I sympathized. Paige could be quite a handful—even when she meant to help.

"Don't worry, dear," Paige said primly. "At my age, it's *all* celebration. What can I get you?"

"I've heard rumors," I mused, "that you might have a small supply of larger paper plates back there somewhere—for special guests? Any truth to that?" I knew the answer, of course. I'd arranged for those plates myself.

Paige gave me a mildly disapproving smile as she went to pull two sturdy eight-inch paper plates out from under the linen-draped table. "When people start asking us where you got these," she said with mock-severity, "I'm going to send them back to *you* for explanations, dear."

"Thanks for the warning."

"And what would you two like on these?" Paige asked with amusement.

"One of everything," I said. "For each of us."

"Oh…wait," said Jen, gazing down the long buffet. "I'm definitely feeling peckish, but—"

"I'll eat whatever you can't," I cut in, "but I'm betting I won't have to. I had to taste every one of these things when I met with the caterers. You'll thank me later."

Jen shrugged. "Okay then. It's your stomach pump!"

We took our plunder well out into the field, hoping for enough privacy to have a real talk before my public found me again—and to avoid calling our big plates to anyone's attention.

"Okay, so, mmm, you may have been right again," Jen said, already halfway through her mound of goodies. "Maybe you should come brainstorm the Barnacle's menu with me. This is going to keep me up all night, I'm sure. But, oh my goodness, what a way to go."

"Didn't I tell you?" I said around a mouthful of my own. "I can't help you, though. This is all the caterers. I just had to make a lot of terrible choices about what not to let them serve tonight." I dabbed daintily at my mouth with a napkin. "Is my lipstick ruined?"

"No. You're fine, of course." Jen poked her plastic fork into what remained of her food, and looked thoughtfully off at the valley beyond us. "What are we going to do now, Cam?"

"What?" Wanting a breather, I bent my knees inside the tight dress and set my plate down on the lawn. "Do about what?"

Jen looked back at me. "This has been the most interesting not-even-a-year of my life. And, well…that's mostly your fault. So thank you."

"Are you serious?" I laughed. "You're the one who took me under your wing, Jen! I'd have been lost here without you."

She gave me a crooked smile. "Okay, fine; it's a draw then. But the play's over now. And I guess the investigation is over too, right? I mean, if they're arresting people, I suppose the murder spree on Orcas is finished." She looked like someone had just eaten her last cookie.

"You're bummed about that? Seriously?"

"No… Of course not. But…what *are* we going to do now?" She set her plate down as well. "We gotta come up with a new project, right?"

Well, between keeping Lisa's estate in order, managing her theater company, and writing new plays for Emerald City Rep, all I really hoped for was a break someday. But when she'd said *we*…I knew what she really meant. "So, you're telling me that four jobs is not enough activity for you?"

"Oh, hon, I don't think I can just go back to cleaning rooms, serving drinks, walking dogs and delivering packages. You've spoiled me! Ever since you showed up, I've had so much more than that; and now…"

"Well…this is great!" I said, seeing the solution—for both of us. "Because, if you're serious, I could sure use some help. I've got a decent handle on the caretaking part of things by now; but whatever you may think, I have no idea how Lisa ever managed that whole theater company by herself. If you're looking for another project, Jen, I have so got one for you!"

"Oh! Seriously? You'd let me help you run these plays?"

"I'm still not sure you really get it," I laughed. "This is not a *favor* I'm suggesting. I'll be thanking *you*, if you agree to this. In fact, I'll probably have to thank you if you're even still speaking to me by this time next year."

"Oh, you are the best *bestie* ever!" she cried. "When do we start?"

"Um…not here, probably. I just bawled Paige out for working through this party; and if she catches us doing the same thing, she'll never let me live it down."

"Right. This is your big night! What am I thinking? Wanna get another drink?"

"Good idea!" I looked down at my plate and sighed. "It makes me want to weep, but…I don't think I can finish this after all. This dress is really tight!"

"I'm so glad to hear that," Jen said, picking our plates up off the grass. "Because if you had finished yours, I'd have had to finish mine, of course. I'm kind of the competitive type—though I'm sure you've never noticed that." She grinned. "But maybe let's find someplace to throw these out where Paige won't see us do it?"

"Smart," I said, looking around. "That can over there should be out of her sightline."

"*Out of her sightline*," Jen chortled. "Listen to you, all theatrical now."

As we headed for the trash can, I became conscious of a nagging sense that something was missing—or left undone? Then I realized what it was, and turned to Jen. "Have you seen JoJo?"

"No… That's weird; he's never seemed the 'miss-a-party' type to me."

"Huh. I have to go check on something." I turned and started back toward the crowd in mounting panic.

"What's the matter?" Jen asked, clearly concerned now. "Is everything all right?"

"I'll tell you later," I called back to her as I hurried off. Could he have decided just to leave tonight for some reason, without even saying goodbye? What if that letter had just been meant to throw me off? Was there some rich-boy helicopter waiting at the airport?

If JoJo had snuck off this way without even giving me chance to say goodbye, I would never, ever forgive him—no matter what kind of undercover spy stories he tried to hand me next time.

I all but ran through the party, looking for any sign of him, but came up empty. So I hurried back inside the barn. *"JoJo?* Are you in here somewhere?"

Nothing.

I rushed to the hallway where the bathrooms were. *"JoJo? Can you hear me?"*

I heard a toilet flush, and waited hopefully, but the man who came out wasn't anyone I recognized.

I turned and ran back past the stage, not even knocking as I rushed into the men's dressing room—and found JoJo sitting calmly at the makeup table, reading a *newspaper!* He twisted around to look at me, and his eyes widened. "Well…my goodness," he drawled approvingly. "Look who's having her diva moment. My sweet little Camikins, all grown up."

"What are you *doing*?" I demanded.

"Reading a paper?" he asked, as if the question confused him.

"That's what I mean," I said, crossly. "There's a cast party out there, if you haven't noticed—and you're a pretty important member of the cast."

His brows rose in mock-surprise. "Is it just the dress doing this to you? Or have you really made the jump that quickly?"

"What jump?"

"Ingénue to diva—in sixty seconds flat, apparently."

"Stop calling me that. You're the diva here, not me."

"You may have a point," he said with a smirk.

"My point is that you're missed out there. Are you coming or not?"

He sighed wearily, and turned back around to pick up his paper. "If I'd wanted to be sniped at tonight, I'd have invited my mother."

Okay… I took a deep breath to unclench myself, and walked over to lean against the table edge beside him. "I'm sorry, but when I realized you weren't out there, I was afraid you might have gone already…without even saying goodbye."

He went on gazing at his paper. "I believe I've said goodbye several times already."

"You mean that note?" I asked indignantly. "After all we've been through, you were going to toss a note at me, and call it good?"

He shrugged, still not looking up. "It seemed the least risky approach."

"Least *risky*? Risk of what?"

"Being misunderstood," he said, his eyes still fastened on the paper as if it were too fascinating to look away from. But it was just a page of advertisements—in the fashion section.

"How have I misunderstood you, JoJo?" I asked quietly. When this got no response, I tried again. "Whatever I've done, can't we at least try to work it out before you go tomorrow? I really don't want to leave things like this."

He set his paper down at last, and turned to me. "I don't want to meddle in your life again. Perish the thought. But could it be yourself, not me, that you've misunderstood?"

Well, that sure made nothing clearer—but at least we were finally talking. "Can you help me understand what that's supposed to mean?"

He just gazed at me in silence at first. "I guess I could try that. But only for you. And only this one last time." I saw no hint of the usual JoJo there now, which was kind of frightening. "Would I be mistaken," he asked, "in assuming that you understand I've trusted you in all sorts of ways I trust virtually no one else? Except for Lisa, of course."

"I do understand that, and I appreciate it, deeply."

"Good. So, can I also assume you understand that I grew up with a family that blamed *me* for every ugly thing in their dark little heads that they couldn't stand to see in themselves, much less take responsibility for—and that pretty much my whole life, out here in the poisonous world, has been carefully constructed as a fortress against that kind of violation?"

"You've...made that pretty clear too. On a couple of occasions," I said, wondering what I'd done to merit this frightening monologue.

"Yes, I thought so, as I've always been careful *not* to do with other people ever, except for Lisa Cannon—the first and only person I'd ever met who didn't try to nail all her shadows to my back, then drive me off into the wilderness—until *you* came along."

"JoJo, hurting you is the last thing I'd ever want to do, but I still have no idea what I've done. Please just tell me what—"

"A few weeks ago," he cut in, "you asked if I had told our law enforcement buddies—behind your back—that you were crazy."

"Well...I never said you *did* that. I just—"

"—just wondered if I *might* have," he cut me off again. "So, maybe you didn't trust me quite as much as I had thought you did—or as much as I had come to trust *you* by then." He shrugged. "All right, that hurt, maybe more than I let on that night, but—"

"I know. And I was sorry. I hope I said that; I think I did, but I thought we'd worked that—"

He held a hand up to stop me again. "I thought we had too.

And I'll give you all the time you want to talk. But I need you to let me finish first, okay?"

I nodded, bracing myself.

"Thank you," he said. "So, yes, we worked that through, and I thought I understood, actually. I may or may not be a wicked cretin in real life, but I do play one very convincingly on TV. I know that, and I gave you a pass, explaining—without tossing in a single joke, if I recall correctly—that I would never betray you that way. You seemed to hear me. All good.

"But then, just two nights later—*'after all we'd just been through'* to quote a distinguished acquaintance of mine—you did it *again*, even more angrily than before."

Did WHAT? I thought, keeping my mouth shut, as promised; but I still had no idea what I could have done to make him so angry. We'd hardly even talked since—*Oh…no!* Our argument? At the gala? That had lasted all of three minutes—before Lisa was *arrested*—which had sure blown our petty quarrel clear out of *my* mind! Could that be what he'd been hanging onto all this time? How juvenile was *that*?

"*Once* is a misunderstanding," JoJo said. "But accusing me of betraying you *twice*—despite my heartfelt apologies and assurances just days before; despite having just gone through everything that happened that night—is a *pattern*. A pattern I don't wear anymore, for anyone."

"Okay, just stop!" I exclaimed. "I never accused you of *betraying* me, *Mr. Diva*. I was tired of everybody—not just you—trying to manage some relationship that doesn't even exist in *my* life; and maybe I got crankier than I should have. Maybe I was even wrong again about what you'd done. But—"

"*Just tell me what you said to make him think that!*" JoJo yelled, coming to his feet. "*That's* what you *shouted* at me. And you weren't just accusing me of something I didn't do. You were accusing *me* of something *you* did!" He'd lowered his voice again now, but that did nothing to hide his anger—or his hurt. "It had never even crossed my mind that Martin might be some avatar of Kip in your head, much less that I should go *suggest* the idea to him." He shook his head and sat down again, seeming more exhausted than angry, suddenly. "That was all *you*, Cam. Not me. And when Kip noticed your little faux pas, the only way you could live with that, apparently, was by making it *my bad*—at the very minute we were losing Lisa." He looked down at the floor between his knees, and said very quietly, "So I lost both of you that night, at literally the same moment."

He just sat in silence for a while. I had no words either.

"I'd known for days what was going to happen to Lisa," he finally went on. "Her arrest, I mean. I was prepared for that. Then Derek showed up. But *you*, Cam…" He sighed. "I never saw *you* coming. I'd thought that…you and I would face the rest of it together." He sounded as broken as he'd seemed that night. But now I wondered how much of the emptiness I'd seen in his eyes then had been…my fault? "I guess that's pretty much it," he said, looking up again. "So if you have things to say, I'll listen now. Go right ahead."

But I was truly at a loss now. It was like he'd just spun the stage around to reveal some completely different play going on behind the set. My head felt stuffed with paper. "I never meant to… I had no idea what any of that meant to you, JoJo—and I'm so sorry. But it all meant such different things to me. I wish we could have talked about this…earlier. But I know I was busy and not paying attention," I rushed to add, not wanting to sound like I was blaming him again, "and I'm sorry for that too. I just don't know what to do now." I felt light-headed, and went to sit in one of the other chairs. JoJo followed me with his eyes, as if deciding whether I was dangerous or not.

"I've done my time in therapy," he said quietly. "I know what PTSD is, and that normal people like you wouldn't feel the way I do about things like this." Normal people like me? I didn't know whether I should laugh or cry. "If you think I'm just a spoiled, self-pitying rich boy who's never even known what hard really means, I wouldn't blame you. But spending the first eighteen years of my life as a household scapegoat for all the people my whole self-image was most dependent on wasn't as shallow a cut as it may seem." He looked at me with a soulful expression like the ones I remembered from our day up at the lake. "To someone like you, I'm sure that argument was just another stupid spat. But it pushed a lot of very old and painful buttons for me..." He looked down again, as if ashamed—a look I'd *never* seen on him before. "For me, getting blamed by someone for their own stuff feels like..." He looked up again, almost skittishly. "I still don't... handle that kind of thing very well."

I understood what he was saying so much better than he thought, of course; but I'd never trusted him with anything at all about my own past. Before I could decide how to tell him that, he straightened up, seeming to draw himself in, and said, with a touch of his usual JoJo bravado, "Just in case it isn't clear, I'm trusting you again right now by pulling all the whiniest, most pathetic cards I've got right out in the open where you can stick a knife in them and laugh if you want to. So, now's your chance. I almost wish you would. It'll sure make leaving here tomorrow a lot easier." Then he sat there gazing at me, looking more transparently defiant, and scared, than I would ever have guessed he knew how to—really seeming to think I might actually laugh in his face. And that just broke my heart.

"First," I said, very quietly, not wanting to do anything that might shut him down completely before I'd had my say, "you might want to save a little room for doubt about assumptions that I'm one of those *normal people* who won't understand what it's been like for you. I spent several years of my childhood in foster care before those parents you met at Thanksgiving adopted me..." I wondered how much else to say. I wasn't anything like ready to tell him things I still hadn't even shared with Jen. "If you come back someday to sleep on my floor and eat all my food like you promised to, maybe we can pull out a couple bottles of that wine you talked about, and I'll tell you why they took me away from my birth parents. We can compare notes on whole lives lived in a fortress." His face was set like stone now, and I realized that if I wasn't careful, he might think I was just trying to compete with him. "But to make sure I don't just exchange one misunderstanding for another one here, I'm not telling you this to compare my pain to yours. I'm just trying to tell you that I do know what it's like to hide all your life—and how it feels when someone touches things like that...in the wrong way." I'd left my whole life in Seattle, such as it was, and run to this island in pain and fury because Kevin had called me crazy one night. He hadn't hit me, or threatened me really, or even cheated on me—that I knew about. He'd just been a narcissistic jerk who'd belittled me and failed to take me anywhere as seriously as he expected me to take him, and then finally touched something he hadn't even known was there, in a stupid, insensitive way... And I'd repaid him for that now, hadn't I? "So, I don't think any of those awful things you want me to about you," I went on, "and I really am as deeply sorry as I should be. It doesn't matter what I *meant* that night. I see what it did to you now, and I get it, like those *normal* people—if there really are any—might not. Does that... help any?"

"You know why I left that note for you?" he asked at last.

"Because you're a jerk?" I answered with a slight smile.

"Well, yes. That goes without saying. But...there was another reason."

"I'm all ears."

"I wanted to have this talk. But I didn't want to be the one to ask for it." He shrugged. "I didn't think I should have to. But I hoped that if I just left a note saying goodbye..."

"It would tick me off enough to make me come find you?" I asked, amazed that his deviousness could *still* surprise me. He had the grace to look a little embarrassed, at least. "You manipulative twit!"

"Yes again. But it worked, didn't it. And…" That's when I realized his eyes were brimming. "I want to thank you, Camikins,
for proving me right—about who you really are, and what you'd
do about it."

Now we were both working not to cry. "Well, I'm sorry to make
your departure tomorrow harder," I said, fiercely determined not
to leave here with streaks of running mascara to go fix. "So…you
really think Kip was right then? About Martin?"

"Well, yes. Why else would you have gotten so upset when he
brought it up?" He made a pained face. "What you did to me
that night—that's a kind of panic, Cam. I get that. And people
don't panic about things they don't feel threatened by."

I looked down and shook my head. Hardly an hour ago, I'd
been standing back there in the theater congratulating myself for
having worked through so many of my lifelong issues. Just when
you think you've got things all worked out…you get a whole new
batch of issues.

How many other people had seen the same thing in my play
that Kip had? I winced at the memory of Larissa's sly smile when
she'd said she was sure that Kip would want to see the rest. Were
all his co-workers laughing at him now? Did they think I'd done
this on purpose—as some kind of *revenge* for…for what? Kip had
done nothing—ever—to deserve revenge from anybody, I was
sure. "What am I going to do now?" I asked, not quite looking
JoJo in the face.

"About what?"

"What I've done to Kip! I've humiliated him, publicly, for
three weeks now!"

"Don't be absurd!" JoJo scoffed. "You just wrote a brilliant play
that's got your own life woven through it in all sorts of ways, just
like every other piece of fiction ever written."

"Don't try to make me think it's all right," I growled.

"Listen, Kip saw himself that night because, in some ways, he *is* like Martin. But I'd bet all my mother's money that no one else saw any of that. We rehearsed that play for two months, and not even you or I ever saw any such thing there. What are the chances that anyone but Kip did after just one sitting? Unless he's dumb enough to call it to their attention—which he is definitely not— no one else is ever going to see what he saw."

Everything he was saying sounded so…convincing, and smart and…*mature*. When had JoJo learned to be mature? "Even if you're right," I said, "I told Kip he was wrong. I told him I would never do such a thing. But I was *lying* to him. And then…I ran away. Like literally ran away from him. I can't just leave it like that. How am I going to make this right?"

"Did you know you were lying?" JoJo asked.

I thought about it, hard, wanting to be honest *this* time. "Not at first. But, if you're right, I must have realized it was true at some level… I guess that's why I ran away."

"So that's it? You told him he was mistaken, and just ran away?"

"Yes," I said miserably.

"Great!" he said cheerfully. "Just stick with that!"

"You're telling me to just keep *lying* to him? Tell him I'm in-nocent, and he's an idiot for thinking something so awful about me? That's major league gaslighting, JoJo. Isn't that exactly what you just bawled me out for doing to you? How can I tell you I'm sorry and just turn around and do it to Kip?"

JoJo sighed. "Cami dear, you just asked me how to make this right. And if that's really what you want to do, then I'm afraid that lying to him is your best shot." He leaned toward me. "If you really never meant to do what he thinks you did—and you clearly didn't mean to—then what he *thinks* you did, and what he thinks it *meant*, aren't the truth either. What hurt him here really never happened—it's all just an innocent mistake." He leaned back again. "So what's going to be made right, for him or for you, by confirming his misguided fears, and the wound he thinks you meant to inflict? Do that, and you cement all this in place.

Just tell him he's mistaken—because he really is, in a way—and you make it possible for both of you just to set this down and leave it behind." He threw his hands up in a triumphant gesture. "Sometimes, sweet summer child, a lie is kinder—and even more honest—than 'the truth.'"

I stared at him for a long time. "Who *are* you?"

"Well that depends," he said, "on who it makes most sense for me to be."

"No, I'm serious, JoJo. I keep thinking I'm finally getting to know you better. But…I've still hardly even met you, have I?"

"You've come closer than most," he said with a sad half-smile. "And it's fun to have a few things left to look forward to, isn't it?"

"I don't want you to leave. Isn't there some way to talk you out of this?"

He gave me an appreciative look, and sighed. "We'd just be sorry if you did. The Feds have Derek now; he'll flip, too, and it won't be long before they go after his funders and put this whole case to bed. I'll be going somewhere far, far away for all the reasons we discussed. Lisa is safe in the gentle arms of the law. And you're now free to go about your life; collecting more wild animals to fill your whole little chicken coop of a home with now that you're encamped in the big chateau, writing more plays and whatever else you want to do." He spread his arms. "Everyone's a winner."

He got up and came to stand in front of my chair. "I told you I was in this to help Lisa. And I think I may have done that, some. My reconnaissance to our federal masters was never delivered without…skillful editing. Things could have gone worse for her without it, I believe. But please don't ever pass that along to her. I imagine she'd be pretty miffed with me."

"She didn't know?" I'd always just assumed they were working together.

He shook his head. "I never told anyone but you, Camikins. Though, I was also able to help her…better understand her part in all of that from time to time—which may have helped a little too. Lisa can be like you sometimes: her own worst enemy. But she has you to take care of her now—which is one reason I can go with a clean conscience."

I still wondered what they really were to each other. But if they'd ever meant to tell me, they'd have done it by now. "I'll do my best."

"I know." He reached out to wrap his arms gently around me. "Thank you, Cam—especially for tonight."

"Thank you. But the night's not over. Won't you come party with us?"

He shook his head. "I'm already done here. I was just waiting for you—and you didn't disappoint me." He let me go, and stepped toward the door. "I'm going home to finish packing, and then…a good night's sleep—for the first time in a long while. Will this do for our goodbye? I can't imagine what we'd say tomorrow that would mean more than all we've just said here."

I was really trying not to pout. But he wasn't helping. "I guess so—if you promise that you really will come back someday—to visit, at least."

"Oh, no doubt of that, Cam. I promise by all the cocktails I hold most sacred. So stock up on that wine—and get a chicken to keep you in eggs. You'll never know when I might suddenly appear." He blew me a kiss, and reached back for the door handle.

"Don't you want your paper?" I asked, going to pick it up in childish desperation to keep him here for even seconds longer.

"No; that's for you."

"Me?" I blinked. "Have you ever seen me read a newspaper?"

"Have you ever seen *me* read one before? This is an especially good one, though. You should really look it over before you throw it out. Do throw it out, though, when you're done." He gave me a wink, turned to pull the door open, and, a second later, he was gone.

Just like that.

I looked down at the page of fashion advertisements he'd been staring at when I came in, wondering if his strange instructions had just been more JoJo patter, or... I flipped the paper closed to look at the front page, expecting a Seattle paper. But it was today's *Los Angeles Times*. Why would anyone around here read the *L.A. Times?*

Then I noticed a tiny happy face, apparently drawn in Sharpie, at the corner of a lesser headline in the page's lower right corner. *"Net Closes In Covert Sting Operation."*

My mouth fell slowly open, as I sat down to read.

A spokesperson for the Federal Bureau of Investigation announced today that a large covert sting operation more than five years in the making had resulted during the past week in a series of as yet unspecified indictments which the Bureau claims may have significant impacts within high-level business and investment circles both nationally and globally; possibly even minor repercussions for the stock market in coming weeks. None of the investigation's targets were named in today's briefing, but the Bureau's spokesperson predicted the release of more specific information by week's end. Informed sources speaking on condition of anonymity have informed the Times that the multinational sting operation originated with a probe into the activities of several administrative staff at a well-established pharmaceutical company in Seattle, Washington...

The article went on for several more paragraphs, managing to say almost nothing of any substance, while implying all sorts of dire possibilities. But the apparent reference to Lisa's company seemed unmistakable—to me at least. This was us!

National and global! The stock market? What had we gotten ourselves into?

When the door rattled open behind me, I spun around so fast, I almost fell out of my chair—expecting mafia hit men, or something. But it was just Jen.

"There you are!" she said. "I've been looking everywhere! People are asking about you. Is everything okay?"

"Oh…sure. I'm sorry, I was…looking for JoJo, and…"

She glanced around the room. "Did you find him?"

I nodded. "He had to go, though."

"Then, what are you doing in here?"

"Um…reading the paper?"

"A *newspaper*?" she asked. "Why?"

"No reason." I crumpled it up and threw it in the nearest waste-basket beneath the makeup table before she could ask to see it. I didn't need Jen, of all people, putting any of these pieces together before the investigation's "terminal phase" was done. "Sorry."

"Well…" she said, looking at me oddly. "There's a cast party out there—and you're the star. You wanna come out and join us, maybe?"

"Oh, yes!" I said, though suddenly our little play on Orcas Island seemed like such a small concern. "Here I come."

CHAPTER 20

"So, he didn't tell you anything at all—just goodbye?" Jen asked.

She and I were at the Brown Bear, having a midday breakfast of savory scones and their silky-smooth ham and leek quiche after sleeping off quite a raging cast party. Even Paige had been dancing up a storm near the end. I vaguely remembered a goat or two dancing with her...but that had surely been the wine. Porter must have done quite well for himself last night.

"Nope," I said. "Just that he's done forever with the JoJo we all know, and going off somewhere to find out what that means."

"Well, I can't really imagine him as anybody else. I bet he gets to Bangladesh or wherever and discovers he packed nothing but himself. People don't leave themselves behind."

"I'd have agreed with you once. But I'm not as sure about that as I used to be."

"Hmmm." She gave me an impish smile. "I guess you may have a point, *Madam President.*"

"I told you, don't even start with that, Jen. I'm serious." I took a sip of my hot chocolate. "He kind of promised he'd come back and visit me someday, so maybe we'll find out."

Jen gave me a sympathetic smile. "It must be hard having everybody just disappear like this, huh? All at once—just as the play ends too? How are you doing with that?"

"I'm fine," I said. And it was true. "As long as *you're* not going off somewhere."

"Are you kidding me?" she laughed. "And quit all these jobs? There aren't enough people on this island to replace me."

"And yet, you want *another* job!" I teased. "Or was that just the liquor talking?"

"Oh no; helping you run Orcas Island Rep is the job I'd quit last, hon! So what's next on the agenda, huh? Could we do *Wicked* maybe? Or what about *The Lion King!*"

"Uh…well," I said, smiling, "those are big budget musicals with giant casts, Jen. And I'm pretty sure we don't have anything like the resources for that here." I almost laughed, imagining what Roland Markus would say if I asked him for sets like those. "We're more in the *Arsenic and Old Lace* catagory here, I think. And sadly, the first thing we need to work on is just getting *Salon Confidential* all cleaned up and…" I stopped short as the door opened and a sweet hunk of a man with blue eyes and gold-kissed sandy curls walked in looking trim, tidy, and achingly well put-together—even out of uniform.

Oh crap… Was I going to have to deal with this *now? Here?*

Jen gave me a questioning look, then followed my gaze to Kip. She immediately scooted her chair back and grabbed her over-sized purse. "Oh gosh, look at the time! So many dogs to walk, so many inns to clean, so many cocktails to invent! Bye hon!"

"No!" I cried. "Don't leave me here! I don't want—"

"Yes you do!" she said cheerfully. "The sooner it's done, the sooner you can all move on." And she darted out the door—right past Kip with a quick wave—and was gone. Kip stood in the doorway watching her go, then turned and saw me. His confused expression was replaced by a determined one.

I sighed. This was just about the last big mess left to clean up in my life. And Jen wasn't wrong: I might as well just get it over with. I gave him a timid wave and the best smile I could manage. He nodded, and approached me like a man on his way to the electric chair.

"Care to join me?" I said when he reached the table.

After just a second's hesitation, he sat down across from me. "Hello, Cam."

Cam? That was new. Or was "Ms. Tate" just part of the uniform he wasn't wearing today?

"Hi," I said. "Must be your day off?"

"Oh, sort of." He gave an abashed smile. "It's…nice to run into you." Could that *possibly* be true? "I've been hoping we…I thought perhaps…" He shook his head. "What I'm trying to say is, I'm a little tired of making a fool of myself." He gave me a small, rueful smile.

Even *rueful* looked so good on him, I had to admit.

He really was about the most appealing person I'd ever met, especially in these normal clothes. "You have *never* seemed like a fool to me, Kip Rankin," I told him. "Not for one moment. You're a marvelous man—and the best deputy on this island. I've always thought so, even though I'm not that fond of cops."

His brows rose in surprise. "You have a problem with cops?" I could see JoJo grinning in my mind. *What did I say about too much truth, Camikins?* "Is that why I scare you so much?"

Now it was my turn to look surprised. "You've never scared me! Except that night on the boat, I guess, but we're way past all that…aren't we? Why would you even think that?"

He looked a little perturbed. "Well…you tend to run away a lot when I'm around."

I looked down, feeling myself blush. "You mean, on opening night."

"That's one good example, yes."

One example? Were there others? *No,* I told myself; *don't even ask.* One mess at a time, please. But…was I really going to take JoJo's advice and double down on the lie now? Or come clean and…hope it didn't just make everything worse? "Kip…I'm so sorry about that. You didn't scare me. *I* scared me. I just didn't—"

"I know," he cut in. "I clearly caught you by surprise with… those assumptions—which makes it pretty obvious I was wrong. I'm sorry. It must have been very strange for you."

So, did that mean it was gone now—like JoJo had predicted? "Well, I certainly wasn't *aware* of doing anything like that. Has anyone else you know of seen anything like that in the play?"

He shook his head. "No…that was just my…overactive imagination, I'm afraid."

Then no one at work was laughing at him either… Maybe I hadn't humiliated him? *Now leave it there*, said JoJo's ghost. "So…you said I've run away from you before that?"

He shrugged. "I've gotten that impression, yes. But maybe that was just my imagination too."

"Like when?"

"Well…that morning at the substation, I guess," he said, averting his eyes as he had at the theater. "You seemed to be running especially hard that day."

"Oh, Kip," I sighed, wondering how I'd ever made such a mess of so many things with this kind, sweet, deserving man. "I was just trying to save your career."

His eyes snapped back to me. *"What?"*

"There were rumors all over that you were in trouble at work—getting cut out of the investigation, being shunned by other deputies. And there were people who thought that…that you and I were…inappropriately involved—which was ridiculous, of course. You'd never said or done a single thing to suggest that, but I could see why they might not believe it if you said so, and—"

He held up both hands, palm out, to stop me. "So you came down and made it clear to everyone that there was nothing to see." He looked away and shook his head again. "To save my job. Oh, that's rich, isn't it?" He looked up again and gazed at me as if weighing his next words very carefully. "So, was it true?"

"Was what true?"

"Was there…never anything there?" I felt my mouth drop open, but before I could respond, he said, "Because I could never tell. There were times when you looked at me like…" He blushed and looked away. "I'm sure it was nothing, of course, and most of the time, you just seemed like I…made you nervous, or something—which, of course I did. And I'm doing it again; scaring you and making a complete fool of myself. I apologize."

He started to stand, but I said, "No, don't leave now. This needs to get cleared up, and…I haven't been completely honest with you…about…" I looked around. The lunch hour was well over by now, and the few people left here were all sitting well away from us. "Please, sit down and let me explain some things I should probably have told you a long time ago, okay?"

He settled back into his seat, uncertainly. "Okay."

Now…what parts, exactly, should I explain—and how? "Kip," I said, scrambling for some way in, "that nervousness you saw; it wasn't about you. I've been scared of almost everything, all my life. Fear's been almost literally my middle name. My childhood was a nightmare I don't even want to talk about, but there were a lot of cops involved in it—before and after I was put in foster care—and…they almost never made anything better—for me, or…anyone I cared about. That's got nothing to do with you; but I came to see cops as dangerous a long time ago."

He looked down, sadly. "I get that; and I'm sorry, Cam."

"Please don't be. If they'd been like you, there'd be nothing to be sorry for now. But I've always been so terrified, of so many things, that I've spent most of my life running away, trying to just…disappear. That's what I was doing when I came here. And I'm so sorry you ever thought any of that was your fault."

He leaned back, still seeming to consider all I'd said. "I can see now what you're saying. But you don't seem so frightened anymore. You sure didn't seem scared up on that stage, or even in that situation with Ms. Cannon."

"Oh, I was, believe me," I admitted. "But I'm learning to manage my fears better now, or trying to, at least. And Lisa had so much to do with that before…she left. Part of that is learning to be more honest. With everyone, including myself. So, honestly, Kip, I don't think any of the confusing signals you kept getting from me were really about you at all."

"I see." He bowed his head briefly. "Thank you for trusting me with all that. I guess there are things I've been less than honest with you about too." He looked up at me. "Remember that talk we had a few months back, when I told you that I'd always wanted to go into law enforcement?"

"I do," I told him. "I enjoyed that talk." *And the way you took my hand… Stop it*, I told myself.

"Well. I've been coming to see for a while now that what I told you then isn't quite true."

I raised an eyebrow.

"What I've really always wanted to do is help people. And I used to think that a career in law enforcement would be a great way to do that. But…I've come to realize that the job is not quite what I imagined—and a pretty bad fit for me in particular. I seem to spend more time getting people in trouble than helping them. I'm usually doing it to help a lot of other people—but they're always somewhere else—living safer because of my work, hopefully—but… My job is about enforcing a bunch of clear and inflexible rules. And I keep seeing that helping people requires flexibility. That gets me into trouble sometimes."

"Well, I can see how frustrating all that must be, Kip; but there were lots of people at the theater a few weeks ago who were very, very glad you were there—including me. I have always felt better when you showed up, Kip. Beginning with that first morning at the Brixtons' house."

He nodded. "I'm glad to hear that, but I've decided there must be better ways for me to help people." He smiled, then glanced up at me with his lovely eyes. "I gave my notice this morning.

Clarke told me to take the day off and think it over. But I'm sure."

"Oh Kip!" I had no idea what to say. I could hardly imagine him as…anything else.

"So," he said with a half-smile, "I'm afraid you put on that whole show down at the substation for nothing. I wasn't in trouble there for anything to do with you, Cam. I was in trouble because I kept trying to do a deputy's job as something other than a deputy."

Then my heart sank. "Does this mean you'll be going away too now?"

"I have no idea. I'm not sure what I want to do instead yet. I've really only just admitted to myself that it wasn't this. And I have enough savings to get me through while I figure it out. No reason to go before I know where I'm going instead, and why."

Tell that to JoJo Brixton, I thought. "Well, maybe you could go into radio. I've always thought you had a lovely voice." *What are you* doing, *Cam?* "And I run a theater company now, which makes me an expert on such things, right?" I added, trying to play it off as a joke.

"Well, I'm glad you think so." He looked bashfully down at his hands folded on the table. I'd always thought his hands were lovely too, actually. "I guess I have the face for radio too."

"Oh stop it! You're—" I just managed to stop myself from saying *gorgeous* "—as good-looking as any man I've ever met."

"That's very nice of you to say, Ms. Tate."

I stared at him. "Really? We're back to 'Ms. Tate' suddenly? If you're not a cop now, we don't need to worry about formalities like that anymore, do we?"

"I guess you're right, Ms. Tate." He said it with a grin, as if afraid I might not get it. But then the grin faded. "But there's one other bit of honesty I guess I owe you—now that I'm laying down my badge."

"Oh?" I said, nervously.

He nodded. "That night on the boat. I've never, um, found the courage to tell you what that was really all about. And before I say another word, I want you to know that nothing I'm about to say requires any kind of response from you. You're not meant to do anything about this. Okay?"

I nodded—three times as anxious now about where we might be going next. But he'd listened to me tell him why I disliked cops, and fair was fair, right?

"Okay..." He took a deep breath. "I can't imagine how you could not know this by now, but I did have feelings for you... earlier on." *You did?* I thought with surprising sadness. *Not you do?* "I liked you pretty much the minute you answered the door that morning at the Brixtons'. But that was entirely inappropriate to admit or act on in any way with a witness involved in an active investigation I was working on. That's one of the things I've realized I hate about being an officer—all the ways we're not supposed to have feelings—even good ones—or act on them anyway. So I was as careful as I could be to avoid any behavior that might...complicate things that way." My head was spinning, but I kept my mouth shut for fear of what I might say before I'd seen where this was going. He cleared his throat, and said, "I hope I did a decent job of tabling those feelings at first." I nodded, and he looked relieved. "But those feelings didn't get any easier to ignore as events unfolded, and we continued...interacting.

"And then we got to that night, on the boat..." His gaze faltered. "Well, that was when it really started to look like you might be...more involved in whatever was going on than just being a witness, and I..." He looked so uncomfortable. "I'm sorry. This is hard to say, even now, but, on the boat that night, I really thought that you were playing me. That you'd been aware of my feelings after all, and using them to..." He shrugged. "...throw a hood over my eyes, I guess. You weren't, of course. That's clear now. But that night, I was convinced of it—the way I was about that thing with Martin a few weeks ago." He gave me an embarrassed smile. "You see? I have way too much imagination to make a good deputy." *Or maybe not*, I thought guiltily. *You might make a better detective.* I *had* been more than a witness that night. I'd been on that boat helping Lisa find a binder, which I suddenly hoped now didn't make me some kind of accessory to something too. "And thinking you'd done that didn't just hurt me," he went on. "It made me…really angry." He looked so miserable. I felt like a slime ball. "You know the rest. They were completely right to put me on leave—and to distance me from the investigation." He shrugged again. "So, now you know. If you're going to be afraid of me, I guess it just seems better to make sure it's for the real reasons."

I was…flabbergasted. This wonderful man had liked me *that much*—all this time! For a minute, I could only stare at him, my head too crowded with reactions to get anything clear in mind at all. And, once again, he misinterpreted my silence.

"Cam, I understand how…uncomfortable this must be for you. I've gotten this whole thing so wrong in so many ways, so many times over now, that I'd be shocked too, if I were you; and I really meant it that I don't want anything from you now. I can't think of anything worse—for either of us—than trying to beat a dead horse back onto its feet, and I'm not asking either of us to try. Whatever your reasons, you were right that day in the sub-station. And I'm fine with that. I just didn't want to leave you… wondering what you'd been through and why. And now that I know more about your past, I'm even gladder that I didn't—no matter what you think of me." He leaned back at last, giving me a painfully embarrassed look—but not glancing away any longer.

My head was so full of noise by then that I wasn't even sure what I'd just heard. "So…you don't have these feelings anymore? Is that what you're saying?"

"Yes, ma'am," he assured me. "That's what I am saying. There's nothing for you to worry about; I've put all that entirely behind me. If you felt able to go on being friends, that would make me very happy—though I can't expect you to after all you've just heard. So, whatever you want, I'm fine with. But all my own confusion is completely settled. And I'm truly sorry for whatever it may have cost you."

"Kip, you've said nothing here that makes me think less of you at all. I'm very touched and flattered that you…ever felt such things for me." I'd *had him*? And I *lost him*…without ever even knowing? Where had I been for all of that? Running away… probably. I was so scrambled inside that I couldn't really tell yet how I felt about that. But my heart ached. "You just try ending our friendship, and I'll show you some serious criminal behavior."

He looked so comically relieved that I almost laughed—or cried. I couldn't even figure that out yet. "You're a very generous woman," he said, gratefully. "Not that I'm just figuring that part out now. So… Well, I should go." He rose gracefully from his chair.

"I need to go too," I said, getting up as well. "But thank you. For all of this. I feel like I've put you through so much, without ever meaning to. I'm…sorrier than I can say."

"Well," he said, smiling a little sadly, "suppose we just agree to let each other off the hook then, okay? No harm, no foul, right?"

"Absolutely." I gathered my purse and started toward the door. "Enjoy your lunch."

"Oh, I'm not hungry anymore." He grinned self-consciously. "All that adrenaline kills the appetite. May I walk you out?"

"Sure."

We headed outside, and at the sidewalk, I gestured up the street. "I'm parked over there…"

"And I'm back there." He waved in the opposite direction.

I looked at his sweet, handsome face, wondering how long it would take me to forgive myself for getting him so wrong. I took a deep breath. "So…"

"So, have a nice life?" He smiled bravely, then turned and started walking away.

I started off in the other direction. But my heart was pounding. *Fear again?* said an exasperated voice in my mind—or, no, in my heart. *Just—stop it, Cam!*

I turned around. "Kip?" He turned back to face me. "What if…I mean, as long as you're…off duty these days… Maybe, we could…go get a meal sometime, or…"

His eyes widened, then he walked back toward me. I was afraid, so very afraid. That feeling ran too old and deep in me to change, but I wasn't going to let it go on ruling me. Not anymore.

"Cam?" he said uncertainly as he stopped, a step or two in front of me. "Just to prevent any further misunderstanding, are you—"

"—telling you I think we might be making big decisions faster than…I would like to."

He came closer, eyes shining, arms open.

I stepped into them. So much more easily than I had thought I could.

Our kiss set the world afire.

<<<>>>

RECIPES

Jen's Ruby Sipper cocktail

1½ ounces cucumber vodka
½ ounce blood orange liqueur (Solerno or equivalent)
¼ ounce raspberry liqueur*
¼ ounce lemon juice

Shake the above ingredients over ice, then decant into a martini glass. Garnish with cucumber slice and lime peel.

*Commercially available, but of course Jen used a funky little bottle made by some friends of hers out in West Sound, with raspberries grown on their property.

Beet-Date-Goat Cheese Salad

Shannon says: Mark and I had something sort of like this in a restaurant in Portland years ago, and loved it so much that we've made it a staple around here. You can leave out the arugula, and have a dense, flavorful vegetable side dish rather than a green salad. It's all good.

1 large or 2 small beets, roasted, peeled, and chopped
½ cup dates, pitted and sliced
¼ cup goat cheese (or more, I don't measure it)
3 or 4 green onions, chopped
Handful of candied pecans or walnuts
Arugula—any amount, zero to salad-bowl-full
Orange balsamic shrub to taste

Combine all the ingredients, toss together, using the shrub as your salad dressing. Start light on the shrub, it's potent. Serve immediately.

Rosemary Salmon

Thanks, Mark!

One half-pound fillet of fresh salmon per person
½ teaspoon of garlic salt per fillet
1 teaspoon fresh rosemary, coarsely chopped, per fillet
2 tablespoons olive oil (or rosemary-infused olive oil if available)

1. Heat an empty nonstick skillet over medium heat for several minutes.
2. While pan is heating, sprinkle chopped rosemary liberally on the fillet's non-skinned side, and pat it down so that it clings to the raw fish.
3. Next, sprinkle garlic salt liberally over the sprinkled rosemary.
4. When the skillet is hot, drizzle the olive oil around the pan, and toss the fillets into it, skin side UP, seasoned fish side DOWN, and cover immediately with a lid to prevent spatter.
5. Cook the covered fillets fish side down for TWO MINUTES.
6. After two minutes, use a non-scratch spatula to turn the fillets over and continue cooking with skin down and browned fish side up for THREE MORE MINUTES.
7. At five minutes, total cooking time, the pan should be removed from the heat. Unless the fillets are exceptionally thick, cooking them longer than five minutes total may result in dry, overcooked salmon.
8. Once removed from heat, fish should sit in the hot pan no longer than another minute or two before being removed a cool serving dish. The middle of the fillet may look undercooked or even raw at this point. But the fish will continue to 'cook' internally for another couple minutes on the serving dish, and should be tender and juicy with a moist custardy texture by the time it is actually served and eaten.

Cinnamon Roasted Yams

Preheat your oven to 375. Cut up two large sweet potatoes or yams into 1-inch cubes, skins on.

In a mixing bowl, combine the cubed potatoes with:

¼ cup olive oil (you can use less, but why?)

¼ cup honey (see above)

1 ½ teaspoons cinnamon

¼ teaspoon nutmeg

A dash of mace if you have it.

Stir to distribute spices and cover the potatoes with oil and honey, then spread in a single layer on a sheet pan. Karen bought a commercial grade sheet pan a long time ago and it's worth its weight in gold.

Roast for 25 minutes until tender.

Serve them sweet, or give your taste buds a thrill and add fresh ground pepper and a dash of sea salt.

These are delicious alongside fish, especially salmon, and the leftovers are wonderful for breakfast the next day under some freshly fried eggs.

Hamburger Stroganoff

Karen says: This recipe—a staple of my South Dakota childhood—came from the back of a Campbell's Mushroom Soup can, the One True Soup for all Midwestern casseroles. It's the ultimate comfort food. Any attempts to make it healthy by using low-sodium soup or low-fat sour cream are pointless and highly discouraged. You're welcome to get fancy by adding fresh sautéed mushrooms as you brown the beef (or canned mushrooms, that's probably more "authentic") but here is the basic recipe.

1 12-oz package egg noodles (the ruffly edge ones, if you're feeling fancy)

1 lb lean ground beef

¼ cup finely diced raw onion
Salt & pepper to taste
1 10.75-oz can Campbell's Cream of Mushroom Soup (use this brand!)
1 16-oz container of sour cream

While you're making the sauce, cook those noodles in salted water. Yes, salted!

Brown the beef and onion together, hopefully in an old, square electric skillet with a questionable power cord. Salt and pepper this mixture because you need more salt in your diet, clearly. When fully browned, drain off the fat, because you're going to be adding enough of that when you…

Stir the (undiluted) soup into the beef mixture and heat thoroughly.

Before serving, stir in the sour cream and reduce heat. You want to heat the sour cream gently, but not too much as your sauce will curdle.

By this time, your noodles should be done. I hope you haven't overcooked them. Drain them well.

On four plates, divide the noodles, top with sauce, and you're ready to serve with, oh, I don't know, frozen petite peas or a can of green beans or whatever excuse for a green vegetable you have. Please note, this is an easy recipe to scale for large groups, should you find yourself needing to feed a herd of hungry Midwesterners.

Pretzel Salad

Karen says: Pretzel salad is real. I heard about it from a friend long ago, and thought he was joking until he arrived at my door, proudly bearing a pan of this oddly delicious dessert that is baked, boiled, whipped, and chilled. It's also delicious, even though every ingredient is processed in some way. You may be tempted to substitute fresh strawberries or real whipped cream, but I warn you, it just won't work. Also, please make this in a clear glass baking dish, so you can see the pretty layers.

Crust:
2 cups crushed pretzels (I use the little mini pretzels, but you can use sticks)
¾ cup butter, melted
3 tablespoons white sugar
Center layer:
8-oz package of cream cheese, softened
1 cup white sugar
8-oz container of frozen whipped topping (we're talking Kool-Whip®), thawed

Topping:
2 packages strawberry flavored gelatin (just use Jell-O®) (the 3-oz size)
2 cups boiling water
2 packages frozen strawberries (20 oz TOTAL) (do not thaw!)

Crust: Preheat oven to 400 degrees. Stir together crushed pretzels, melted butter and 3 tablespoons sugar; mix well and press mixture into the bottom of a 9x13 inch glass baking dish. Bake 8 to 10 minutes, until set. Set aside to cool. Let it cool! Seriously! Center filling: In a large mixing bowl cream together cream cheese and 1 cup sugar. Fold in whipped topping. Spread mixture onto **cooled** crust.

Topping: Dissolve the two packages of gelatin in 2 cups boiling water. Stir in still-frozen strawberries (they help cool it!) and allow to set briefly. When mixture is nicely cool and starting to set, pour and spread over the cream cheese layer. Refrigerate until fully set. Then you can cut and serve—this makes about 12 squares.

COMING IN 2023

Orcas Afterlife
Tales from the Berry Farm, volume 1

Just when Camille Tate thinks life may finally be done throwing her curveballs…

…Act Three takes her completely by surprise!

When Lisa Cannon left Cam to manage her estate and repertory theater company on Orcas Island, no one foresaw the coming global pandemic. During the shutdown, no plays were staged, and island tourism dropped precipitously; Cam's friend Jen came to live with her, having lost all but one of her former jobs.

Now the world is reemerging from its years of pandemic isolation, and Lisa is coming home from prison to resume her former life. Fortunately, she still needs Cam's help as her personal assistant, and she has generously offered to keep Jen on as well, as her new caretaker.

As Cam prepares to move back into the charming A-frame cabin she occupied before Lisa's arrest, she looks forward to the busy, whirlwind existence she briefly knew in the "before times"…until a very strange letter from a good friend arrives, and Cam's world is suddenly thrown on its side *again*.

ACKNOWLEDGMENTS

The still-imaginary Laura Gayle would like to once more thank the very real authors Shannon Page and Karen G. Berry for bringing her to life, so that she could write yet another book.

Shannon and Karen would like to thank our husbands, Mark and Tony, for their continued love, assistance, and enthusiasm. We are particularly grateful to Mark for his editing and plot help, in addition to the gorgeous cover; and we are deeply indebted to Tony for sharing his community theater expertise.

Thank you again to the whole team at Book View Café for production help on this book, particularly Sherwood Smith for her careful proofreading and character suggestions, and Jennifer Stevenson for her lovely formatting of the ebook.

A million-billion-*trillion* thanks to Jenny and Kelly and Becky and the rest of the team at Darvill's Bookstore on Orcas Island for their AMAZING support.

And thank YOU, our dear readers, for continuing on this ride with us! This chapter in the lives of Cam and Jen might be ending here, but you've spurred us on to start another one, coming next year!

Photograph by Mark J. Ferrari

Laura Gayle is the nom de plume of two friends who love to collaborate.

Shannon Page was born on Halloween night and raised without television on a back-to-the-land commune in northern California. Her work has appeared in *Clarkesworld*, *Interzone*, *Fantasy*, *Black Static*, Tor.com, and many anthologies. Books include the contemporary fantasy series The Nightcraft Quartet; fiction collection *Eastlick and Other Stories*; personal essay collection *I Was a Trophy Wife*; hippie horror novel *Eel River*; cozy mystery series the Chameleon Chronicles, co-written with Karen G. Berry; and *Our Lady of the Islands*, co-written with the late Jay Lake, as well as a forthcoming sequel co-written with Mark J. Ferrari. Her many editing credits include the essay collection *The Usual Path to Publication* and the anthologies *Witches, Stitches & Bitches* and *Black-Eyed Peas on New Year's Day: An Anthology of Hope*. Shannon is a long-time yoga practitioner, has no tattoos (but she did recently get a television), and lives on lovely, remote Orcas Island, Washington, with her husband, author and illustrator Mark Ferrari. Visit her at www.shannonpage.net.

Karen G. Berry has lived in or near Portland, Oregon, for forty years, but remains solidly Midwestern in outlook and recipes, which is why you never find any of hers in the recipe sections of the Chameleon Chronicles (until this one!). She has one wonderful husband, three wonderful daughters, two wonderful grandsons, and several thousand books. A marketing writer by day, Karen is a prize-winning poet and has published seven novels and one non-fiction book, *Shopping at the Used Man Store*. As a committed underachiever, Karen finds all of this fairly amazing. Visit her at www.karengberry.mywriting. network/.

Made in the USA
Monee, IL
13 May 2023